GAUNTLET OF FEAR

GAUNTLET
OF FEAR

David Cargill

Matador
9 Priory Business Park,
Wistow Road, Kibworth Beauchamp,
Leicestershire. LE8 0RX
Tel: (+44) 116 279 2299
Fax: (+44) 116 279 2277
Email: books@troubador.co.uk
Web: www.troubador.co.uk/matador

ISBN 9781780883236 (pb)
9781780883243 (hb)

British Library Cataloguing in Publication Data.
A catalogue record for this book is available from the British Library.

Typeset by Troubador Publishing Ltd, Leicester, UK
Printed and bound in the UK by TJ International, Padstow, Cornwall

Matador is an imprint of Troubador Publishing Ltd

For Alan and Jane

Dedicated to my beloved wife Sheila
1931–2010
Her love and inspiration meant everything to me

MY THANKS TO...

Chris Robinson – Doctor and friend for anaesthetics circa 1967.

George W. Randall – Historian and passionate researcher of time capsule and **E. Douglas King** – one time Honorary Secretary KCFA

Iain & Joy Morrison – Friends and critiques for advice and transportation around the Devon countryside to get my facts right.

Bob Pearson – For introduction to airfield "that never existed"?

My thanks also to **Alex, Bill, Hilary, Joe, John** and **Norma** for their support and lunchtime tongue-in-cheek offering of big words – never used. I hope the "magnificent six" have as much enjoyment reading this piece of fiction as I've had writing it.

CONTENTS

Chapter 1

AND IT DIDN'T EXIST?

It was still very cold, but at least the frost was out of the ground, as Freddie Oldsworth steered his red Triumph Spitfire into the already crowded car park, at Kempton Park racecourse, on the morning of twenty-seventh December, 1966. The Boxing Day racing card, that had been lost due to the bad weather, was now scheduled to take place a day later.

Freddie eased the gear lever into neutral, engaged the handbrake and switched off the engine. He was thankful he was soon to be involved in his favourite pursuit, which would take his mind off the anxiety he had for his companion.

He brushed both hands through his mop of curly light-brown hair before turning to gaze at the recumbent figure fast asleep in the co-driver's seat.

A faint smile broke out at the corners of his mouth as his steel-grey eyes took in the slim form, in the charcoal-grey suit, slumped, in total oblivion, beside him.

The smile lengthened into a broad grin with the realisation that the sprawled heap, with the shock of dark hair prematurely greying at the temples, looked less like the professor he really was.

Professor Giles Dawson, historian and lecturer in "Stage Magic and the Great Illusionists", had shared common interests with Freddie Oldsworth since RAF days. They were both members of the Magic Circle and the Ghost Club, and their mutual love of horse racing had started with a visit to the 1947 Grand National at Aintree, whilst stationed near Liverpool. On that occasion dense fog had made it impossible to follow the Tom Dreaper trained favourite, 'Prince Regent', in his bold attempt to carry top weight;

the horse finishing in fourth place behind a 100/1 outsider.

Now, almost twenty years later, both men were arriving to watch another Tom Dreaper favourite continue his extraordinary steeple-chasing career in the King George VI Chase.

Despite the smile, as he looked at his companion, Freddie couldn't help a feeling of foreboding. The Prof, as he was known to his closest friends, had spent the Christmas vacation, with Freddie and his wife Penny and their two little girls, at their Cotswold home in Evesham. During that time, Giles had been moody and depressed.

Freddie wondered if the events at Maskelyne Hall, near Lockerbie, had caused the problem. The Prof had told a tale, stressing three words that provoked a shudder. He would have to wait for a more detailed explanation and he knew that might take time. The three words were '*Gauntlet of Fear.*'

Putting those to one side, Freddie knew the name on everyone's lips, in the horse racing world, was '*Arkle*'. Owned by Anne, Duchess of Westminster, such was the esteem, in which an endearing public held the horse, that he was known only as '*Himself.*'

A full two minutes passed before the heap, known as The Prof, stirred, opened flickering lids to reveal clear blue eyes and then struggled to sit upright.

'Have I missed anything?' he enquired sleepily.

'No, not really, but you've been asleep for the best part of an hour. We've a helluva lot to do before racing starts.'

'You're spot on, as usual, Freddie. I'm afraid I haven't been the best company lately and I was having a dream about that mysterious business at Maskelyne Hall. It's less than a month since I arrived at a solution and I continually have nightmares about whether I could have prevented…you know! I still blame myself for what happened at the end.'

'Take my word. You have a clear conscience.'

Giles nodded, but without conviction. His eyes closed as he sat for several moments in contemplative thought about the complex mystery surrounding the death of the owner of the big house near Lockerbie. The truth behind 'how a bottle opener can open more than bottles', and the significance of 'The Statue of Three Lies' that had finally helped him arrive at a solution.

Now it was the equine hero of the age they were about to admire. Both men would readily admit, history had a nasty habit of repeating itself and, hand-in-hand with destiny, was capable of wrecking dreams just as often as making them come true.

'Is there anything you want me to do?' Giles asked once they were inside the racecourse proper.

'Yes! Nip over to that kiosk where that crowd is gathered and pick up a race card. I'll meet you over at the rails, in a few minutes, and then we can grab some light refreshment at the bar. My stomach thinks my throat's been cut. Oh, before I forget young Katie usually attends to the race cards so you might deal yourself a good hand if you just…smile a little. I was going to say 'be yourself' but I'm not sure that would help. Cheer up, for God's sake!'

Both men were soon enjoying a sandwich and a beer in the nearby bar when Giles handed over the race card.

'So you found our little Katie then?' Freddie said as he opened the card and appraised the runners for the big chase.

'No! As a matter of fact I was out of luck – the kiosk was empty.'

'Don't tell me you missed out getting the girl again,' Freddie sighed with a wry smile on his face. 'You keep doing your Bob Hope impression like in those great Road films.'

Freddie was always ragging Giles about his seeming failure to have any success in the marriage stakes; ever since The Prof's fiancée had…! But that was another story.

'Anyway, how did you manage to get this then?' Freddie asked, brandishing the card.

'As I was saying, before I was rudely interrupted, the kiosk was empty when I got there; people were turning away saying the girl had gone for more cards – something to do with the exceptional crowd for today's meeting because of Arkle,' Giles hesitated. 'I was about to do the same when a voice asked if he could help me.'

'He?'

'Yes, it was a man's voice. I looked into the booth but couldn't see anything. It was fairly dark inside…and then my eyes got accustomed to the surroundings. I spotted a face with distinct features.'

'Here we go again with another bout of your imagination! I suppose it had the horns of a goat and bloodshot beady eyes and…!'

'No!' Giles cut his friend short. 'But it did have a military bearing, a waxed moustache and large bushy eyebrows. Hardly the features you'd expect in a girl or, for that matter, a goat. It was also wearing a smart flat cap at a jaunty angle and not many goats wear those, clever clogs.'

'That must've been Katie's father,' Freddie spouted forth knowingly. 'Ex sergeant major, and, ever since leaving the army, he's been a regular at Kempton Park carrying out all sorts of necessary odd jobs like repairing fences or replacing turf at the jumps. He'd be helping his daughter.'

'So that solves another problem.'

'Yes! A great guy and one who could make even you jump when he barked out a command. Did he say anything?'

'Not much. He passed over the race card with a low whispered "You can 'ave my copy guv…I don't think I'll be needing one today." I lost sight of him in the darkened booth so I thanked him and left.'

Freddie looked slightly perplexed as he digested what he was told. 'Strange! That's not like the sergeant major I know. Never mind, let's look at today's runners and make decisions.'

The early races were enjoyed by the vast crowd as they awaited the one they had all come to see. Freddie had a couple of wagers – but the big race was the main attraction.

The crowd that encircled the paddock, where the small field for the King George VI Chase were being led round, was a tribute to Arkle as racegoers continued to pay homage to this equine hero.

Freddie cast his expert eye over '*Himself*' and his challengers, while Giles disappeared to make a phone call to book a table at Simpson's-in-the-Strand for their evening meal. On his return he found his friend in a state of agitated excitement.

'What's up?' he asked as the jockeys began to mount. 'Have you noticed something of a problem?'.

'Indeed I have!' Freddie replied, smacking his lips. 'But not inside the paddock. Outside and it made me wonder. I bumped into that filly you missed. You know…Katie…and I told her your story…about how you got the race card.'

'Yes?'

'She looked slightly bemused; then she smiled in a kind of quizzical fashion which turned to one of loving understanding – like my wife Penny occasionally does at home. She said she hoped to meet up with you before we left the course. Then she dashed off, carrying a large bag, saying she was going down to one of the fences to watch the race.'

'How interesting! I'd love to meet her, though how we'll see her in this crowd beats me.'

They watched the race from the stands and, as Giles focussed his binoculars on the leaders, he began to feel that an upset might be on the cards.

As the field approached the second circuit, he could sense that Arkle wasn't jumping with his usual freedom, and a bad blunder at the fourteenth fence caused Giles to lower his glasses briefly and look across at Freddie whose face registered his concern.

When the leaders entered the straight for the final time Woodland Venture was still there and appeared to be going slightly the better until he hit the second fence from home and came down.

Arkle, the 9-2 on favourite, was left in the clear – but something was wrong. Arkle was stopping fast and Dormant belying his name came from the last to lead close home and win by a length. *'Himself'* finished lame and a vast crowd of admirers were left in little doubt that the great horse had completed his final race on three legs.

Both men left the stands in silence and made for the unsaddling enclosure when a voice from behind stopped them in their tracks.

'Well now, Freddie, aren't you going to introduce me to your professor friend?'

Giles turned to see a young woman with rosy cheeks. She was well wrapped up against the cold, but slightly out of breath from running.

'Katie, this is Giles Dawson, the prof I was telling you about. Giles, please let me introduce Katie…I'm sorry but I don't know your surname.'

Pleased to me you,' she said, holding out a delicate hand as she removed her glove. 'Starters, Katie Starters. Born and bred in Ireland…like Arkle! Freddie told me your story.' Her slight London-Irish accent created an atmosphere of intrigue. 'I'd love to hear it again, but first I think I should explain. The kiosk was closed because I needed more race cards and…' she hesitated before continuing, 'there was another important task I'd promised to do for him!'

'For your father?' The Prof asked gently.

'Yes,' she replied.

'There you are then! That solves our little mystery! Putting two and two together I'd say it would be himself that gave me his very own race card… military bearing, waxed moustache, bushy eyebrows and smart flat cap set at a jaunty angle. He said he wouldn't need one today! Am I right?'

'That's m'dad all right. Sergeant major Bert Starters – firm but fair, even when barking out the orders on the parade ground. Now retired…!' Her eyes misted up.

'So mystery solved then?' Giles glanced at Freddie who was now shaking his head.

'No…not quite!' Katie had a tear at her eye as she spoke. 'You see, dad died ten days before Christmas.'

'The same day you were running the *Gauntlet of Fear* thing!' Freddie chipped in.

Katie wiped the tear from her eye. 'He was cremated at Golders Green crematorium. It just had to be Golders Green, you see, because of the two G's in the title…you know, gee gees…m'dad was always keen on the horses… and my orders were to have his ashes scattered here at Kempton Park. I was down, near his favourite fence, doing just that while the kiosk was empty and today was the first day *he wouldn't be needing his card!*'

'I'm sorry!' Both men spoke as one.

'That's quite all right,' she said, with affection. 'His ghost will be welcome here. He'll always be the greatest; I doubt we'll ever see the likes of himself again, but now I know where he is and where he'll be forever!'

'We'd both like to echo that sentiment,' the Prof said. 'And after today the same thought might have to be applied to that other Himself…Arkle.'

'Wouldn't it be rather strange if the two of them were to end it all at the same course and on the same day?' Katie reflected and started to move off. 'Anyway I did what he wanted me to do,' she called back, over her shoulder, as she melted into a subdued crowd. 'And all because of himself, Bert Starters. God bless him!' Her laughing voice trailed away in the freshening breeze. 'And all because I was under *Starters Orders!*'

Giles and Freddie waved farewell to the disappearing Irish colleen who had captured their hearts, before they turned to do likewise to the nation's steeplechaser…Arkle, who, due to his exceptional talent, had instigated a complete transformation of the handicapping system in National Hunt racing.

Simpson's-in-the-Strand was heaving with guest diners, that evening after racing; diners who didn't have to say grace as they knew what they were about to receive.

'Can you try to explain how you've managed to get involved with this latest fiasco?' Freddie asked after they were seated. 'And I'd like to hear it from the beginning, please, because I've certain reservations, about which I'll say more later.'

'From the beginning? Yes, of course – I'll try to do that, but I don't want to spoil our meal!'

'You can't do that, Giles. Simpson's will not allow that to happen… believe me!'

'I believe you!' Giles smiled, and the tension in his face relaxed, as he sipped a little of the red wine.

'It was in the St James's Club, at 106 Piccadilly.' he nodded to the gentleman pouring the drinks. 'It's a gentlemen's club once tenanted by the Coventry Club and, during the Second World War, was briefly occupied by Ian Fleming, the creator of James Bond. It was ten days before Christmas and I was giving a lecture to an invited audience of stage magicians and circus proprietors. I was expounding on the impact that feats of disappearance could have if performed in the circus ring, as opposed to those exhibited on stage.'

Giles paused and took another sip of his wine.

'Go on!'

'Don't be impatient, Freddie. I'll get there, in time. I just want to collect my thoughts. Now where was I?'

'You were giving this lecture about how stage magicians could transform the circus.'

'Yes! So I was! The circus ring is so different to the theatre stage. It is set in a large tent and is totally surrounded by the audience. There can be no trapdoors, nor are there any drapes to prevent those watching from seeing hidden wires or mechanical devices. It appears to be entirely open so any disappearance, in full view of the audience, could be devastating.'

'No doubt about that, Giles. Bums on seats! That's what it's all about these days, especially when the circus is going through a lean period, what with the threat of animals being removed.'

As the roast beef was being carved, Giles continued to put Freddie in the picture.

'When the lecture was over, and questions answered, we were all offered a glass of Champagne. Several magicians approached, introduced themselves and agreed that the evening could be the answer to many of the problems of the Big Top, notwithstanding those of the stage magician who was also going through an uncertain time in entertainment.'

'I'm sure they're right, but I'm still waiting to hear about the *Gauntlet of Fear* bit!'

'I'm coming to that, but, before I do, let's give this roast dinner the accolade it deserves.'

They thanked the waiter, clinked wine glasses, and then set about enjoying the best roast beef available in this great city of London – beef that came from Scotland.

As always, Freddie knew he might have to be patient, and wait, before Giles came to the crux of the matter. But the excellence of the meal made the wait exceedingly bearable.

Giles wiped his mouth gently with his napkin as the wine-waiter poured the two men another glass of Bordeaux claret.

'Where was I?'

'You were enjoying a glass of Champagne...'

'Was I? That's right, so I was! My glass was all but knocked out of my hand. The culprit was tall, dark and would have been handsome...but I digress! He bumped into me with such force it could only have been deliberate. He had dark hair, well-brushed back, and a heavy moustache. His eyes were almost as dark as his hair but they were terrified beyond belief. He was trembling as he gripped my arms with vice-like strength, and he spoke English but with a Portuguese accent.'

Freddie nodded as he ordered the sweet.

'Did he give his name?'

'Yes.'

'Well?'

'Oh! He said his name was Ramon Mordomo.'

'And…?'

'He said he desperately needed my help.'

'And…?'

'He revealed he was the owner of a circus, and one that he was establishing in Britain, after starting in the United States. One that might revolutionize the circus world but was now experiencing accidents that he felt were being fiendishly created to try and make him give up ownership of the circus. He believed he was running a '*Gauntlet of Fear*'. Those were his chosen words. He could barely utter them so stricken, he was, with fright.'

'So how did that make you feel?'

'I wanted to help but didn't know how I could.'

'Did he say why he was contacting you?'

'Yes. He said he'd read, in one of the Sunday papers, a piece about the Maskelyne Hall affair in Scotland, and he was impressed about my ability as a detective.'

'That must've pleased you.'

'Yes, it did.'

'That's all very well, Giles. But the family in Scotland were mostly known to you and those in this circus would be total strangers. Have you considered that?'

'Yes, I have.'

'And…?'

'I'm going to give it a go.'

Freddie looked distinctly perturbed and remained silent for several seconds.

'What, exactly, does this Portuguese gentleman want from you?'

'I understand he is actually Cuban, but of Haitian descent. He wants me to visit his circus and find out who the hell is trying to make him give it up.'

'Aha! Haitian you say! Now that smacks of zombies and voodoo worship, and someone may have a grudge against him…and there may be more than one!'

'Zombies and voodoo worship? You're being very melodramatic, Freddie! Dare I ask if that has anything to do with the reservations you had?'

'No, not really, but it does bring me to the point which certainly concerns me. It was something you mentioned when you were with me, and my family, over Christmas. Something I found strange in the extreme.'

'What was that?'

Freddie, with dessert spoon raised over his sweet, pondered for a moment, looked straight into the blue eyes of his friend, and uttered the words 'RAF Winkleigh!'

'Why should that have been strange in the extreme?'

'Because,' said Freddie, pointing his spoon directly at Giles. 'It never existed!'

'What?'

'The place you said where this circus was spending their winter quarters, RAF Winkleigh, in Devon. Well I looked up the three volumes of the RAF airbases during World War 2. I left you dozing by the fire one day and checked several sources and I found something strange about your RAF Winkleigh.'

'And…?'

'And it didn't exist!'

Giles turned his head and looked round at the other diners. He seemed unsure of what he'd just heard. He spooned several mouthfuls of dessert before he spoke.

'But he gave me instructions on how to get there and a contact number to call.'

'So?'

'You say it didn't exist but I'm sure I'd heard that name before.'

'Another one of your dreams, Giles?'

'No! What he said rang a bell. Something that happened at RAF Padgate when I was called up.'

'What was that?'

'Well, as recruits, when we were on parade, there were fighter pilots, in flying jackets, lounging on the grass, waiting for demobilisation as the war was over.'

'And…?'

'Well I managed to get in conversation with some of them and what one guy said has remained with me to this day.'

'What was that?'

'He said he'd survived several years flying Lysanders at a Devon airfield named RAF Winkleigh.'

'You don't say!'

'Yes, I do say,' Giles pushed his plate to one side, with a satisfied look on his face. 'And it didn't exist?'

Back at the flat in South Kensington Giles suggested a nightcap before the eventful day was over.

Freddie was due to spend the following day racing, before returning to his Cotswold home, and Giles had decided to spend the next few days relaxing, but the conversation at the evening meal had made such an impression that a change of plan was contemplated.

A serious talk over a whisky and Crabbie's Green Ginger resulted in a phone call to Evesham, to confirm Freddie's return home for the New Year, and a phone call from Giles to a number in a Devon village, for God knows what.

A visit to an airfield, which according to the RAF didn't exist, was to be the target for tomorrow – the day after the strange incidents, involving Arkle and Katie Starters.

A visit to the winter quarters of a circus, at a place which didn't exist, was something anyone interested in magic and the paranormal, couldn't resist. Giles was no exception. It just could be a place where someone had murder in mind!

Chapter 2

FUNAMBULISM, IMPALEMENT AND KHAN

The journey, by rail, to North Devon, gave Giles a chance to catnap and concentrate his thoughts on what he was about to encounter.

It was hard enough to realise that, in the space of less than eight weeks, he'd been asked to solve two different problems. One was the strange death in the locked room at Maskelyne Hall near Lockerbie. Now a circus was about to test his wits. One thing, for sure, he was determined to analyse all the facts, with meticulous care, and not jump to conclusions.

His pal, Freddie, had expressed concern, but he was only a phone call away and would leap at the chance to help him if he hit the buffers.

Giles was convinced that the stage magician could create a resurgence of interest in the travelling circus. But what he found, when he got to RAF Winkleigh, might change all that.

The final part of the journey, from Exeter St. David, was a steady climb. Passing the freight yards of Exeter Riverside, the twenty-one mile journey to the station at Eggesford was enriched by the North Devon rolling countryside. Thatched roofs in some rural villages gave the area, noted for red sandstone, a peace that countered the disquiet Giles had about his impending task.

It was almost dusk, when Giles got off the train at Eggesford, acutely aware that the station was lit by only an oil lamp. The solitary lamp, combined with the eerie silence, gave the place a creepy atmosphere that was heightened by the dark, unoccupied, Victorian buildings Giles could see on the other platform.

There was no traffic noise nor street lights outside the station buildings.

In fact there was no village or town outside the station. The station appeared to be at the back of beyond; a ghost station that sent a shiver through Giles' body. Fortunately his apprehension was short-lived

He was soon greeted by someone in his mid-to-late forties. The stranger, his face bursting into a huge grin, grabbed his hand and shook it, demonstrating upper body strength.

'You must be Professor Dawson,' the man said, with an American accent, as he lifted Giles' bag. 'If you follow me across to the other side we'll get you to base in double quick time.'

Giles followed the man out to the battered old Cadillac noticing the man leading the way had a slight, but unmistakeable, limp. He made a mental note of that in his cranial filing system, and was about to speak when the stranger said 'You hop in while I put your bag in the trunk.'

Giles moved to open the door when a voice warned him tactfully, 'Not that side Professor, unless you want to do the driving!'

Giles shook his head and, moving around the car, said apologetically, 'Sorry, I was forgetting it was an American car. And you must be… American…hmm?'

'Yes, I am! I'm all the way from the sunshine state of Florida. At your service! The name's Hank, Hank Findley.'

'Okay, Hank. Take me to your circus.'

'Sure thing, Professor.'

Over the railway at the level crossing, it wasn't long before Giles became aware of the difficult driving conditions on the narrow tree-lined road which climbed for most of the four mile stretch towards their destination.

'I'm not at all sure I'd take you up about driving around here on a journey to a place that doesn't exist.' exclaimed Giles, his tone expressing playful nervousness.

'So you've heard the stories too. None of us are very pleased that Whitehall has denied the existence of RAF Winkleigh but I can assure you it did exist; I was there.'

'You were stationed at the airbase?'

'Yes! For longer than I sometimes care to admit. I was with the USAAF. We lived in Nissen huts that were hard to heat when fuel was difficult to get. Rest wasn't easy.'

'I'm sure it wasn't. Can you say what you did?'

Yes! I flew Dakotas by the seat of my pants. Oh, the place existed. It existed alright. It sure did and part of it still does, which is more than can be said about those guys from Britain, Poland, Canada and The States, who didn't come back'

'You lost a lot of friends?'

'Yes I did. And, if the local rumours are true, you might meet some of them during your stay!'

'You're not suggesting…?'

'I sure am buddy. Many of us think it's the ghosts from the past that's causing the accidents. I've had one myself.'

'What…a ghost from the past?'

'No siree…an accident.!'

'Oh yes, I wondered about that.'

'Don't be surprised if you hear aero engines at night or the sound of men scrambling to get airborne. You might even smell oil burning or get a whiff of kerosene. It could frighten the hell out of you if you can't keep your imagination under control.'

'I'll keep that in mind.'

'The boss doesn't go along with that theory. He believes someone is hell bent on relieving him of his circus. He feels he's running the gauntlet. A *gauntlet of fear*, he says to everyone. If that's the case, the accidents could get worse. Senhor Ramon will fill you in when you get there. He speaks very good English, by the way.'

'Yes, I know.'

For the next few minutes Giles sat back and admired the way his American driver handled the car; his thoughts went back to those heady wartime days as he visualised a younger Hank Findley at the controls of a Dakota.

Giles broke the silence as Hank negotiated a sharp bend.

'Do you mind if I ask you how you had the accident?'

'Not at all. Ask away.'

'Well?'

'Hmm…I'm afraid I didn't feel too clever when it happened. I'm a funambulist, you see!'

'A what?'

The American stopped the car but left the engine idling

'I'm a wire walker!' Hank smiled as he turned to face Giles. 'I've been a wire walker since I joined the circus but while practising, a few weeks ago, the wire suddenly started to vibrate. It was so violent that I had no chance of correcting the sideways motion.'

'Did you fall?'

'Yes! I slipped, tried to grasp the wire as I fell, but only managed to break the fall before hitting the ground. Luckily I only twisted an ankle and bruised a foot, whereas I might have broken a leg, or worse, and that could have kept me out of action for the rest of the season.'

'Don't you normally use a net?'

'Yes, but my circus act will be without a net so, periodically, I practise without one.'

'And that was one of those occasions?'

'Unfortunately, it was. And that's what makes the wire vibration so suspicious.'

Giles closed his eyes as he puzzled over the statement of his American friend. The horrendous possibility of a vibrating wire occurring, during a performance, involving a wire walker, possibly carrying someone on his shoulders, fifteen feet or more above the ground, without a safety net, was something too devastating to even think about. And yet Giles was all too aware that many of those in a circus audience went there in the expectation that danger was a constant possibility in every act.

'I know what you're probably thinking,' the American broke the silence as Giles Dawson looked across at him. 'Most people expect circus performers to take risks every time they go into a cage with wild animals, or fly in a trapeze act or walk a high wire. It's that dicing with death that makes the circus the greatest show on earth. I accept that, but I'm sure you'll agree that each performance is hard enough without added complications being brought into the equation.'

'Of course you're right there. I was trying to visualise what kind of person would put his, or her, circus colleagues at risk in order to gain control of an organisation that might just have lost one or more of it's top stars.'

'Well it has to be someone with the capability to run an outfit as large as this. But Senhor Ramon will, no doubt, point you in the right direction.

And you'll meet him again very soon cause we're almost there.'

The American paused, reached over and grabbed Giles by the shoulder.

'Before I take you the rest of the way, Professor Dawson, let me explain why I stopped the car,' he tightened his grip and looked at Giles, his eyes piercing his passenger.

'The first was to let you know about funambulism; the art of wire walking! The second...' there was a brief hesitation before he continued. 'I thought I'd let you know that, if you'd taken a taxi from the station at Eggesford, some cab drivers would've stopped here and made you walk the rest of the way. It is only a few hundred yards but some of them believe this place is haunted!' Hank released his grip.

'That is interesting. My pal Freddie would enjoy a visit.'

The smile on the face of Giles said everything as Hank released the handbrake and set the Cadillac on the last part of the journey, to a place the RAF had said didn't exist.

The area they approached was a grassy plateau high up on the moor. Wagons and trailers filled a large part of the grassland; many of them emblazoned with the colourful lettering – *Circus Tropicana.*

As they got nearer Giles could make out what must have been the airfield control tower and two large hangers.

The remains of the tarmac landing strip became obvious as they entered and Giles was left in no doubt that RAF Winkleigh had, in fact, existed.

The noise of men going about their business filled the air but it was another noise that stunned Giles as he got out of the stationary car. It was a noise that reminded him of the fictional hound of Conan Doyle's tale of the Baskervilles on nearby Dartmoor – a throaty blood-curdling roar that threatened an unimaginable death of being torn apart by the claws of an animal with great strength.

The American retrieved Giles' bag and looked across at the professor whose face showed anxiety.

'Don't worry, Professor! That'll just be Khan. He's probably still hungry and is asking for an evening meal.'

'Khan...?'

'He's our Royal Bengal Tiger. We still manage to use the big cat despite animal rights protests. And he's big, believe me.'

'I'll take your word for that.'

'The boss will introduce you and you'll see for yourself. One thing you can be sure of – you can stroke him off your list of suspects right away. And you can remove me too – we're both gentle pussycats!'

A movement of the head and a chuckle signalled Professor Giles Dawson to follow the American tightrope walker in the direction of a large trailer where he knocked on the door and entered.

Giles followed him into a spacious cabin full of expensive bric-a-brac.

The place was well lit and the gentleman, Giles had met in St. James's Club, was seated at an ornate desk at one end.

Senhor Ramon Mordomo rose, came round from behind the desk, and shook Giles by the hand. 'It is good that you come to our great circus and I'm sure that you will already experience our hospitality,' he ventured as he took the bag from the American driver and laid it carefully on the floor. His English was easily understood though delivered in a clipped Portuguese accent.

'My wire-walking friend is, I believe, capable of matching members of the Wallendas family; a group he worships as the greatest high wire performers in the history of the circus. But he is also one who can pull the wool over your eyes, as is said in your country. Everything he says must be taken with a pinch of your salt.'

Giles smiled as he assimilated the collection of mixed metaphors spoken by the Portuguese circus owner, who ushered the American wire-walker out of the trailer.

Senhor Mordomo closed the door, arranged a couple of comfortable arm chairs and invited Giles to sit down.

'Did he explain about Khan? I'm sure he did.'

'Yes, he said he was a gentle pussycat, like himself, and that I could stroke both of them off my list of suspects.'

'There you are then. Do not take everything he says at face value.'

Ramon Mordomo got to his feet and moved towards his desk. When he turned he was holding a box from which he produced two large cigars.

'Hank Findley may be correct about Khan not being a threat to me and my circus – but a gentle pussycat, he is not. He is a wild animal and could turn at the drop of the ringmaster's hat. As for Hank himself, there may also be a part of the wild animal in him. If I were you I would not stroke him off your list!'

Ramon handed one of the cigars to Giles.

'I hope you will join me and accept one of my best Cuban cigars. I have read that you occasionally smoke these when under some kind of stress,' his tone was jocular. 'But let us relax and I shall explain what I really want from you and how you will be well repaid.'

Giles took the cigar, noticed it had already been clipped, held it up to his nose to admire the flavour of the tobacco and nodded appreciation to his Cuban host.

'Do you always pre-clip your cigars?' Giles asked as he rolled the cigar between his fingers then held it to his nose to enjoy the aroma.

'Not really! I only do the honours in advance when I know I am about to have guests who enjoy fine cigars or I am leaving my trailer and know I am going to smoke them in the very near future.'

'I will gladly join you in a smoke,' Giles said before putting the cigar between his lips and crossing one leg over the other. 'But,' he removed the fine Havana, before continuing, 'Let me make it clear that I have not yet decided to help you. From what I saw, on my way into your winter quarters, there must be upwards of a hundred or more people involved here and to find out who is trying to take over your outfit could be an impossible task.'

'Do not worry, my friend. The men you saw are the riggers; those who erect and dismantle the big top. Most of them have neither the know-how nor the inclination to take over my circus and are more interested in their sex lives and other amusements. The suspects can be narrowed down to a select few amongst the elite in our show and I shall introduce each one of them to you before you make a decision.'

Ramon produced an ornate cigarette lighter and, as he bent over Giles and lit the cigar, his dark eyes pierced deep into the clear blue eyes of the Professor.

'I am a very rich man,' the circus supremo disclosed as he straightened up. 'You will be well rewarded…if you are as successful as you seem to have been in solving the Lockerbie problem.'

The lines at Giles' eyes creased a little more as he remembered how he'd cracked the mysterious death of the patriarch of Maskelyne Hall in Scotland. He nodded and took several deep puffs of his cigar.

'I have to agree you make it all sound quite feasible but I shall reserve judgement until after I meet those who are your top performers. For the moment the jury is out!'

'Thank you my friend,' the Cuban circus magnate said as he passed the wooden cigar humidor across to Giles. 'Take a good look at that while I get you a drink. Will a Cognac do?'

Giles nodded, took the humidor and opened it to face an array of the finest Cuban cigars, complete with wrappers. The wood appeared to be a mixture of walnut and, Giles guessed, Spanish cedar. There was no smell of ammonia, which usually came from cigars that are very young. These were mature Havanas being correctly humidified. Giles was impressed.

Senhor Mordomo passed over a large Cognac.

'I see you are impressed, my friend. Cigar smoking is an art not a science – just as enjoying a Cognac is. Walnut is a fine wood to choose but it is the Spanish cedar lining that is the big plus. It not only aids as a buffer against the outside climate, but discourages pests and transmits a flavour to the cigars which many smokers appreciate.'

Giles relaxed back into his chair. He was warming to his companion and slowly coming to a decision that might plunge him into a situation that...could end in murder.

Enjoying his cigar the Professor, who lectured in illusions, couldn't help but admire the artefacts of quality that purveyed the roomy trailer. Handing back the humidor his eyes caught sight of an object of great significance.

This was no illusion. It was a classic vintage car mascot in a prominent position on the luxurious desk.

'Can that possibly be a Lalique? He enquired, pointing at the objet d'art.

'Yes, Professor! That is *Spirit of the Wind-Victoire*. It is one of the twenty nine pre-war car mascots produced from high quality glass by Rene Lalique.'

Giles took hold of the object; a female head with the hair shaped as if flowing backwards to a point. As he caressed it Senhor Mordomo continued.

'It is one of my prize possessions. These mascots were produced to grace cars of Hispano Suiza, Bugatti and Bentley among others. Now drink up and we'll have a meal brought to us. You must be hungry?'

'I have to admit I am a little peckish!'

'I can satisfy that. How would you like some roasted pork with black beans and rice and after that I will take you to see Khan?'

'Thank you. That will do nicely.'

The Cuban lifted a telephone, pressed a number and spoke in Portuguese.

He laid the receiver down, looked at his Rolex Oyster Perpetual watch and said 'Our meal will be here shortly, but we have a guest about to join us. She should be here very soon.'

At that there was a knock on the door. It was opened and in stepped a fair-haired young woman in her late twenties.

'Come in my dear. Let me introduce Professor Dawson, a historian in magic and illusion, who is here to cast his spell over our circus before we take to the road in April. Giles, may I present Miss Ingrid Dahlberg.'

'Delighted to meet you, Miss Dahlberg.'

'Please call me Ingrid, Professor. I do not wish us to be too formal. And…may I call you Giles?'

'Indeed you may.'

'Splendid, splendid!' Senhor Ramon's enthusiasm was catching as he continued. 'Ingrid is one of our exceptional performers but I doubt if even you could correctly guess what act she does that excites audiences so much.'

Giles loved conundrums and here before him stood a physical one.

He took his time and his gaze absorbed details of an incredibly beautiful specimen of femininity.

She was petite, with blonde hair cascading down her back. Had there been a wind blowing her head and hair would have come close to resembling the car mascot he still held in his arms. Her blue eyes and pert nose gave her an endearing boyish look. Her long neck, slim arms and wrists complimented a slender but firm body.

She was dressed in a tight pink sweater that accentuated her small, but perfectly formed, breasts. Her sky blue slim line trousers, with matching shoes, completed the ensemble.

Giles was almost lost for words as he stared at this stunning woman. She reminded him of another girl he had cast eyes upon, not so long ago, on a station platform in Scotland. The colour of hair and eyes were different but the effect on Giles was electric. He quickly put the flashback out of his mind.

'You want me to guess what role she plays in your circus? Well I think,' he said hesitantly. 'She could be either a trapeze artist, a bareback rider on one of your horses or…' Giles paused as a thought sprang into his mind. 'She might even work with your Bengal Tiger, Khan!'

'Neither,' said Ramon, grinning. 'Ingrid is an impalement artist, or knife thrower, and the best in the business.'

Giles' gaze shifted between Ingrid, Ramon then back to Ingrid.

He struggled to say something but words died in his throat.

He fought to gain composure and, at last, could only conjure up 'Well I never!'

'I agree it is difficult to believe but, in her profession, she is, as I said, a knife thrower or better known in circus parlance, as an impalement artist.'

Giles shook his head and his mind wandered back to similar acts in theatrical magic and illusion.

'Most are male,' Ramon continued. 'With the female role being that of the target figure and, although there are a few pairs with roles reversed, Ingrid is most definitely one of the best.'

There was a knock at the door and two waiters entered with several dishes which they put on a dinner table set for three. Giles was shown where he could freshen up and when he returned he was seated opposite a slip of a girl who was capable of throwing knives at a male target figure – intending not to draw blood.

Dinner was exquisite with fine Portuguese wine. Conversation was mostly about the exceptional talent this Cuban circus had at its disposal; Giles having already met two of them. The first being Hank, the funambulist, as the Cuban owner described him; the second being the girl opposite him at the dinner table, who was an impalement expert making a living throwing knives at a human target.

'You are incredibly silent, Giles,' it was Ingrid who woke Giles out of a spell of vocal inactivity. 'You seem miles away.'

'I'm so sorry,' Giles replied, then cleared his throat. 'I have to admit that you are not the first person to suggest that. In my defence, however, I can assure you I accumulate more top class information, as a listener, than…'

'Could it be that you wish to ask me about myself but are reluctant to do so?' Ingrid's blue eyes sparkled and her lips had a provocative smile.

'As a matter of fact I was hoping an opportunity might arise.'

'Well here's your chance, so ask away.'

'An impalement artist is surely a slight misnomer,' Giles began, tongue in cheek. 'Correct me if I'm wrong but I believe impalement is something such an artist would be trying to avoid. What induced you to start a career throwing knives?'

Ingrid's smile became more pronounced. She looked towards Ramon then back to face Giles. 'It was easy! I never had any doubts, from an early age. My father was a knife thrower! He learned his skills in Sweden and Germany before moving to the United States where I grew up watching him perform in burlesque shows. I never wanted to do anything else.'

'But isn't it usual for the girl to be the target rather than the other way round?'

'Of course. But my father made it clear that the safest place to be was at the throwing end.'

Giles nodded. 'Your father was more than a knife thrower. He was a shrewd gentleman. I can see that. If someone got hurt, it would be unlikely to be the knife thrower and would be classified as an accident.'

'My father was one of the best and he taught me well and I make it my business to prevent an accident.'

The circus boss had been silent throughout this exchange between Giles and Ingrid, but now spoke with eager delight, 'Ingrid is practising very hard and is working on her own version of the Wheel of Death which involves throwing knives at a revolving circular board on which an assistant is strapped. She might even become a funambulist and impalement artist at the same time as she is learning to walk a tight rope while throwing knives at a revolving target.'

Ramon rose and filled the wine glasses before proposing a toast. 'To the Wheel of Death!' he said.

Giles responded, sipped from his glass and wondered what was next on the list. The circus owner soon clarified that doubt.

'When you are ready I'll take you to see our Bengal Tiger after which I'll get someone to escort you to your accommodation and you can have a good night's rest.'

The remainder of that first evening at RAF Winkleigh was something of a blur to Giles. How he came to find himself in a strange trailer, lying on a bed that somehow lifted to a dizzy height when he tried to sit up, was a complete mystery. He'd had that feeling before…after a hectic Hogmanay. His lasting memory, before sleep grabbed him, was Khan.

It was almost one o'clock in the morning when Giles looked at his watch. He struggled to get off the bed, realised that he was still fully clothed, and then became aware that his travelling bag was on the floor within reach.

Once he'd changed into his night wear, and slipped between the sheets, he lay awake for a while searching his memory bank to access what he remembered from the previous night.

The informed discussion at the evening meal had centred on the circus greats such as The Flying Wallendas, famous for their seven-and-eight-person pyramid wire walks, and another German group, The Gibsons, knife throwers who were credited with bringing the Wheel of Death to America, and were featured in Ringling Brothers' and Barnum and Bailey's shows.

Thinking back; it had become evident that the circus boss, with his wealth, was aiming to surround himself with circus greats.

As memory came flooding back, he recalled the circus owner taking him to a caged area, comfortably warmed by generators, where he came face to face with a specimen of Bengal Tiger that defied belief.

Khan was a royal animal in every sense of the word: a magnificent creature which would rank alongside the other artists for top billing, but only if he was kept under total control and not allowed the freedom of the place.

The superb colouring of his stripes and, in particular, the musculature of his massive frame, alerted Giles to the fact that, if Khan ever got free, he could destroy, not only those in his path but the future success of the circus as well.

It had been at that point that Giles had experienced a rapid increase in heartbeat and the cold sweat on his brow bringing him back to earth with a jolt. His hand had been shaking as he pointed to the door of the cage: a door that was clearly unlocked.

A grateful and relieved Ramon had thanked Giles after securing the cage door. He was clearly shaken as he cited the episode as yet one more example of a deliberate attempt to make him relinquish ownership.

But that was last night and sleep beckoned as Giles drifted into a fractured land of nod where he found himself, wearing thin and flexible leather-soled slippers, trying to balance on a violently vibrating wire, whist dodging knives being thrown at him by a fair-haired girl doing her best to make him fall into the path of a waiting Bengal Tiger below.

Chapter 3

THE PLOT THICKENS

Pale soft sunlight was filtering through his trailer window when he next looked at his watch. It was after nine o'clock.

A note had been pushed under the door.

Take your time. When you're rested visit our canteen and have breakfast. Spend the day meeting the artists then come to my trailer at seven for dinner and we can talk terms.

Ramon

After a hearty breakfast Giles went to one of the two hangers where he met a group of clowns rehearsing a scene where they were rescuing a maiden from a burning building. It was here he was told that the burning effect, to be used, was created using lycopodium, a dried Mexican club fern processed in New Jersey.

Giles was aware of the substance which had also been used in demonstrations by magicians. When it is in a container, it is not flammable but, when blown into the air and in contact with a flame, it makes a dramatic fireball that looks real but doesn't burn. It had been used in the "Wizard of Oz" movie. It was an illusion that could be part of a variety of magic routines but, as Giles was only too aware, could also be replaced with real fire by anyone seeking to create panic in the circus.

The leading clown introduced himself. He was a Canadian in his mid-to-late forties by the name of Chuck Marstow and he informed Giles that the trapeze artists would be working in the hanger in the afternoon if he would like to get acquainted.

Much of the day was spent wandering around the two hangers where he also met a group planning circus routines and he got to know the ringmaster, band leader and the circus magician. They were some of the people he wanted to meet as, in his estimation, all of them were possible suspects capable of trying to oust Senhor Mordomo. He'd been given their names and nationalities but his head seemed unready to absorb those and he knew all he had to do was consult the circus boss and he'd be given a proper list. He would interview each one of them, individually, at a later date.

He watched Eastern Europeans perform elementary moves on the trapeze using a safety net, saw an Australian juggler and twin Chinese girls practise an acrobatic balancing act. He scrutinised each individual, making mental notes he could use later, if deciding to take up Ramon's request. It seemed enough for one visit.

Daylight was fading when he went to what had been the airfield control tower. As he entered he was immediately conscious of the past. There was an unnerving presence about the place. The building had been tidied and made more amenable for use as a control centre with chairs, tables and a few circus posters, but nothing could remove the atmosphere of wartime triumph and disaster that had elated and destroyed the hopes of so many men and women. He was about to leave when he heard the noise of something landing on the floor beside him. It landed with a heavy metallic sound.

He moved a few yards and switched on a light. What he saw made his flesh creep.

On the floor, just a few feet from where he stood, was a gauntlet; the heavy metal glove that was used by men, wearing armour, in days gone by.

Giles looked upwards to see if the object had fallen from the ceiling but he couldn't detect where it might have come from.

Nothing was evident but one thing he *was* sure of. It had been thrown there by someone who was following him. Someone who knew where he was all the time. And it had been thrown down as a challenge.

The stubborn streak in Giles asserted itself. He was now very clear about how he was going to react that evening, when dining with Ramon.

It was approaching seven o'clock when Giles reached the trailer of the circus boss. His dander was up and he was ready to throw down the gauntlet himself.

He knocked and entered to find Ramon with female company different from the previous night.

'Come in, come in, amigo. I want you to meet Madame Zigana.'

Giles immediately admired what confronted him. The girl was diminutive in size with jet black hair showing beneath a colourful scarf which adorned her head. She wore a full-length sari-type dress in bright orange that came down to her feet, but nothing could hide the fact that she had a presence that was greatly in excess of her stature.

Giles took her tiny hand in his and bent down and kissed it. 'I'm charmed!' He said, still holding her hand in his.

'It's my pleasure to meet you Professor Dawson,' she spoke with a slight American accent with a lilt that Giles found irresistible. 'Senhor Mordomo has shown me newspaper cuttings of your recent accomplishments in solving the death of the magician in Scotland and I've wanted to make your acquaintance.'

'Madame Zigana is American, but she insists her family had connections with gypsies associated with this area,' Ramon enlightened Giles. 'Her Hungarian name means Gypsy girl and she is our resident fortune teller. Some of her relations were unfortunately chosen for total annihilation at concentration camps, like Dachau and Ravensbruck, when Hitler saw the gypsies as a race that he believed needed to be made extinct. She now has a wonderful record of success in offering hope to the lives of others.'

Dinner that evening was succulent sweet grilled lobster and discussion centred on whether Giles was willing to accept the task of helping Senhor Mordomo eliminate the succession of accidents in the circus and, if possible, discover who the perpetrator was.

Madame Zigana implored Giles to take on the job and bring the circus back to being trouble free.

'I predicted,' she claimed. 'The circus would encounter many problems but I had no idea about how or why.'

Giles listened to the terms explained to him and, although he knew exactly what his decision would be, he stretched out his doubts before finally agreeing with a shake of the hands.

Ramon produced a sheet listing the names of those he considered capable of a circus takeover and passed it to Giles who scanned the names with lots of interest and much astonishment. The first few names on the list were, as yet, unfamiliar but he would meet them in due course; he was sure of that.

There were at least two names on the list that Giles found surprising and one of them was in the room with him. He scanned the list again.

Ramon Mordomo suspects:

Sebastian Capuzzo	Ringmaster
Felix Reiser	Band Leader
Velazquez Trio	Trapeze Artists
Chuck Marstow	Clown
Hank Findley	Funambulist (Wire Walker)
Ingrid Dahlberg	Knife Thrower
Eva Zigana	Fortune Teller
Michael Wagner	Magician

Enough to be going on with, he thought, but there may be others. He folded the list and put it in his pocket. It was something he would give serious consideration to later on.

Senhor Mordomo produced cocktails and conversation turned to Madame Zigana.

Giles was keen to know if she would attempt to tell him his fortune. Her answer came as a surprise when she agreed; a radiant smile lighting up her entire face. She said she had brought her crystal ball with her for that purpose.

Giles looked at the circus boss who got to his feet and went over to his desk and returned carrying a heavy object covered with a dark purple velvet cloth which he laid down in front of Eva.

'I have to warn you, Madame Zigana, that I once had my fortune told when I visited a booth in Lytham St. Anne's and nothing, that was said then, has come true!'

'You are still a young man, Professor. Don't be so impatient and please call me Eva.'

'Very well, Eva, and please call me Giles. I await your predictions with interest.' He ran his tongue along his lips.

Eva Zigana removed the velvet to reveal a large crystal ball which displayed a myriad of colours absorbed from the lights, and vibrant objects, scattered around the interior of the trailer.

There was an extended silence before Eva spoke once more.

Giles sat transfixed as the lady opposite gazed intently at the crystal globe.

'I see that you are a sceptic, Professor, but one that can give some benefit of the doubt to those who may deserve a second chance. Am I right?'

'Close enough!'

'You do not classify yourself as a detective but have already excelled with a successful conclusion to a case that lay unsolved for a considerable number of years.'

'Yes! I suppose so!'

'I predict a future for you in the field of detection that will rival the literary giants of detective fiction, the names of which I need not express.'

'So far so good Madame Eva, but what you have disclosed is hardly rocket science. Most of what you've said was available from some newspapers at the end of last month and you yourself did mention that you'd read the newspaper cuttings of the Maskelyne Hall affair in Scotland.'

'That is true but I now come to what lies ahead for you.'

'I'm sorry; I did not mean to be disrespectful. Please carry on.'

The diminutive lady adjusted her head scarf before gazing once more into her crystal.

She paused then her intake of breath startled Giles. As he waited to hear what had caused the disturbance he remained silent.

'You have agreed to assist Senhor Mordomo in his quest to solve the riddle that haunts his circus; his *gauntlet of fear* as he describes it to everyone here at the circus. You made that abundantly clear earlier this evening, but you were doing so without any prior knowledge about the outcome?'

'And…?'

'Well, you'll be glad to know that you will probably succeed but only if you travel to some far off spots in this country of yours and overcome problems on the way.'

'Well now, that is interesting as I am joining a cruise of the Scottish Hebrides and the Shetland Isles in March. I'm giving a few lectures on magic and the history of the subject and the Hebrides and Shetlands are about as far off spots in this country as I care to admit! Yet…on the face of it, your prediction might just have been gleaned from some magazine article, so I remain unconvinced!'

'Aha! Your scepticism still shows but time may alter that.'

The look on the face of the circus maestro was one that puzzled the Prof. 'I was not aware that the predicted cruise ships were already in operation.' Ramon questioned.

'Neither was I until recently. One of the first is a small German ship, built two years ago, and it will be my home for a short spell in March next year.'

'There you are then,' said a jubilant Gipsy. 'Perhaps your scepticism has lessened since my latest prediction about travelling to far off spots in this country. And, as I said, you will have to overcome problems on the way. In fact I believe you may already have had a problem before coming here this evening and I am afraid it will not be the last.' Her expression showed concern.

'What makes you say that?'

The clairvoyant's gaze turned from the crystal ball to Giles and her next words came as a warning.

'When I look into the future I make a point of analysing what I already know and the future prospects then become more likely to happen than not. It doesn't take an expert in psychic phenomena to conclude that, whoever is wreaking some distress on our circus boss, he or she will do everything to succeed and bring about your failure.'

Giles responded with an enlightened nod of the head.

'And,' she continued. 'I believe that you are being followed and that will surely continue.'

'Now that you have a portent of the future do you still wish to carry out my assignment?' The Portuguese circus boss asked Giles as he filled the wine glasses again.'

The Prof took the slender hand of Eva Zigana in both of his as he replied. 'I have never shirked trying to solve a puzzle whether it is in magical entertainment, or in real life, and I don't intend to start now!' he said giving Eva's hand a gentle squeeze.

'There is a friend of mine,' he continued, 'who will be interested in what I have to tell him and will grasp at the chance to assist me in solving this complex mystery.'

'Freddie!' said Eva, with laughter in her voice as her turquoise eyes penetrated the crystal ball in front of her. 'I remember the name from those newspaper clips! You can tell him the good news.' she quipped; the radiant expression on her face signifying delight. 'Please let him know that his horse will win the Grand National in April.'

'That would obviously interest Freddie but as his namesake, the Scottish-trained steeplechaser, *Freddie*, has been placed twice in the big race I doubt if he will run next year.'

'I think you may have misunderstood me,' Eva retorted with a mischievous turn of her head. 'Your friend will have to do better than look at his own name to arrive at the winner. I suggest he puts two and two together to make eight and, at the same time, not to overlook his lucky number.'

'Your cryptic remarks remind me of a conundrum that recently brought me into the detective game but I'll convey your observations to Freddie when I see him next.'

'This brings me to something I meant to say to you,' Ramon said as he came over and put a reassuring arm on Giles' shoulder. 'Next time you come bring your friend with you. I'm positive he would enjoy my circus even though a circus is not a circus if it's not in a tent!'

'I'll keep that in mind. I go back to London tomorrow but I will return sometime in the New Year and I'm convinced I shan't need to use the big stick to persuade Freddie to come with me.'

'Good! That's settled then. Before you go tomorrow I'd like you to watch a full rehearsal of my troupe of clowns performing their fire rescue routine in the large hanger. After that, Hank will drive you to the station.'

'I did see them having a workout this afternoon but the complete routine would be something special.'

'Splendid, splendid! Now one last thing before you go. I'm giving a party in Soho on New Year's Eve and, if you can attend, it will give you an opportunity to meet and talk with the stars of my show, some of whom are on that list I gave you. Do you have a Panama hat?'

'Yes! As a matter of fact I do.'

'Good! I'll call you when you are back in London and give you the details.'

Giles left Eva and Ramon shortly afterwards. It was a little after midnight as he picked his way through the many trucks and trailers.

As his own trailer came in sight he caught a glimpse of a dark figure who appeared to have just left the trailer door and was scurrying furtively into the darkness beyond. It was difficult to tell whether the figure was male or female as it headed towards Khan's cage.

He followed as quickly as he could but, try as he might, he lost sight of the figure in the intense gloom.

Returning to his temporary trailer home he went in and closed the door. Nothing appeared to have been moved. The room was as he'd left it, except that someone had been there in his absence.

There was no doubt about there having been a clandestine visitor for on his bed there was a piece of paper, which had not been there before.,

He picked up the note which had four names on it.

William Henry Pratt

Archibald Leach

Frances Ethel Gumm

Erich Weiss

His bewilderment didn't last long once he read the last name on the list. Whoever had placed the note on his bed had deliberately used the name of one of the greatest magician illusionists of all time to clarify what was meant even if the other names weren't at all evident. They were all names at birth or baptism of people who later became well known under a different name; nom-de-plumes or pseudonyms.

William Henry Pratt had been better known as Boris Karloff, who'd played the monster in the early Frankenstein movies, Archibald Leach was the birth name of Cary Grant and Frances Ethel Gumm changed her name to Judy Garland. The last name, Erich Weiss, had been the original name of Houdini,

Someone was informing him that there was a person involved who was not what he or she seemed. He would keep that in mind. A member of the circus was obviously baiting him.

Giles quietly started to do what he was often accused of doing; he started talking to himself. He pursed his lips before softly uttering three words. 'The plot thickens!'

Next morning Giles was awakened by a knock on his trailer door. It was

Hank, the wire walker, who entered to say he'd be back in an hour to take The Prof to the hanger, to watch the clowns rehearse, before driving him to the station for his return journey to London.

Giles shaved, showered, and packed his bag, and was ready when the American who was on Ramon's list of suspects, called to escort him to the comical display of the group of clowns led by the Canadian Chuck Marstow.

He'd hardly sat down before the band started playing one of the songs from the musical movie "Singin' in the Rain". It just had to be "Make 'Em Laugh", and the sound filled the large hanger with merriment.

In centre stage there was a two-storey mock-up building with a lady, holding a baby, silhouetted in a window.

As the band kept playing, flames appeared near the upstairs window. Sirens screeched and lights flashed on and off as a fire wagon entered from behind a screen.

Clinging on precariously to the wagon were six clowns, in full make-up and wearing old style firemen's helmets.

Clowns were trying to connect a hose to a fire hydrant that unusually wouldn't remain in one place. Other clowns were wearing large flat shoes. They got in each others way and were tripping and colliding. It was total chaos but beautifully choreographed.

Upstairs the lady kept screaming for the clowns to come and save her baby, while down below the hose got wrapped around one clown and another couldn't get a ladder to stay upright. The Keystone Cops image, portrayed by the group doing a slick well-performed slap-stick comedy routine, took Giles back to his boyhood days.   Kids attending the circus would love this he thought.

There was a chill in the air with a touch of frost that morning and Giles had been glad to get into the large hanger and out of the icy wind. Now he was warming to the situation that was being played out before him

As the chaos continued the band began playing, with gusto, "There'll be a Hot Time in the Old Town Tonight".

Cymbals crashed and so did the clowns. Giles watched the hose get straightened but it then knocked one clown off his feet. Another got a bucket of water over his head and all the while the lady kept screaming for help.

Giles watched open mouthed and made valiant efforts to stem tears of laughter.

But now the screams began to sound more urgent. The lady shrieked obscenities that could be heard clear above the band music and several assistants moved forward carrying fire extinguishers.

The flames, which should have just looked real, because of the lycopodium, were beginning to take a hold of the structure holding the lady.

She, herself, was now in danger of catching fire and it was only the swift action by the circus attendants that prevented a major catastrophe.

The clowning on the floor of the hanger ceased as Chuck and his comical clutch of comedians were pushed to one side.

The fire was speedily brought under control, and the girl clutching her dummy baby was safely taken away for treatment.

It all happened so quickly. Giles could hardly comprehend what was going on; never suspecting, for one minute, that one of the terrible circus fears, that of fire, had taken place before his very eyes.

Circus staff started to clear the hanger making sure no traces of fire were still evident. Hank Findlay grabbed Giles by the shoulder and said it was time for them to head for the train.

Giles shrugged him off concluding that another so-called accident had just been added to the growing list that circus owner Ramon dreaded, as he ran this gauntlet of fear.

'Who was the girl playing the part of the young mother in the burning building?' Giles was confronting the American tight rope walker as he asked the question.

'She is the magician's assistant but performs several roles when required.'

'Does she have a name?'

The American frowned as he looked at Giles and answered with a cynical 'Yes she does! Funny you should ask! Most of us circus folk have names would you believe. Her name is Allison. Allison Somerfield. I think she's from Raleigh, North Carolina. Now I think we should be heading for that train!'

'My question was necessary,' said Giles, with the annoyance in his tone as he cleared his throat. 'But the information I required has been received and noted and I thank you for that.'

Giles then smiled with a nonchalant shake of the head and made a mental note of the name Allison; adding her to the list of suspects he had in his pocket. He would review that list once he was on the train and bound for London.

Before leaving the hanger Giles said he wanted a quick word with Chuck, the head clown, and, before Hank could restrain him, he darted across to confront the anxious comic.

'As the Head Clown I wonder if you can tell me what you think went wrong?'

'To be honest I don't feel much like a clown after what has just happened. I've been in this business a long time and nothing like this has ever taken place. It's scary and I don't like the look of it!'

'I agree. And if that had happened during a circus performance in front of a large audience it could have caused a panic of terrifying proportion.'

'And loss of life as happened in the States during the circus fire in Connecticut. It's a disaster we circus folk dread.'

'Would you mind if I have a talk with you when I come back. I'm travelling back to London now but you may be able to throw more light on things once you've had a chance to give it some thought.'

'No problem! I'd like to offer all the help I can.'

'There's one other thing I'd like to know. Does the circus carry any medieval pieces of armour?'

'Yes it does. I believe they're planning a magical act involving an armoured English knight.'

The smile on Giles' face was all he could register, in reply, before Hank, the wire walker, dragged him away.

The journey from RAF Winkleigh to Eggesford was uneventful, with his American wire-walker driver being silent for much of the way. Giles had time to think about his future plans and on the train was able to concentrate on what he intended to do next.

The train was quite busy with passengers heading east to celebrate the New Year but he managed to get a seat and he drew out the list of possible suspects and added the name Allison Somerfield. He wondered about the clown he'd had a conversation with. Why had Ramon included him on that list in his pocket? He'd seemed like a decent guy and one to be trusted but, on occasions, first impressions could be deceptive. Giles smiled as he realised that theatrical magic was based on that premise.

His two nights at a place that had never existed had whetted his appetite for an attempt to solve a conundrum that was becoming more enigmatic by the hour. He rubbed the palms of his hands together and grinned at what he had to tell Freddie next time they met.

Before that, once he was back in his place at South Kensington, he must look out the Panama hat he often used when he and his ex-RAF friend went summer racing on the Sussex Downs.

Darkness had descended quite early that night when the taxi brought him to the door of his London flat. He went in, closed the door and immediately poured himself a whisky and green ginger.

He picked up the phone and made a quick call to Evesham to give Freddie news of how the visit had gone and to ask him when he was likely to be back in the big city for a tête-à-tête.

Giles had a couple of drinks from his crystal glass while he ran a hot bath.

His thoughts went back to his stay with the circus at Winkleigh. He recalled the events trying all the time to make some sense out of them.

As he undressed he commenced talking to himself again. 'The plot thickens.' His tired mind was starting to work overtime.

Searching for the Panama hat would have to wait till morning.

Chapter 4

DEATH BY A THOUSAND CUTS

The last day of the year began with a lengthy call on the phone from Senhor Mordomo who gave full instructions as to how Giles should get to the circus showpiece in the Soho strip club.

Tropicana was to be a Cuban-style extravaganza for invited guests to bring in the New Year and signify the emergence of a circus designed to bring back audiences in Britain which had been declining.

Patrons were being asked to wear linen suits or summer dresses with gentlemen in Panama hats to give the whole proceedings the aura of the authentic entertainment, by the same name, in Cuba's capital city of Havana.

The circus boss hoped Giles would be there, not only to enjoy the show, but to meet the circus stars, some of whom were on the list Giles took back with him to London.

The Professor pondered for a while; an evening in a Soho strip club was hardly the venue Giles would choose to spend Hogmanay but beggars can't be choosers and, with a job to do, he convinced himself that the visit might pay dividends.

He found the Panama in a hat box in his wardrobe and the linen suit, that hadn't been worn since last summer, was given an airing in the bathroom with the window slightly open.

He phoned for a taxi to come for him at about 7.30 p.m. and spent the remainder of the day relaxing and making a few notes about his stay at the circus winter quarters.

Hank Findley, the tightrope walker, Ingrid Dahlberg, the lady knife thrower, Eva Zigana, the fortune teller, and Chuck Marstow, the clown, were possible suspects in a conspiracy to topple Senhor Mordomo.

There was also a suspicion about the magician's assistant, Allison Somerfield, though Giles couldn't quite explain why, apart from the fact that she could have been responsible for the fire in the clown scene.

He had a bite to eat at a local bistro and plunged himself into a receptive mood for the evening ahead.

The black cab arrived bang on time and Giles was greeted by a cabbie who was hooting with laughter as he opened the door.

'Strike me pink! You're not thinking of going racing are you guv? Glorious Goodwood doesn't take place till the end of July. You're seven months too early. And it's bloody dark out 'ere.'

Giles got into the cab shaking his head and almost losing the hat in the process.

The irreverent-sounding cabbie closed the door and dashed smartly round the other side.

'I know', he said with deference as he got in. 'You're going to a fancy dress ball. Where can I drop you off?'

The Prof sighed disconsolately as he adjusted his hat and tried to steal a glance in the driver's mirror.

'As a matter of fact I'm heading for Soho…'

He got no further as the cabbie looked over his shoulder. 'Ooh you naughty boy! I can't blame you though as it's not a bad way to end the year.'

'The place I'm going to is Tropicana.' Exasperation showed in Giles' voice. 'It's a special show by a bigwig Cuban circus owner who wants his guests to be dressed like they do when the show is on in Havana. That's the reason for the Panama hat, smarty pants!'

'Well sit back and I'll get you there but what you're wearing shouldn't be called a Panama hat. For what it's worth a lot of us cabbies are real life smarty pants. It seems a lot of us have an enlarged hippocampus which is located towards the back of the brain.'

'Is that so? Not many people know that! And when I bought this hat it was called a Panama!'

'All I said was it shouldn't be *called* a Panama. You see they're made in the small town of Montecristo, in Ecuador, so they should be renamed Ecuador hats!'

'So why are they called Panamas?' Giles was reaching the stage of mild excitement when he was confronted with co-incidence.

'I suppose it's because Panama was where they were primarily sold. The most expensive ones are made from the Toquilla Palm Leaf grown in the coastal lowlands of Ecuador...'

'You have just made my day!' interposed a cheerful Giles as he settled back in his seat. 'You have given another interesting example of something that goes by a name that isn't strictly correct. And I'm beginning to see the light.'

'I'm very glad to hear that. We're nearly there, guv. Give me a call when you're ready to go back. I'm on till late tonight.'

'I most certainly will. You've been great company.'

Giles got out and paid his fare refusing to accept any change. He doffed his hat in deference to the cabbie and smiled at the lucky break he'd had of being driven in a black cab by a driver...with an enlarged hippocampus.

The neon sign that glowed above the dingy building had the single word TROPICANA in coloured lettering and the light rain on the pavement outside glittered with splashes from an artist's palette.

Inside he was told he should keep his hat on by the girl at reception and he was then shown downstairs to where a band was tuning up.

He was immediately greeted by Senhor Mordomo who shook him vigorously by the hand and led him to a large table where several men and women were seated.

The room was spacious and was lavishly decorated giving it a Mardi Gras effect; more so than one could have imagined from the upstairs reception area.

Long-legged girls in short skirts came round with drinks and trays of Cuban delicacies and Giles was speedily engaged in conversation with some of the people he'd met at RAF Winkleigh.

A resounding roll on the drums followed by a crash of cymbals brought everyone's eyes towards the band where the circus supremo was on his feet with a microphone in front of him.

'Ladies and gentlemen of the Press, welcome to Tropicana. You are invited to a preview that I hope will have you giving my circus first class coverage in your newspapers and magazines. Before the evening is over you will be entertained by the kind of show visitors to Cuba's capital city regard as the best.'

'Prior to the evening's entertainment, which will include a mind-blowing act never before seen in any circus, allow me to introduce certain of my celebrities whose skill, artistry and mystery will captivate audiences, young and old, nationwide.'

Firstly he introduced the leader of his band who bowed to his audience. He was a well-built individual with thinning brown hair by the name of Felix Reiser.

Next in line was Sebastian Capuzzo, the Ringmaster. He was tall with dark hair brushed well back and Giles put his photographic memory into action. Both men were on the list, given him by Ramon, and both looked more than capable of leading a circus if they wanted to.

Each of those at the table where Giles was seated stood at the mention of their names. All of them were on that same list except Rodrigo Gomez who was the trainer of Khan, the Bengal Tiger. He was a swarthy character with a weather-beaten face, broad shoulders and slim waist and hips.

Giles was the final person to be announced: Ramon describing him as someone the circus was proud to have assisting with new ideas about the use of illusion in their show.

When the applause died down the circus magnate then encouraged everyone to partake of the refreshments before the evening entertainment started.

The short break that followed the introduction of the circus elite gave Giles the opportunity to chat and get to know each of them. The broad profile of everyone on his list was mentally catalogued for the next meeting with Freddie Oldsworth when Giles would proceed to let his friend have their details before his next visit to the winter quarters.

A roll on the drums brought conversation to a halt. Sebastian Capuzzo, the Ringmaster, stood with a microphone in his hand, in front of the band.

'Ladies and gentlemen, Circus Tropicana is proud to present our tribute to the authentic Tropicana floor show that is Havana's greatest entertainment. Tropicana is possibly the oldest and most lavish cabaret in the world and we hope we can recreate, in miniature, the spectacularly colourful show once enjoyed by the author Hemingway, and his associates.'

The band struck up immediately with lively Latin American music and a group of scantily clad dancers took to the floor. What little costumes were in evidence were brilliantly exciting and the dancing was slick and stimulating.

Giles was captivated and as each act ended another began with a different set of dancers. Vocalists interpreted the music which jumped between Cuban and Brazilian.

When the breathtaking spectacle was over, with a crescendo of percussion instruments, the Ringmaster appeared as the loud applause began to subside.

'Thank you for your show of appreciation but, as I made clear earlier, you are now about to witness an act never before seen in any circus.'

He pointed to the clock in the room. 'It is less than an hour until the New Year is welcomed in your country. In a short space of time you are going to see a balancing act with a difference. Because of the serious nature of this act I must ask you all not to applaud until the act is over.'

While he was speaking several assistants entered carrying two heavy metal stands. They were triangular in shape and, when placed side by side, two to three feet apart, with metal struts joining them together, they formed a staircase up one side and down the other.

The Ringmaster paused for effect; his eyes searched his audience. Five girls entered wearing colourful diaphanous pantaloons, with matching tops. In their hands they each carried two swords.

'The swords you see are Falchion – one-handed single-edged swords similar to the Persian Scimitar. These large-bladed weapons, shaped like a large cleaver or machete, combine the weight and power of an axe with the versatility of a sword.' The ringmaster's words had the full attention of the visiting media.

The girls slipped the swords into grooves on each stand so that they lay parallel with the metal struts but with the cutting edge uppermost.

When the girls had completed their task a young man entered the arena; he was wearing flesh-coloured tights but was stripped to the waist, demonstrating his fine physique.

'Ladies and gentlemen when you enter a circus you buy a ticket for a fantasy. It is now my pleasure to introduce Leonardo from Ecuador. This will be the very first time members of the public have been privileged to see his balancing act – the act of the century.'

The young acrobat rubbed the palms of his hands with a white powder.

'The Death of a Thousand Cuts was a barbaric form of torture practised in China,' the ringmaster continued his explanation to a hushed audience. 'It lasted from the tenth century until it was abolished around 1905. Leonardo will now attempt to defy the death of a thousand cuts by climbing up and down the staircase of swords while balancing on his hands.'

A gentle roll on the drums led the ringmaster into his final announcement.

'There is a metal spar running alongside each sword to assist balance but his hands have to come into contact with the cutting edge of each blade and any slight altering of his weight can result in serious injury. I therefore ask you to remain silent throughout the performance. Thank you.'

The drum roll stopped and slowly the Ecuador athlete began his hand balancing act. He placed both hands on the floor and little by little eased both legs upwards until he was in an upside down position.

He approached the foot of the Falchion staircase and with a slight sway of the legs from the waist he placed one hand on the cutting edge of the first sword.

Holding that position for a few seconds he followed by placing the other hand on the same blade.

The balancing climb continued to the second sword as spectators held their breath.

Every eye in the room was fixed on the lean figure as he climbed to the third rung of the sword ladder. His lithe body swaying slightly to the rhythm of each hand movement had a hypnotic effect on those who watched with unblinking eyes and quickening pulses.

The fourth rung was reached when a slight cough in the room caused a tiny tremor in the balanced form.

There was only a momentary pause then Leonardo was at the top and beginning his downward movement. It was as his hands moved on to the second blade from the top that, for the first time, a distinct sign of pain appeared in the body of the balancing artist.

Giles stiffened when a red fluid slowly oozed between the fingers of the acrobat as he moved down one more rung. The fluid was apparently mixing with the whiteness of the resin type powder on the young man's hands and was now starting to cover the blades on which he was balancing.

Balancing was now in the past tense: for the body, which had been upside down for more than five minutes, was already losing equilibrium.

Giles was a fraction too late as he dashed out of his seat. The young Ecuadorian tumbled from his perch slicing an arm and a thigh in the process.

'Is there a doctor in the house?' Giles asked in a voice with no intention of flippancy. 'Will someone please call for an ambulance…for God's sake?'

Ambulances can sometimes be held up for a variety of reasons, particularly on New Years Eve, but on this occasion the paramedics from the Soho Centre for Health and Care came fairly close to breaking records. By the time they arrived Leonardo had been given first aid and was ready to be whisked away to the nearby hospital on Frith Street.

Giles went with him missing the ringing of the bells bringing in the New Year.

Doctors confirmed that although the injuries to Leonardo were serious they were not life threatening and as the acrobatic young man had never lost consciousness Giles was able to have a brief conversation with him before returning to the Tropicana venue.

'They were at the wrong height!'

'I beg your pardon?'

'The blades…some of them were higher than they should have been!'

A tired but articulate Leonardo surmised that a few of the grooves, which were designed to hold the blades on to the stands, must have been altered making the cutting edges slightly higher and thereby deadly dangerous.

Giles concluded that the alterations had been deliberately done to cause the accident to happen. But who could have done it?

The alterations could have been made just prior to the performance and everyone on his list of suspects had been at Tropicana that night. It could have been any one of them.

Another thought struck him. The adjustments might well have been done before the stands were moved to London so someone not on his list could be the culprit.

Before leaving the injured Leonardo at the hospital Giles was able to glean from him information about the Panama hats. The cabbie had indeed been correct as, believe it or not, Leonardo had been born and brought up in Montecristo and despised the error in naming the hat as if coming from another country.

Back at Tropicana the Prof asked to be excused as he'd had enough for one night. He phoned the number given him by the cabbie who'd brought him to the show in Soho and, before leaving, said he would get in touch with Senhor Mordomo and give dates for when his next visit to the winter quarters would be.

On the way back Giles was able to obtain the name of the cabbie and to confirm with him the observation made by the injured sword balancer about the Panama hat. In return he was given the lowdown of the historical data as to how the South Downs racecourse of Goodwood became associated with the hat and the linen suit.

Colin Forbes, the cabbie with the enlarged hippocampus, elaborated about the origin of the Goodwood summer meeting and the Panama hat. It seems Edward V11 had turned against convention one summer and donned a linen three-piece suit and on his head had placed a Panama hat. From that day on, a uniform was born for the summer meeting at what became known as Glorious Goodwood.

Giles put Colin Forbes and his contact number into his memory bank. There was just a possibility he would use him again at some stage.

The South Kensington flat was quiet when Giles got home. He removed his linen jacket, hat and shoes, poured himself a drink and put a call through to Freddie and his wife Penny at their Evesham home to wish them a Happy New Year.

He consulted his diary for the year ahead and pencilled in dates when he and Freddie might pay a visit to the Devon quarters of the Cuban circus.

There was going to be much to do in the succeeding weeks with a couple of lectures thrown in. Also he did contemplate a return trip to the Ramsden home near Lockerbie, to do some research in the library which housed a unique collection of volumes relating to the circus.

That trip might have to wait until the end of March when he was determined to fulfil a promise made to a member of the Maskelyne Hall household who was possibly going to ride in the local point-to-point.

Giles finished his drink, had a good look at the list of supposed suspects and made a few notes. He looked at his watch, his bleary eyes coming to grips with the fact that it was the First of January 1967 and today would be a welcome day of rest.

Chapter 5

THE WRAITH OF KHAN

It was late when Giles awoke and, after breakfast, he spent much of the day noting down all the so-called accidents that he'd witnessed or been told about. Freddie would expect first hand notification about each and every incident and who'd had opportunity.

As was his wont papers with little notes and names on them were strewn around the floor and Giles took painstaking efforts to arrange them eventually in some form of chronological order. Freddie would insist he got it right.

He went out for lunch, had a walk in the brisk winter weather while his brain mulled over the events and tried to piece together some semblance of logic.

There was no disguising of the fact that this quest for truth was going to be entirely different from his previous case. Earlier he'd tried to figure out what had happened in the past and this time he had to deduce what might happen in the future and who might be to blame.

That first week of January seemed to fly past. Giles was heavily involved; interviews with the Press became a priority as journalists were anxious to know what was going on and why he appeared to be so important to the Portuguese circus owner.

Some newspaper headlines had exaggerated the happenings at Tropicana and others were quick to claim that supernatural irregularities were engulfing the circus to such an extent that delay of the seasonal opening had to be inevitable.

After a night at the theatre, to watch a comedy mystery, Giles returned to the flat just as the phone was ringing.

It was Freddie.

'Hello Giles,' the familiar voice said. 'Can you please tell me what the hell is going on? I've just had a call from someone whose voice I didn't recognise. All it said was "Do not believe all you see or hear." Is this some kind of a joke or are you up to your neck in circumstances out with your control.'

'I'm sorry, Freddie. I'm afraid I'm none the wiser. Such a lot has happened and I really need to meet up with you as soon as possible.'

'You sound as if you're in a spot of bother again, old son. Expect me in a few days time and we can maybe get to grips with whatever is the problem.'

Freddie was true to his word. His arrival was greeted by Giles with welcome relief though he could detect, in his friend, a disturbing anger. Freddie had said, later in his phone call, that he would meet up with Giles, at the flat, after racing on the first Thursday of the New Year and stay the night, before returning to his home in Evesham for the week-end. He was hardly in the door of the flat when the first outburst came.

'I'm a fairly patient man Giles but I do think it's time you told me what's going on.' Freddie's blunt words made his friend sit up and take notice.

'You're right, Freddie. I'll go over everything that's happened so far but, before I do, I think we both need a drink.'

'Is it that bad?'

'No, not really, but I'm puzzled about the whole set-up. I guess a little snifter might just help us both to fathom out some meaning and put some logic into everything.'

'Well I've had a disappointing day at the races and a little nectar might put me back on an even keel again before I get confused by what you are about to tell me.'

'I'll do what I can to fill you in,' Giles declared as he laid a glass of brandy in front of his pal. 'After that we can look at some of the common denominators and try to find a pattern.'

'Cheers!' Both men clinked glasses.

'Let battle begin!' said a more relaxed Freddie after taking a sip from his glass.

'I'll start by listing the so-called accidents I've either been told about or have seen for myself.' Giles produced the list of suspects given to him by Ramon Mordomo. 'Here is Ramon's list of suspects. I've added to that but the list may not be complete.'

'When you've let me know about the accidents we can maybe tie in who may have had the opportunity to cause them. If a pattern should appear that would be a step forward.'

'I'm not convinced it'll be as simple as that but it's worth a go. I must also tell you about certain happenings that weren't accidents but were unnerving and need explanation.'

'Yes…like that phone call to me warning me not to believe all I see or hear. I'd certainly like an explanation for that!'

'I'd like to have an explanation for that as well.'

'While we're on that subject…how did the caller know who I was and how did he get my number?'

'Getting your number would be easy. Knowing who you were would be a little more difficult but as the fortune teller had read newspaper cuttings about the last case we solved she knew about you and there could be others.'

'Hang on a bit Giles! What's this about a fortune teller? I thought neither of us totally believed in premonition.'

'Well as you know there have been classic cases of foretelling the future but I'll come to Eva in due course.'

'You're getting ahead of yourself, old son. Who the hell is Eva?'

'Eva is the fortune teller. That's her name… Madame Eva Zigana…but I'll come to her later.'

'I hope so…but let's get on with those accidents.'

'The first one was told to me on the journey from Eggesford to RAF Winkleigh.'

'Where the dickens is Eggesford and what were you doing there?'

'Eggesford is a railway station in North Devon. It happens to be the last stop on the way to RAF Winkleigh.'

'The place that didn't exist!' said a smiling Freddie as he took a sip of brandy.'

'Yes.' nodded Giles in response.

'A driver picked me up there. He is a funambulist.'

'A what?' exclaimed an incredulous Freddie.

'Yes, I felt the same way when I heard it. That's one f word I didn't know the meaning of.'

'Well…?'

'It means a wire walker or tight rope artist.'

'And…?'

'He'd had an accident on a tight rope that started to vibrate violently causing him to fall when he wasn't using a safety net.'

'What was his name?'

'Hank. Hank Findley.'

Freddie grabbed a piece of paper and a pen from his pocket and wrote something down on it.

'Any number of people could have been responsible for that vibrating wire,' said Freddie looking up at Giles. 'But one person stands out a mile as a possible culprit…Hank himself!'

Giles nodded, realising full well how easy it would be for the wire walker to make the wire vibrate and imitate a near disastrous fall.

The next incident, the unlocked cage of Khan, the Tiger, presented Freddie with a slight difficulty. He made a note of the incident and wrote down the name, Khan, with a question mark.

He continued writing as Giles described the fire scene during the clowns' act that went wrong.

Freddie checked the list that Freddie gave him, noted the name, Allison Somerfield, and then looked up at Giles.

'What makes you think she may be a suspect?'

'I'm not sure. She wasn't on the list given to me by Senhor Mordomo. I added her to that list after watching the clowns' act involving the fire. It's just the fact that she could have been in control of the lycopodium as she was the only one at the place where the fire started.'

'She certainly fills the same role as Hank on the tight rope. I'll give you that. But she doesn't strike me as someone prepared to take on a circus of this size.'

'I suppose you're right…but she could be an accessory for someone else…perhaps even the magician himself as she is his assistant.'

'Hmm! You could be right. We'll keep her on the list.'

Freddie looked decidedly concerned when Giles briefed him on the injuries to Leonardo at the Tropicana show in Soho. He accepted the

Ecuadorian athlete on his list but suggested that any number of people could have been involved. Once again though Leonardo could have arranged the swords so that he might receive cuts without them being life threatening.

The recounting of the incidents involving the throwing of the gauntlet in the former control tower, the clandestine visit by the shadowy unknown figure to Giles' trailer with the note listing names of celebrities who'd later changed their names, and the comments made by Eva, the fortune teller, all had a bewildering effect on Freddie.

'Why are you prepared to have this gypsy girl on your list? You must have had a very good reason.'

'She seemed to know that I was being followed and we both know, that when that happens, there's a pretty good chance that they're in cahoots with the one doing the following.'

Freddie nodded in acquiescence.

'How many people knew of Ramon's concern that he was running, as he described it, this *gauntlet of fear*?'

'Why do you ask?'

'For the very simple reason that whoever threw down that iron glove in the control tower had to know of Ramon's latent fear and that could conceivably narrow the list of possible suspects. Also the unknown figure who left the list of names in your trailer – we don't even know if it was male or female.'

'No, that's true…but he, or she, did head in the direction of the tiger's wagon, and that might lead us to think it was Khan's trainer or someone connected with the animal.'

'So far it's all a hotchpotch of uncertainty. We're going to need more information about persons who might have been involved.'

'Yes, and I'm certain there's more to come. You know I have a shrewd idea that the accidents could occur when I return to the winter quarters! Do you fancy a trip with me sometime? Two heads are better than one!'

'That might not be a bad idea! Penny's taking the girls to spend a few days with their gran before they go back to school so I could drive you down to Devon and that will get me acquainted with this circus of yours.'

The two companions talked well into the night. Freddie wanted to know more about the fortune teller and became intrigued at the predictions about the 1967 Grand National. He couldn't quite work out the puzzling words of Madame Eva Zigana and how his lucky number came into the equation, but experience had taught him that strange unexplained premonitions had been involved in his previous racing encounters.

The Grand National, run at Aintree, was only a few months away and Freddie would be giving the race a good check once the entries were known. It could be interesting to examine Eva's predictions, and try to decipher them, as the race drew nearer.

Some days later Giles was heading back to RAF Winkleigh but this time in the passenger seat of Freddie's red Triumph Spitfire.

Freddie breathed a sigh of satisfaction as he approached familiar territory near Exeter racecourse.

'I've spent quite a few pleasant days at the Devon and Exeter meetings here,' he confided. 'But we have to get a move on if we want to get to your non-existent airfield before dark.'

'Yes, we don't want to have our journey interrupted by the ghosts that apparently haunt the place. We have enough on our plate trying to rectify Ramon's problem.'

Giles surveyed the scenery as he returned to the winter quarters by a different route this time. He was now travelling between Exeter and Winkleigh and, looking at his watch, he guessed he should be there in about an hour or so.

He looked across at his colleague and smiled as he recalled "Two heads are better than one!" Confidence was returning.

Senhor Mordomo welcomed both men when they arrived, and had someone escort Giles and his friend to their trailer with instructions for them to join him for the evening meal.

The spell before dinner was the chance for Giles and Freddie to go over the catalogue of incidents and potential suspects. It was also an opportunity to give Freddie a look around the site and make him familiar with the lie of the land.

Freddie had a good look at the note Giles gave him. His concentration deepened the lines in his brow at what lay in front of him.

Giles interjected with 'Not much to go on but I suppose you haven't heard all that's happened so far.'

Freddie had another look at the short list of events and the people who were present.

Incident	Present
Hank Findley's vibrating wire	All suspects?
Khan's cage unlocked	Giles and Ramon
Fire in clown scene	Allison and others?
Gauntlet in control tower	Giles himself
Clandestine visit to Giles' trailer	Unknown?
Swords balancing act	All suspects

'No, not much to go on there, old son! I'm afraid we'll have to keep a very close watch on things before we can start to eliminate anybody.'

'You're right, Freddie, but, I've only just started and we may have more to go on over the next day or so.'

Giles looked at his watch. 'Let's pop over to the big chief for a spot of dinner. Tomorrow will be soon enough to get a grip of things.'

Dinner was a cordial affair with Ramon, the host, offering Freddie the same amenities as he had previously extended to the Prof.

Talk centred on the main suspects and included a distinct possibility for Freddie to meet with Madame Zigana to clarify her previous prediction about himself given to Giles.

Before the evening was over Senhor Mordomo proposed that Giles should take his friend to see the noble jungle beast which was the apple of his eye in the circus – the Royal Bengal Tiger, Khan.

The two men left the congenial atmosphere of the lavish trailer in a cosy, if slightly, groggy state of mind. They picked their way in the dark among trailers and wagons lit by subdued lamps.

The hushed silence heightened the eeriness of their surroundings as they made their way towards the large wagon, with the extended tented awning, that housed the cage of Khan – the Tiger.

There was nobody outside the door and the door was unlocked.

Giles turned the handle and pushed. Inside the warmth and animal smell was mildly comforting as both men stepped in and Freddie shut the door. As their eyes adjusted to the faint light they could distinguish the bars and the straw-covered floor beyond.

'He's probably asleep,' whispered Giles. 'So let's not make a noise.'

'I'm trying my best, but the pounding of my heart isn't helping me. My ears feel as if they're fit to burst. Can you see him?'

'No, not yet. He's probably lying down. But don't go too close to the bars.'

Two pairs of eyes searched the straw then both men turned to look at each other and shook heads.

It was the soft rustle of an animal's movement that brought two pairs of eyes back to look at the area beyond the bars. Nothing could be seen…but something could be heard.

It was the prolonged but muffled throaty growl that seemed to come from the inner depths of a huge animal's body…and the sound came from behind them.

Both men turned slowly and came face to face with the black and orange markings of the huge beast from Bengal. The white spots above the animal's eyes appeared to glow in the dim light and the large mouth opened to reveal menacing teeth.

'Don't move a muscle!' a voice uttered from the gloom. 'The cage door has been unlocked and if you make any sudden movement you'll be in grave danger.'

The voice belonged to Senor Gomez, the animal's trainer, who managed to gently persuade an inquisitive Khan back to the open door of his cage… much to the relief of Giles and Freddie.

'What are you doing in here?'

'Senhor Mordomo thought I should let my friend see your magnificent animal,' Giles disclosed with a slight tremor in his voice.

'He should have known better!' The outrage in the voice was clearly evident. 'You must not visit this area without someone in charge. You could both have been killed. Please contact me if you want to visit Khan. I'll make sure that everything is secure. You will then get a chance to enjoy the encounter.'

'Thank you. I'll remember that. Freddie and I have no wish to provoke the wrath of Khan. And we would prefer to avoid the wraith of Khan that we experienced a few moments ago.'

'That was some pussycat!' said a terrified Freddie as he and Giles left the caged area. 'It's me that's having kittens!'

Giles just shook his head and wiped the tears from his eyes.

Chapter 6

THE LADY VANISHES

The circus canteen was busy when Giles and Freddie joined troupers and workers, next morning, for breakfast.

The big strong lad next to Giles was very keen to converse and he spoke English with a slight but detectable local accent

'I know who you are,' he said. 'You're that magician chap what's here to revitalise the circus and make sure this Big Top becomes top of the bill.'

'Not quite correct, I'm afraid. I'm really a historian, but I don't deny I'm a historian of magic.'

'Of course, you're the man who solved the mystery that was in all the papers not so long ago?'

'Well…yes. I suppose I did get a bit of coverage in the press. My name is Giles, Giles Dawson. And you are?'

'Lawrence…but I like to be called Larry.' He leaned over and shook hands.

'You sound local!'

'And so I should! I'm from the Exeter area. At my interview, the boss offered me a job that kind of made my boyhood dreams come true.'

'Great. So what line of work are you in?'

'At the moment I'm one of the assistants whose job it is to prepare the ring for each act.'

'A very responsible job and quite onerous, I suspect.'

'Yes, it is,' he said, cramming the last piece of buttered toast into his mouth and washing it down with a mug of hot tea. 'But there's always the chance of something big coming along.'

Giles glanced at Freddie as this remark took on a sinister connotation.

'You seem to be in a hurry? What's the rush?'

'Oh I'm due to get everything ready in that tented area near the control tower. There's a special practice to be held there shortly and I recommend that you watch her.'

'A girl, you say?'

'Yes, a Devon girl and she could be a sensation before long. She's going places. Take my word.'

'What does she do?'

'She rides a horse.'

'She rides a horse? Is that all?'

'Yes, but like nothing I've ever seen before.'

With that he was gone.

Giles looked at Freddie who was devouring scrambled egg, bacon, beans and tomato.

'When you're finished I think we should visit that tent and have a look at this girl on an animal that doesn't instantly remind us of Khan.'

Freddie looked up, his face breaking into a grin and, with a turn of the head, he winked approval.

There was a buzz of excited anticipation when Giles and Freddie arrived at the tented area. The ring was surrounded by technicians who seemed to be eagerly awaiting something spectacular.

Into the ring came a white Andalusian mare with a girl astride her. The girl was dressed in a costume more befitting a trapeze artist than an equestrian rider...and she was riding bareback.

A small group of musicians started to play a tune in waltz time and the white horse and her rider began to move in dressage fashion.

For upwards of ten minutes Giles and Freddie watched the walks, trots and canters of a supremely calm, supple and flexible animal. The confident, attentive and understanding display controlled by a young girl with no saddle or reins to give the horse instructions, was truly memorable.

No climax was necessary but the performance didn't close until the animal had completed a group of techniques accomplished to a varied musical background: showing the rhythm, gait and tempo of top class equestrian pursuit. The finale culminated with the horse jumping into the air and kicking both hind legs…with the rider kneeling and then standing on its quarters. Jumping to the ground, the girl moved to the head of the Andalusian; the act ending with both horse and rider bowing to tremendous applause.

'Come on Freddie. We must meet this young lady. I have an idea it might just work in our favour.'

Rushing outside the tent Giles was just in time to catch the girl as her horse was being led away by stable lads.

'Congratulations on a quite brilliant performance Miss…?'

'I like to be called Lizzie! Lizzie Lisbet is my name and I know who you are…and why you're here.'

'Oh you do, do you?'

'Yes.'

'And…?'

'I believe you're here because of the accidents we've been having and you want to discover why, and by whom.'

'You seem to be a very knowledgeable young girl. Have you been with the circus long?'

'Not very long, but I've been watching things happen…and I don't want to be involved in an accident myself.'

'Do you happen to believe that they're being caused by someone or have you another explanation?'

'Well I don't believe the ghosts of this place are causing them, so something or someone has to be responsible.'

'Hmm! I understand that you're a Devon girl?'

'Yes. My home is not far from here. My dad is a farrier and I've been riding ponies since I was born…I think. Someone told the boss about me and, after a rehearsal with the mare, I was hired. They also want to train me for the trapeze.'

'You say you know why I'm here…would you like to help?'

The young girl looked a little surprised. She stared enquiringly at Giles; her slight frown showing bewilderment.

'How could I possibly help?' she questioned, and her pretty face began to indicate eagerness.

Giles turned to look at Freddie before answering.

'Just keep doing what you've been doing. Keep watching things happen but come and tell me if you have any suspicions about the causes. That will give me an extra pair of eyes and your astuteness could prove very valuable to me.'

'I'd love to help, but I'll talk to you later. At the moment I'm starting to feel cold in this costume. Please excuse…!'

'I'm so sorry, Lizzie. You mustn't stay out in this temperature after a performance like that. Off you go and get dressed. It was stupid of me to keep you hanging around like this.'

Lizzie turned and was gone in a flash.

Giles was grabbed from behind by a rather disturbed Freddie.

'Don't you think you might be asking for trouble? After all, this girl might be one of the suspects causing the problem you're trying to solve. You could be falling into a trap.'

'Come off it, Freddie! Surely you don't think a girl, just recently hired by the circus and most likely after some of the accidents started, is now trying to take over the running of the entire circus. That's pretty far fetched, don't you think?'

'Yes! I suppose you're right. I never thought of it like that.'

'What do you think we should do now?'

'I wouldn't mind paying a visit to that control tower where the gauntlet was thrown. A proper examination of the place might reveal things.'

'Yes, that's true, and there may be information listing all the rehearsals that are taking place. We can then make plans for the rest of the day.'

A short walk from the tent where the young girl gave her unbelievable demonstration of equestrian art saw the two men reach the control tower.

Giles knocked on the door. There was no reply but they entered.

When they were inside and the door closed Freddie moved around and discovered that the ground floor consisted of more than one room.

'When you came in here for the first time did you go upstairs?'

'No!'

'Well I suggest we do that now.'

Upstairs the area was clean and tidy with a table and a small cabinet with drawers full of documents which on closer scrutiny both men felt were irrelevant.

On the walls were several posters in vivid colour of some of the great circuses of bygone times plus a notice board listing the timetable of acts due to be rehearsed.

'This is what we were looking for,' said a gleeful Freddie, pointing to the notice pinned to the board. 'And that is what we've just been watching.'

Giles gazed at where his companion's finger made contact with the list. 'It just says "White mare and rider" and that's an understatement if I ever saw one.'

'Yes…' expressed Freddie, his expression rapidly changing from incredulity to concern. 'But look at this!' he said, pointing to a number of newspaper articles from "The Hartford Courant" of July 1944.

Both men read graphic accounts of one of the worst fire disasters in the history of the United States.

The fire had occurred during an afternoon performance of the Ringling Brothers and Barnum and Bailey Circus in Hartford, Connecticut, which was attended by more than six thousand people.

The death toll was one hundred and sixty-seven, many of them children, though some estimates put it higher, and more than seven hundred were injured.

'You don't think…?' a disturbed Freddie asked his colleague as he turned away from the newspaper cuttings.

'I hope not! I sincerely hope not!' Giles retorted before biting his lip, his gaze somehow suggesting a past remark. 'But this extract gives me the shivers!' he said pointing to one of the articles.

Freddie looked at his colleague with concern. 'Is some past remark bothering you, old son?'

'Yes, I'm afraid is does! Something Hank, the tightrope walker, said when he drove me here that first time. He was suggesting that ghosts of past airmen might be the cause of the accidents…but there was something else.'

'Well…?'

'He said there may be the sound of aero engines at night or the smell of oil burning and that…*I might even get a whiff of kerosene! It could frighten the hell out of you!*' That's what he said.'

'I don't like the sound of that. But surely you don't think someone would attempt to start a fire that could possibly destroy everything they were trying to take over? And anyway, why would there be kerosene in a circus?'

'Yes…good question, Freddie. Kerosene may have been used as an ingredient in aviation fuel during World War 2, though I can't be sure of that, but you wouldn't expect it to be in use at a circus. This article might cause us to think again,' Giles said, pointing to the notice board. The disquiet in his voice transferring alarm to his companion as Freddie read the newspaper report.

"One possible cause of the disastrous fire at Hartford may have been due to a common waterproofing method for canvas at the time. It appeared that the large tent had been coated with paraffin dissolved in gasoline (some sources say *kerosene*)."

Freddie looked at Giles. His face, tanned by many racecourse visits, was beginning to take on the shade of one confronted by a ghost.

'I don't know about you but I could do with a stiff drink. Or maybe there are some other attractions to have a look at, like that Lizzie and her performing horse.'

'Yes, Freddie, a drink could come in handy, but let's look at that notice board again and see if there is something listed that might entertain and not frighten the hell out of us.'

'Here we are. This should be just up your street,' said a jovial Freddie, pointing to the item listed on the notice board. The Lady Vanishes – magician and assistants. 'This might be exactly what you were advocating at the lecture in St James's Club.'

'I do hope so. I think we could both do with a bit of magic.'

'It's to be in the big hanger so that should be a good disappearing trick on a solid floor.'

'Yes, Freddie! A good disappearing trick, just as long as everything goes according to plan.'

The twinkle in Freddie's eyes, as this statement was made, clearly expressed that he was on the same wavelength as his colleague.

The main hanger was almost empty apart from a tall gentleman, in evening dress; a girl, wearing a long blood red gown; several male assistants, standing beside a number of large vehicle tyres; and two female assistants in short dresses carrying a crimson cloth.

The two pals seated themselves to watch the show and, after an acknowledging nod and wink from the gentleman in evening dress, the performance was ready to begin.

Giles' attention was directed to the central performer. This was the first time he'd seen the circus magician in action.

Without any spoken words the magician, using a display of arms, introduced his assistant. The girl in the red dress moved slowly to the centre of the hanger demonstrating to her imaginary audience.

This was immediately followed by two assistants rolling one of the large motor tyres towards the centre of the hanger, lifting the tyre and placing it over the girl's head and body.

Another two assistants followed this routine with a further tyre and this was repeated until the girl, whom Giles recognised as Allison, from the fire episode with the clowns, was hidden by the pile of tyres.

The two female assistants moved towards the tyres unfolded the large crimson cloth and draped it over the pile, thus covering the girl.

The magician walked around the tyres covered by the cloth, clearly showing that there was no way for the lady to leave her hiding place, without being seen.

At a signal from the magician, the two girl assistants removed the cloth and, one by one, the large tyres were removed from the pile and rolled away by the male assistants until the final tyre was taken away to reveal nothing but a blood-red dress lying in the centre of the hanger…the lady had disappeared.

The magician bowed to all sides of the hanger before pointing towards the applauding Giles. As both Giles and Freddie were giving the magician a well-deserved ovation, Allison, the magician's assistant, stepped from behind them.

Freddie looked at Giles and nodded.

Giles got to his feet and approached both the magician and his assistant.

'That was a very slick performance,' Giles said, with admiration in his voice as he shook the magician by the hand. 'It will be even more spectacular when performed in the circus ring, under the lights, with the band playing.'

'Thank you, Professor.'

'I'm not sure I caught your name when you were introduced at the showpiece in Soho.'

'Wagner, Michael Wagner.'

'Haven't I seen you before?'

'I attended your lecture in the St James's Club, in London, when your optimism, regarding stage magic in the circus, was well received.'

'Of course…I remember seeing you in the audience that night. It was the start of what could now be a lengthy and difficult undertaking, I'm afraid.'

'Senhor Ramon is convinced there is someone hell bent on forcing him to relinquish his hold on the circus, but I've spoken to a few others who are not so sure that is the case.'

'Have you been with the circus long?'

'Not really. I joined last year when artists were being recruited for the circus. I applied thinking that illusions could be performed despite being entirely surrounded by an audience. Senhor Ramon appeared to agree and I'm looking forward to a good year ahead.'

'When do you expect to make your first public performance?'

'Well we start in York, at the racecourse, at the end of April. But we are due to give a performance here at Winkleigh, sometime at the end of February or beginning of March.'

'I'd like to see that. It would give me a good chance to scrutinize the entire programme and make my mind up about certain things that disturb me.'

'You'd be most welcome and everyone would co-operate.'

'I'm due to give lectures on a cruise ship in March so I hope that doesn't coincide with the Winkleigh show. Have you any other illusions ready for March, apart from the one I've just watched?'

'We're working on another depicting a knight in shining armour. There's still a bit of work to be done and there's also a chance we might use Khan, the tiger, in a disappearing act substituting the animal for Allison, my assistant.'

Giles smiled as his gaze turned to the girl. 'You are involved in more than the magic acts although there was quite a bit of magic used in your escape from the fire.'

'Michael doesn't object to me working with other acts.'

'Just so long as the accidents don't rob me of someone I rely heavily upon,' the magician said as he put an arm around Allison's shoulders.

'Do you ever employ doubles?' Giles asked.

'Funny you should ask,' Michael smiled gently as he answered. 'I'm considering an illusion involving Senhor Ramon, our circus supremo. There is someone here, who shall be nameless, who is the exact double of Ramon.

All he requires, to complete the likeness, is to wear a false moustache. After that you'd be hard pushed to tell them apart.'

Giles turned to Freddie, who had approached the group. He'd been silent throughout the exchanges. 'Let me introduce my close friend. Freddie Oldsworth.'

'I read about you when the newspapers had articles about the Lockerbie affair,' Michael Wagner commented as he shook Freddie by the hand. 'The whole business interested me as the mystery involved the death of the magician cabinet-maker.'

'I played a supporting role, much like your assistant today.'

'That is true. But today it was the supporting role that created the illusion to complete a successful performance.'

As Giles and Freddie left the hanger Freddie pulled his friend to one side.

'It occurred to me,' he said. 'When Mr. Wagner told us he was considering a magical act involving a knight in armour; we didn't see the gauntlet in the control tower when we were there. Do you know what happened to it?'

'No I don't. I think we should pay another visit.'

There was a cold wind blowing as they trudged towards the control tower. It was unlocked and they were glad to get some kind of shelter.

A search downstairs revealed nothing resembling the iron glove that had been thrown at Giles on his first visit to what would have been the hub of the airfield throughout those critical war years.

Upstairs the result was the same. Everything was as they'd found it the last time they were there.

The notice board still had the cuttings about the great circus fire of the Barnum and Bailey, Ringling Brothers disaster.

They were about to leave when Freddie observed an additional notice pinned to the board. It was addressed to Giles.

Freddie took it from the board and handed it to his friend.

The envelope was unsealed. Giles held it in his hands for what seemed an age. He looked totally mystified and appeared reluctant to open it and read the contents.

On occasions like this Freddie knew it was best to keep a watching brief and not interrupt his close friend.

Several moments passed before Giles removed a sheet of paper and started to read. Lines on his furrowed brow deepened and a shake of the head was the only other indication of his puzzlement before he handed the sheet over to his waiting colleague.

It was headed: To Professor Dawson

I am well aware that you enjoy a conundrum, Professor, so if you solve this riddle you will go a long way to unravelling the predicament you are in at the moment. But a word of warning. Do not believe all you see or hear.

Go in the direction of a Hitchcock movie
Whose leading man had two names?

Seek out the KC on a forbidden isle and
Retrace half a century from March Twenty-first.
Learn of a Race that never was
On grassland that, unlike RAF Winkleigh, is now an airfield.

Near where the Seats of Rhouma stay
Is the secret you wish to solve one day?

'I'm not entirely sure what this is all about,' Freddie said as he handed back the note. 'But whoever wrote this was the same person who spoke to me on the phone.'

'What makes you think that?'

'Do not believe all you see or hear. That's in the letter and that was what was said to me on the phone.'

'What does it all mean?'

'I don't know…you're the one who loves conundrums.'

'I think a phone call to a house near Lockerbie might help. I know someone there who loves to solve little brainteasers like this.'

There was a smirk on Freddie's face as he remarked 'Yes…the lady is just the person to call. Why don't you do that now?'

'North by North West has to be the Hitchcock movie. That's fairly clear, and I'm heading in that direction, in March, on my lecture cruise. But the rest is obscure. Yes, a phone call to that house in Scotland might just be what is required. I'll do that now.'

Chapter 7

THE BLACK SQUADRON

When Giles returned to the control tower he found Freddie studying the cuttings pinned to the notice board.

The letter with the cryptic conundrum was still in Giles' hand.

'Did you make the call? Freddie asked with eager anticipation.

'Yes, I did, but it was answered by Doreen, the housekeeper. She said Mrs. Ramsden was having a nap and her daughter was out. I said I'd call again later.'

'Let me have another look at that riddle, Giles. There may be something we can fathom out with a concentrated effort.'

Both men grabbed chairs and sat down at one of the tables.

Giles spread the letter out, leaned back in his chair and looked at Freddie.'

'One line, in particular, bothers me somewhat.' He said.'

'What line is that? They all bother me apart from the opening one.'

'It's the one with the KC on it. You know how I constantly correct you when you describe Horse Racing as the Sport of Kings?'

'Yes, you keep telling me it ought to be the Sport of Queens because we have a lady as the monarch. But I always insist that, although we have a Queen on the throne, Racing is still the "Sport of Kings" and will remain so.'

You may be quite correct, Freddie, but the line that mentions the KC strikes me as odd for the simple reason that a King's Counsel becomes a Queen's Counsel when a lady is our monarch.'

'So you think the KC should be QC?'

'Yes I do.'

'But, just for the sake of argument, supposing the KC is quite correct.

Maybe it is not an abbreviation for King's Counsel…but for something entirely different?'

'I never thought of that, but, if what you're inferring is correct, what could it possibly mean?'

'I'm afraid I don't know, but it's something to be considered very seriously.'

'If only I had an enlarged hippocampus!'

'What, on earth, are you drivelling on about now, Giles?'

'I'm sorry, Freddie, I seem to be inundating you with a collection of extraordinary expressions.'

'Yes! Funambulism and impalement were just about as much as I could take a short while ago. But where the dickens did you get this hippo thing? Don't tell me it's another name for a 'potamus?'

'No, Freddie. It's not.'

'Well…?

'It was a term used by the cabbie that drove me to the Tropicana show on New Year's Eve. He told me he had an enlarged hippocampus. Apparently it's a structure in the floor of the brain that enables lucky individuals, who have this abnormal configuration, to develop an extraordinary memory.'

'We could do with him right now.'

'Who?'

'Your cabbie friend; the one with the enlarged thing. Next time you see him ask some questions and try and get some answers.'

The two colleagues headed for the canteen, in a jovial mood, though still trying to puzzle what the wording of the riddle meant. A spot of lunch and a conversation with a few of the riggers prompted Giles, accompanied by Freddie, to visit the circus barbers.

The usual "no racing tips, no politics" was a prelude to a trim as Giles sat down in the barber's chair. Meanwhile Freddie had a few words with some of the other hairdressers.

What Giles gleaned from his visit was that he should keep an eye on two of the main characters; the Ringmaster and the Band Leader. Both were considered to be leading protagonists if a bid to usurp Ramon as circus owner was being made.

The early part of the afternoon was spent watching a few jugglers on stilts, after which Giles proposed that a return trip to the control tower might reveal further details of forthcoming rehearsals.

Late afternoon gloom was shrouding the winter quarters of the circus as Giles and Freddie approached the control tower. There was a light on as they entered and they could hear someone upstairs.

'Is it all right for us to come in? Giles called out as Freddie opened the door.

'Be my guests,' said a familiar voice. Giles recognised it as the first voice he heard when he was met off the train at Eggesford station.

It was Hank Findley, the wire walker. He was busy pinning more information sheets on the notice board.

'How's the leg doing? Giles enquired when they were upstairs. 'Are you almost ready to resume your act?'

'It's coming along and I should be able to walk the wire in a week or so. I want to be ready to perform when we give a show to the Devon folks at the end of February,'

'I'd like to see that. If you're not too busy can I ask you something?'

'Sure…go ahead.'

'Does the circus have more than one telephone?'

'Yes there are several. The boss has one. I think there are two in the canteen, one in each hanger and, believe it or not, there's a phone here in this building.'

'I haven't seen one in here.'

'No, you won't unless you know where to look. Come on, let me show you.'

Hank took Giles aside to a tiny alcove where, on a shelf and under a protective cover, there was a phone. To the astonishment of the professor of illusions there was also something else under that cover. It was a gleaming gauntlet; the very same gauntlet, he presumed, he'd last seen under his feet.

Giles made every effort to conceal his surprise. 'Can I use this phone on the odd occasion?' he said.

'I don't see why not. Only the circus celebrities are allowed in here and you come into that category.'

Hank replaced the cover and both men returned to find a thoughtful Freddie studying the notice board.

'Do you mind if I ask you a question, Mr. Findley?' said Freddie as he turned to face the wire walker.

'Not at all; please do. And please call me Hank.'

'I gather you told my friend that he might hear aero engines at night or the sound of men scrambling to get airborne? I think those are the very words you used? What did you mean by that?'

'Oh, that…that's easy. It was the Black Squadron!'

'I'm sorry, I don't understand.'

'It was all very hush-hush during the war years at most aerodromes; this one in particular. That's probably why the Ministry of Defence or the RAF have always denied the existence of this place.'

'But the Black Squadron…?'

'161 squadron had Lysander aircraft, painted black that were used in clandestine stealth missions to drop spies and secret agents into occupied Europe. The men who flew these dangerous assignments, on moonless nights, undoubtedly influenced the outcome of the war and it's probably no wonder that the RAF have never admitted the existence of this place. Few of these men knew the big picture and many never came back.'

'Is it true that some local people still hear the sounds?'

'So I've heard.'

'You were here, Hank.' Giles cross-examined. 'Do you still hear them?'

'Yes, I was here. And it was my suggestion that we use this site for our winter quarters. Yes, I still hear them, but I can never be sure if what I'm hearing is the wind swirling around the hangers and control tower, or my imagination. It can be quite eerie here at times. Excuse me, I have some important work to do.'

The American tightrope artiste gathered some papers and started to go downstairs. As he left the building he shouted back. 'Don't be afraid to use the phone; that's what it's there for.'

Upstairs both men looked at each other and smiled.

'Why don't we have another look at that written conundrum, Giles? Someone, who knows you intend travelling has to be the one who wrote it. If you can produce a short list of people to whom you mentioned your intended trip, that might clarify things a bit more.'

'I agree. The only problem with that is that whoever heard it from me could have inadvertently passed it on to someone else.'

'Point taken! But it would do no harm to go over those you told about that lecture cruise of yours.'

A thoughtful professor pondered, for what seemed an age to his friend, before uttering his conclusions. 'The first time I mentioned my trip was to Madame Eva Zigana, the circus fortune teller. I did say to her that I would be joining a cruise of the Scottish Hebrides and the Shetland Isles in March.'

'That's a good start. The Hebrides would conform to the part about the Hitchcock movie and the month of March is mentioned significantly in the puzzle.'

'That is a good start, as you say, but, if I remember correctly it was Madame Zigana who first brought the idea of travel into the conversation. She said I would probably succeed in my quest to solve Senhor Ramon's problem if I travelled to some far off spots. She could have read that in any one of several magazines and as a fortune teller the most important way to influencing an individual before attempting to predict their future, would be to read as much about them as possible.'

'Yes, Giles, I suppose that's true. And if Madame Zigana could read up about you so could anyone else who was determined to lead you up the garden path.'

'The Magician, Michael Wagner. I did mention my cruise after I congratulated him on his Vanishing Lady Illusion but he wouldn't have had time to construct the conundrum. He did, however, attend the lecture I gave at the St James's Club in December and it's quite possible I gave that information to my audience there. He told me he'd been there and had also read a great deal about me in the newspapers. I may even have mentioned it to Hank Findley while he drove me to the station. I just can't be sure. Regarding Hank, what did you make of his remarks about the Black Squadron?'

'He seemed genuine enough. The entire operation was of stealth and we're both aware that, during any war, such exploits can have dire consequences. They don't always go according to plan.'

'I have no problem with that, but what did you make of those phantom sounds and the possible odour of kerosene that he stressed?'

'Well we both know there are Second World War airfields with a history of spectral images, but our connection with the Ghost Club impels us to be a bit more sceptical even though certain incidents are often difficult to explain.'

'Imagination can distort things and auto-suggestion invariably lures the unsuspecting recipient into believing they see what they're intended to see. Isn't that the secret ingredient of the magician and illusionist?'

'Do not believe all you see or hear,' Freddie recapped.

'Now where have I heard that before?' Giles expounded further. 'In close-up magic the onlooker is directed to look at a certain object while the manipulator is performing elsewhere.'

'The quickness of the hand deceiving the eye, you mean?'

'Not every time, Freddie. The converse can be just as effective. A slow movement may give the innocent bystander a false sense of security and a confidence that is misplaced. Hank gives the impression of being trustworthy in all he does or says, yet I'm not sure whether to take him at face value or not?'

'He seems just a bit too plausible at times and maybe requires close scrutiny.'

A glance at his watch alerted Giles to get to his feet. 'I think I'll make another call to Lockerbie.' He called out as he moved towards the alcove.

Freddie nodded acquiescence.

When Giles reached the alcove and removed the cover he was caught a little off guard. As he picked up the phone and started to dial it became clear that there was no sign of the gauntlet that had been there a short time ago. It had disappeared. Had it been there in the first place and had Hank removed it, or was it all a figment of his imagination?

At least fifteen minutes passed before Giles returned from the alcove.

'Did you have any luck this time?'

'Yes, Laura was back home and I gave her all the information about the riddle.'

'How did she react?'

'She agreed about the Hitchcock movie and, as it co-responded with my trip to the Inner Hebrides in March, she was of the opinion that the first line of the riddle had been written by someone who already knew of my intended journey to the North West.'

'Did she have any clear thoughts on the other lines?'

'No. not really, but she did say she would make some inquiries about the forbidden isle.'

'It would obviously help things if we knew that. The KC puzzle might then have more meaning. Did she say anything about that?'

'She agreed with your idea that if KC was not an abbreviation for King's Counsel then the identification of the forbidden isle could make an awful difference…KC could possibly be the initials of someone important living on the isle.'

'Did she say when she might have a solution to those clues?'

'No, she didn't say. But she asked if there was any likelihood of me travelling to visit her in Lockerbie around the second week in February when she expected to have made some progress about the forbidden isle. We could then both think things over like we used to do in those long ago days of the early forties.'

'Don't tell me, Giles, let me guess. You are going, aren't you?'

'Yes, I am. How did you guess?'

'It's your face, old son. The look on your face made everything abundantly clear. As an ex-teacher of mathematics it didn't take me too long to work out that the second week in February usually comes fairly close to the fourteenth, and if my information is correct that is St. Valentine's Day and that might play a significant part in your getting together.'

'You're at it again, Freddie. You invariably, at some stage, try desperately to get me involved in the marriage stakes.'

'With little or no success, I'm afraid. Still it's always good to remember that the grey days of Winter are repeatedly followed by the colours of Spring.'

'No comment, Freddie. Now are you ready for a visit to the circus canteen for a bite of dinner? We've had a busy day and the inner man requires a bit of sustenance.'

Freddie gathered up a few notes as he prepared to leave but it was Giles, grabbing him vigorously by an arm that stopped him in his tracks.

'What on earth is that noise?' The words that poured from Giles' voice box were uttered with an incredulous alarm and a power that equalled the pressure on Freddie's arm.

'If I was on an airfield, that was still an airfield, I'd say it sounds like an aircraft coming in to land.'

'But this is no longer an airfield, Freddie. It can't land here.' The tremor in his voice increased as did the grip on his colleague's arm.'

'It sounds much too real to be an aircraft of the Black Squadron…and what the hell is that smell?' posed a perplexed Freddie as he broke free from the grip on his arm and pushed his companion outside before closing the control tower door.

The odour was quite distinct in the cool evening air.

'That has to be kerosene, if I'm not mistaken!' Giles' anxiety was pronounced.

The aircraft engine noise grew louder as two pairs of eyes scanned the darkness. But, as the racket gradually began to decrease, as if signifying an aircraft coming to a halt, another sound grew. Was it the sound of men scrambling to get airborne as described by Hank, the walker of tightropes? No! It was the commotion of men running around urgently attempting to rectify a major problem.

The uproar came from where the overpowering smell of kerosene was evident. It came from the area close to the canteen – an area where the inky blackness of the night was starkly illuminated by the flames that were now engulfing a section of one of the tents.

The two ex RAF men rushed towards the fire like moths to a candle flame. Striding over ropes, cables and metal poles they joined a group of men, dressed in black, who were dismantling a section of vinyl canvas. The pungent smell of kerosene was potent but the damaged section was being speedily brought under control.

Senhor Ramon was spotted by Giles near to where the fire was being extinguished. Giles approached him and inquired. 'How did this happen?'

'I'm not sure, but I suspect it was yet one more attempt to create an accident and make my hold on the circus more precarious.'

'Did you see how it started?'

'No, I came out to meet my visitors who were arriving by plane.'

'So that's what we heard?'

'Yes, my visitors are from a leading film studio. They have come to collect some circus background they might use in a future movie.'

'But I thought this was no longer an airfield.'

'That is basically a correct description of this place but the runway can still be used though only by light aircraft. It will no doubt deteriorate as each year goes by. Now if you'll excuse me I'll go and meet my guests.'

When Ramon had gone Giles moved across to where the fire had been.

He introduced himself to one of the men clearing the burned debris. He was a short stocky man with a jockey's tan and a wrestler's handshake. He was perfectly willing to answer Giles' question.

'Is it normal practice to use kerosene as a waterproofing agent for circus tents?'

'No. Not that I'm aware of. We tend not to use chemicals that are highly inflammable. Why do you ask?'

Giles gave a shake of the head and a rather vague 'No reason. I was just curious, that's all.'

He looked across to Freddie whose face registered disbelief in the harsh light from the head lamps of one of the circus wagons.

Chapter 8

"DOUBLE, DOUBLE TOIL AND TROUBLE"
William Shakespeare

Sitting down to a meal in the canteen was a welcome relief after the excitement and clouded contention of the previous hours.

With dinner finally over, Giles and Freddie decided that a night cap, in the artist's bar area, would make a deserving end to an interesting day.

They were hardly inside before they were joined by the two gentlemen Giles had been advised to keep an eye on while he was in the barber's chair earlier in the day.

'Professor Dawson, let me introduce my colleague, Felix Reiser,' Sebastian Capuzzo, the ringmaster said as he made the introduction. 'Felix is our outstanding band leader. I'm not exactly sure if you spoke with him at the New Year's Eve celebration at Soho in London?'

'We had a few words, that tragic evening,' Giles ventured as he shook hands with both men. 'Neither of you have met my associate, Freddie Oldsworth. Please join us.'

Greetings done with, Giles gave Freddie a sneaky wink accompanied by a sly grin.

'Do you mind if I ask both of you a few questions?' Giles looked at each of the two talented individuals as he spoke.

'I have a good idea you are about to ask us our opinion of tonight's unfortunate incident. I have no hesitation in offering you my total co-operation and I'm sure Sebastian will agree with me. That happens to be one of the reasons we came over to join you.' The band leader's self-confidant tone was received with suspicion.

'And what were the other reasons?' asked Giles.

The two circus professionals glanced at each other before the ringmaster replied.

'We'd like to know what you think of the situation we seem to be faced with. We both have come from circus backgrounds and I doubt if there has ever been a circus, large or small, that travelled without the occasional accident happening.'

'I assume you are stating what appears to be the obvious; simply because of the nature of this form of entertainment which deals with danger. I am, however, reluctant to accept that a circus of this magnitude, with the immense skill at its disposal, can stomach so many so-called accidents in such a short space of time without a realistic questioning of the whys and the wherefores.'

Freddie nodded approval of his friend's speech.

'Professor Dawson, I don't accept that the spate of minor accidents are the norm in a circus of this quality but I really am unconvinced that everything has been deliberately staged in an attempt to relieve the circus of its present owner.'

'Minor accidents, did you say?' Giles' disapproval of Sebastian Capuzzo's trivial definition of the accidents was evident as he continued. 'I would hardly call the fire that happened tonight or the one in the clowns' scene as minor. Nor the sword act, that occurred on New Year's Eve. And certainly not the several times when Khan's cage has been suspiciously unlocked.'

'I wasn't aware that our Tiger's cage had been unlocked. No-one has told us about that.'

'Well,' stated a ruffled Giles. 'I am telling you now! And I would be very interested to know how you two gentlemen appraise the situation?'

The look on the circus artistes' faces showed evasion and a reluctance to continue their own line of enquiry.

'I'm sorry if what I said sounded flippant. The particulars you mention about the possibility of Khan leaving his cage make all the difference to the predicament we're in.'

The apology by Sebastian was immediately followed by the ringmaster taking a drink from his glass and then removing a black silk handkerchief from his pocket.

As he used the piece of black silk to dab his upper lip the expression on Giles' face had an instant effect on Freddie. It was such an impact that

Freddie knew he was certain to quiz Giles about it once they were on their own.

It was sometime later that evening when a tired Giles and Freddie made their way back to their trailer.

They were hardly in the door when Freddie swung his compatriot around.

'I know what you're about to ask,' said Giles. 'You want to know what startled me a short time ago when we were speaking to the ringmaster and band leader.'

'It was the look on your face, old son. A dead giveaway…but why?'

'It was something Michael Wagner, the circus magician, said when I asked him if he ever used a double. He implied that he intended using a double with Ramon in one of his acts. He didn't give a name but said there was someone in the circus that was the exact double. All he had to do was wear a moustache to create the likeness.'

'So I assume you saw the likeness when Sebastian brought the black silk handkerchief up to his mouth?'

'Exactly. Although both men are not quite the same height, as doubles they would never be seen together.'

'I wonder what he plans to do with them?'

'No doubt we'll find that out in due course. Now then, Freddie, I believe I saw you make some notes when we were in the control tower. Have we got something important to watch tomorrow? I'd like that to be our last day for a while as I have some important business to attend to. I'm sure you'll need to get back to the family and plan a few outings at race meetings.'

'Yes, its time I was back but I would like to see the Trapeze act tomorrow,' Freddie said as he fumbled for the notes he had in his pocket.

A note was pushed in front of Giles. It read: The Flying Trapeze, Velazquez Family.

'I haven't put down the date but it's tomorrow,' said Freddie. 'It's to be in the large hanger at eleven o'clock in the morning.'

'That will be worth watching,' Giles said, rubbing his hands together. 'It will also give me a chance to meet, and get to know, the final members on Ramon's list of suspects.'

'It says Velazquez Family,' said Giles. 'Did the notice board give any more details about them?'

'Only that they are two brothers and a sister. They are Puerto Ricans; Miguel, Cordero and Luisa. We'll know a bit more about them tomorrow. Until then I suggest we get some shut-eye.'

Next day the first port of call for Giles was to the trailer of Senhor Mordomo. He informed him of how things had progressed so far and let him know that he and his friend would be travelling back to London that afternoon and could be away from Winkleigh for some considerable time.

Before he left, Giles asked Ramon to keep a note of any further incidents and possible suspects. He could then weigh up such developments when he returned for the first official opening performance of the circus due to be scheduled for Tuesday, 7th March, before an invited audience of North Devon residents.

The big hanger was quiet when Giles and Freddie entered. The trapeze and all the trappings were in place along with a large safety net. Both men wandered around the set, looking up at the equipment with worked up anticipation; this was the first time either of them had been in close proximity to the gear used by "The Daring Young Men, and Woman, on the Flying Trapeze."

They were so engrossed with the apparatus that a near accident almost took place that had nothing to do with making the circus supremo run the gauntlet of fear.

With eyes skywards, Giles just about fell over a body that was lying on the floor. The body was that of a young man dressed in a leotard and he was one of three persons, similarly dressed, who were engaged in a warm-up routine that stretched to nearly half-an-hour.

'I must congratulate you, old son,' said Freddie as he pulled his friend to one side. 'You deftly side stepped that athlete like a steeplechaser avoiding a stricken rider in an event at Cheltenham.'

'It's a good job another accident was prevented or I might have been added to that list of suspects,' Giles said with thankful relief.

'That would put the cat among the pigeons and no mistake'

'And it would certainly end any prospect I might have of emulating Arthur Conan Doyle's Sherlock.'

'If you had fallen over that trapeze artiste you'd have had more than your pound of flesh. More like Shylock than Sherlock, old son.'

A silent chuckle from both men was the forerunner as they waited and watched the completion of the vital warm-up.

Several assistants entered the hanger and it was fairly obvious that their entry coincided with the termination of the trapeze artistes' warm-up.

Everything appeared to be going like clockwork and each assistant moved to specific spots with a diligence that signified absolute attention to detail for a dangerous act that was about to begin.

The younger man and his sister started to ascend ropes that were held securely by circus helpers. They climbed to a platform next to a trapeze using only hands and arms but with their legs free.

The older artiste did likewise climbing to the second trapeze. For upwards of five minutes the brother and sister, at one end, took turns moving through the air from one trapeze to the other while the older man ensured that the timing of the trapeze swing, at his end, gave the aerialists perfect synchronisation thus allowing the grace of the act to be admired by the spectators.

With unblinking eyes Giles and Freddie watched the talented twosome with high regard yet, at the same time, the sweating palms of the two men somehow acted as a warning of things to come. The act was poetry in motion but inevitably, in a circus act, there was another side to the coin. The act was undoubtedly danger in motion and could end in disaster.

There was a pause in the proceedings as the older brother hooked his legs over the bar of the trapeze at his end and, with upper body hanging downwards below the bar and facing the trapeze at the flyer's end, started to swing with his arms stretched. He was now ready to play his role as the catcher.

The aerial act commenced once more with the younger pair taking it in turn to swing towards the catcher changing from one trapeze to then grasp the arms and wrists of the catcher before the 180 degree return to their starting trapeze and swinging back to the platform.

Tension was building as the moves on the flying trapeze took place; tension and danger increasing when the young man and girl began to practice the complicated next act of transfer. As the girl reached and was caught by the catcher, the younger brother was on his way back and both boy and girl switched in mid air before returning to the platform, having changed places.

The complex manoeuvre was attempted three times but on the third attempt the male athlete missed the catcher's arms and fell to the safety net.

The aerialist wasted no time in climbing back to his base on the platform. One more time the trio tried the tortuous trapeze turn which they completed with success.

After a very short interval the young masculine flyer started to add a somersault to the act. The acrobatic move was done between leaving the trapeze and being caught by the catcher. This he achieved three times before finally doing a double somersault. On his return to the platform both Giles and Freddie applauded his effort with a prolonged handclap.

They were clapping as the trio, one by one, swung on their trapeze and, letting go, dropped safely to the net below.

They were still applauding as the assistants rushed forward to give the flyers their dressing gowns. Giles moved forward to greet them.

'You must be Miguel,' Giles said, as he prepared to shake hands with the older brother.

'That's correct. And you are Professor Dawson. Allow me to introduce my brother and sister. Luisa, my sister, is the youngest in the family and Cordero is my younger brother.'

Giles introduced Freddie before announcing his high regard for what they'd just watched. 'I'm sure I speak for both of us when I say how riveting your performance was. It was a privilege to be so close to the action.'

'Thank you. We aim to please.'

'As you probably know I am here to take note of accidents that are troubling the owner of the circus. I was wondering if your trio has had any bad luck that might have been construed as deliberate acts of sabotage?'

'Well, you may have noticed that we pay close attention to checking each and every part of our equipment before and during our performance. The attention to detail has worked in our favour and only last week we came across a smear of Vaseline on one of the trapeze bars. How it got there we don't know but it could have been disastrous had it not been discovered.'

'I'm interested to know if your fall was an accident,' Giles asked Cordero, the younger brother. 'Or was it a calculated part of the act?'

Cordero smiled as his sister answered the question. 'A return to the action immediately after a fall always gets an ovation from the spectators,' Luisa explained. 'Will that answer satisfy you?'

It was Giles' turn to smile.

'Our routine is aiming for something we did not rehearse today,' Miguel disclosed. 'The double somersaults Cordero executed will be followed by an attempt at the triple aerial somersault first performed by Alfredo Codona. That will be done with the safety net for obvious reasons, though Alfredo did it without a net'

'One further question before we leave you,' said Giles. 'What is your opinion of the "toil and trouble" that is persistently causing grief to Senhor Ramon?'

'I simply cannot fathom it out,' Miguel affirmed. 'He is a stoical leader of our circus and has helped us every step of the way. Not many outsiders realize that he also has the ability of many of the top performers in their various acts.'

'That is interesting and I thank you very much. I look forward to witnessing that triple somersault.'

Final congratulations and handshakes were exchanged then Giles and Freddie turned to leave.

On the return journey to London in Freddie's car Giles was morose and silent for much of the way.

As usual, when mood swings like that took over, Freddie had the good sense not to interfere. Eventually, though, the question had to be asked.

'What's bothering you, Giles? Something's puzzling you and talking about it might just help.'

A slight irritating cough from Giles preceded his reply. 'Yes, Freddie, something is definitely bothering me, and it's to do with what happened in the hanger.'

'Well, let's be having it.'

'Can you remember what happened when the aerial trio finished their act and left the safety net?'

'Yes I can. You went over to speak to them.'

'No, Freddie. I mean before that.'

'You're talking in riddles again.'

'Perhaps I am. But you'll see what I'm driving at when I mention…that when the Velazquez trio left the safety net three assistants went over to them and helped them with their dressing gowns.'

'That surely was the right and proper thing to do, Giles. Aerialists, like all other circus performers, have to be kept warm. That prevents ailments such as torn shoulder ligaments. Racehorses have rugs placed over them after a race. Even you know that.'

'Sure I do, Freddie. But the point I'm making is this. The Flying Trapeze act has had no accidents, but there was another stunning act we saw that has had no accidents either. In each of these acts something didn't happen there that might well have been an accident and it didn't register with us.'

'I'm not sure I follow you.'

'Do you remember when we watched Lizzie doing her equestrian act?'

'Yes.'

'Well, after she dismounted and left the ring, her horse was taken away by stable staff but Lizzie was never given a dressing gown. It was a cold morning and she was starting to shiver. Surely someone should have given her something to put on. Or was that a deliberate act of sabotage?'

'I think you've hit on something quite serious, Giles. But, who could have been responsible?'

'That, I'm afraid, is what I have to discover.'

Once they were back in London and, after Freddie had left to head back home, the days and weeks passed in no time at all. Giles was kept busy: interviews with the press, visits to museums and libraries gave him plenty to think about, yet there was hardly a moment when his mind was not occupied either with the circus riddle or the thought of going back to Scotland and the house near Lockerbie.

He was anxious to crack that conundrum about the KC and the forbidden isle and he knew full well who might help him do that.

With January out of the way Giles took a good look at his diary and decided to take the train north on or around the seventh of February.

A call to Maskelyne Hall, the big house on the outskirts of Lockerbie, was again answered by Doreen, the housekeeper. She was afraid that Laura was sleeping; she hadn't been too well she said, but Giles would be welcome to come. That might cheer Laura up.

Giles decided there and then to travel on Tuesday 7th February and gave Doreen the details when he'd be likely to arrive.

Giles managed to obtain the services of Colin Brown, the cabbie with the enlarged whatnot, when he was all set to travel by train. On the way to the station Giles told Colin about the mystic conundrum that was puzzling him.

The cabbie was stumped about the KC, and the forbidden isle, but he was positive he could figure out the part about the grassland that was now an airfield.

'I would like to know what your idea of that could be,' asked an interested Giles.

'The thing that springs to mind is Gatwick,' said the cabbie with an air of confidence.

'Why Gatwick,' asked a bemused Giles.

'Gatwick is now an airport,' the cabbie said smugly. 'And it used to be a racecourse! The Grand National was run there during the First World War.'

The journey to Lockerbie was a pleasant one as Giles contemplated what he'd been told by Colin Brown. It all made sense though he couldn't work out why. A race had been mentioned in the riddle so maybe he was a step nearer the truth.

An elated Giles was met by George, the Maskelyne Hall lodge keeper. The feel good emotion Giles had was short-lived and the reason was the look on George's face.

'Is there anything the matter, George?' Giles asked. His bothered tone matched the worried look on his face.

'I'm afraid I have bad news for you. Laura is in hospital!'

Chapter 9

LOVE AND THE FORBIDDEN ISLE

The news of Laura's illness brought numbness to the newly arrived Professor and melancholy set in on the familiar car journey over the bridge and up the hill.

The joyous mood, Giles had when he arrived at the market town's station, was now gone. Anxiety took charge and all Giles wanted was to hear what necessitated Laura having to go to hospital.

'What, exactly, is the problem?' Giles asked as the silver-haired lodge keeper steered the station wagon on to the B7068.

'It all started with a sore throat,' explained George as he changed gear. 'We called the doctor and he thought it might be tonsillitis. Laura had a high temperature and the swelling made swallowing difficult.'

'Did the doctor prescribe anything?'

'Yes, he put her on a course of antibiotics but when he came back, a few hours later, he diagnosed a Quinsy throat. There were abscesses that might require surgery so Doctor Richardson decided that a hospital visit was essential.'

'Did she go to the cottage hospital?'

'No, Giles. She is in the Royal Infirmary at Dumfries. After dinner I'll drive you there. I know Laura will be glad to see you. She's been in a lot of pain and there was just the possibility it could have been life threatening, but we've been told she's over the worst and could be home in a few days.'

'I'm certainly relieved to hear that.'

Isabella Ramsden, the septuagenarian widow of cabinet maker Jack Ramsden was having an afternoon nap when George carried Giles' bag into the big house.

Doreen Gardner, the housekeeper, was preparing dinner as Giles walked into the kitchen. The hugs that ensued were reminiscent of his earlier visit, in the previous October, when Giles had come back to solve the mysterious death of Jack Ramsden.

Jack, a magician who also designed and built masterly props for stage magicians, had been a mentor for Giles while he'd stayed with the Ramsden family, on holidays during his boyhood.

The library at Maskelyne Hall contained a large collection of books on magic and illusionists but it was the historical works on the great circuses that Giles wished to examine.

They would have to wait. Giles' immediate interest was to see Laura and help her regain her health.

Dinner with the matriarch of Maskelyne Hall was not quite the same as Giles had expected despite the presence of Doreen Gardner and her husband George. Isabella had requested their company believing their presence would help Giles overcome his anxiety at Laura's absence.

Conversation was subdued though Isabella did her best to put Giles at his ease.

'I believe George is taking you to see Laura this evening, Giles. I'm sure that will do her an enormous amount of good. I've prayed for her…we all have and we want her back home as soon as she's strong enough.'

'Have you any idea how it all happened?' Giles inquired with concern.

'We don't really know,' declared George. 'But she was cleaning out one of the drains down at the stables and that may have had something to do with it. Laura was always a girl who helped anyone who needed assistance. She was never afraid of hard work and mucked in with the rest of us.'

When dinner was over Doreen cleared the table and started washing up. Giles got himself ready to accompany George to Dumfries for what was to be an unexpected visit to a girl he might have lost if George's account of Laura's illness was correct.

The drive to the county capital was completed in record time and, as George parked the station wagon at the hospital, the pounding of Giles' heart increased. This was not quite the way he'd expected to meet Laura again even though the effect on his heart was the same as when they had met on his previous visit to Lockerbie.

Before going into Laura's ward Giles had a word with one of the nurses who confirmed that, at one stage, the staff thought they might be in danger of losing Laura. The patient's strength of will was, fortunately, a force that helped to turn things around and the treatment soon took effect.

'She is ready to see you, Professor Dawson,' the nurse said and her smile and words gave Giles the necessary encouragement he required to step into the hospital ward and meet the girl he had looked forward to seeing so much.

Laura was sitting up and talking to George when Giles moved across to her bedside. Lodge keeper George, who was also groom, gardener and general handyman, rose, gave Giles his chair and said he would go and search for a cup of tea and leave the two alone for a wee while.

The auburn hair, with the titian highlights, framed Laura's face, as her head lay back on the white pillow. Her hazel eyes gazed out at Giles and a tiny smile lit up her pale face; the scarlet lipstick contrasting starkly with her skin.

'You look lovely,' Giles said, rummaging for the right phrase to use. He sat down, held her hand and looked longingly at her as he continued. 'I so wanted to see you.'

'That's not a bad start for someone as reticent as you, Giles. I'm pleased to see you too.'

'How are you feeling?'

'I can honestly say I feel much better than I did, now that you're here.'

'I'm glad,' said a relieved Giles as he squeezed her hand. 'I believe I saw a little colour come into your cheeks and that means so much to me. May I kiss you?'

'No, Giles. Please wait until I come home to Lockerbie.'

'Patience is a virtue, as they say. If I have to wait a bit longer then so be it, but I will ask you again. Have you any idea how long you'll be here?'

'The doctor thinks I could be leaving here by the week-end.'

'Good,' said a delighted Giles as he still held her hand in his. 'I'm pleased to hear that.' He lifted her hand up to his face caressing one finger as he did so before giving it a little kiss.

'What are you thinking, my dear Giles?'

'I was thinking that this particular finger might look a little better with something on it. It deserves something very special and maybe that can be arranged. Get well soon, my dear.'

The reaction from Laura was more than Giles could have envisaged. Her other hand grasped his and he glimpsed a tear drop appearing at the corner of Laura's eyes.

They were still gazing fondly at each other when George reappeared.

The run back to Lockerbie was a lot more enjoyable than the earlier trip to the hospital; the meeting with Laura had bucked Giles up no end. When he was about to leave the ward he turned to look back at Laura. She was waving her left hand and stroking the finger he'd caressed.

That gesture conveyed a meaning Giles would cherish for God knows how long. He leaned back in his seat and breathed a hearty sigh of relief.

George glanced briefly across at his passenger and nodded before concentrating on driving the professor safely back to the country house near Lockerbie.

Isabella was sitting by the fire when George and Giles got back to the house. Doreen made some tea and Isabella produced some glasses and a bottle of brandy.

Giles sat for a while chatting to Isabella. Mrs. Gardner put a couple of logs on the fire but when Isabella's eyes began to close the housekeeper escorted the old lady upstairs to her bedroom.

After Giles said goodnight and retired to bed he found sleep difficult. His muddled thoughts wandered between Laura and her recent escape from death and the distinct possibility that death might soon happen at a circus with a problem he'd been asked to solve.

It was a rather bleak morning when Giles went downstairs. To his surprise he was ushered into the cosy kitchen by an ebullient Doreen who sat him down and, in no time at all, prepared breakfast.

Fragmented sleep had left Giles in an agitated state of mind, but a bowl of hot porridge with grilled bacon and scrambled egg to follow, plus the company of Doreen and her husband, George, who came in from the stables, was excellent therapy for his condition.

As the library was the intended destination for Giles, after his breakfast, he told housekeeper Doreen that he might spend most of the day there browsing over the books. Doreen said she would bring him a cup of tea mid-morning but would otherwise not interrupt him.

The library was ghostly quiet when Giles entered; the door opening on well-oiled hinges.

The oil painting of the female dancer in a Spanish costume of scarlet and vermillion still hung on the wall opposite. It instantly brought disturbing memories of the immediate past; the objects carried by the dancer were so diametrically different which bothered him. The fan she carried in one hand signified gaiety and merriment while in the other hand was a portent of tragedy.

Giles had difficulty of ridding his mind of that object that had been a pivotal component in the investigation of *The Statue of Three Lies* not so long ago. That object was...! Giles shook his head and, talking to himself, said 'That, thankfully, is over and done with. The mystery was solved!'

With composure returned to normal, Giles closed the door, moved to the extensive book shelves and removed several volumes, which he took over to the long mahogany table.

Before he sat down in one of the leather arm chairs he noticed there was already a book lying on the table. It was a collection of Grimms' Fairy Tales. He frowned, glanced at the painting on the wall and made a mental note that he would ask Doreen about that when she came in with the tea.

He switched on the standard lamp nearest to him as the morning light was barely good enough for reading by.

The first volume Giles opened was one that had a detailed history of the Ringling Brothers Circus. He thumbed through it until a section on the Codona Family caught his attention.

The Codona Family, a Flying Trapeze act, had apparently owned a circus before becoming famous with the Ringling Brothers. One member of the family, by the name of Alfredo, had first appeared in a circus while balanced on his father's hand. He had only been about seven years old at the time but as an adult became the most noted member of the family.

Reading on, Giles learned of the act that was known as the Three Codonas. Alfredo and his sister, Victoria, were flyers and their brother, Leo, was the catcher. Alfredo was the first performer to master the triple aerial somersault and was also first to realise that trapeze swings and their timing could be affected by the slope of the ground. That was another reason which could be responsible for an accident during a trapeze act thought Giles.

The next item to capture the attention of Giles was about Alfredo's marriage to Lillian Leitzel, a petite aerialist, born in Bohemia, who pivoted while suspended by a rope looped around one of her wrists. Leitzel fell when part of her rigging broke and she died a few days later from her injuries.

It was clear to Giles, as he read such details, that accidents have always occurred in circuses; and the more difficult the aim of the performer, the more likely that an accident might happen. Giles knew that the Velazquez Family at the Tropicana Circus were aiming to emulate the Codonas and that meant that an accident might be waiting to happen.

The problem with the circus, which was wintering at RAF Winkleigh, was the quantity and frequency of the spills it was encountering.

Further information about the Codonas was more disturbing. After his wife, Lillian Leitzel, died from her fall, Alfredo married again. He became reckless and tore shoulder ligaments in a fall that ended his career. When his second wife sued for divorce Alfredo shot and killed her and himself.

These revelations tempted Giles to scan through some of the other volumes until he came across what were described as the Seven Sins of the Circus. They were listed as arson, bigamy, rape, bestiality, group sex, organised crime and murder.

The first of those sins had already taken place at Winkleigh; that of arson, Giles was certain the fire had been deliberate. The penultimate sin of organised crime might even be the cause of the recurring accidents and the last one of murder might well be inevitable, as he'd just read about Alfredo's sins. Giles could not discount the possibility of such a crime happening at some stage in his probing of the *"gauntlet of fear"* proceedings. That was something he feared might happen.

Biting his lower lip Giles got to his feet and started to wander around the library. Could any of the Velazquez family be remotely thought of as the culprit? Was it conceivable that all three could be involved? Giles doubted that. So far, there had not been any problem with their trapeze act but that might support the idea that they were concerned in damaging others.

Perhaps they were not only aiming to emulate the Codonas' aerial act but aiming to achieve what that family had originally possessed – their own circus. A possibility, perhaps, but Giles had no obvious reason to suspect the Velazquez trio.

If only Freddie was here, he thought. He would then have someone to exchange views with. Still there was always Laura and she might be here in a few days.

Giles looked up at the oil painting of the Spanish dancer. Apart from the colouring of the hair it could be a portrait of Laura. With that thought in mind he smiled and was about to sit down when Doreen entered.

'You'll be ready for this, Giles,' she said laying down a small tray with a cup of tea and a biscuit.

'Yes, Doreen, that will keep the inner man satisfied!'

'I have something else that might satisfy you, Giles. We've had a phone call to say that Laura should be allowed home early tomorrow afternoon. It seems your visit last night has worked wonders.'

'That's great news. There's so much I want to talk to her about.'

Doreen was on her way out of the library when Giles stopped her in her tracks. 'Tell me, Doreen,' he said. 'Who has been reading the book of fairy stories?'

'Oh, that was Laura. I'm sure she'll tell you about it when she comes back home. I understand she may want your help.'

With that enigmatic remark Doreen scuttled out of the room.

A shake of the head and a smile from Giles signified that all was well at Maskelyne Hall. It was like old times.

Back to the business in hand, Giles poured through more of Jack Ramsden's wonderful collection of circus histories. The more he read the more he became aware that even the greatest circuses were only a hair's breadth away from serious danger.

Many of the top artistes had been seriously injured or had ended their lives performing their acts. The Mexican trapeze artist, Tito Gaona, who perfected the triple somersault while blindfolded, was somebody spectators flocked to see.

The Flying Wallendas had been involved in a serious accident while performing their seven-person chair pyramid on the wire, without a safety net. Three fell and two died. Giles had read about that disastrous incident which had happened only a few years previously.

The list went on; it seemed endless. Giles was now beginning to realize that he would have to sift through all the accidents and distinguish the ones which were truly accidental from those that were caused deliberately by a malicious person, or persons, so far unknown.

One thing he was clear about; someone in the circus, who possibly had a grudge against Ramon Mordomo, was challenging Giles to discover who that person was and openly defying him to achieve a result. That challenge Giles was prepared to accept. He was coming to the conclusion that he himself was running the *gauntlet of fear* along with the circus proprietor.

A brisk walk down to the stables was next on the agenda for Giles, who desperately wanted to clear his head.

George was busy in the tack room when Giles appeared.

'I've had news from your wife, George. Laura will probably be allowed home tomorrow afternoon.'

'That's great news, Giles. I bet Doreen will prepare something special for her coming home. And we'll have a cosy fire on so you can do your usual business of telling stories late into the evening.'

'Now when did I ever do that?'

'Come, come Professor. You've been doing that ever since I knew you.' George was grinning all over his face as he added. 'Let's hope Laura recovers her health and fitness in the next few weeks. I think you know that she intends riding in the local point-to-point at the beginning of April, and I truly believe she has a good chance of success in the Ladies event; both the gelding and the mare seem to be in great form.'

'I'm hoping to be there to see that, but I have to be in North Devon for the first public performance of the Tropicana Circus and then I'm giving lectures, as a guest, on a cruise ship.'

'Sounds like you're having a busy time, Giles. I'm sure you prefer it that way. You always wanted to be a detective, even as a small boy, so we all want to know how you're doing in the world of detection.'

'Well, George, let me say that as soon as I know how well I'm doing you'll be one of the first to be told. At the moment I'm stumped, but Laura may be able to assist me when we have her back home. She may have some news I'm waiting for.'

'I'll pick her up from the hospital tomorrow, Giles. I'll give the Royal Infirmary a phone in the morning to find out when she'll be signed off.'

Before he left the stables Giles paid a visit to boxes where the two hunters had their heads looking out at him. His mind went back to his last meeting with the horses and his dramatic ride on one of them. That episode inescapably brought back emotive memories of a girl he lost years ago at a point-to-point.

He stroked the muzzle of one of the animals and whispered, 'Take care of Laura for me. I don't ever want to lose her.'

Doreen served a snack lunch in the kitchen where Giles was joined by Isabella and George. After that, he returned to the library, had a look at the Fairy Tales by the Brothers Grimm and wondered why Laura should be interested in this particular book. The cryptic remark, by Doreen, that Laura might want his help, was hard to fathom. It was another puzzle in a minefield of confusing posers.

He was going round in circles and yet there was always a glimmer that kept shining through on one person.

Dinner that evening was a favourite of Giles. Doreen's steak pie was something to behold and afterwards, in the lounge with a log fire, Giles was on the verge of sleep.

Isabella prodded him awake.

'You are very quiet, Giles. Something is bothering you and I have always found that it's much better to talk about things and bring them out in the open.'

'You mean a problem shared is a problem halved,' murmured a sleepy Giles. I suppose you're right, Isabella.'

'Well then, Giles?'

'The quandary, in which I have allowed myself to become involved, is such that although I am unable to put my instinct into play and decide who might be the guilty person or persons, I continually come back to one name. I have faith in my intuition but...'

'There is nothing wrong in having faith, Giles.'

'That is so true, Isabella, but I did read somewhere that faith is a belief in something for which there is no evidence. And evidence is a commodity I don't have.'

'Perhaps it will come, Giles. And often, when you least expect it. If you'll excuse me I think I'll have an early night. Help yourself to a drink, Giles and I'll see you in the morning. Tomorrow we'll have Laura back with us.'

'I'll certainly drink to that, Isabella. Goodnight and sleep well.'

Pouring himself a cognac, Giles settled down with the fire embers as a cheerful companion. He was speedily coming to the conclusion that he must stop feeling cross with himself. His truculence would have to be kept under control. The outcome at the circus and his relationship with Laura could depend on it.

He looked at his watch and calculated that he might be holding Laura's hand again in fourteen or fifteen hours. He lifted the glass of cognac to his lips and, before taking a sip, muttered, 'I'll certainly drink to that.'

Giles was up bright and early the following morning. He'd slept soundly and was ready for what the day had to offer.

He was just finishing breakfast in the kitchen when George came in with the news that Laura would be ready to come home in the afternoon. The hospital staff said there could be a slight delay as certain papers had to have signatures but any delay would be kept to a minimum.

On the basis that two's company and three's a crowd Giles decided to stay and give Doreen any help she needed for the homecoming, thus allowing George to go to Dumfries and collect Laura by himself. George also had instructions from Doreen to do some shopping before going to the hospital.

While the housekeeper made preparations for a roast chicken dinner Giles and Isabella set the table in the dining room for the evening meal. Candle holders were put in place for what was to be a romantic spread even if it became apparent to Giles that Laura might not be able to consume a hearty meal.

Throughout the afternoon Giles was constantly looking at his watch. He shook it on occasions to check if it was still working. There were times when he felt like giving himself a shake to see if he was still working; such was the state he was in.

The noise of the station wagon pulling up on the gravel drive had Doreen and Giles scurrying to the front door.

The wait was over. Giles rushed down the steps to open the car door. Laura almost fell into his arms and as she did so she laughingly said, 'Yes, you can kiss me, Giles. I'm home once more. And you can be a good Professor and help me up the steps.'

A willing Giles did as he was told, He kissed Laura lovingly on the lips then, putting his arm around her, he escorted her up to the big house while Doreen and George collected Laura's case and coat. Isabella was at the top of the steps at the front door and hugged her daughter before taking her inside to the warmth of the log fire.

Dinner was served to Isabella Ramsden, her daughter, Laura and Professor Giles Dawson in the dining room at Maskelyne Hall. Doreen Gardner and her husband George had their meal in the kitchen having decided that it might be a fitting start for Laura, on her first night at home, to have the company of only her mother and Giles.

The candle lit feast was a delight for Laura. Her appetite was such that she was unable to eat as much as normal and although conversation centred on her stay in hospital she appeared at ease with her condition.

After the meal was over, Isabella, Laura and Giles retired to the lounge and Doreen said she would bring in coffee when she'd cleared away the dishes.

Mrs. Ramsden settled in her favourite armchair then turned to Laura and Giles who were cosily seated on the sofa.

'There was a strange look in your eyes, Laura, while you were at dinner,' Mrs. Ramsden hinted in a slighted worried way. 'And that same look is still there now. Is there something wrong?'

'No, no, nothing wrong Mother dear. It was just the candles at dinner and we have them here in the lounge. I was reminded of the time when the lights suddenly went out when Giles was here at the end of October. I think we were all in the dining room then and we had to light the candles. I think we wondered if the lights going out might be the work of…ghosts.'

A shiver went through Laura's body as she spoke. Giles put an arm round her and held her close to him.

Laura smiled and glanced at Giles. 'I'm feeling warm and loved,' she said in a low voice. 'And the past can look after itself.'

'*You* were also very limited in your chat, Giles. Can you explain why?'

'I'm sorry, Isabella,' Giles answered with contrition, as if trying to explain to the teacher at school. 'I have so much to ask Laura but there is a time and a place for everything and, although this may be the place I don't think tonight is the right time.'

'I know what you want to ask, Giles,' a patently understanding Laura said. 'There's one question I may have the answer to…I'm just waiting for confirmation and I expect that to arrive any day now. The other question I shall answer when the timing is right.' Her coquettish glimpse at Giles sent a tremor of excitement through his body.

At that moment Doreen appeared with the trolley of coffee and said she would take Laura to her bedroom in about half-an-hour.

The final moments of Laura's first day back at Maskelyne Hall were spent in cheerful chat before bedtime.

The next few days were occupied getting Laura well on the road to a successful recovery. Walks and talks and visits to her majestic horses seemed to work in her favour.

Evenings were enjoyed exchanging views on a variety of subjects. At one of those Giles enquired about Grimms' book of fairy tales and, to his surprise, was told that Laura had been asked by a theatre company to assist in the production of a stage play based on one of the stories. She'd be required to come up with some stage illusions for a mystery play; a dark rendering of Cinderella and she was hoping to enlist the help of Giles.

By Monday 13th February, Laura seemed ready to answer everything asked of her.

On that day, the day before St. Valentine's Day, Giles ventured to ask if Laura could make some sense out of the conundrum he'd received at RAF Winkleigh.

'I imagined the best way to tackle this problem was to take it one lap at a time,' Laura explained. 'In the same way as I do in a point-to-point race.'

'That sounds reasonable to me, as it would to Freddie. So what did you come up with?'

'I got in touch with the West Highland Museum in Fort William. That, from my point of view, was the best place to ask about the forbidden isle; Fort William being one of the few towns close to where you are going to be on your lecture cruise.'

'Were they able to help?'

'It was very interesting. What they said was that, although they couldn't be adamant about the term, there had been some talk about the Isle of Rum, one of the small isles on the West coast of Scotland, being classified as the forbidden isle.'

'Why, on earth, would that be?'

'Something to do with someone on the isle not wishing to have visitors, I think.'

'Interesting, but strange. Very strange, indeed. Did you ask about the KC?'

'Yes, I did. They were going to try and make some enquiries and would get back to me. I have a premonition that we'll have some news before very long.'

'I hope your vibes are in fine order, Laura. Someone in that circus is playing a game with me and I also have a premonition; more a prediction really. Someone is going to die and the death will not be from natural causes. I don't know who that person will be and I have no idea why that person will die...or when. And the most horrid thing of all is...I will be unable to prevent it happening.'

The following day, St. Valentine's Day, was always going to be a day Giles would remember...for several reasons.

When he went into the library, Laura was already there. She had a letter in her hand and Giles looked at her quizzically.

'Is that from Fort William?'

'Yes, Giles, it is. And the KC is not the King's Counsel, as we correctly thought. Nor is it the initials of a person living on the isle.'

'Well?' questioned an eager Professor.

'The KC, it would appear, is the biggest house on the isle. It is the name of the house and the KC, in the riddle, must stand for Kinloch Castle!'

The rest of the day was spent rummaging over the other parts of the conundrum. Kinloch Castle must have some connection with Gatwick if the London cabbie's inkling regarding the grassland was correct but Giles could not come up with any reason for the two parts of the riddle to be linked.

When Giles and Laura were left alone in the warm lounge after a sumptuous evening meal, they talked small talk for a while until Giles changed tack and became serious.

'Laura, your father was an inspiration to me. Without his help I would not be the historian I am now. If he was alive today I would be asking him…'

Laura interrupted before he could go any further. 'He is not here, Giles, and he no longer will be except in spirit. Why don't you just get a grip and put me in place of my father!' She was wearing her provocative face as she continued. 'Get down on your bloody knees, Professor, and pop the question. That's how my daddy might have said it. Pop the question before St. Valentine's Day is gone for this year and, perhaps, gone forever.'

Giles tried to get to his feet, stumbled in the process and fell to his knees. He struggled to get his torso to the vertical; Laura grabbing his hands in hers and looking him straight in the eyes, blurted out. 'The place is right and you're in the correct position, Giles…you'll never have a better opportunity.'

The pause was electric; the only sound in the room was the crackling of the logs in the fire and the breathing of two persons who couldn't take their eyes away from each other.

'Will you marry me and be my wife, Laura, my love?'

'Yes, Giles,' she said as she bent down to kiss him. 'That wasn't too difficult, now, was it?'

After being helped back on to the couch, Giles and Laura lay in each others' arms while the logs in the fire gently hissed and spat their approval.

Chapter 10

POLE AXED

How he got to his bed on St. Valentine's night Giles never knew. In the morning he was alone between the sheets but he could've sworn that there were two in his bed at sometime during the night…much like a previous encounter in the same bedroom.

'You are like a pussycat with a saucer of milk, Giles,' Doreen Gardner commented when he came into the kitchen for breakfast.

'With good reason,' said a chirpy Professor. 'Laura and I are engaged to be married, though how I managed to propose is beyond me.'

'Congratulations, Giles,' said the cook, with a tear in her eye as she hugged him. 'I so desperately hoped it would happen. You deserve each other and I hope you'll both be very happy.'

The weather on the days following St. Valentine's was not conducive for early Spring walks. There was a drizzle in the atmosphere but the rain that came couldn't dampen the spirits of two lovers who meant so much to each other.

There was plenty to discuss between Laura and Giles. Decisions had to be made about an engagement ring for Laura and a possible wedding later in the year.

It was decided that no final arrangements for a wedding were to be made until Giles' business with the circus at RAF Winkleigh was resolved.

There was always the lecture cruise to be considered and the letter from the West Highland Museum in Fort William had stated that the large building on the Isle of Rum was not open to the visiting public. The Nature Conservancy, the body responsible for the Castle, makes special concessions to academics carrying out relevant research. It was agreed that Laura should contact the Nature Conservancy for permission to allow Professor Dawson, as a historian, a brief stay in the Castle to complete some research. If the large building, known as Kinloch Castle, was the KC which was in the circus riddle, he was determined to go and find out why a visit was deemed so necessary.

Plans for Laura to return to her occupation as a choreographer, working with theatre and film clients, were to be put on hold until her health and fitness were no longer in doubt. Giles wanted to know more about the Cinderella production that Laura might be involved in. It was to be a Comedy Thriller, she told him, based on the original story but completely different from the Walt Disney version produced not so long ago as a feature length cartoon. Giles said he would love to help her in planning stage illusions; it would be a pleasant change from the present problem he had with the circus.

The cruise to the Scottish Isles and the next visit to RAF Winkleigh for the public performance of the circus to the North Devon people, were Giles' priorities for the immediate future.

If there were further accidents at the circus they could escalate out of control and the repercussions might make it impossible for Giles to continue. His reputation would be short-lived and could slide down the scale to absolute zero. That was quickly put out of his mind. Giles was confident he was on the right road to a successful conclusion. He only had to keep focussed and not be diverted from the task in hand.

The short voyage on the recently built German cruise ship which was to leave Tilbury docks on 17th March was something that could be a pleasant interlude and Giles made all the necessary arrangements to be put ashore on the Isle of Rum. He was convinced Laura's letter to the Nature Conservancy would bear fruit.

There was a lump in his throat as Giles waved goodbye at Lockerbie's railway station. He hated goodbyes but was ready to get a grip, as Laura had instructed him when he was about to propose to her. He knew he would have to knuckle down and reach a solution to the enigma he'd become involved in.

On the train to London Giles consulted his diary. He was due to be at

RAF Winkleigh for the North Devon residents' performance in early March. That was to be followed by the trip to Rum starting on the 17th of the month. After that he must be at Lockerbie for Laura's point-to-point meeting which would take place at the beginning of April; and there was a visit to Aintree, near Liverpool, for the Grand National, shortly afterwards. His diary was very full. Freddie would be at Aintree and Giles hoped Laura would also be there to watch the race with him. The main interest, apart from the excitement of the steeplechase, would hinge on the prediction of Madame Zigana, the circus fortune teller. Her enigmatic forecast of the race result warranted scrutiny.

Before leaving the big house at Lockerbie Giles had made a suggestion that he and Laura might spend a week at York at the beginning of May. The Tropicana Circus was starting their tour at the racecourse and there was an old coach house, where the engaged couple could stay. It would be a good opportunity to enjoy a few days together and, at the same time, keep a watching eye on happenings at the circus.

When Giles was completely settled in his South Kensington flat he made a phone call to Freddie, at his home in Evesham, to explain about the forbidden isle and the KC in the riddle. It brought an instant reaction from his ex RAF colleague. Freddie was fairy certain that Giles' London cabbie was on the right track in his conclusion that Gatwick was the grassland in the conundrum. If only the previous owner of Kinloch Castle had somehow been connected to the Sport of Kings and had raced at Gatwick things could become clearer. It was at that point that Giles related what had occurred when he reached London.

The services of Colin Brown, the cabbie with the enlarged hippocampus, had been enlisted by Giles on the way from the station to his flat and Giles had mentioned about the large house on the Scottish Isle. The cabbie said he'd heard about an English industrialist who'd had a large house built around the turn of the century on some island off the West Coast of Scotland and that gentleman had owned racehorses. One horse, Golden Myth, had won the Ascot Gold Cup. Another, Campanula, had won the One Thousand Guineas. But the most interesting one of all was Ballymacad, a steeplechaser which had won the Grand National during the First World War. That was in 1917 and the strange thing was,

Aintree, the home of the famous steeplechase, had been out of action at that time and the race had been run at Gatwick…and the race had been denied the title of the Grand National. It was another case of something that had never existed.

Giles couldn't believe his ears. The pieces of the jigsaw were beginning to fit into place and a picture was starting to make sense. A visit to this island Castle could be full of interest and intrigue…but why was he coerced into this visit. Someone had an ulterior motive and that someone was the person he had to ferret out.

There was a pleasant surprise waiting to greet Giles when he returned to the winter quarters of the Tropicana Circus.

A note from Michael Wagner, the magician, which he found inside his trailer, asked him to get in touch when he was back as a special illusion was ready for him to watch.

The Prof met with Mr. Wagner who intimated that the rehearsal would take place that evening in the tent in which the equestrian show had been staged.

A short meeting with Senhor Mordomo gave Giles the chance to say that he was to sail on a cruise ship starting on the 17th March. He made no mention of the fact that a visit to Kinloch Castle, on the Isle of Rum, was on the cards. It was best to keep that information a close secret. One person knew, or suspected it might happen, and that person was the one who concocted the conundrum.

The circus ring was well-lit when Giles took his seat in the rehearsal tent.

Michael Wagner greeted him saying that the illusion he was about to perform had been having some small problems which he could eliminate with a few more rehearsals. It seemed that the timing of everything was of the greatest importance, and if it was not yet of the highest quality tonight it would be by the time of the North Devon public performance.

A nod from the magician towards the tent entrance was enough to get the act started. This had to be an illusion that could be done completely surrounded by viewers. An edge-of-the-seat magic act was what Giles expected. He was especially interested because of what he'd advocated in his lecture at the St James's Club on the night he was asked to help the circus boss.

His gaze was riveted on what was being pushed into the ring by male assistants. It was a steel cage on wheels. It had a covered roof and the cage was empty.

When the cage reached the centre of the ring the assistants rotated it to demonstrate that the cage was completely empty. A cloth curtain was attached to the back of the cage but the rotation allowed anyone, wherever they were, to see through the bars and be convinced that there was nobody inside.

The magician beckoned to a girl who had taken her place at the ringside. As she moved towards the centre of the ring Giles recognised her as Allison.

The magician made a great presentation as he met his female assistant. He opened the door of the cage and guided Allison into the empty compartment and closed the door.

The cage was rotated once more showing that it was now occupied by the girl. Two female attendants came into the ring and, taking the ends of the drape attached to the back of the cage, pulled the cloth curtain around the other three sides until the cage, with the girl inside, was entirely hidden.

Once the ends of the drape were closed together four steel cables descended from the ceiling and were attached to the covered roof of the cage.

At a signal from the magician the cage was lifted off the ground and suspended in mid air. It was clear that there was no way for anyone to get in or leave the cage without being observed.

A roll on the drums alerted the girl assistants who had retained hold of ropes attached to the cloth covering the cage; the ropes were pulled dragging the cloth curtain away at the same time.

The suspended cage, now in full view of the onlookers, contained the Royal Bengal Tiger, Khan. The disappearance of Allison, which Giles knew was expected to take place, had somehow gone disastrously wrong: for Allison was clearly still in the cage with the enormous tiger.

The panic that ensued was professionally handled by the male attendants. The cage was rapidly, but gently, lowered to the ground. One assistant crossed over to the cage with some meat in a bucket. As the meat was offered to Khan, to keep the animal interested, Senor Gomez, the animal trainer was instantly at the door of the cage. He speedily opened it and led a petrified Allison out to safety. Giles watched this whole tableau with alarm and, as Allison was approaching him, he could see fear in her eyes.

With the cage securely closed again assistants wheeled it out of the ring.

Michael Wagner came over to Giles. He was markedly embarrassed and full of apologies. 'I'm so sorry about that, Professor Dawson,' he said. 'That, of course, wasn't meant to happen. And it wasn't one of the minor problems we were having.'

'I am aware of that Mr. Wagner; Allison and the big cat were meant to change places. But that particular illusion is dependent on timing and the ability of the girl in the cage to release parts within the structure…or you could be landed with a situation that not only spells disaster as far as the illusion is concerned, but could end in death.'

'Once I've had a talk with Allison I'll know much more about what went wrong,' volunteered the magician. 'The worry is that it's the second time my assistant has been in danger. The first being the fire in the clown act and now this. Why should Allison be a target?'

'I don't know, Mr. Wagner, but I would certainly like to find out.'

'If you'll excuse me I'll go and see how she is.'

'By all means. Please give her my best wishes. If it is at all possible perhaps I could have a word with her?'

'I will arrange that. I'm sure she will have no objections. We all want to get this problem sorted out.'

Retiring to his trailer Giles sat and gave the incident he'd just witnessed some serious thought. It was true that Allison had twice been involved in accidents and yet, on examining the facts, it was clear that she had been in a position to create each accident herself. The first one in the clowns' fire scene she could have had complete control of the fire had she wanted to. The second, ending up in close proximity with Khan, the Bengal Tiger, might have had life-threatening consequences. But that didn't take into consideration the possibility that Allison and Khan might have some kind of friendly relationship between them that Giles had no knowledge of. His thoughts went back to a remark Hank, the wire walker, made regarding Khan. He described the tiger as a pussycat.

His thoughts were interrupted by a knock on the trailer door.

The door opened and in stepped Allison. She seemed perfectly calm and composed and the fear in her eyes was no longer there.

'Michael said you'd like to have a word with me.'

'Come in and sit down, Allison. This is the first real opportunity I've had to make your acquaintance.'

'I've wanted to meet you for some time now, Professor Dawson, but I know you are quite busy with the scary happenings that we all want stopped.'

'Please call me Giles. I've been calling you by your first name and I'd like to continue doing that. Do you have any idea what went wrong in the illusion you were performing?

'Yes I do. As you will know, being a historian in stage magic, the timing is critical. It was my job, and mine alone, to ensure that the false back panel, discreetly hidden by the drape, was released along with the floor panel to allow my escape into the bottom of the cage. When I activated the dual release the floor panel didn't operate. That left me with Khan, the tiger. Had it happened in front of an audience I have no doubt there would have been huge applause because most spectators would not have known what to expect.'

'Had that happened before?'

'No! We've had little problems like the drape curtain not remaining secure and covering the cage sides; and the steel cables not lifting the cage without the cage tilting, but nothing as dangerous as what happened a moment ago.'

'Have you ever been in the company of Khan before?'

'What exactly do you mean?'

'I'm trying to establish if you and the circus tiger have had a previous understanding. That neither of you would attack nor harm the other.'

'Are you suggesting that I might have deliberately caused the accident to happen?'

'No, I'm not suggesting that. But I do have to eliminate all possibilities.'

'Am I a suspect in your investigation, Professor?'

'Let me just make it clear that everyone is a suspect and will remain so until I'm convinced of the truth.'

When Allison, the magician's assistant, had gone, Giles decided to pay another visit to the control tower and make a phone call to Evesham and talk to Freddie.

The upshot was that Freddie was due to make a trip to the meeting at the Devon and Exeter racecourse and he thought he might come to

Winkleigh, which was a little over an hour's drive away from the racecourse, and assess what was going on.

That was just the ticket as far as Giles was concerned and a tête-à-tête would be like old times again. Both men could exchange views and, if Freddie could stay a few days, they could watch the first public performance of the circus together.

On leaving the control tower Giles wandered around until he found exactly where Felix Reiser's trailer was. Giles had not yet had an opportunity to talk to the Band Leader on his own and as Reiser was present when the barred cage illusion went so wrong, Giles believed this might be a good time to question the man.

The band leader was going over some sheet music when Giles entered Reiser's living quarters.

'Do come in, Professor. Please be seated and make yourself comfortable.'

'Thank you. I hope you don't mind but I'd like your opinion on certain things.'

'I'll be glad to help, if I can. Can I get you something to drink?'

'That's very kind of you. I'll have a small drop of whatever you're having yourself.'

'I'm having a Southern Comfort myself.'

'I'll join you. I'm at the stage where I need a bit of comforting.'

'I know what you mean. I'm sure you are referring to the illusion that we both witnessed today.'

'Yes, I am! I wonder what you made of it. You are the one person who must be present at every act in the circus.'

'That's not strictly true, I'm afraid. All members of my band are usually present and so, of course, is the ringmaster.'

The dubious smile that wreathed Giles' face showed how he thought of the two men in the circus he'd been warned to keep an eye on; the band leader and the ringmaster.

'You ask what I made of the illusion that went wrong,' stated Felix Reiser as he poured two drinks. 'Well, that accident plus what you told Sebastian and myself regarding Khan's cage being unlocked leads me to accept that we have a problem at this circus that needs to be resolved as quickly as possible.'

'I'm glad you see it that way. But do you have any idea regarding these calamities. Have you ever seen so many mishaps in your previous experience?'

'No, not really, though I have to admit I was a member of the band that was playing when the Big Top went on fire at Hartford, in Connecticut.'

'Were you? Now that is interesting.'

'I'm sorry but you make it sound as if you suspect all who've been in the vicinity of tragedies.'

'You could be right. In fact I told the unfortunate Allison, after her close encounter with Khan, that, in every case I'm involved in I suspect everybody until I have a clearer picture that leads me to a credible conclusion.'

'And how many cases have you been involved in where you had to clear up a mystery?' asked the band leader in a tone of voice that could only be described as smug.

'Just the one, Mr. Reiser, just the one. That is, until I've finished this case, when I can double that number.'

'You sound confident, Professor. I admire your conviction and I'll give you all the assistance I can offer.'

As Giles left the band leader's trailer he mentally recorded Felix Reiser's holier-than-thou attitude. The band leader was certainly one to have on the list of suspects. However there was no evidence yet to implicate him or, for that matter, anyone else on that list. Giles was looking forward to his next meeting with his pal, Freddie, and to let him know which member on that list was nagging away at his vitals; a member where Giles' faith in his idea was a belief in which there was no evidence…as yet.

A few days later Freddie's arrival, after racing at Exeter, was just what the doctor ordered. After an evening meal in the diner the two best friends got down to brass tacks as they usually did when Freddie stayed at the South Kensington flat in London.

After describing the latest fiasco with Allison and Khan, Freddie agreed that it was a distinct possibility that Allison and the Bengal Tiger might well be so placid, when together, that the cage illusion, which seemingly went wrong, might not have been as disastrous as was first thought. The problem was there was no evidence to support that theory.

'You mentioned on the phone, Giles, that there was one name on that list of suspects you suspected above all others. Would you care to mention a name?'

'Please don't insist at this moment. In my subconscious this person's name stands out, but I have no proof. Someone is going to lose his or hers life and there may be others. If that should happen, Freddie, I will have failed.' The concern on his face, as Giles paused, changed to a look of consolation. 'The strange thing is I may be that much closer to realising my gut instinct about the name on that list.'

Leaving the diner after their evening meal the two ex- RAF colleagues were threading a path back to their trailer in the semi darkness when a near calamity happened.

Rounding one of the stationary wagons Giles was suddenly felled by a heavy metal pole that struck him a glancing blow across the side of the head and shoulder.

The soft, sensuous lips of a young female caressing his parched mouth were the first vibrant awareness of Giles' awakening from his brief, but alarming, unconsciousness.

He opened his eyes attempting to focus on the blurred face that observed him from above.

A silky smooth hand was being laid on his clammy forehead as the indistinct façade gradually became clear. His immediate recollection that he was being tended by an angel, was a momentary reaction that changed to a realisation: the angel was indeed the angel on horseback he'd been privileged to see giving a heavenly display of equestrianism.

He tried to call her name but the Lizzie he wanted to articulate died in his throat.

'Lie still for a while, Professor. Your friend, Freddie has gone for some medical help and I don't think you should move until that help arrives.'

Yes. That was the spectacular Lizzie's voice; his memory and vitality were returning.

When he sat up, with the assistance of Lizzie and a circus nurse, Giles looked around him. In the evening darkness, sporadically lit by occasional lamps, he could see he was not far from the Big Top where Allison and Khan had held their unscheduled meeting.

The area around him was strewn with ropes, metal poles and steel cables. 'What on earth happened?' he eventually asked, putting a hand up to his head as he spoke. 'Did anyone see what hit me?'

'It was that pole,' young Lizzie said, pointing to the heavy metal structure lying on the ground nearby. 'You could have been killed.'

'Well he wasn't! But you certainly were pole-axed, my son,' said a relieved Freddie.

Chapter 11

EVIL INTENT

Once Giles was in bed the circus doctor came to the trailer to check his condition. He advised a rest for a day or two but not necessarily to stay in bed.

The doctor's words before he left were weirdly prophetic. 'The circus is an environment where disaster and tragedy lie in wait and you and your friend should take constant care to avoid injury.' The circus doctor uttered that advice with such profound sincerity that made Giles wonder. Were those words genuine advice, or were they uttered as a warning threat?

Freddie made a cup of tea and settled down in a chair to keep watch over his long-time buddy.

'How are you feeling now?' he asked. 'Is there anything I can get you to make you more comfortable?'

'No, I'm fine. But there is something I meant to tell you and it seemed to slip my mind.'

'Well spill the beans if you feel up to it.'

'When I was at Maskelyne Hall…'

'Yes…take your time,' ventured Freddie. 'I'm really in no hurry.'

'Well, when I was with Laura at…'

'Yes, you've already said that,' interrupted the slightly perturbed bedsitter. 'Well…?'

'Laura and I got engaged to be married.'

The stunned silence was broken by Freddie choking on a biscuit and spilling his tea. 'Lie still and stay calm, Giles. Perhaps the doctor hasn't diagnosed your condition properly. You seem to be hallucinating and that bump on the head may be more serious than any of us thought.'

'No, no, Freddie. You've got it all wrong,' said Giles, wincing with pain from the shoulder as he adjusted his pillow. 'Laura and I…we're engaged. Cross my heart!'

'Look, Giles, the painkillers will take a little while to kick in. Listening to what you're gibbering about, I think I myself should've taken some of those tablets, but it's too late now.'

'I'm serious, Freddie. But I don't know how I managed to propose. I was down on my knees at the time.'

'Stop right there, Giles. You sound delirious and that worries me. A bump on the head can cause all sorts of complications.'

'But I didn't have a bump on the head when I asked Laura to marry me.'

'You never cease to amaze me. For years I've done my best to get you entered into the marriage stakes, to no avail…and now it seems you really are under starter's orders. Congratulations, sport.'

'Thanks, Freddie. We haven't set a date for the wedding yet. That, I'm afraid, will have to wait until I'm successfully finished with this circus business.'

'Do you think Laura should be told about your mishap with the metal pole?'

'No! For the moment, no news is good news.'

With those few words Giles drifted off to sleep while his friend took advantage of the interlude and attempted to doze off in a chair.

The next two days were restricted to occasional walks around the circus where they noticed arrangements were being made to erect a main tent with seating accommodation. This was obviously a preparation for the first public performance of the season.

A visit to the control tower notice board put them in the picture as regards the date of this event which was less than three days away.

This was the first time either of the two men had the opportunity to watch the arduous and delicate process of erecting a circus tent, or "big top" as it is often nicknamed.

Tons of heavy canvas, laid out on a wide area of level ground, was examined for tears. Large metal poles were equipped with bale-rings to which the canvas was attached. Many workers meticulously brought the poles to the vertical and the bale-rings with the canvas were hoisted upwards.

Everything was done with strength and efficiency, until finally all parts of the big top were fastened securely. The circus tent then looked as it always did in the best adverts and was ready for the bleachers to be installed which would seat a huge audience.

Nothing was left to chance and Giles watched every detail as it unfolded. The horror of a collapsing tent and falling poles of toughened metal, once a crowd of people were seated inside, would probably mean the end of this form of entertainment. But logical reasoning suggested to Giles that an accident of this nature would not only deprive Ramon of his circus authority but would make it impossible for anyone else to take over the show.

When the day arrived, for the performance to North Devon guests, the tent was a blaze of coloured canvas and welcoming lights. As the afternoon daylight began to go the old airfield, which had once been a place of secrecy and dark foreboding, was now transformed by the gaiety of the music from the circus band, and by the Tropicana Big Top with all its illuminations.

Crowds arrived and before long the large tented area was filled to capacity. Giles and Freddie had two of the best seats and were looking forward to an exciting evening along with the rest of the spectators.

At the same time Giles was anxious about the likely possibility of an accident which might have repercussions for Ramon and his circus.

A fanfare from the circus band brought the ringmaster before the audience.

Sebastian Capuzzo, dressed in red frock coat, white shirt with wing collar and white tie, black top hat, black dress trousers and boots, held a microphone in his white-gloved hands and addressed the crowded spectators.

'Ladies and gentlemen, boys and girls, welcome to the Circus Tropicana. This circus is proud to present some of the finest artistes in the circus world. They come from all parts of the globe. So sit back and enjoy the best entertainment available. As Cecil B. DeMille once said, *it is the greatest show on earth.*'

The band started playing some of the Souza marches in rapid time as a group of jugglers entered the ring and performed their amazing routines to great applause.

The costumes and the lighting brought a new dimension to the acts that Giles had watched in rehearsal. He was rapidly becoming more relaxed as clowns came on to create mayhem around the ringside while riggers entered and checked everything for the high wire act.

The wire walker, Hank Findley, entered the ring to a rousing reception while the band played tunes in waltz time. Hank was wearing fine, loose fitting trousers in a bright aquamarine colour. A light jacket, in the same colour, was open at the front over a bare chest. Carrying a pair of very soft leather flexible slip-on shoes he climbed to a platform at one end of the tight rope and paraded to the spectators.

There was no sign of the limp that was clearly evident when Giles first met him at Eggesford railway station and his body language demonstrated supreme confidence.

He changed his footwear, slid one foot on to the wire and moved forward maintaining an assured balance using arms to assist as he travelled, with swagger and aplomb, across the wire to the platform on the other side.

He followed that by crossing to halfway and removing his jacket which he threw to the ground.

A hushed crowd watched his daring and skill as he collected a skipping rope from one end and, moving to the centre, once more, started to skip while balancing on the wire. A slight wobble in his performance caused a moment of anxiety to those watching but that seemed to cause greater distress to the spectators than it did to the performer.

The realisation that they were watching a human being, like themselves, whose physical achievement and co-ordination appeared beyond their capacity, moved the spectators to emotional distress at moments of extreme difficulty for the performer when his survival on the wire was in grave doubt.

This was an edge-of-the-seat act that brought gasps of alarm from spectators when the performer had even the slightest totter on a wire that had no safety net below to protect the artiste if he should fall.

The finale, which was a somersault on the tight rope, received thunderous applause from the enthralled crowd.

Wiping sweaty palms Giles was no exception. He clapped and welcomed the fact that the first really dangerous act had finished without mishap. He was constantly on the alert for any sign of equipment that might have been tampered with and his brain had to cope with the demeanour of those on that blasted list of suspects.

But what if the perpetrator of the circus accidents was someone not on that list? That was something Giles could not envisage but it was still a possibility.

As Hank left the arena to a standing ovation, the band played rousing music that introduced a bunch of clowns with their gaudy costumes and made-up faces. Falling about on the floor and getting in each other's way they had the crowd in stitches. Even more hilarious was the sight of a couple of the clowns scrambling their way to the tightrope platform.

They started taking it in turn to attempt a wire walk displaying shaking legs and heart stopping antics before collapsing back on to the platform. It was all good fun but those who stepped on to the wire and displayed their dodgy capers were anything but novices. They were skilful in their own rights.

A few minutes of merriment closed with the circus band playing a fanfare and an announcement by the ringmaster introducing Michael Wagner, the magician, as someone who was proud to present illusions where the audience, wherever they were seated, could see all around each act which was to be done without the use of backdrops or mirrors.

It was at this point that a small cage was wheeled into the ring by several male assistants. Giles looked at Freddie with a hint of apprehension. The cage, which was covered on the top, had a draped curtain attached to the back bars. The assistants rotated the cage so that all the spectators could see that the cage was empty. Giles had a shiver move up his spine; danger had been the end product when he'd last witnessed this act.

The magician gestured to his female assistant, Allison, who proceeded to glide into the ring wearing an impossibly tight bikini in a strikingly rich mauve colour. Was mauve or purple the colour of death thought Giles?

The magician opened the door of the cage and helped his assistant to enter before closing the door again. The male assistants rotated the cage once more thus allowing all spectators to see that the cage contained the lovely Allison and nothing else.

Two girls, in colourful costumes, entered. Taking hold of the ends of the curtain, the girls pulled it around the other three sides of the cage completely hiding the girl inside. Four cables were lowered from the roof of the tent and attached to hooks on the cage top after which the cage was gently raised off the ground.

The band, played a medley of mysterious music, then developed into a roll of the drums that ended with a crash of cymbals. The two girls who still held cords from the curtain pulled the entire cloth away from the cage to reveal that the cage no longer held the bikini-clad girl captive. Instead the cage was filled by the orange and black striped frame of the Royal Bengal Tiger, Khan.

The cage was gently lowered to the floor, the cables unfastened and the cage containing Khan, wheeled away from the ring to thunderous applause. Michael Wagner bowed to the audience, looked across to Giles and winked. Giles wiped his damp hands on his trousers, turned to Freddie and exhaled a breath he'd been holding for more than half a minute.

A group of clowns, some on stilts, some juggling clubs or coloured balls, cascaded around the ring causing amusement and laughter from the younger members of the audience and rapturous applause from the adults.

Into the ring came a galaxy of shapely young females in strikingly rich costumes while attendants carried in springboards which they positioned on a sheet covering the ring floor. The acrobatic act which followed was action packed as girls, standing on the specially designed boards, were sprung into the air by a colleague jumping onto the other end and propelling them upwards to land on the shoulders of a partner in a perfectly balanced position.

While the band continued to play some stirring music the slickness of the lively act went down well with the crowd and, when it ended and the ring was cleared, on came a mock-up building, several stories high, that immediately brought back unpleasant memories of the fire Giles had witnessed in the hanger.

The magician's assistant, Allison, had been so nearly involved in a life-threatening incident during that rehearsal and as Giles scrutinized the young woman, carrying the baby, going into the building and climbing up the stairs, he became instantly aware that the young woman was not Allison.

The act had obviously been changed and, as the fire started to take hold in the building, Michael Wagner, the magician, came over to Giles and whispered that it had been felt that Allison had appeared in too many acts and a decision was made to substitute someone else in the fire act with the clowns.

An understanding nod from Giles sent Michael on his way and the Keystone Cops scene by the hilariously comical clowns went off without a hitch to a great reception by an appreciative audience.

The ring was cleared as the band played gentle music in waltz time. Several female assistants began to build a staircase of swords and Sebastian Capuzzo, the ringmaster, announced the outstanding balancing act by the Ecuadorian gymnast Leonardo.

When Leonardo had stripped to the waist he moved to the staircase and paid special attention to the position of the swords. This was something he hadn't done when Giles watched the act on New Year's Eve at the Soho venue in London.

The tension in Giles' face increased as the Ecuadorian athlete moved into the handstand position and advanced towards the large swords. Giles' jaw tightened and the muscles of his upper back started to ache while his eyes searched carefully for any sign of bleeding from Leonardo's hands.

It was probably the longest few minutes of Giles' life as he watched and waited for the harbinger of doom. He expected something to happen at sometime during this performance before the public. Not knowing when, or at what point an accident would occur, was agonizing but it was much worse having no knowledge of just how serious it might be.

Relief was very much in evidence when Leonardo safely completed his act, took his bow and left the ring. The ringmaster waited until the applause had finished before he introduced what he described as the equestrian showpiece sensation of the century…Lizzie Lisbet and her Andalusian mare.

From the moment she entered on her imposing white horse she took the spectators by storm. Many of those watching were almost certainly knowledgeable about horses and a considerable number of them would be riders who were well versed about the many difficult manouvres being executed by a young girl riding bareback.

Once again Giles was enthralled by this horse and rider whose performance ended the first half of the circus programme. The interval that followed was a chance to compare notes with Freddie and thank some divine intervention that, so far, nothing amiss had taken place.

The second half of the circus presentation started with a group of young, scantily-clad, females performing intricate and aesthetically pleasing balances involving as many as five at a time. It was a good start and a buoyant precursor of things to come.

The ringmaster, who was thoroughly enjoying being allowed to introduce a succession of class acts, welcomed back the magician, Michael Wagner and Allison his charming assistant. Michael was dressed in an Ali Baba outfit and Allison wore a fetching Arabian Nights' costume.

Several males in Eastern outfits brought a large round wicker basket on a pedestal with four legs, into the ring. The basket was wider at the top than it was at the bottom and had a square shaped wicker lid on top.

The magician had one of the assistants remove the lid and then he assisted Allison as she stepped into the basket.

Once Allison was in the basket the open top was covered by a black cloth that was pushed down into the basket. The lid was put in place at the same time as the cloth was removed.

Four swords were brought to the magician who, taking one at a time, pushed the swords through a hole in the lid making sure each sword came out through the lower part of the basket with the final sword being plunged straight down through the middle.

One by one the swords were slowly removed. The lid was taken off and the cloth replaced. The magician stepped into the basket pushing the cloth downwards, with his feet, as he did so. As he stepped out the cloth started to rise from the inside of the basket, finally being removed to reveal a smiling Allison who was assisted out on to the ring floor by Michael Wagner, the magician.

This first live performance, to the general public, was almost over without a single fault in the proceedings and that was comforting to Giles. A look at the programme showed that more mad mayhem from Chuck Marstow and his clowns was to be the next act.

That was due to be followed by a number of acrobats performing a sequence of intricate balances using ropes, poles and swings. This would climax with a girl acrobat attempting a tumbling shoulder swing on a rope.

Other acts yet to come included Ingrid Dahlberg with her knife throwing "Wheel of Death" and Giles was in no doubt that this could be where there was a fine line between success and failure. Accident was always going to be a possibility without a third party being involved. That thought brought back the words the circus doctor had spoken regarding disaster and tragedy lying in wait. Giles knew that circus performers risked their necks twice a day and the knife-throwing act would be no exception.

The spectacular trapeze performance by the Velasquez Trio, which would bring this top class programme to a close, was one more instance where lives were at stake.

As Giles handed the circus leaflet over to Freddie he suddenly became conscious that he had his own fingers crossed. He uncrossed them and looked around in a rather embarrassed way.

His gaze focused on Ramon, the circus proprietor, who was standing in the artistes' entrance way. Giles rose and went over to the one man who could possibly be more apprehensive than he himself was.

'The show has gone very well Senhor Mordomo. You ought to be a very proud man.'

The circus supremo tilted his head and stared at Giles. 'You are, of course, correct in what you say but…I can never eliminate the stress that comes from an expectation that catastrophe may be just around the next corner. You know how it is sometimes said that the show is not over until the fat lady sings…well, in our case we do not have a fat lady and there are several acts still to come where accident, contrived or not, could ruin what has gone before. That, in hindsight, would be the occasion when I'd wish we'd had a fat lady singing.'

A brief musical introduction and an announcement from the ringmaster, inviting patrons to take their seats, gave Giles a chance to lay a hand on Ramon's shoulder giving him a squeeze of encouragement before returning to sit down beside Freddie.

It was unusual for Giles not to be totally entranced by the antics of circus clowns but, as the second part of the show began, for some reason Giles was much too aware of a premonition of disaster. The hard work done by Chuck Marstow and his entourage had a wonderful effect on the large audience, but Giles sat with staring eyes at the melee in front of him as his head ruled his heart…his brain seemed in no doubt that tragedy was about to take the place of comedy. But when and how?

The comical concoction by the clowns came to an end with a female aerialist taking over. While suspended by a rope looped around one of her wrists the girl began swing overs. Each somersault she performed was given a drum roll and the audience was encouraged to count the number of swings. Giles was conscious of the fact that in 1931 Lillian Leitzel, who was the wife of the world famous trapeze artist, Alfredo Codona, fell while doing this act when part of her rigging broke. She had died of her injuries a few days later and the possibility of a similar occurrence had Giles on the edge of his seat.

As the count went beyond the fifty swings the nervous tension in Giles' body increased. It was then he realised that the aerialist was Louisa Velazquez, the girl in the trapeze act. When the swings reached the one hundred mark without mishap Louisa left to a deafening applause, and a sigh of relief from Giles.

A look at the circus programme showed that there were still two acts where a dangerous accident could spoil the party. The "Wheel of Death" knife throwing act and the pulsating Trapeze Performance by the Velazquez Trio which would be the climax of the show. Before that, however, the magical disappearance of Allison entitled "The Lady Vanishes" would delight and mystify.

The tension in Giles eased a little as the magician welcomed his glamorous assistant into the centre of the ring. Allison was wearing the long red dress as she'd done in the rehearsal and at last the contours of a smile appeared on Giles' face.

The large motor tyres were brought on, one by one, by male assistants, dressed as mechanics. They looked the part wearing blue overalls, peak caps in the same colour and dust masks covering nose and mouth. Each tyre was placed over Allison until she was hidden from view. A cloth was placed over the top tyre and the magician walked around the pile of tyres making arm movements as if summoning the supernatural.

The cloth was removed and, one by one, each tyre was lifted from the pile and rolled away. With only two tyres left the first signs of confusion and alarm broke out among the assistants.

The final tyres were speedily removed and set aside to reveal the red dress lying in the centre of the ring. The red dress was still being worn by Allison but the girl was lying inert on the ground. The ringmaster rushed forward, a stretcher was summoned, and the cloth was arranged around the figure of the girl while she was attended to.

Ramon Mordomo appeared and after a brief interval lasting not more than forty-five seconds the ringmaster asked everyone to remain seated and announced that Allison had just fainted and would be fully recovered after a short rest…the show would go on.

The stretcher and Allison were quickly taken away from the ring and the magician came over to Giles to suggest that Allison had probably fainted due to extreme pressure of work.

The knife throwing act was in full operation as Giles left the ring to get first hand knowledge of Allison's condition. But when he entered the rest room the news from the nurse was as if someone had impaled him on the Wheel of Death.

Allison was dead…but not from natural causes.

Chapter 12

FROM BEYOND THE GRAVE

When Giles went aboard the MV "Blenheim Palace" at the Port of Tilbury on the morning of 17th March 1967 the words of the circus nurse were still ringing in his ears.

The inexplicable and sudden demise of Allison, after her fainting spell, had a dreadful effect on the Professor of Magic. The circus nurse had tried to explain that, although no definite conclusions as regards the cause of death could be made until after a post-mortem examination, the tell-tale signs of a bruise, on Allison's arm, possibly caused by a hypodermic syringe, appeared to indicate something other than natural causes.

The intervening days since the tragedy had not been easy for Giles. He had great difficulty coming to terms with events. Why had Allison died? Could it possibly be murder? He was forced to return to the prediction he had made to both Freddie and Laura: that someone would die though he knew not where or when, and he despaired as he would be unable to prevent it happening.

Having been driven back to London by Freddie, the Prof had the chance to prepare for his Small Isles cruise and to collect his thoughts about what had taken place.

The first thing he did was to put down, on small bits of paper, the names that were on Ramon's list of suspects, and then attempt to place their whereabouts when Allison had her fainting accident.

The data he produced was the enlightenment he so desperately, required…it was the first time he was able to link so many of those in the list of suspects with a major circus incident.

Now that he was safely aboard the small cruise ship Giles settled down in his well-appointed cabin to review that list again.

The incongruous thought that brought a gentle smile to his worried features, before studying the list, was the knowledge that the cruise ship, named after the birthplace of one of the great Prime Ministers of history, had been constructed in a German yard within the last three years.

The tremendous improvement in flying had tended to decrease the use of ocean liners but a new craze was taking shape: that of cruising around coasts using ships with shallower draughts thus allowing them to visit shallow ports.

Circumstances beckoned him to go back to that list of suspects and his scribbled handwriting.

The notes showed that the ringmaster, Sebastian Capuzzo, was one of the first on the scene when it was apparent that Allison was in trouble. Michael Wagner, the magician, was also quickly in attendance and, after talking to Giles, he had followed the stretcher to the resting tent.

The chief clown, Chuck Marstow, was one of those who'd helped clear the way for the stretcher; and the circus nurse, when asked, confirmed that the fortune-teller, Eva Zigana, had been in the rest area when the stretcher was brought in.

That meant that four members on that suspect list were in close proximity to Allison at some moment following the incident. The number, however, was doubled to eight when Giles learned that Ingrid Dahlberg was about to leave the rest area to perform her knife-throwing act and the Velazquez Trio were relaxing in the same area prior to performing their aerial trapeze finale.

From the original list of suspects only Felix Reiser, the band leader, and Hank Findley, the wire walker, were unaccounted for. But that had all changed when Lizzie Lisbet, who'd been keeping a sharp look-out for any signs of wrong doing, informed Giles that the band leader had disappeared from the band stand when Allison was stretchered from the ring. Where he had gone remained a mystery.

As the cruise ship was about to set sail from the Port of Tilbury Giles was summoned by a steward; there was a telephone call from Exeter hospital.

The news was devastating. The post-mortem examination seemed to show that Allison had been initially rendered unconscious by a powerful anaesthetic as yet unknown. At some point after losing consciousness it appeared that she may have been administered with a muscle relaxant. Without the use of a ventilator she would succumb being unable to breathe. Full details were not clear, but the circus authorities would be notified when the post-mortem was complete. No needle had been found. The matter was now in the hands of the Exeter police and murder was suspected.

During that first day of sailing the white cliffs of Dover were enjoyed by the passengers as the ship navigated its way along the English Channel. After passing the Isle of Wight, the cruise ship docked at Plymouth. Two small parties were given a guided tour of the Black Friars distillery where the superlative Plymouth Gin has been made since 1675.

Most of the day Giles spent making notes for his evening lecture although his train of thought was continually directed to pondering over the possible killer of Allison.

Evening dinner at the Captain's table was a suitable prelude to a lecture that was very well received. Giles' talk centred on the early exploits of Maskelyne and Devant and, as he voiced the name of Maskelyne, he was constantly reminded of that house near Lockerbie and his fiancée, Laura.

At the end of question time Giles had suggested that members of the audience, who wished information on specific illusionists, could fill in one of the cards available and he would try and make every effort to accommodate them in future talks.

Six cards were given back to Giles who put them in his jacket pocket. Later, that evening, when Giles had a look at the cards, alarm bells started ringing when the words on one of them were "Do not believe all you see or hear". The harrowing truth dawned on Giles. He was being followed by someone from the circus…and that someone was here on the boat with him.

The next two days, the 18th and 19th of March, were close to a blur for Giles. After leaving Bideford, where most of the materials for the construction of the World War 2 airfield at RAF Winkleigh were landed, Giles was distracted from the beauty of the West of England coastline by disturbing thoughts of being shadowed. Why was he being followed? Someone had suggested that when he first arrived at RAF Winkleigh. He tried to recall from his memory bank…Madame Zigana the Fortune teller springing into mind.

A phone call to Maskelyne Hall when he went ashore at Douglas, Isle of Man, was some encouragement for the disconsolate professor. His conversation with Laura lifted his spirits. She was well on the way to a complete recovery and was anxious to help Giles as he journeyed north with an unpredictable conclusion.

During their discussion Laura hinted that it might not be a bad idea if she drove up to the Lochaber area in the West Highlands of Scotland. She could be there when eventually Giles left the Isle of Rum and crossed to the mainland.

The busy fishing village of Mallaig seemed the most likely place to land after a boat journey from that forbidden isle and Laura would somehow make a phone call to the house on Rum and arrange for their possible meeting.

Once they were together again a short stay, probably in the Fort William area, would be a good idea for a brief rest and a chance to catch up on plans before heading south again.

By the end of the third day the cruise ship had negotiated the Irish Sea, sailed past Wallasey on the Wirral where Giles and Freddie had met in the RAF and travelled northwards to Scottish waters.

Most of the passengers enjoyed the sight of the Scottish Isles of Islay, Colonsay, Tiree and Coll. Most, that is, except Giles.

His attention span seemed much shorter than the norm. His lectures and demonstrations of close-up magic were interspersed with the examination of his audience for some sign of recognition of a face he'd seen at the winter quarters of the Circus Tropicana.

All to no avail however. He was beginning to doubt his sanity as each face he scanned assumed expressions of guilt. Getting to the big house on the Isle of Rum could not come quickly enough. What could possibly happen there he wondered? To be alone for a spell and have the chance to concentrate on the task in hand would be more than welcome.

But why was he going to this strange building on a remote Scottish Isle? Seeking the truth was one of Giles' pursuits and he had every reason to believe that this time- capsule might supply a hint of the truth.

A tiny smile crossed his creased face as his thoughts of wanting to be alone reminded him of the Hollywood actress of those early movies, who had been associated with the alleged saying "I want to be alone."

On the morning of the 20th March the MV "Blenheim Palace" sailed past Ardnamurchan, the most westerly part of the mainland and through the Sound of Rum skirting the Small Isles of Muck and Eigg and into the shelter of Loch Scresort.

The Sound of Rum is frequently battered by violent gale force winds from the Atlantic and regularly lashed by accompanying rain storms. This morning, however, the water was relatively calm and passengers were out on deck hoping to catch a glimpse of porpoises and minke whales.

One person though was much more interested in casting an eye on the largest of the Small Isles…an island with its volcanic past that, in the next couple of days, might erupt once more in a different way. As the cruise ship entered Loch Scresort and approached the Isle of Rum slipway the professor of magic and mystery, concentrated his binoculars on the red sandstone building which is the dominant feature at the head of the bay.

Was this the KC of that enigmatic riddle posted on the notice board in the remains of the control tower at RAF Winkleigh? Did it hold the secret that might lead to a solution of the *gauntlet of fear* puzzle? Giles was about to find out.

When he was put ashore Giles was met by one of the Nature Conservancy staff who drove him along a pot- holed dirt track to the rear entrance of the late Victorian-cum- early-Edwardian extravaganza, a symbol of debauched gratification.

As Giles walked into the courtyard his bag was taken inside. He was then welcomed by the caretaker and his wife who came out to meet him.

Angus Mackintosh, ex-military, had been given a temporary appointment as caretaker of Kinloch Castle and he and his wife were thrilled to have the pleasure of showing someone round.

Angus readily intimated that Poet Laureate, Sir John Betjeman, had been one of their previous visitors. He had written about his experience in visiting an undisturbed example of pre- 1914 architecture.

Having been taken to his bedroom on the first floor Giles was then shown up a short flight of stairs to a small antiquated bathroom. Angus, the caretaker, said he would return to collect his guest and take him from his room to have a bite to eat before starting a guided tour of the building.

The room Giles was allocated was one of the oak bedrooms at the far end of a long corridor leading from the front of the house. Here he unpacked his bag and took a little time to become acquainted with his surroundings.

The gothic-style four-poster bed was directly opposite the panelled fireplace. The posts were ornately carved and the double bed filled much of the room. Two windows, which were on the opposite wall to the bedroom door, looked out to the woodland at the rear of the house. Giles gazed out onto a variety of trees that were being blown about by a breeze that was steadily increasing. Coming away from the windows he looked upwards at the elaborate panelled ceiling.

His thoughts, as he noted the amount of wood panelling, were deeply engaged in trying to surmise who might have stayed in this room and slept in this four-poster bed a long time ago. He didn't have much time to dwell on that as he was interrupted by a knock on the door.

It was Angus who'd come to escort him downstairs to the kitchen area.

'I think there's a wee bit of a storm brewing,' the caretaker said. 'I'd like to show you this magnificent building from the outside first and I suggest we do this before the rain becomes heavy.'

'That's fine by me,' expressed Giles, eager to start his thorough examination of this enigmatic mansion on a forbidden isle. 'I'm ready to begin when you are.'

Downstairs, in the servants' quarters, Giles was given a cup of tea and a venison sandwich before starting his travels with the caretaker. Outside beyond the open courtyard Giles tried to get his bearings. As he faced towards the west side of the house Giles looked up to the windows on the far right of the first floor; the windows which he believed to be the ones he'd looked out of when he was in the oak bedroom. For a brief moment he saw what appeared to be someone looking down at him. Only for a brief moment then it was gone. But someone was in his bedroom and was keeping an eye on him. Of that he was certain.

They turned left at the corner which had a large turret and started to stroll along the South facade of the big house.

'Surely the sandstone that was used to build the house wasn't local?' Giles questioned as he studied the extravagant stone.

'No, you're quite correct. But there's some doubt as to where it came from originally. Some sources suggest the stone was quarried on the Isle of Arran while others say it came from Annan, in Dumfries-shire. I'm afraid, since coming here, I can't believe all I see or hear!'

The last statement of the Highland caretaker was accepted with more than a little interest as Giles noted the almost identical words heard before by both himself and Freddie.

As light spots of rain were beginning to fall Giles was glad that his tour was along the glass-covered walkway surrounding three sides of the building.

When they reached the East Main Entrance the caretaker led his guest down the steps from the stone-floored verandah where Giles had his first glimpse of some hardy Rum ponies grazing on the grass leading down to the bay. The ponies were bay coloured with a prominent dark line along their backs.

The rain was beginning to get heavier as Giles turned to look at the magnificent, but unusual, building that would be his home for the next few days. It was just conceivable that, if the conundrum was all it alleged to be, this building, with rounded turrets at each corner, might hold the secret which could unlock the mystery he was deeply involved in.

Moving forward towards the main entrance Giles was fascinated by what he saw. The steps to the front door of this time-capsule, unchanged by the passage of years, were flanked by large Greek-styled stone ornaments.

'You look a wee bit stunned by what you see, Professor Dawson,'

'That, I'm afraid, is an understatement,' expressed Giles; his eyes taking on that vague look. 'I can't quite get over the conscious fact that, such a long time ago, the stone this house was built with had to travel by sea before construction could begin.'

'Seventy years ago, around 1897, I believe, the first stones quarried somewhere else in Scotland were transported here. I'm as flabbergasted as you, Professor, but let me take you inside and you can begin your research.'

'So Queen Victoria was still on the throne when the foundations were laid?' Giles surmised as he went up the steps and approached the front door.'

'Yes. And by the time it was built King Edward V11 would be in charge so the place you are now entering has a great deal of Victorian and Edwardian grandeur still intact. But more than that I can promise you a few surprises.'

The rain spattering on the covered roof of the verandah was becoming more noticeable as Giles was ushered into the front hallway and through a door on the right that took him into the Great Hall.

Immediately stopped in his tracks, Giles couldn't quite believe his eyes.

A little in front and to the left was a Steinway Grand Piano and on the floor were the skins of two beasts of the jungle…a leopard and a lion.

Upwards on the left were five deer heads above the ornate archways that led to a corridor. The entire area of intricate woodwork, the inglenook fireplace and stained-glass windows had the look of a magnificent setting for a presentation of stage magic. To crown it all was an eye-catching bronze of a monkey-eating eagle.

Looking upwards to the first floor gallery Giles could spot what appeared to be two large Japanese urns. He turned to his guide and shook his head in disbelief. 'This hall is large enough in which to hold a dance.' he said in wonderment. 'Do you think it might have been used for that?'

'I doubt it…surplus to requirements as you will see when I take you to the Ballroom!'

Giles just shook his head as Angus escorted him into the corridor leading to the room on the right.

'This is the Dining Room,' said Angus with a warm glow in his voice as he gesticulated with a sweep of his arms to the large dining table with sixteen chairs around it. The wood-panelled room had a fireplace in the wall backing on to the Great Hall and, to the left of that in the corner of the room was an opening into an alcove.

'What would that be used for? An inquisitive Giles asked as he wandered through the opening in the wall.

'The alcove was apparently an afterthought,' the caretaker remarked. 'An original access for dinner guests was through a secret room to the right of the fireplace in the Great Hall. It was eventually sealed off leaving this alcove.' The caretaker smiled knowingly as he continued. 'And this would be where the piper would sit with his dram of whisky while the guests were at dinner.

A nodding Giles was as good as a wink from this professor of magic. 'The chairs around the table look different,' he said changing the subject, 'and I'm not sure why?'

''You're quite right,' Angus agreed as he obligingly proceeded to explain. 'The chairs came from Sir George's ship the "Rhouma". Most of the wood in here also came from that ship.

The grip Giles made on the caretaker's arm brought his remarks to an abrupt halt.

'Good God, Professor, what's the matter...have I said something to cause you distress?'

'Nothing the matter, I hope!' Giles explained as he released his grip. 'But your words remind me of something sent to me in a conundrum...one of the reasons why I'm here I believe. Would you repeat what you just said?'

'I think I just said...what's the matter?'

'No, Angus. Before that.'

'I'm not sure.'

'You were explaining about the chairs being unusual.'

'Oh yes. I think I mentioned that the chairs came from Sir George's ship.'

'Yes that was it. And the name of the ship? Would you spell it?'

'The Rhouma...R-H-O-U-M-A.'

'The seats of Rhouma,' said an enlightened and relieved Giles. 'Where the seats of Rhouma stay. That was part of the riddle.' Giles' eyes once more had that faraway look as he spoke. 'I'm in the right place but I'm really none the wiser as to what it means!'

'Sorry I can't help you any more but there's a painting of Sir George's ship in the corridor. As I said earlier much of this room came from *the Rhouma*. The chairs or seats in your riddle were fixed to the floor in his ship as is usually the case with sea going vessels.'

'You've been most helpful, Angus. If only I can put everything in perspective I'd have a clearer picture. The secret is here...I know it is. It is now up to me to make some sense of it. Why ever do you think he furnished this room from contents of his ship? It must have had a special meaning for Sir George.'

'It certainly did. It was because of his ship that he was given a knighthood. Without *the Rhouma* he might never have been Sir George.'

'Really?'

'Yes he allowed *the Rhouma* to be used as a hospital ship during the Second Boer War and George was knighted by King Edward V11 in 1901 for his services to King and Country.'

'Yes, I can see why it was very special.'

'The ship was Clyde built in 1895 and we Scots are very proud of that fact, especially as shipbuilding on the Clyde is no longer what it used to be. Sir George sailed around the world and, in particular, to Japan where he became a friend of the Emperor. The monkey-eating eagle was one of the many gifts he received as were the incense burners in the Great Hall. We'll come across a few more gifts in some of the other rooms.'

When the two men left the Dining Room they moved across the corridor and entered what the caretaker named as the Billiard and Games Room.

'This part was where the gentlemen smoked their cigars after dinner and Sir George had vents installed in the ceiling that extracted the smoke,' Angus clarified with seeming approval. 'He also had air conditioning introduced under the billiard table; possibly the first of its kind this far north.'

'He must have been a remarkable man with such foresight to have modifications like that put into this structure.'

'I think you're right, Professor. Much of what you'll see in this building will have been the thoughtful deliberations of a man's world; the deer heads, the large fish you'll see in glass cases and all the paintings.'

'Not forgetting the billiard table,' said Giles pointing through the opening to the full size table in the next area.'

'That's right. It was his marriage to Lady Monica that changed things somewhat. It was she who brought the feminine touch to some rooms.' As they were about to leave the Games Room the caretaker host astonished his researching guest by declaring that the windows in the place were double glazed; yet another incredible innovation from years gone by.

Leaving the room, they retraced their steps along the corridor that passed the Great Hall, now on their left. On their right Giles stopped to look at a painting of the large yacht from where the dining chairs came. Giles' thoughts returned to the conundrum he'd received at RAF Winkleigh. His thoughts were short-lived as Angus pressed a switch and organ type music blasted out from behind. Turning to face an ebullient caretaker Giles was unable to converse as the vast musical contraption, complete with drum, played part of Rossini's William Tell Overture.

Struggling to make conversation audible Angus pressed close to the ear of his guest. 'What you are hearing is coming from the German built

"Orchestrion". One of only three of its kind and, probably, the only one that is still capable of playing. It is motor driven and plays perforated card rolls.'

'That takes me back,' shouted Giles in playful mood. 'It reminds me of a piano that did something similar in an ice cream shop in Dumfries when I was quite young. I think an Italian by the name of Fusco owned the shop.'

'This one was supposedly made for Queen Victoria,' said Angus whose words bellowed out in the still quiet as he switched off the machine. 'Quite possibly another bit of news that may not be entirely true.'

'I'm afraid the truth is a hobby of mine,' said Giles. But there seems no doubt at all that Sir George Bullough was a man before his time.'

'Sir George was, in every way, a big man,' said Angus pointing upwards to the portrait on the gallery wall. 'He was six feet eight inches in height and, among his many technological gadgets, he established electric lighting, marble top central heating, double glazing, power showers and also had the powerful music-playing Orchestrion installed.'

The next stop was Lady Monica's Drawing Room where her feminine influence was very much in evidence.

On to the Empire Sitting Room where the laurel wallpaper gave the room the atmospheric tradition of a Great Britain long since gone.

On leaving the Empire room the caretaker took Giles across the corridor to the Ballroom with its sprung floor and the Minstrels' Gallery where musicians from *the Rhouma* played. Giles was impressed by the magnificent chandelier and the silky wall covering. He was also curious about the windows facing out to the open courtyard.

'I'd like to know why the windows are placed so high on the walls.'

Angus smiled as he replied. 'The placing of the windows was done to prevent outsiders looking into the ballroom yet allowing daylight to enter. It would never have been proper to let others look in at ladies and gentlemen in their finery dancing the night away.'

Both men crossed the spacious dance floor and left by the far door. 'That is the Library,' said Angus pointing to the south-west end of the house. I was going to show you that interesting Study today but someone was trying to get in there earlier and to prevent that happening my wife locked the door and she has the key. I'll take you there tomorrow.'

'That's one place I really want to visit. I have an idea that a little research there might reveal some important results.'

'Have no fear, Professor. That will be a vital port of call tomorrow.'

'How did your wife get to know that someone was trying to enter?'

'That's easy! She was in the library doing a spot of tidying when there was a knock at the door. When she called out "who's there" there was no reply. She heard a scuffle but when she opened the door there was no-one outside and the corridor was empty. There are several places where one could hide and the impression she got was that a stranger was in the building who wished to remain unseen.'

'What an unnerving incident!'

'That's not the only one we've had recently.'

The questioning and puzzled expression on Giles' face prompted the caretaker to continue.

'Yes, I had a phone call in the library yesterday and a voice spoke in a whisper when I answered.'

'Has there always been a phone in the building?'

'To his credit Sir George had a phone installed when the building was in the early stage. I understand it was an undersea cable and would give him a chance to communicate with those in Newmarket regarding his racehorses. He'd probably had a phone in the library and in his general quarters. The Nature Conservancy have now had several installed for the use of their staff.'

'You sounded surprised and a little mysterious when you said the person on the phone whispered?'

'It made no sense at all,' replied Angus, stroking his greying beard. 'The voice said "This is Allison calling from beyond the grave. Please make your visitor aware there will be others". We had no visitor yesterday and I don't know anyone called Allison. The whole thing made no sense especially the words…there will be others.'

'Was the voice female?' Giles asked insistently.

'Do you know, I can't say…it was so faint?'

'I know someone who'd say that was spooky,' offered a bewildered Giles. 'I don't suppose you've had any more calls like that?'

'No, it's not the kind of call we normally get here. Let me guide you back to your room. You can freshen up and make any notes you want, then I'll contact you when dinner is ready.'

It was raining quite heavily when Giles got back to his bedroom. He removed his shoes, lay down on the bed and tried to fathom the meaning of that sinister phone call the day before he arrived. It was obvious he was continually being harassed by someone belonging to the circus group he was investigating. Someone who knew what was going on and was probably the killer of Allison…someone who was most likely aware of what was to take place in the future. And that someone was taunting Giles; believing all the time that Giles was incapable of coming to any successful conclusions.

Giles got up from the bed, put on his shoes, and grabbed a towel that had been laid out for him. He then climbed the short flight of stairs to the small bathroom where he sponged his face.

Once back in his room he looked out the windows overlooking the trees at the back of the house on the West side. The rain was sluicing down the panes and the trees outside were blowing wildly in the strong wind.

It was getting quite dark outside and Giles began to feel the atmosphere of this strange building of a bygone era and his thoughts turned again to those eerie and ghostly words spoken in a whispered voice.

Chapter 13

YOU'RE TALKING TO YOURSELF AGAIN

After dinner Giles sat for a while with Angus and his wife who were exceptionally intrigued by their guest's association with magic and illusion. Angus, in particular, was well informed about the great Jasper Maskelyne's efforts in the Second World War for British military intelligence when, in the North African desert, he created mock-up vehicles to outwit Rommel.

A long and informed discussion was followed by Mrs Mackintosh deciding that an early night was what she desired. When she'd gone her husband suddenly came to a decision. Slapping his knee with a distinct thump he rose, faced Giles and, for a brief moment, remained silent before he spoke.

'If you have no objection I'd like to let you see the rooms on the first floor. That will give you some idea of the layout of the place. You can then move around the place on your own tomorrow and research to your heart's content.'

Looking up at the caretaker Giles was conscious, for the first time, that this Highlander was wearing the kilt. The tartan-clad gentleman, with the military bearing, was now giving the impression that his trust in Giles was overwhelming. 'The kilt is not the Mackintosh tartan, if you're a little confused, Giles,' the caretaker said as he noticed his guest's look of surprise. 'I'm wearing the Murray of Atholl tartan. The Atholl Highlanders, the regiment I was proud to serve in was in the private employ of the Duke of Atholl. That meant it was Europe's only private army.'

'I suppose that means it was never part of the British Army...one more important institution that never existed?'

'You could say that…but we existed alright. The regiment was the first to attack the English at Culloden.'

'Your offer to explore upstairs is welcome, Angus. I'd very much like to see other parts of this exceptional building even in the subdued lighting.'

'Let's go then. We'll head back to the stairs beside the Orchestrion.'

Before they climbed the stairs Angus pointed towards a large fuse box. 'The lighting is controlled from there,' he said. 'We try to keep it to an acceptable level without putting too much strain on the generators. In the evening and throughout the early morning darkness, the lighting is kept to a minimum until daylight appears.'

The stairs led to the first floor gallery within the Great Hall. It was there that Giles examined the large Japanese vases and the painting of Sir George Bullough. Even in the subdued light and despite the gap in their ages Giles was rapidly coming to like this giant playboy from a vastly different era and background. He was gradually coming to the conclusion that this man, of much foresight was, like the building itself, deserving of great sympathy. According to his host Sir George had died in 1939 while playing golf

'The First World War obviously made a huge impact on visits by guests of Sir George and Lady Monica. It is her bedroom we'll visit first.'

Lady Monica's Bedroom was situated in the South-East corner of the house. It oozed her feminine charm as they entered a part of the house quite different.

'Some reports state that Lady Monica was related to Napoleon but that appears to be another of the myths of the Castle folklore and its larger-than-life owners. As I keep saying…do not believe all you see or hear.'

There was a long pause as the caretaker studied Giles' face. 'Is there something wrong, Professor Dawson…you've suddenly gone a little pale?'

'It's just that saying of yours! I've heard those words several times before from an unidentified person. A person involved with the circus I'm investigating. If I knew who that person was I'd be much closer to the truth. The evidence may be staring me in the face…if I can only interpret it.'

'Do you honestly think this house harbours the clues that you seek? Whatever mystery you're attempting to solve, can you possibly find the clues here which can put that mystery to rest?'

'Yes I do! Why else was I directed to come here? I firmly believe the answer to the puzzle is here but I'm equally convinced that whoever wanted me to visit and research this Edwardian time-capsule did not think I would be successful. I have to prove that person wrong!'

'Perhaps the little grey cells of Agatha Christie's Belgian sleuth may be what are required, Professor, don't you think?'

'You may not be too far from the truth, Mr. Mackintosh.'

'The truth is never the easiest commodity to find. I realised that during my career in the Army. This castle has countless works of art; ornaments and paintings among them. In a moment you will see a nude painting of a woman. It is a three-quarter rear portrait purported to be that of Lady Monica. But is it Lady Monica or did someone else pose for the artist? Truth, or another myth, Professor?'

'Listening to you as you expound about everything on show, I rather suspect you were well respected during your Army days, Angus?'

Angus smiled before answering. 'Many in the regiment joined the 3rd Transvaal Scottish which took part in the relief of El Alamein with the Eighth Army. I reached the rank of Major before I retired...not Sergeant Major. A little bit further up the ladder you understand.'

'The beam on Giles' face matched that of his guide.' I think, from this moment on, you deserve to be addressed as Major Angus Mackintosh'

'As you will, Professor! As you will!

The two men shook hands and were about to leave Lady Monica's Bedroom when a deafening roar from the Orchestrion stormed and blasted their ears from below the stairs.

'What the bloody hell!' cursed an angry Major as, with a swirl of the kilt, he descended the stairs in double-quick time to try and discover exactly what had started the blaring music.

Left alone Giles made a mental note of the music. He recognised the prelude to Lohengrin and the wheels of cognition sprang into motion. The music stopped abruptly but into his brain was implanted one word. The word was the music's composer. That word was Wagner.

Wagner was the same name as the circus magician. Was that another clue or was it much too obvious. The circus magician was certainly one person who had access to interfering in Allison's unconsciousness and her resultant death. But surely that was so blatant...or was it?

What had started the music and why was it so different from the piece he had heard previously? Was someone deliberately creating certain incidents in order to give him a clue? Or was it meant to distract him, put him off the scent and, like the stage magician, create suspension of disbelief?

The footsteps of Major Angus, as he climbed the stairs, prevented any further cogitation.

'Sorry about that, Professor. I've never known that to happen before. Something must have caused the switch to be pressed.'

'Something or someone!' expressed a dubious professor of magic. 'Usually, even in magic, someone has to do something in order to make things happen.'

'Since I arrived to act as temporary caretaker I've delved myself to get to know as much as possible of the history behind the objects in this house and that includes the rolls of music played by the Orchestrion. In particular the piece you just heard...the prelude to Lohengrin.'

'As a historian I'd like to know more about Lohengrin...apart from the composer.'

The caretaker stroked his chin before answering. He paused as he delved deep into his memory bank. 'Lohengrin was a knight of the holy grail. I'm not sure whether he was factual or fictional but in the play by Wagner he was sent in a boat pulled by swans to rescue a maiden who can never ask his identity.'

At the mention of a boat and swans Giles held up a hand as he apparently was reminded of Swan Boats on a different continent...but that was another story that eventually came to a successful conclusion. 'The attempt to rescue a maiden who must never ask his identity intrigues me,' said a more enlightened Giles with a ring of mild assurance. 'It takes me back to my problem at the circus where I'm led to believe that the identity of the culprit may only be properly known under a different name before the mystery is finally solved. This whole episode is beginning to make more sense than I think it was meant to.'

They moved on to the next room which was Sir George's Bedroom where the baronet's lengthy boots were still standing as if the master of the house had just returned from a ride on his favourite horse.

'He was very much involved with horses then?' Giles inferred questioningly as he anticipated news that would add conviction to what he already knew.

'Why yes! Very much so! He had a residence in the horse racing capital of Newmarket where his wife, Lady Monica still resides.'

'She must now be a fair age, Angus?'

'I believe she is ninety-seven or ninety-eight years old, but in poor health.'

'That means she has outlived her husband by around twenty-eight years?'

'Indeed! Though I'm afraid it won't be too long before she is joined once more with Sir George in the mausoleum on the other side of the island at Harris.'

They retraced their steps to a door opposite Lady Monica's Bedroom. 'Let me show you one more innovation of Sir George's,' Angus said as he opened the door that led into a unique bathroom; unique for a house built at the beginning of the century. 'This bath has a walnut shower hood which allows water to be sprayed at various angles using high-powered jets; almost the equivalent of what Jacuzzi is starting to produce now.'

'Incredible!' Giles said shaking his head in disbelief. 'Such hygienic and therapeutic culture as well as leisure enjoyment for those who travelled to this rather remote but beautiful island is unbelievable'

''I couldn't agree more. Especially when I know of some houses who only have the use of a tin bath in front of the fire. And that has to be filled with kettles of hot water. Now I think we've seen most of the interesting rooms except for the Library. I'll take you there tomorrow. What about joining me for a nightcap? That would be a good end to the evening.'

'That's very kind of you, Major. A bit of highland hospitality, if you please.'

They left the innovative bathroom and the caretaker opened the door leading to the first-floor gallery within the Great Hall. At the far end of the gallery Angus opened another door that led to an area which he described as the manager's domain.

Going into one of the flats Angus beckoned his guest to be seated. 'The rooms we're in now were Sir George's private quarters, complete with bedrooms, sitting room and bathroom.' The Major brought out two glasses and a bottle of twelve year old malt whisky. As he poured generous portions of the amber liquid his face lit up. 'Uisge beatha,' he beamed, handing a glass over. 'That's Scottish Gaelic for the water of life,' he said, noting the rather puzzled expression of his guest.

They chatted for a couple of hours as if they'd known each other for ages. It was quite remarkable how they had become good friends in such a short space of time.

Angus talked about how the outside grounds of the house had been transformed. Apparently the garden was so big it required twelve full-time gardeners to look after it. Exotic fruits were grown in heated greenhouses and turtles and alligators were allowed to roam around in pools until frightened staff had them removed.

'Tell me, Angus,' said a sceptical Giles who was desperately trying to grasp all he was hearing. 'Are these myths and figments of someone's imagination that make this place even more remarkable than it obviously is?'

'I think you have to make a valued judgement because so much was done to this Highland holiday home that it is difficult to separate the wheat from the chaff. I say that because you haven't heard the whole story. It seems that a nine-hole golf course and a bowling green were also established.'

'I see what you mean, Angus. I must say I even find it difficult to make up my mind about the red sandstone this building was built with.

'Why do you say that, Giles?'

'Well in my home county of Dumfries-shire a lot of the buildings are built of the red stone and that leans me to believe that Annan may have been where the stone was quarried.'

The talk continued and more than one glass of the water of life was imbibed before Giles returned to his oak bedroom. It was after midnight and the rain was lashing on the windows as he made ready for bed.

Stillness and silence was persuasive as he went up the short flight of stairs to the small bathroom to brush his teeth.

When he got back to his room the only noise came from the rain against the window panes. It was when he switched off the light that the atmosphere of an age gone by was starkly re-created. The combination of fatigue and whisky had a welcome effect as he climbed into bed, for he was soon fast asleep.

It was almost eight o'clock in the morning when Giles looked at his watch after a good night's sleep. The rain had stopped and today was to be the day when a visit to the library of this house of fantasy would emphatically reveal more details of a baronet who'd built a haven in the North West of Scotland where he could enjoy his leisure time.

When breakfast was over the ex-army caretaker said he was ready to show Giles to the room he most wanted to visit.

The Library, in the South West corner of the house, was reached along the corridor passing the Empire Sitting Room and Ballroom.

Once inside Giles was allowed to have a good look around the place and make notes. There were bookcases along the walls, some with glass fronts and Giles noted that many of the volumes could probably do with some cataloguing and placed in an order that made location easier. On reflection he was convinced that eventually some order would be restored with the books given their proper place as in a modern library.

The entire collection of Encyclopaedia Britannica was there as was a Century Dictionary and a Dictionary of National Biography. A glass case contained Bismarck, My War, the Life of Gladstone, The Story of a Soldier's Life and The First World War. Victorian and Edwardian History nestled behind glass awaiting a researcher's look at the past.

Elsewhere Sir George's travels around the world had an immediate impact. There were books on Africa, China and Japan. Others on Ceylon, India, South Africa and Tasmania gave a strong impression of a visit to the headquarters of National Geographic.

The fictional influence of the pre First World War era was not neglected for in a bookcase the Works of Dumas had pride of place. But the admiration for what was in the room was put to one side when Giles spotted a few books on the mantelpiece over a fireplace which had a large ornate Japanese screen in front of it. That image took Giles back to another library in Scotland when he was involved in the mysterious locked-room affair that had been entitled "The Statue of Three Lies".

'You are looking at the fire screen, Giles, with that same faraway look I've seen before.'

'Yes, it reminded me of the immediate past and a problem I was trying to solve and that made me aware of why I'm here now and this new problem that requires a solution.'

'The screen was another present from the Emperor of Japan which gives you some idea how well thought of Sir George must have been. But to get back to your problem…do you see anything in this room that may give you a glimmer of hope?'

'Yes, those books on the mantelpiece! They are Weatherby's Racing Calendars and one in particular is for the year I'm interested in. Can I examine it?'

'Of course you can. I know you'll be very careful with it. Which one would you like?'

'The one for the year 1917 please. The words of the conundrum were "Retrace half a century from March twenty first. Learn of a Race that never was, on grassland that unlike RAF Winkleigh is now an airfield." Today is the twenty-first of March, 1967 and if I retrace half a century, the fifty years take me back to 1917.'

Major Angus handed over the 1917 Racing Calendar and Giles carefully turned the pages until he arrived at the date he wanted. On page 49 was Wednesday, March 21st. Listed below were the races for that day. First was Chequers Selling Hurdle Race with owner, name of horse and jockey. Next was Crawley Hurdle Race with details and that was followed by Stayers Handicap Hurdle Race.

On page 50 were the details of the Stayers Handicap Hurdle Race and below that came the words that sent a shiver of excitement through Giles as he read them. "Wartime National" Steeplechase, Sir George Bullough's Ballymacad- E. Driscoll.

That cleared the line in the conundrum about "A race that never was.' The fact that the race was run at Gatwick and not Aintree meant that it was classified as not being the Grand National. It also verified the part concerning "grassland that was now an airfield" as Gatwick is now one of London's largest airports.

So far so good was the reasoning of a thoughtful Giles. But there was no disguising the fact that one very important discovery had to be made during his brief visit to this controversial and remote mansion.

Contemplation of the situation came to a halt with the ringing of the telephone on the desk at which Major Angus was now sitting. Giles watched with a little trepidation as the caretaker answered, looked upwards and said 'It's for you.'

As he took the phone Giles looked down at Angus who was mouthing the words 'It's a woman.'

'Hello, Giles Dawson speaking.'

'It's so good to speak to you, Giles. But you sound rather detached. Is there anything wrong?' It was Laura on the other end.

'No, there's nothing wrong, Laura darling. I wasn't expecting your call and I thought it might be from someone else. I'll explain later when I see you. How are you feeling?'

'I'm fine, Giles and I'm waiting for you in Fort William.'

'How did you get there? It's quite a distance from Lockerbie.'

'By car, silly. I can still drive. The problem with the throat doesn't prevent me from driving my car and I'll be in Mallaig waiting for you when you leave the Isle of Rum.'

''That's tremendous, Laura. But when did you arrive and where are you staying?'

'I travelled yesterday and managed to wangle staying for a few days in a little cottage designated for one of the estate's assistant factors. It's a few miles outside Fort William at a place called Torcastle and I'm sure you'll love it.'

'I'm just about finished here and with a bit of luck I could be in Mallaig tomorrow so long as the weather is not too bad. Give me a call about nine o'clock in the morning and I'll let you know if I'll be able to sail across.

How long will it take you to drive to Mallaig?'

'I've been told it could take at least two hours. Part of the road is single track with passing places but they tell me that someday the road will be much better. Don't worry, Giles. Once I know you're going to sail across I'll set off for the fishing village. I should be there before you are.'

'You certainly will if you drive the way you did when I was in your car last October.'

'Exhilarating wasn't it, Giles? I'll call you tomorrow and I'll have my fingers crossed.'

'That will suit me fine. God bless, darling.'

After he handed the phone back to Angus, Giles started to saunter around the room; his brain struggling with the conundrum that concerned his visit to Kinloch Castle. It seemed to him that most of the riddle had been successfully solved. Most, but not all. And the part that was still to be solved was the most important part of all.

'Near where the seats of Rhouma stay is the secret you wish to solve one day.'

'You're talking to yourself, Giles. Is there a problem?'

'The problem,' said a rather sheepish professor, grappling to find words. 'The problem I have is to solve a secret that must lie here in this house. I wish to solve it one day, according to the conundrum, and today would be a good day to do just that.' He turned and, looking at the Major, said 'Would you mind if I took another look at the Dining Room and those chairs from the yacht?'

'Not at all, Giles. I'm sure you know your way around the place. You're free to wander. I can get on with office work here in the library. If you need help you'll find me in here.'

Making his way past the Great Hall Giles entered the Dining Room. He walked around the large table examining the chairs as he did so. Neither they nor the panelled walls offered any clues. Nor indeed did the fireplace or the alcove where the piper would sit while the guests were at dinner. The alcove was a small space but was comfortably furnished and large enough to keep essentials for the dinner table. It was also a place where someone could use for quiet study. But that was all…no secret jumped out at Giles.

The only other areas close to those chairs were the combined Billiards, Games and Smoking Room or the Great Hall which backed on to the Dining Room.

Stopping for a moment Giles wondered how his close friend, Freddie would tackle the situation.

'Go back to the conundrum. That's what Freddie would have done. You're talking to yourself again, old son.' Giles muttered under his breath.

He went back to the conundrum. The second line stuck out like a sore thumb. What was it? Something like the leading man had two names. The leading man in the Hitchcock film "North by North West" had two names in real life and, in the movie, he played a character who was suspected of having two names.

Two names? The note left in his trailer with the strange birth names of leading actors and actresses. That had listed men and women with two names. The riddle mentioned a man. Could he be the main suspect? But what if it was a woman? He was going round in circles but the two names… could that be the vital clue? Should he search for a person or object with two names? Maybe, but where did he start?

The Billiard Room had a table that was set for a different game… snooker. That was what had struck him as slightly odd. Billiard or snooker table? Two names but difficult to find any secret there; but that was a start.

When he examined the 1917 Racing Calendar in the library a race was listed as the "Wartime National" not the Grand National. Two names for the same race but the Library was a fair distance from the chairs and the conundrum suggested the secret was close to the chairs.

He strolled into the Great Hall. Did the monkey-eating eagle have another name? Was there a double name for Steinway of piano fame? Could the leopard and lion skins have even a remote connection to Khan, the Royal Bengal Tiger?

He couldn't see the wood for the trees. He was confusing himself. He suddenly stopped as if hitting a brick wall. The wood and the trees. Were there alternate names for oak and mahogany? He remembered the difficulty he had when trying to open the safe at Maskelyne Hall the previous year when he was involved with another problem. Logical thinking had to be the order of the day. The secret was close by. He just had to think things through and perhaps a word or a phrase might set the wheels in motion again.

It was funny and strangely comforting but Freddie was somehow by his side and aiding his thought processes as if he'd been transported there by some time machine.

With that reassuring attitude Giles went to lunch having got rid of his previous despondency. Angus and his wife were already there and apparently talking about a person in great detail. The words he heard were "he was the most trusted man." Angus turned to greet his guest.

'Come in Giles. You're just in time. We were talking about a gentleman who was obviously a very close friend of Sir George Bullough. His name was Sir William Bass and his room was named as such. The room, he occupied when here, is on the South West corner of the first floor which is the one round the corner from your oak room.'

'It seems,' said Mrs Mackintosh, joining her husband in the conversation. 'Sir William Bass was a British racehorse owner whose family traced back to William Bass, the founder of the brewery company.'

'I can see why they'd be good friends. Both titled men with wealth and interested in racehorses.' Giles expressed his views assuming, as he did so, that Sir William Bass was the person being described as a most trusted man. 'He must have been a very trustworthy pal.'

'That's very true, Giles.' Angus continued where his wife had left off. 'Sir William was very much involved with cinematography theatres but was most noted as Billy Bass for his ownership of racehorses. He was a steward of The Jockey Club and had success in the Cesarewitch at Newmarket.'

'Was Sir William married?'

It was Mrs Mackintosh's turn to enter the conversation once more. 'Yes he was,' she said. 'He was married to a leading sportswoman, Lady Noreen Hastings. Sir William outlived her by several years and, as he had no family, when he died he left his fortune to his wife's nephew, the racehorse trainer, Peter Hastings. Peter later changed his name to Hastings Bass.'

The wheels were turning again as Giles listened to the story about the racehorse trainer. Two names once more.

When lunch was over Giles informed his caretaker host that he wanted to spend a bit longer in and around the Dining Room. He would also like to have another look at the Library to avoid missing anything. Angus declared there was no problem. Giles could spend as much time as was required in any of the rooms. It would be a shame if he left this house without finding the data he required.

The first return visit was to the Library. Once inside he closed the door and had another look at the vast collection of books. The place was steeped in history; the historic involvement of a man who'd travelled the world, been involved with war, and yet was a passionate owner of racehorses and had resided in the home of the racing world: Newmarket.

It was that thought that brought his attention away from the volumes around the room; his eyes concentrating on objects he'd missed on his first visit. Those objects were a set of racing plates; the shoes racehorses wore when they went into the serious business of competing on the turf. As he lifted a shoe Giles thought Freddie would love this. The plates had been worn by Ballymacad when he won the Wartime National at Gatwick racecourse. Next time he saw his ex-RAF friend he must tell him about this and research a bit more about the Grand National that apparently never was.

The walk to the Dining Room was accomplished with ease. Giles seemed to know his way around the ground floor as if he'd stayed on many occasions.

Sitting down in one of the chairs around the dining table he contemplated those lines in the circus conundrum that mentioned the seats of Rhouma.

'The Dining Room has to be the place,' he muttered under his breath and looked around to see if anyone was within earshot. He needn't have worried. The place was quiet. Deadly quiet; his thoughts turning to Allison whose final bow at the circus was on a stretcher.

The light from outside appeared to struggle to enter the Dining Room windows and the shadows took on strange shapes giving the empty space a feeling that it was filling with spectral figures bent on mischief. Giles tried to stifle the shudders flaunting fleetingly over his flesh.

He took a deep breath and, giving himself a vigorous rubbing with his hands, brought the circulation back into his fingers. He sighed, looked around the room at the fireplace, the alcove room where the piper may have sat when guests were at dinner, the magnificent table and the seats of *the Rhouma* where Sir William Bass and Lady Noreen Hastings had sat, along with Sir George and Lady Monica and their invited ladies and gentlemen… and possibly even King Edward V11 himself.

With his eyes closed Giles concentrated on the room he was in. His trance-like state of mind searched for some divine intervention that would focus on the secret that might lead him to the conclusion he needed.

His gut feeling was…that secret was here. It was here and not far from where he sat. Something someone had said? Was that it? Some seemingly incongruous remark he'd heard but taken out of context?

Powers of recall went into action and, as the hours went by and the evening gloom approached, Giles came gradually to a conclusion that awakened him with a sudden start. The name Billy Bass etched into his brain.

Was it possible? Words that someone had said not so long ago came flooding back to him. Were they words that could have been applied to a place close to the seats of Rhouma where he was seated? And there was just a slim chance that, if those words could be connected to a person on Ramon's list of suspects, the person that Giles had a suspicion about might not be too far away from the truth. He would then see a reason for Allison's tragic death plus the inevitability of at least one more killing.

The flicker of a smile on Giles' face, as he rose and made his way to dinner, was deceptive. The smile wasn't there because of his prognosis of further murder. It was because of what Freddie would have said had he been in the room listening to Giles' thoughts.

Freddie would have said "You're talking to yourself again, old son!"

Chapter 14

TWO CAN PLAY AT THIS GAME

When dinner was over Giles excused himself and retired to the oak bedroom to mull over his eventful stay at the Castle.

It was getting very dark outside and the weather was deteriorating by the minute. Heavy rain was cascading down the windows and Giles was doubtful if a sailing to the mainland tomorrow would be possible. The caretaker, however, was optimistic that a contingency plan could be put into operation as several Nature Conservancy staff had business elsewhere.

Taking off his shoes Giles lay back on the bed and drifted off into sleep. A strange thought, entering his mind before sleep enveloped him, was that in a lifetime the average person spent almost a third of that time with his eyes shut. The important thing for him now was to make good use of that time by not only recharging the batteries but allowing the brain to overcome problems and bring them to a successful outcome.

He must have been asleep for some considerable time for when he looked at his watch, in the dim light, it was almost midnight. His fuddled brain took a few seconds to realise what had wakened him. It was the sound of his door closing. No doubt about it…someone had been in his room. But this time he had been in the room with the intruder and that intruder had now left in a hurry.

He got off the bed, dashed to the door, opened it and glanced down the oak room corridor. The corridor was empty but a door at the far end was being shut. He scampered past the oak bedrooms on the left and the stained glass windows, which overlooked the courtyard on the right. When he reached the staircase leading down to the kitchen area he realised for the first time that he was in his stocking soles. That was just right he thought for he was making no noise.

The lighting on the staircase was so bad that it meant braving the dimly lit stairs to the floor below without losing his footing. He was positive that whoever had entered his room had gone down before him but he had a spooky sensation that an unwanted presence was creeping up behind him. That sensation was so strong it had an unnerving effect on him and he gripped the banister with increased firmness.

On reaching the ground floor he heard another door close. He wasn't far behind and he hurried his step along past the kitchen area, through a door and into the main corridor with the Dining Room on his left and the Billiard and Smoking Room on his right.

He could just make out a figure at the far end close to the Orchestrion but, as he hurried, he realised he was too late. The lights suddenly went out and, as he stumbled and fell in the darkness, he knew the figure had tampered with the fuse box.

Having bruised a knee he got to his feet but, with the open archways of the Great Hall not allowing him to have a solid wall to get his bearings, he blundered through one of the gaps and, reaching out with hands and arms as he fell again, he found himself lying close to something stretched out on the floor.

At that moment the lights came on again and, raising himself, he found he was staring into the lifeless head… of a lion whose skin was spread over the Hall floor.

Bringing his head and shoulders upwards and leaning on an elbow Giles could observe that the area close to the fuse box was entirely clear. There was no sign of the intruder but the noise in his head was deafening…only the noise wasn't in his head. It was coming from the Orchestrion and it was the prelude to Lohengrin. Wagner again! Was someone doing everything to misdirect him in the same way as a stage magician uses artistic skill? Or was this a genuine attempt to put him off the scent?

Making his painful way towards the stairs Giles switched the music off and started to climb to the floor above. His stocking-soled feet made no sound in the dramatic silence that now existed and that brought back a memory of a previous soundless experience during his attempt to solve the Lockerbie mystery.

Putting that memory out of his mind he made his way back to the oak bedroom. It seemed to take an age and, being physically exhausted, he wasted no time in preparing for bed. Before passing out his final thoughts were of the action-packed witching hour that had just passed.

Dreams can work in mysterious ways. They can descend into grotesque nightmares causing blood pressure and breathing to go haywire which can leave the sleeper near to cardiac arrest. They can also go to the other extreme and induce clear thinking combined with compensating powers of reasoning.

Despite the distressing events of the evening before sleep took over, Giles' dream covered the other happenings during his stay at Kinloch Castle. Certain words and places jelled into a comprehension that somehow endorsed some of his previous assumptions.

If, as some have said, dreams invade the mind just before the sleeper awakes, Giles would certainly subscribe to that for he awoke feeling refreshed and went to breakfast with a *joie de vivre* outlook.

Major Angus had been told that the boat that was to take the Nature Conservancy staff to Mallaig was not going to sail because of the bad weather, but a small covered power boat was coming from another of the Small Isles and would make the sailing.

There had also been a telephone call from Fort William to enquire about travel arrangements and the lady, making the call, had been told that Professor Dawson would be in Mallaig sometime before noon.

With lots of bustling Giles packed his bag and brought it downstairs to be told by a girl on the staff that in about an hour a van would take him to the jetty. He thought he'd take a last look at the place and wandered along the downstairs rooms. Why had he come here? It was patently obvious that the circus riddle was responsible and he could only surmise that someone in the circus was not only hounding Senhor Ramon but believed that Ramon was wrong to hire Giles. It was up to Giles to make that person pay for that incorrect belief.

As he paid a final visit to the area around the Dining Room, certain facets from his dream came flooding back convincing him that during his brief visit some words and places had important meaning. He would now expound his theories to Laura and to Freddie during their next get-togethers.

A final farewell to Major Angus and his wife after a light breakfast and a sincere thank you for their helpful support, was followed by a walk out to the van and a last look at a time-capsule of how the wealthy lived their lives during the reign of King Edward VII.

It took more than two hours to cross to the fishing village of Mallaig but in that time the boat was pounded by heavy seas as it bounced its way across the water.

Windscreen wipers were constantly in use, struggling to clear the deluge of rain and the crashing waves. The extremely poor visibility and the up and down and side to side movement of the small boat as it ploughed its way through the torrent of water made it difficult for the skipper to navigate with any degree of certainty. The man at the helm however was experienced and knew this stretch like the back of his hand. After moments when the boat felt like it might break up it was then in calmer water in the Sound of Sleat – between Skye and the mainland round Mallaig. The outline of the fishing village came into view and the sandstone battlements of Kinloch Castle were a distant memory of the past.

Once in the harbour and sheltered from the storm Giles spotted Laura's colourful sports car. With his heart-beat increasing, like the acceleration of Laura's car when they left Lockerbie railway station the first time they met as adults, he climbed the steps to the top of the pier and watched his fiancée coming toward him.

They were in each other's arms in a jiffy and their wet faces were soon in pleasurable contact. The weather conditions still raged beyond the harbour, but the rain that made standing outside uncomfortable, had almost stopped.

They were hardly in the car when Laura looked quizzically at Giles. 'When I called you yesterday you sounded rather remote. You said you would explain later. Were you really expecting another call?'

'No, I wasn't but there had already been a call the day before I arrived and the caller apparently sounded as if he or she was speaking from beyond the grave. I didn't want another call from the same person.'

'You're not serious, Giles? You're talking in riddles again. How could you know someone was calling as if from the other side when you weren't there? And why the he or she part? Was the sex of the caller not evident?'

'It was the caretaker who answered and the caller, who mentioned the name Allison, spoke in a whisper that made it difficult to know whether it was a man or a woman who was speaking'

'But why should a girl's name make you think…?'

'Because, my dear Laura, Allison died a few days ago and I'm very much afraid it may not have been an accident. Now I don't believe the dead can lift the telephone and dial a number in the West Highlands that even I don't know. But someone at the circus who knew there had been a fatality called and tried to act as if…' He never finished the sentence.

'Let's have some lunch and we can go over what you've just been telling me.' Laura said. 'After that we'll drive to Fort William where I can pamper you before we head back to Lockerbie.'

'Good idea my love. But I think we could stop off in Glasgow and choose a ring.'

Laura smiled, leaned over and kissed Giles on the cheek. She started the car, and drove into the main street where she parked the car overlooking the bay.

A short walk took them to the bar restaurant of a local inn and, after enjoying some of the best fish and chips they'd had in ages, they continued the conversation they'd started at the pier.

'You say there's been a death at the circus?'

'Yes, but it's not just a death. It's more like a killing.'

'You mean a murder, Giles?'

'I'm afraid so, Laura.'

'I'm thinking back to what you said when we were together at Maskelyne Hall.'

'What did I say?'

You said you expected the death of someone but didn't have any idea who might die or where or when it might happen.'

'That about sums it up, Laura. Allison would not have been my idea of the likely victim of murder. Nor did I think it would happen the way it did. The mystery goes even deeper…I haven't the foggiest idea how it could be done or who could have done it. I must be losing my grip.'

'I don't think you are, Giles. Losing your grip, I mean. There are so many mysteries and I just hope I don't have another one for you. What I'm about to ask can clear things up if I get the right answer?'

'Ask away, Laura!'

'While I was in hospital, did you ever mention to anyone at Maskelyne Hall the name of the circus you're investigating?'

A puzzled expression came over Giles' face as he pondered for a moment. 'I believe I mentioned it to George. I may have done so to your mother, though I doubt it. Why do you ask?'

'Well I'm pretty sure you've never told me the name of the circus but, when I drove all the way from Lockerbie, a small van seemed to be following me. I came across it everywhere I went. The last time I saw it was close to where we'll shortly be staying…Torcastle. And that's really out of the way.'

'A mere coincidence, Laura. I'm sure you're putting too much emphasis on something that has a perfectly logical explanation. Why are you so suspicious?'

'You could be right, Giles. It was the name on the van that gave me concern. The name Circus was on the van.'

'So you put two and two together and thought you were being followed by someone from the circus I'm investigating. Did you not consider it might be a small circus searching various areas for one night stands.' Giles paused giving his fiancée a gentle smile of encouragement. 'Was the name of the circus on the van?'

'Yes there was but it meant nothing to me since I never knew the name of the circus you were involved with. You never mentioned it to me.'

The muscles of Giles' jaw tightened and he looked at Laura with apprehension written all over his face. 'What was the name on the van, Laura?' he asked gripping her hands tightly.'

'Tropicana!' said Laura. 'It was Circus Tropicana!'

Nodding his head in a kind of resigned fashion Giles gave Laura's hands a gentle squeeze. 'You *were* being followed, Laura!'

'But why?'

'Someone would make a shrewd guess, if you were going north, you'd be going to meet me. They're keeping a close eye on me Laura. I was followed on the cruise ship and I'm sure I was followed on Rum. I'm a threat and they know that.'

'You keep saying they, Giles. Do you think there's more than one person involved?'

'I can't answer that with any certainty. I'm not sure if it's a man or a woman or if it's more than one I'm up against, but my short stay on the Isle of Rum has given me an idea that coincides with my previous thinking.'

'Tell me, Giles. If I was being followed why would the name be on the van? Surely that gives the game away?'

'Yes it does, darling. But I think someone wants to let me know I'm being followed. He or she is trying to alarm me and make things difficult. And the closer I get to the truth the more worried that person will become. Two can play at this game!'

The journey of forty or so miles to their destination was accomplished in comfort despite the stormy weather. The sports car was driven at a speed much slower than previous experiences due to the single track. The passing places had to be used with consideration for other drivers and though Giles was near to sleep he was able to admire the skill of Laura at the wheel.

The skilful handling of the lively sports car reminded the sleepy co-driver of his own driving ability. It had been neglected during his stay in London where public transport, or a jaunt with a jovial cabbie with an enlarged hippocampus, was much more pleasant than driving in city traffic.

The winding and twisting road along the coast passed through villages with romantic names like Morar and Arisaig and when they were passing Cameron-Head's Inverailort House, which was on their right when they reached the small hamlet of Lochailort, Laura said she'd been told that the techniques used by Commandos were coached there during the War years.

As they passed through Glenfinnan, Laura pointed out the memorial statue of a MacDonald commemorating the rising of Bonnie Prince Charlie on the right and the railway viaduct on the left.

The car gathered speed alongside the single track railway line with Loch Eil to the South. It was the job of Laura to point out another landmark that could barely be seen through the covering of cloud. The misty shape of Ben Nevis, Scotland's highest mountain, made it clear they were nearing Fort William. After going through the village of Corpach they made a left turn at Banavie with the Caledonian Canal and the unique section of canal locks, called Neptune's Staircase, on their right.

The road for the next two miles had more twists and turns than Giles had been involved with at RAF Winkleigh. The last half-mile was also single track and Laura slowed at a sign for Muirshearlich and turned into an opening on the right. She switched on headlights as she drove the car down a sloping path towards a dark tunnel.

'We're about to go under the canal,' she explained. 'It's dripping wet but we'll get through all right so long as I don't stall.'

'Where are we?'

'This is where the Tor Castle was, once upon a time, and we've got the use of a little cottage for a few days.'

There was barely room enough to drive a car through the dripping wet tunnel but, once through, the track opened up again.

A gurgling burn on the right broke the silence of a wooded glade as Laura guided the car to a destination, a few hundred yards on, beside a ruin.

A little cottage with a small garden surrounded by a fence came into view. There was smoke coming from the chimney.

'Here we are for a day or two.' Laura said as she stopped the car. 'Once inside you can relax while I rustle up a meal for two.' She looked up at the sky where patches of blue peeped through. 'I think the weather looks much more inviting and we might be able to explore this area tomorrow. But first things first…let's go inside!'

The interior was warm from a Raeburn cooker in the kitchen. Laura replenished the cooker with some logs, Giles took his bag into one of the bedrooms, then Laura made him sit down and poured him a brandy.

The small kitchen table was set for two with two candles in their holders which Laura lit.

Sitting in that comfortably warm kitchen with a brandy in his hand Giles was captivated as he gazed at the beautiful Laura. Having been absorbed by events that had happened over the past few days since leaving London on the cruise ship it was marvellous to realise just how much he was in love.

He'd tried to put all the events neatly into some kind of order, in the same way as he did in his London flat when he used scraps of paper and moved them about to make sense of them.

Laura's tale of the circus van convinced Giles that his original assumption, that he was being followed, was correct. He was, more than ever, positive that this would continue, and, as long as he was pursued in order to make him more anxious and not to put his life in danger, he'd come up trumps. But why was he threatened in this way? Was it really to make his task more difficult or was someone there to keep a constant check on his rate of success? There was always the distinct possibility that if he was thought to be making real progress, his own life could be in danger.

He took another sip from the glass that was cupped in his hands. Some gut feeling over the last few days was being reassured that he was indeed making progress but he was confident that no one else could be aware of that. The death of Allison would be followed by another, if his theory was correct, but he did not wish his own demise to be the next one in the chain of events.

'Can I give you a hand?' he asked, as he watched his beloved Laura preparing vegetables and chicken pieces.

'No, my dear Giles. It's just so pleasant to get the chance to cook our first meal, all by myself.' She wiped her hands, pulled a chair over and sat down beside him. 'I've been watching you and there were times when you seemed so far away.'

'You can read me like a book, darling and I know you've seen me in this state before. My mind has the unfortunate habit of wandering off at times but thankfully the spin-off is usually very productive.'

Pouring herself a brandy she then topped up Giles' glass before giving his hand a squeeze. 'Let's drink to a continuation of those wanderings, my dearest Giles, and hope they may not only be wanderings of the mind!' her coquettish smile giving way as she bent over and kissed him. They clinked their glasses, linked arms and Laura, with that flirtatious look on her face, proposed a toast. 'To many years of wander lust!'

'I'll certainly drink to that!' Giles said as he lifted his glass to his lips.

Dinner that evening was a triumph. Laura produced a bottle of wine and Giles did the necessary with a corkscrew. With the lights out, the candles gave the place a romantic setting and the problems of the *gauntlet of fear* circus dissolved and were eliminated from Giles' often-tortured mind.

The chicken was cooked to perfection and afterwards the washing up was accomplished by the engaged couple.

When everything was cleared and they were seated by the warmth of the cooker, Laura looked anxiously at her fiancé. 'Can I ask you a serious question, Giles?'

'Yes, by all means.'

'When I was watching you earlier you were away on a different planet and we both agreed about your occasional wanderings,' she said with that smile of hers. 'But there was one instant when I did detect fear in your eyes as you thought over your problem. Did that fear concern us or was it because of the dilemma you're involved in?'

'Fear, my love, is a normal emotion. I believe it prevents us from going too far into the unknown. As far as we are concerned I have no fear about going into the unknown with you…the further the better. As for the circus, the fear is because of what might yet be to come. I will solve whatever lies ahead…I know I will. I'm well on the way there already and whoever is responsible will be the one who'll know the meaning of fear at the finale.'

'Why don't you get some sleep and we'll put in a full day tomorrow before we go home to Lockerbie?'

When Giles went into the little back bedroom the sheets were turned down and the bedside lamp was on. He'd washed his face and brushed his teeth and as he slid between the sheets he reminisced about the previous night in the oak room in Rum's Edwardian mansion and the eventual wild goose chase around the building at midnight.

He was about to switch off the lamp when the door opened and a vision stood in the doorway wearing black silk pyjamas. The last time he'd had the pleasure had been one night at Maskelyne Hall when he was trying to explain the death of Laura's father. But that had been a rear view as Laura disappeared along a darkened corridor. The black pyjama against the blackness of the corridor was the same effect used by the stage magician… that of almost total invisibility. This was different. The full frontal figure of his fiancée in those revealing pyjamas lit by the bedside lamp was as eye catching as any man could wish.

He switched off the lamp as she slid between the sheets and snuggled up to him. 'Have no fear, my dear,' she said. 'Two can play at this game.'

Chapter 15

ENTER THREE MURDERERS

The early morning sun shining through the bedroom window wakened a sleepy Giles and the aroma of bacon and eggs explained why he was the only one in bed. He got up, put on a dressing gown and went through to the kitchen.

Laura was standing at the cooker. The singing of Shirley Bassey coming from the radio was loud enough to make Laura unaware that there was anyone behind her; that is until Giles' hands reached around and gently caressed her, simultaneously kissing her on the neck.

The sensation that Giles felt through his fingers, travelled all the way up his arms and into his whole being. She turned, looked into his blue eyes and smiled. He pulled her towards him and kissed her on the mouth.

'How wonderful it is to know that you are still determined to wander, my dear Giles.'

He held her close and kissed her passionately. It was only the hissing and spitting of the bacon in the frying pan that caused them to break apart.

'I know we're going to be a wonderful team darling,' said Giles, the quaver in his voice matched the tingling quiver that remained in the tips of his fingers. 'Last night was heaven, and holding you in my arms this morning is a magical moment.'

'Last night I think we both had a little too much to drink, Giles. You fell asleep and I did soon after.'

'Well the more practice I get the luckier I should become.'

Laura gave a gentle laugh at that remark and Giles placed a hand tenderly under her chin and said, 'I love the way you wrinkle your nose when you laugh.'

Standing back, Laura, looking a little anxious asked, 'Do you remember anything of last night Giles?'

'I certainly remember everything…before I fell asleep; that is something I'll never forget. But after I fell asleep…well I drifted off to cloud nine.' Laura just shook her head.

With breakfast over both Laura and Giles walked down to the River Lochy and sat for a while. Their talk centred on the problem at the circus where Giles was wrestling with a puzzle which appeared to defy belief. Laura made it perfectly clear that she was determined to assist as much as she could. Along with Freddie she believed they could help steady the ship and assist Giles in his quest for a speedy solution to what seemed an impossible situation.

The improvement in the weather from the storm of yesterday was spectacular. It was unbelievably warm for late March, so much so that they were both reluctant to leave the swirling river.

After a lunch of sandwiches Laura suggested she take Giles to an interesting spot nearby. She pointed out there was a possibility they might catch a glimpse of deer on their travels. When Giles asked if that was the reason for the high fence around the cottage garden she said she'd been told that the deer apparently were a problem if there were vegetables growing and other food was scarce.

The walk along a rough path took them down to a mysterious avenue lined on both sides with beech trees. It lay between the Caledonian Canal and the River Lochy. Giles reminisced about the fact that in the science room at the school in Lockerbie, when he was there as a young boy, there was a chart showing the locks on this canal known as Neptune's Staircase. He'd never have dreamt that one day he'd be so close to that stretch of Telford engineering.

The avenue they'd come across seemed to begin and end in the middle of nowhere, yet it was wide enough to drive a carriage and Giles wondered if it might have been part of the approach to the Tor Castle of which only part of a wall now remained.

'This place is called Banquo's Walk,' declared Laura in the manner of the best tour guide. 'It is supposed to be haunted by the ghost of Banquo as he walks alone and contemplates the three witches' prophesy. Spooky, don't you think? Though today it looks quite benign'

'I wonder if Banquo really existed, Laura? Was he just a character in Shakespeare's play, Macbeth? Just another example of a non-existent force… another myth?'

'Funny you should say that, Giles. I've heard it rumoured that William Shakespeare may not even have written the plays or the poetry. Is that possible?'

'Perfectly possible, though I doubt it. It does seem that a few intelligent persons in history believed it unrealistic to accept that someone having left school early, and with no great knowledge of the countries that appear in his plays, could write such literary masterpieces.

But I have an idea. Let's go back to the cottage and we'll carry on there.'

'Oh Giles…if I didn't know you better I'd say you were suggesting a naughty carry on at the cottage! You must be getting bolder, but I'm game if you are.'

The exasperated shake of the head from Giles was all that was necessary to provoke another chuckle from the girl now on his arm.

Back at the cottage Laura made a cup of tea. Giles stoked up the Raeburn and they then settled down to a cosy conversation.

'You said you had an idea, Giles. What was it?'

'It was Shakespeare and the mystery of who was the real author of those wonderful plays. It made me start to think. As a historian I've come to the conclusion that some of the greatest historical mysteries involve a case of mistaken identity. That includes some of the great names in stage magic.'

'Do you think that Shakespeare had an identity problem?'

'I really can't answer that, but out at Banquo's Walk I mentioned men of intelligence who were of that opinion. I know of two. One was Sigmund Freud, whose enigmatic riddles we've always loved to solve, and the other was the great actor, Orson Welles who is alive and well and probably still kicking at the studios that've refused to let him have his head. Strangely enough, he is interested in stage magic. I thought I would name-drop and bring my favourite subject into the conversation. I mention Welles because, not only is he a great actor, but he has directed some top class theatre productions, and one of them was Macbeth, believe it or not. Another one of my coincidences, you'll probably say, but when I associate certain events with others the wheels start coming up with notions I find difficult to ignore.'

'Orson Welles rings a bell, Giles. Didn't he do a radio play that caused such a commotion in America?'

'That was in 1938, I believe, when he made a radio adaptation of "War of the Worlds" which caused panic to listeners who thought the country was being invaded by aliens. Well, that was what reports said but they were mostly false. Yet another example of "Do not believe all you see or hear."'

'You said Welles was interested in magic. Did he ever perform?'

'Unfortunately he was often described as an amateur but he performed in Las Vegas and I understand he played "The Great Orso" in the 1944 film "Follow the Boys" when he sawed Marlene Dietrich in half, though I never saw the movie He usually acted out his tricks while smoking a large cigar… yes he is a professional…he certainly is. All this rather obscure data brings me back to the many myths of historical celebrities with identity problems. I'm in no doubt that the person making Ramon Mordomo run his *gauntlet of fear* has an identity problem.'

'Ramon gave you a list of those he considered suspects. After dinner I think we should go over that group of names and we may be able to narrow it down.'

'That's a good idea, Laura. History, I'm afraid is littered with greats who, when they died, may really have been murdered. Napoleon was possibly one of them…but why Allison? She wasn't one of those historical greats, nor was she so important that Ramon would give up the circus because of her death. No, that wasn't an accident. There was a reason behind her death and if we can find that reason…! Your idea of looking at the names of those suspects might just be of great help. I'm certain the culprit is on that list!'

After the evening meal Giles searched his bag and brought out the original list of suspects given to him by Ramon.

Ramon Mordomo suspects

Sebastian Capuzzo	Ringmaster
Felix Reiser	Band Leader
Velazquez Trio	Trapeze Artistes
Chuck Marstow	Clown
Hank Findley	Funambulist (Wire Walker)
Ingrid Dahlberg	Knife Thrower

| Eva Zigana | Fortune Teller |
| Michael Wagner | Magician |

There were three more names that Giles had added; one of them Giles now regretted.

Allison Somerfield	Magician's Assistant
Rodrigo Gomez	Tiger Trainer
Leonardo	Sword Balance Artiste

'I have to stroke Allison's name off and although Gomez and Leonardo remain as possible suspects they don't figure in the same category.'

'So you think the guilty party is on that first list?'

'Yes, I do. But, as yet, I do not have any proof.'

'You're doing something with your face, Giles.'

'What can you possibly mean by that?'

'You do something with your face when you come up with an idea but are reluctant to let anyone else know. You suspect one person…I know you do! And you're not going to tell me? Is that correct?'

'That's right, Laura. And I'm not going to tell you… well not until I have a bit more to go on.'

'Spoilsport! Did the visit to Rum assist in any way?'

'To be quite honest I'm sure it did. Everything that happened has been stored in my head. All I have to do now is to decipher everything just as they did with the enigma machine during the War.'

'Do you think a visit to that Detective Inspector you saw while you were helping solve Daddy's death would be of any help, Giles?'

'Ex-Detective Superintendant, my dear!'

'Sorry!'

You know that might be worth a try. We could go there together.'

'Let's have a look at that list again. What is the ratio of men to women?'

'On the original list there are seven men and three women. We must remember there are two men and one woman who make up the Velazquez Trio.'

'And if you include the Tiger Trainer and Leonardo that brings the number of men to nine.'

'That's quite a large number and Leonardo doesn't strike me as someone who could afford to take charge of a group like Tropicana. He can stay on but must be considered as a lesser suspect.'

'What about Rodrigo Gomez? Some circuses are now facing the threat of having to do without wild animals? Could he really want this circus if his tiger had to be removed?'

'You're quite right, Laura. I doubt if he'd want to continue without his Royal Bengal Tiger, but I will keep him as a suspect for the time being. I somehow think Khan is going to play a major role when a dénouement is eventually arrived at.'

'Is that another gut feeling, Giles?'

Giles smiled. 'Have I done something with my face again, my love?'

Laura's nodding gave Giles the answer he expected.

Conversation strayed to the days and weeks ahead. One of the first things Laura was looking forward to, after choosing an engagement ring, would be checking on her mount for the local point-to-point meeting. After that there was a visit to the Grand National at Aintree and a holiday in York with Giles, to have her first encounter with the Tropicana Circus and a chance to help her fiancé in much the same way as she once did as a girl.

The remainder of the evening was spent on a sofa in front of the Raeburn while Giles described the events he'd experienced during his stay on Rum. The warmth from the cooker, and from their two bodies, was conducive to a feeling of well-being and, when bedtime approached Giles retired in the most relaxed state for many days. Several ideas resulting from his talk with Laura were now giving him the confidence he sought and his mind was extremely focused on that name on Ramon's list...a name he was not yet going to repeat to Laura.

The slight sound at the door made him turn. Laura was framed in the doorway but this time she was not wearing her black silk pyjamas...she wasn't wearing anything. The fumbling to put out the bedside lamp was accompanied by the pounding of his heart, but that sight of her framed in the doorway was something he would not forget in a long time.

The car journey south meant using the ferry at Ballachulish as the proposed bridge was not yet complete.

Once they were across the water they travelled through Glencoe where the mountains still had a covering of snow. The journey alongside Loch Lomond was tricky because of the narrow winding road but their early start saw them in Glasgow in time for lunch at the Rogano. After that they sought and bought the engagement ring.

Leaving the city behind, the A74 was covered in time to arrive at Lockerbie before the daylight had gone. A meal was being prepared. Doreen had been contacted by Laura before leaving Torcastle, giving her an indication of their arrival time and that allowed the engaged couple to each enjoy a bath using the double bathroom. Sharing was an option that would have to remain as a future delight.

When they went downstairs together they didn't have long to wait before the first course of a scrumptious meal was served in the dining room.

Isabella Ramsden, the matriarch of Maskelyne Hall, was in a talkative mood and wanted to know how their trip north had gone. Laura and Giles looked at each other and smiled. It was almost impossible for Laura to stifle a guffaw. She managed to do so with the help of Giles who created a diversion by asking Isabella if she would be having coffee in the lounge when they could discuss everything that had happened…with some exceptions.

There was a lovely fire on in the lounge as Giles escorted Isabella through to her usual chair while Laura went to the kitchen with Doreen to prepare the coffee and, no doubt, recover some of her composure.

The lady of the house suggested that her intended son-in-law get a bottle and glasses from the drinks cabinet so they could all celebrate the engaged couple's homecoming.

The rattling of the trolley heralded the arrival of coffee and coincided with the production of four glasses and a bottle of Courvoisier. 'I hope I'm not presumptuous,' Giles bent down and whispered to Isabella. 'But I brought out four glasses if you have no objection to Doreen joining us.'

'Please stay a while with us, Doreen. It gives us a chance to welcome the family back home.' Isabella insisted stridently giving Giles a little wink.

'What about George? Shouldn't he be here?' Laura glanced in the direction of her mother as she spoke.

It was Doreen who answered. 'I'm afraid my husband is extremely busy down at the stables. He's been there most of the day. One of the Hunters has had a bit of heat in a leg and George is doing his best to provide the most suitable treatment. With the point-to-point meeting only days away it is vital the horse is sound in all limbs.'

Isabella inclined her head as she looked forlornly at her daughter. Laura headed for the door but Giles caught her by the arm. 'I'm sure there isn't much you can do this late in the day,' he said. 'George will be giving one hundred and ten percent as he usually does. I think it's best to wait until morning!' Laura nodded in a disconsolate manner and returned to help Doreen with the coffee.

'I intended riding my horse tomorrow but if that's not possible we could give your detective friend in Dumfries a ring and arrange a short meeting with him.'

'I don't see why not! You'll find him a very interesting character and you'll love his wife. He might suggest some little thing I may have overlooked. It's certainly worth a try.'

'You haven't been smoking your cigars, Giles. You usually reach for the tobacco leaf when you are a little bit anxious or worried.'

'That's true, Isabella, but I believe I can wait until I'm about ready to reveal the final solution to the circus problem I'm wrapped up in.'

'That's the dénouement as they say in the best detective novels.' Laura expounded as she squeezed Giles' hand.

It was at that point Isabella decided to retire for the night. Doreen tidied away the coffee cups and glasses and made it abundantly clear that she required no help.

When they were left alone Laura asked Giles if he fancied a walk. 'Yes I don't mind,' he said. 'And I know where you want to go.'

'Down to the stables, you mean?'

'Of course, my love. Where else?'

They put on warm coats as the evening was turning cold and, arm in arm, they made their way down towards the stables. There was a light on in the tack room where silver-haired George was busy giving saddles the treatment necessary to keep the leather in tip-top condition.

The discreet cough from Giles made the groom turn and give his two visitors a welcoming smile. 'So you're back then? It's great to see you and you're both looking so well.'

'Does that mean we're better than Samson, George? Is he going to be fit enough to run in the Dumfries-shire point-to-point, or do we have to give him more time?'

'I'm afraid he has a bit of heat in one leg. Even though it doesn't appear to be too serious if we run him he might break down and that could be the end of his racing days.'

'I'll leave it with you, Gee Gee! Giles was right when he said your one hundred and ten percent efforts with the animals always paid dividends.' Giles smiled at Laura's use of the initials of the stocky little man; Gee Gee being her nickname for George Gardner, the groom.

'I had intended riding out with him tomorrow to let him have a good blow. But that's out of the question now so we hope to visit the ex-detective in Dumfries who gave my dear Giles the advice to go to the States. It was there he found the inspiration as to how my Daddy died.'

'It's getting quite chilly out here so I suggest you go back indoors. I'll be finished shortly after I have a last look at Samson and Delilah.'

The groom's final words had a distinct influence on the engaged couple's actions, as they gave him a pat on the shoulder, before turning and heading for the two boxes where the Hunters were relaxing.

They went into the house by the kitchen door and, after a brief conversation with Doreen, said they were going off to bed. It was all that Laura could do to keep a straight face as her serious professor was doing his level best to remain sincere.

At the top of the stairs Giles gave his bride-to-be an embrace and a passionate kiss before going into his bedroom where he undressed, put on a dressing gown and went to the bathroom.

A lot had happened in the past few days since he'd set sail on the cruise ship. He went over everything in his brain before sleep finally grabbed him. He knew he'd sleep soundly throughout the long night and that it would most likely take brilliant daylight in the morning to waken him. But he was so wrong!

It was still dark outside and he wondered if he'd slept the whole of the following day when he was awakened because he sensed there was someone or something in the room with him. The dream of the intruder in his room at the house on Rum was alarmingly unmistakeable; that is until he stretched an arm behind him and his fingers came in contact with a texture…that was undeniably silk.

He turned on to his other side and the soft-skinned warm body that was Laura kissed him on the mouth. His own frame was once more fighting a losing battle and only survived when the black silk-pyjama-clad maiden slid from his grasp.

'Sorry, darling,' she said. 'But I just had to say goodnight.' The black-on-black vision that was the magic design of Magician Chung Ling Soo disappeared out of the bedroom door and was gone in a twinkling. This time he knew it wasn't a figment of his imagination.

The weather was reasonably mild as Laura steered her sports car through the village of Lochmaben and onwards to the county town of Dumfries. For a brief spell they travelled with the hood open and the noisy rush of the morning air, though exhilarating, prevented any form of conversation.

Ex Detective Superintendent "Bulldog Drummond" must have seen the car approach as he was outside waiting to greet his visitors. 'Come away in. you're in good time as my wife, Anna, is just making a cup of tea.'

He ushered both his guests inside, took their coats and led them into a living room. The clinking of cups announced the timely arrival of the petite fair-haired lady who Martin Drummond introduced as his wife.

'You remember Professor Dawson, Anna,' he said. 'This lady is Laura, my dear. I believe she intends making an honourable man of him.'

Anna Drummond, despite her small frame, gave Laura a big hug and suggested that, after tea and biscuits, she take Laura for a look round the house leaving the men to get down to brass tacks.

With the tea-tray gone and the ladies gone with it Martin Drummond produced a couple of cheroots, offering one to his companion. 'I know from Freddie that you sometimes indulge in a smoke when you are just a little perplexed. Please join me and we'll see if we can ease your dilemma.'

A couple of puffs of the small cigar were enough to get Giles in the mood for relating, to the experienced former detective, the entire problem of the circus accidents and, in particular, the tragic death of the magician's assistant, Allison.

The ex Scotland Yard man, who was now heading a security team for

North of England Racecourses, listened attentively. When Giles had finished explaining how the tyre act had ended in disaster, Martin sat back in his chair; his huge frame tensed and his breathing became more pronounced.

After a short pause he leaned forward. 'Was this illusion, during which the assistant became unconscious, the first time you'd seen it performed?'

'No! As a matter of fact I'd watched it once before.'

'Now that's interesting and I'll tell you why. In my experience whenever a serious criminal act is carried out during a routine, which normally never deviates, there is usually something, however minor, that takes place thus allowing the crime to happen without the observer being aware of it. Did you notice anything that had changed?'

'I find that quite difficult to answer. Comparing the two illusions, they were both as I expected them to be?' Giles paused as he thought back to the events at RAF Winkfield.

'What I'm driving at is did you notice anything like a change in the size of tyres being used? Was the number of men bringing the tyres into the ring altered? Were the outfits worn by the participants, on each occasion, different?'

'I'm trying to think back. As a magician the whole routine was carried out as normal…but now that you mention it one thing sticks in my mind.'

'Go on Giles. This could be important.'

'At the time I believed the slight alterations were done to improve the quality of the performance.' Giles paused, drew on his cheroot and rubbed his chin. He looked at his host. 'The girl arrived at the centre of the ring, the tyres were rolled in by the assistants and placed, one by one, over the body of the girl, but the assistants were…!'

'Yes, my friend. You're doing extremely well.'

A slap on the coffee table and a nod from Giles made the ex-detective superintendant smile. Giles looked up at the bulky man opposite. 'The assistants were dressed as garage mechanics…wearing overalls, peak caps and…!'

'And what, Giles?'

'Dust masks. They were wearing dust masks.'

'That covered the mouth and nose I presume?'

'Yes.'

'Splendid! Absolutely splendid! I can tell you that in all the years I was at the Yard I never found anyone who could describe a scene without omitting some matters of importance. I commend you on your observation skill and I'll bet the clothes and masks were there to act as a disguise.'

I'm going back to RAF Winkleigh before I visit Aintree for this year's Grand National and I'll make a point of watching the tyre illusion one more time. That will focus my attention on the exact choreography of the trick… but that would surely mean that whoever was involved in the change was probably responsible for all the previous accidents.'

'Exactly! And that same person will be the one who will instigate future accidents and…possibly murder! Your circus problem won't have ended with the death of Allison.'

The nod from Giles intimated how much he agreed with that statement as Martin "Bulldog" Drummond continued. 'You said earlier that you were going to Aintree for the National. I shall be there with my team on security business and no doubt Freddie will be there as well. We can have a joint meeting to discuss how things are going.'

'I'll look forward to that. By that time I'll have spoken to everyone on the suspect list and may have come to certain conclusions without giving the game away.'

'Good man, Giles.'

Anna and Laura entered the room and Giles got up to leave. He turned to shake hands with the ex-Superintendent,

'A few days ago,' he said. 'I was standing in an avenue that was named Banquo's Walk and my thoughts were directed at the Scottish play. "Enter three murderers" was the phrase uppermost in my mind and it just occurred to me that the same phrase could conceivably be significant in the death of Allison.'

'You could be right, my friend. But one thing is certain. If changes were made in the illusion you described you were undoubtedly *a witness to murder* and so were a few hundred others in the circus audience without anyone having a clue about what they were watching.'

'Not only that,' said an enlightened Giles. 'But this was the exact opposite of a locked room murder. This was the prelude to a killing that took place in a space lit by many lights and watched by hundreds sitting only yards away and viewing from all sides.'

Chapter 16

THAT NAME WAS…?

On the way back to Lockerbie Laura happened to glance across at her sleeping partner…only he wasn't asleep. He was deep in thought. His eyes were closed but he had both hands on his face. She had seen him like this before and knew he was absorbed with a problem…a problem, she was convinced, he would eventually solve.

Bringing the car to a halt at the front of her home Laura said, in jest, 'Come on, sleepyhead. It's time to join the living and not think too deeply about the dead.'

'I wasn't asleep, Laura. I was just resting my eyes.'

'And working out how Allison died in full view of all those observers. I can read you like a book, Giles, and I love you for it.'

Inside it was the smell of baking emanating from the hallway that drew them towards the warmth of the kitchen and Doreen, the housekeeper.

A freshly baked scone and some home-made jam can work wonders and the opportunity wasn't wasted by Giles. He slipped off his shoes, settled down in a chair and tucked in to one of Doreen's delights. As he looked across at the lovely girl of his dreams he warmed to his fortunate position in life. At last he was, as Freddie would put it, about to enter the matrimonial stakes. Not only that, but the afternoon meeting with the jovial detective had somehow clarified his previous thoughts about the perpetrator of the circus accidents. The name on his mind was now starting to appear in bold type.

The last Monday in March came all too soon for Giles. As always he hated goodbyes at railway stations but waving to Laura, as the London express moved out of the station at Lockerbie, he was consoled by the fact that it would be less than a fortnight before he was with his beloved Laura at Aintree's Grand National meeting near Liverpool.

Approaching Carlisle, Giles was already engrossed with planning the questions he would put to every one of those on Ramon's list of suspects. He was determined to extract the truth even if it required some trickery. The wry smile that spread across his features demonstrated how much he looked forward to employing the art of the illusionist when he interrogated those on that suspect list.

British Summer Time was only a week old when he arrived at his South Kensington flat. London was drenched in Spring-like sunshine and his elation was complete when he phoned Laura in Lockerbie.

He showered before going out for a meal and once he was back in the flat he poured himself a brandy and listened to his Frank Sinatra records.

A phone call to the circus at RAF Winkleigh, giving details of his return in two days, was welcomed by Senhor Ramon who looked forward to the latest news from the person he'd hired to solve his *gauntlet of fear* problem. Hank Findley the wire-walker would pick him up at Eggesford station and a good meal and a sizeable cheque would greet him at the circus.

The old airfield at RAF Winkleigh in North Devon was a hive of activity when the American tight rope artist drove The Prof on to the grassland which had been the winter quarters of the circus for several months. The quizzical expression on his companion's face prompted Hank Findlay to explain to Giles that, as plans had been changed, the circus was now preparing to get ready to move to York racecourse. He added that Senhor Ramon would provide full details when Giles joined the owner for the evening meal.

After freshening up in his allotted trailer, Giles walked over to introduce himself once more to the man who'd hired him to solve the problem of the spate of accidents which had eventually ended in the death of the magician's assistant.

He knocked on the door of the luxurious trailer and went inside. The Portuguese circus owner was seated at his lavish desk smoking one of his large Havana cigars. Ramon rose and came across to shake Giles by the hand.

'Welcome back, Professor. I hope you had a pleasant cruise and are now eager to get to grips with the task in hand.' He reached into a pocket and brought out a cheque which he handed to Giles before returning to the desk and producing the box of cigars. 'Please join me in a pleasurable smoke before we have dinner.'

'Thank you. I notice you were expecting me to join you.' Giles remarked as he removed the one cigar in the humidor that was unwrapped.

'So you remember what I said when you were here on your first visit?'

'You really have them unwrapped when you expect them to be of immediate use. I made a special note of that.'

'I can see I have hired the right man for the task. Now put that cheque away once you're satisfied with the three noughts after the first digit, and you can let me know how well you're doing.'

Sucking his tongue, before drawing on his cigar, Giles scrutinised the suave circus supremo who'd produced a flame from his ornate lighter. The complacent holder of a four figure sum, in pounds sterling and not dollars, put the cheque in his inside pocket then sat down when his host, with a show of hands and a nod of the head, indicated that he should do so.

'The lectures on the cruise ship were well received. It also gave me time to mull over the tragic death of the magician's young assistant'

'That was most regrettable and whoever is out to destroy my ownership of this great circus...surely the death of this girl was totally unnecessary and such a person must be stopped.'

'Have the forensic people come up with information about the cause of death?'

'I believe they are almost ready to announce details but, until they do, I don't think we should jump to conclusions.'

'If it turns out to be a case of murder and early indications appear to suggest that might be the case, I have more than a suspicion that the perpetrator is one of the names on your list of suspects.'

'That is interesting, Professor. *Obrigado!* I was convinced that one of them was involved, but I'll leave you to make the decision and provide the proof.'

'When I arrived at this disused airfield a short moment ago it was obvious that a change of venue seemed imminent and...?'

'I'll bet my wire walking friend hinted at our change of plan.' The nod from Giles was the signal for Ramon to continue. 'We have brought forward the opening day at York racecourse,' said Ramon. 'Our first performance at the Knavesmire will be on Monday 17th April and after a seven day spell there we move to London's Alexandra Park. I'd certainly want you at both venues in the hope that you might reach a stage when you can offer a dénouement as they say in all the best crime novels.'

'I seem to have heard that response somewhere before. Anyway I aim to arrive at a decision in the not-too-distant future and I intend interviewing each suspect over the next couple of days before I leave for the Grand National.'

'Ah, yes. Didn't our fortune teller, Eva predict an unusual ending to your famous race which might be of benefit to your friend by the name of Freddie?'

'That's correct. But as neither Freddie nor myself have much faith in the teller of fortunes the jury is out on that one. It doesn't detract from the fact that the final result of the race will be of interest especially when coincidences have had a major part to play in my life.'

'Can I offer you the use of the old control tower for your interrogations and, if you so wish, I will also arrange for the personnel to be interviewed in the order they appear on that note I gave you.'

'That would be ideal and we can start first thing tomorrow if you have no objections.'

The conversation at the sumptuous evening meal centred on what little had happened since the death of Allison. The entire circus company seemed stunned by the untimely fatality. The large audience who watched it happening, had no idea how serious it was until reading about it in a North Devon newspaper. The circus artistes just got on with their training despite unfortunate disasters. Preparing each act in readiness for the start of the season ahead was always of prime importance.

The combination of good food and fine wine had the effect of inducing a desire for sleep when Giles finally made his way to his trailer. He was well aware that he must be alert in the following day's interviews which might reveal some vital secrets, and he must avoid jumping to conclusions.

When he approached the old control tower, after a good night's sleep, Giles found someone there to meet him...someone he had already trusted to supply him with any information of wrongdoings in the circus. That someone was the person whose lips had awakened him from the nasty result of being pole-axed. It was the young equestrian artiste Lizzie Lisbet.

The smile from this young woman was like a breath of fresh air to a professor who was gearing himself up to put a series of leading questions to the group of high-class performers in an attempt to extract information which might lead to a conviction.

'Senhor Ramon has asked me to act as intermediary and escort the ladies and gentlemen you wish to speak to. I will bring each one here in the order given to me unless you decide otherwise. You are to use the area upstairs for your interviews.'

'Thank you my dear. Senhor Ramon could not have chosen better. If you can inform the ringmaster, I will see him first.'

Upstairs Giles arranged chairs suitable for an informal discussion and he'd barely finished when the door opened and in walked Sebastian Capuzzo.

Shaking hands with the man who could almost act as a double for Ramon, if he grew a similar moustache, Giles then invited Sebastian to be seated.

'May I call you Sebastian?'

'Please do. I realise you wish to ask a few questions and I'm sure you'll find that everyone will co-operate.'

'That's very encouraging, Sebastian.'

'Before you begin, may I ask you a question?'

'Of course.'

The ringmaster leaned forward looking a bit more aggressive. 'Am I a suspect?'

'I'm afraid,' Giles paused as he cleared his throat. 'I'm afraid everyone connected with this circus has to be regarded as a suspect. During our discussion I will have to decide who the least likely suspects are. Much will depend on how frank each person is. Does that satisfy you?'

'It will have to do for the moment!'

'Have you ever taken drugs, Sebastian?'

'I'm not sure I'm obliged to answer that question.'

'Where were you when it was evident something was wrong with Allison during her magic act?'

'I was where I normally am.'

'And where was that?'

'At the ringside where I announce each act.'

'What did you do when the alarm was given that the act had gone wrong?'

'I immediately rushed to the tyres to see if help was required.'

Did you make contact with Allison?'

'No! When I was informed the girl had fainted I made that clear to the audience. The last thing I wanted was panic. That is something no circus wants.'

'Are you a wealthy man, Sebastian?'

'Why do you ask?'

'Could you afford to take over this circus?'

'I'm sure I would manage with the elite group of artistes at this establishment…but I have no intention of doing so. Let me make that clear!'

'One final question, Sebastian. Have you ever heard of the Rhouma?'

'I'm afraid I don't know which rumour you mean, there are so many in circus life.'

'That will be all for now,' said a gleeful Giles. 'Thank you for your co-operation.' Giles smiled as he shook hands.

When the door opened and Felix Reiser, the band leader, entered Giles beckoned him to be seated.

'Good morning. Let me put you at your ease, Mister Reiser. Better still, can I call you Felix?'

'Yes! Please do.'

'What do you fear most in a circus, Felix?'

A short pause was followed by the single four letter word 'Fire!'

'You were involved with such a calamity were you not?'

'Not involved as such but I was there when the tragedy happened at the Barnum and Bailey, Ringling Brothers' circus.'

'If I told you there are no such things as accidents would you believe me?'

The band leader frowned and inclined his head before answering. 'I'm not sure I follow you but I think I know what you're inferring.'

'Where were you when Allison had her…accident?'

The Band Leader's hesitation was an obvious demonstration of how uncomfortable Felix was becoming. 'I had left the bandstand and gone to my trailer before the magic act had started and was not aware that Allison…!'

'Can anyone verify your whereabouts?'

'I'm afraid not!'

'Have you ever heard of a place called Kinloch Castle?'

'Is that another of Britain's royal palaces?'

'Answering my question by asking another was not what I was hoping for, Felix, but you have told me all I wish to know at present. That will be all for now.'

Both men rose and Felix Reiser left the room in a slightly nonplussed manner. Giles put a tick against the name on the list.

Next to be interrogated were the three members of the Velazquez Trio of trapeze artists. Giles sat them all down, smiled and said 'I won't keep you long. I would, however, like you to answer my few questions as honestly as you can.

'When did you realise the circus was in real danger?'

The young aerialists looked at each other as if trying to come up with a concerted answer. 'I think we all felt there was a real problem when we learned that the boss had hired you.' The nodding heads of the two younger members of the trio endorsed the answer given by the older brother of the group.

'Do any of you know the name of the cruise ship I was sailing with recently?'

'I didn't know you were on a cruise recently,' stated Luisa. 'I was not even aware you had left the circus.'

'I don't think we pay too much attention to who's here,' added Cordero, the younger of the two brothers. 'We are too involved in trying to achieve the impossible.'

'Much like the stage magician,' declared Giles. 'I too am trying to achieve the impossible by solving the problem at this circus. Now I know you would like to emulate the great performances of past aerialists…but would you also like to own the circus?'

The credulous looks as the family trio glanced at each other delayed a response until Miguel ventured a reply. 'I speak for all of us when I tell you that, although we have always longed to own our own circus, the main object is to become the best aerial act in the world.'

'Where were you when the magic act went wrong?'

'We were in the rest area after completing our warm-up when Allison was brought in on a stretcher.'

'Did you notice anyone in particular approaching the stretcher?'

'There were several people milling around as everyone seemed concerned.'

'Thank you, Miguel, Luisa and Cordero. You have been most helpful… and good luck in your attempt at perfection.'

When Chuck Marstow appeared, complete with his clown make-up, Giles had difficulty restraining his desire to chuckle. 'Come in, Chuck and please sit down. All I want to do is get to know you a bit more and ask a few questions.'

The genial comic sat down and immediately stood up again as if he'd sat on a whoopee cushion. Giles chortled as the likeable comedian turned, swept the seat with both hands before carefully sitting down once more and placing both hands on his knees.

'When Allison was involved in the fire scene in your very entertaining clown act and again in danger with Khan, the tiger in the magic act, did you ever think she would be in jeopardy during another performance?'

'No, Professor. She was the least likely person to have an accident. She was so professional.'

'You say so, Chuck, but you have to acknowledge that there were many occasions where she had to take risks when things could go drastically wrong?'

'I admit that, Giles, but she was such a lovely person and I think she felt that someone had it in for her.'

'You followed her into the rest area when she was taken there on the stretcher?'

'That's correct!'

'Did anyone appear to touch her while she was lying on the stretcher?'

'There were several people around her but I heard boss Ramon tell everyone to get back and give the girl air.'

'Do you believe Allison's death might put an end to the problems this circus has endured?'

'I sincerely hope so, but I fear not! To be a clown when things are going so wrong around you leaves me distraught.'

'Thank you, my friend, for being so helpful.'

Hank Findley walked into the room with the toe-forward steps of the skilled funambulist. He nodded before sitting down and crossing his legs. 'I know you are about to ask me where I was when Allison took ill,' he said. 'Well my act was over for the day and I was relaxing in my caravan. And before you ask...no, I don't think anyone can vouch for me. I was alone!'

'It's kind of you to save me asking a few pertinent questions, Hank. There is one I would love an answer to. You knew I would be travelling northwards on a cruise ship. Did you know where I was headed and for what reason?'

'Yes to the first part and no to the second. Does that answer your query?'

'Well it helps, Hank. I want to count on you as a friend for the simple reason that we both need to ensure the safety of this circus.' The wire-walker leaned back in his chair and gave a few meaningful nods of his head allowing the historian of magic to continue. 'Have you heard of a man by the name of George Bullough?'

'Was he a magician?'

A thoughtful smile from Giles accented his next remark. 'A magician? Yes I suppose he was in a way but one who never really appeared in front of a huge audience.'

The frown that registered on Hank's brow was the signal for Giles to ask for another answer. 'Do you enjoy working for this Cuban boss?'

'He's Portuguese, Professor!'

'He comes from Cuba and, as an American, you are probably not too keen to give him the credit for what he's achieving. Would I be correct in saying that?'

'Let me just admit I wanted to work in a big circus and returning to the airfield where I had much of my wartime experience was a sort of bonus.'

'Have you ever killed anyone, Hank?'

'I told you I was a pussycat like Khan.'

'So you did...though I've been informed that Khan is certainly no pussycat so where does that put you?'

'Are you trying to tell me something? Am I one of your suspects?'

'I'm afraid you are, Hank. Just as all the others are that I've been questioning this morning. You are, however, free to go but I may need to have a word with you some other time. Thanks for your co-operation.'

As the tightrope walker left the room there was a gentle knock on the door. It was Lizzie Lisbet with a tray on which there was a pot of tea and some biscuits.

'I brought something to keep you going. When you've finished I'll send in the three others you wish to see.'

Refreshed after his tea and biscuits Giles prepared himself for his next interview. A cursory glance at the list in front of him revealed that Ingrid Dahlberg, the impalement artist, would be the next person to have the chance to remove her name from that suspect list.

Following the knock on the door, it opened before Giles had the time to say anything, the alluring figure of the petite blonde-haired damsel stood framed in the doorway. The Professor of illusions couldn't take his eyes off the stunning female: but it wasn't her slim voluptuous figure or her blue eyes and sensuous lips that transfixed him…it was the two throwing knives she carried, one in each hand.

Swallowing hard, Giles made an effort to keep a low profile and tried to speak in a welcoming voice. 'Come in Ingrid. And, if you have no objection, please get rid of the objects you hold in your hands.

He'd hardly got the words out when the whish of a blade passing close to his left ear was immediately followed by a thudding crash as the knife embedded itself in the wall behind him. Miss Dahlberg, her empty right hand still in the air, stepped forward and placed the remaining knife on the desk in front of her interrogator.

'You have now had an opportunity to see me at my best mister Professor, Sir. I thought it was worth giving you a demonstration as I doubt you'd ever agree to becoming a target on my wheel of death.

'You have never spoken a truer word, Miss Dahlberg.'

'Ingrid please, Giles!'

'My dear Ingrid,' his composure was gradually returning as Giles spoke. 'Have you ever, by chance, caused an upset when throwing a knife?'

The Swedish impalement expert paused briefly before answering. 'Yes,' she said smiling. 'I believe I have: in fact I'm certain I have!'

'And when was that?'

'Just a moment ago, when I threw one past your ear!'

'Touché, my dear.' Giles cleared his throat, with a little irritating cough, before continuing. 'Now what were you doing when poor Allison was brought into the rest room on a stretcher?'

'I was being rushed into my wheel of death act as the tyre illusion had been cut short. Unfortunately I didn't have an opportunity to be with Allison but if I took every circus mishap to heart I could be on the verge of a nervous breakdown.'

'I don't think I need trouble you any more, Ingrid. Thank you for your help. Before you leave would you please remove your lethal weapon from the wall behind?'

Ingrid detached the knife and as she was about to leave was halted by Giles' questioning words. 'Have you ever made a phone call to Kinloch Castle?'

Ingrid turned to face her inquisitor. 'I find that a very strange question, Giles'

'I hoped you would, Ingrid…I certainly hoped you would! Thank you for your frankness.'

Making a few notes on the suspect list, as Ingrid left the room with her knives, Giles finished by clenching both hands and speaking to himself again. 'Yes! Yes! Yes! Now we're getting somewhere.'

The entry of Madame Eva Zigana came as yet another breath of fresh air. The diminutive lady with the dark hair made a silent theatrical appearance.

'Please be seated, Eva. I have just a few questions to ask.'

'I will answer as best I can, Professor.'

'Please call me Giles, Eva.'

'Certainly, Giles'

'You predicted I would travel to far off places, but I believe you already knew I was going on a cruise ship before I explained where I was headed. Is that correct?'

'That is correct, Giles. I'm sure your friend Freddie and you are well aware that it's only by getting to know all the facts about a person that you can have any success about making a prognostication. I do my homework and it pays dividends.'

'Do you always have success?'

'No…but I have more successes than failures.'

'As some prominent poet once said about a game having two pleasures for your choosing…one is winning, the other's losing. I must, nevertheless, confess I hate to admit defeat.'

'I appreciate that, Giles and I am convinced you will, like myself, do your homework and will rarely have to admit defeat.'

'Is that a prognosis, Eva or just a stab in the dark?' As he spoke Giles turned to look at the mark on the wall where the throwing knife had embedded itself. He turned back to face the clairvoyant. 'Will you do something for me?'

'I will, if I can.'

'Would you please whisper in your quietest voice the following phrase?'

'Is this a kind of audition for a movie, Giles or are you inviting me to incriminate myself?'

'Neither, Eva. I'd just like to hear you say these words. *This is Allison calling from beyond the grave.*'

Eva stiffened, her face displaying extreme tension as she began to whisper! 'This is Allison calling from beyond the grave.' She paused, looked up at Giles and said 'Now do I get the part?'

Scribbling on his sheet of paper Giles remained silent before addressing the slender clairvoyant. 'Madame Zigana, I think your name can now go up in lights. I'm entirely satisfied with your answers and I have no further questions…except one. Do you still insist that my friend, Freddie Oldsworth, will have success in this year's Grand National?'

'For the reasons I gave about numbers and their sums- yes I think he can win if he jumps to the right conclusions. But if I could predict the winner of every race I would not have a booth at the circus. I would be very wealthy and could afford to buy the circus without the need to put fear into our Cuban boss.'

Professor Giles Dawson rose, came round from his table and gave Eva Zigana a gentle hug before escorting her to the door. 'Do you mind if I ask you one more question?'

'Not at all, Giles.'

'Do you believe I may be in danger?'

The fortune teller looked into Giles' blue eyes, took both his hands in hers and gave him this warning. 'Yes, I'm afraid you may be in grave danger but it will not be until we go to York. So be very much on your guard!'

The final session of questioning was imminent and Giles was anxious to avoid making accusations which could prevent obtaining the truth from this very important suspect, Michael Wagner, the magician.

There was quite a delay before Michael Wagner's footsteps were heard coming up the stairs of the old control tower. Giles was beginning to wonder if the magician had spirited himself away just as his assistant had done in the circus acts but no, his apologies rang true: he had been rehearsing the tyre illusion with his new assistant – the one who'd replaced Allison.

'Please excuse me,' he said, slightly out of breath. 'It is very important that my new assistant achieves the proficiency that Allison brought to my act.'

'I realise that, Michael, especially as the time is now short with the start of the season at York having been brought forward. What is your new assistant's name?'

'Annette. Annette Wagner!' The surprised look from Giles prompted the magician to continue. Annette is my daughter and she is making good progress.'

'There are some vital questions I need answers to. You can help by being as accurate as you can with the truth. Who made the decision to add the caps and dust masks to the outfits worn by the mechanics wheeling the tyres into the ring?'

'I really believe I did because I wanted to distract the audience from what was about to take place.'

'You mean the disappearance of the girl in red?'

'Yes! I talked it over with Ramon and he gave his approval. The additions seemed to provide an air of authenticity to the performance.'

'How many men were used to wheel the tyres into the ring?'

'There were four or five but it all depends on who is available at the time.'

'Could you identify each mechanic?'

'That would be difficult because of the overalls and the men were chosen because their build was similar. Identification would be even more difficult due to the caps and dust masks and the lead up to the lady in the red dress disappearing was intended to misdirect the audience.'

'Was it possible for the number of mechanics bringing the tyres into the ring to differ from the number removing them at the finale?

'I suppose so, but I'm not sure why you're asking that question.'

'I don't doubt that, Michael, and there are a few other questions you may not be able to guess why I'm asking them.'

'What did you do when Allison was taken ill and removed on a stretcher?'

'I followed her to the rest room. I was afraid she'd been over-exerting herself and was concerned for her well-being.'

'I fully realise that a magician's assistant often has to make strenuous efforts to achieve an end result while the stage magician is not required to exert himself to the same degree and the strain can be severe on the assistant's frame.'

The nodding head of the magician appeared to acknowledge the comments of his questioner.

'Did you try to speak to Allison or attempt to touch her?'

'No, I wanted her to rest and recover.'

'Have you any knowledge of Lohengrin?'

'Do you mean the classical piece of music by my namesake?'

'You are answering my question by asking another, Michael. But yes, I do mean the piece of music by Wagner.

However you need say no more. I'm satisfied and you can return to your rehearsals.'

Alone in the room once more, Giles closed his eyes and was deep in thought as he ruminated about the results he'd obtained from his questioning of those suspects.

He eventually came to a decision. What he mustn't do was jump to conclusions. But what he'd heard from the ten people he'd questioned was leading him to the one name he was already suspicious of. That name was…?

Chapter 17

DEADLY SERIOUS

The days following the interrogation of those on the suspect list were occupied by taking a close interest in the final preparations of the varied acts which would constitute the circus programme at York. In particular, Giles paid special attention to the illusion with the tyres. He was most impressed with the contribution from Annette, the magician's daughter. The caps remained as part of the mechanics' dress but the dust masks had been dispensed with.

The trapeze act was reaching new heights with the triple somersault destined to get the circus audience on the edge of their seats; and the Wheel of Death was so full of tension it would surely bring gasps from a York public made up of local residents and visitors on holiday from all parts of the globe.

Annette, who was also replacing the deceased Allison in the disappearing illusion with Khan, the Bengal Tiger, was not performing with the clowns in the fire act. Her father had obviously come to the conclusion that to ask his daughter to perform in so many routines was a terrible mistake.

After watching the circus at full throttle Giles was almost at a stage where he felt stressed out and yet wanting more. Everything was so high-powered and expertly presented that he had no hesitation in accepting the description of the circus as The Greatest Show on Earth.

A relaxing few days at a race meeting was going to be a welcome relief and Southport, on the Lancashire coast, was close enough to Aintree to allow a reasonably short journey to the Grand National.

Giles had taken one of the salubrious flats in the town. With Laura due to drive there later, on the night before the race meeting started, he was keen to enjoy a reversal of roles. So he set about preparing a meal in the well-appointed self-catering apartment.

He'd be meeting Freddie on the opening day of racing and there was every likelihood that there would be a chance to exchange views about his conclusions so far.

It was late evening when Laura eventually reached the apartment building. Giles had been looking out the window for some considerable time awaiting her arrival and when he spotted the car entering the drive he dashed downstairs to welcome her and give her a hand with her case. It was a joyous re-union

She was exhausted and Giles wasted no time in getting the meal ready and making her comfortable before insisting on an early night.

When Laura was safely tucked up in bed, Giles sat for a while contemplating on the days ahead of him. Three days of racing were certain to be a pleasant change from the stress of waiting for something sinister to happen in an environment where deadly disaster was always a threat.

It was clearly evident that circus performers, however skilled they were, lived on a knife edge knowing full well that a slight imperfection in their death-defying performances could mean an end to their career.

Setting the travelling alarm for an early start Giles put the lights out and climbed into bed. Laura was fast asleep and cuddling into her warm body Giles was soon likewise.

The first day of the three-day Grand National meeting dawned after a welcome night's rest. A piece of buttered toast and a cup of hot tea sufficed for breakfast and they were soon on the road to Aintree.

The short journey from Southport to the racecourse was well sign posted. Laura approached the track by way of the Melling road and was able to cross the racecourse not far from where the first fence of the famous race was situated. The road which led into the centre of the track was always covered with tan before racing began and the car was driven to a convenient spot: there being few vehicles at the racecourse early in the morning. Laura enthusiastically watched the horses, due to run on the first day, out at exercise with their riders.

The vans supplying hot food were already in action and the smell of frying bacon and sausage pervaded the chill morning air. Giles procured a couple of sausage filled morning rolls which he and Laura tucked into, washed down with hot tea while sitting in the car.

With the inner man satisfied a short snooze was called for and it was the gentle warmth of a hazy sun that wakened them. Giles escorted his fiancée across the course close to the water jump and when he purchased a race card he was instantly reminded of Katie Starter, the girl he'd met at Kempton Park several months earlier. Laura was fascinated by the tale Giles told of that extraordinary meeting. She was quite sure someone in her family would have called that spooky.

They headed for the stand, produced their booked-in- advance tickets and met Freddie where he'd said they would find him. They then accompanied him to the Clerk of the Course's office where the former Scotland Yard detective Superintendant, Martin Drummond, was likely to be found.

Freddie decided to be the perfect gentleman and take Laura for a coffee giving Giles and "Bulldog" freedom to talk over the problems at RAF Winkleigh.

'Did you manage to watch another demonstration of the tyre illusion, Giles?' the larger than life ex detective asked as he opened the conversation.

'Yes I did and, although the mechanics' caps were retained, the dust masks had been dispensed with.'

'That figures! And of course the magician now has a new assistant, so it's business as usual I suppose?'

'Yes, that's circus life; the show must go on. The new assistant, believe it or not, is the magician's daughter.'

'Now that is interesting. In fact it's more than just interesting…it's bloody suggestive. It provides a motive for murder. And there was opportunity as the magician was always in close proximity to Allison and he could also have had the means.'

'I agree, it's something to be considered but I'm not convinced!'

'Can you explain why you have doubts?'

'Well, for the simple reason that the magician, who was in sole charge of the illusions in the circus, could have sacked his assistant and replaced her with his daughter. One more sin to be added to the seven deadly ones of circuses I suppose.'

'That would certainly be much easier than murder, Giles. I grant you that.' Martin Drummond paused as he scrutinised his companion. 'In my considerable experience,' he said. 'I always paid special attention to facial expressions, whenever anyone made certain assertions, and I was taken by your look when you made your observation.'

'Funny you should say that. Laura tells me I do something with my face when I am about to make a decision.'

'I knew it, Giles. I believe you have a shrewd idea of who the guilty person is and you are keeping your thoughts very close to your chest. Am I right?'

The wry smile on Giles' face was the only confirmation "Bulldog" required.

The two men met up with Freddie and Laura in the restaurant and Freddie was let loose to complete some wagers with leading bookmakers on the rails.

When Freddie returned, Martin left to supervise the racecourse security team. Giles and Laura wandered off for a spell before joining Freddie again for lunch.

Although people were arriving in numbers, Aintree was never crowded on the first two days of this meeting. The afternoon was a delightful change from the problems at the North Devon airfield. Freddie got on with the business of decision making after studying the runners in the paddock before each race; and Laura was in her element watching the riders and their variety of riding techniques and stirrup lengths as they went down to the start.

Giles, on the other hand, became more and more involved with the final stage of each race. In particular he noted that horses playing a major role in every finish had been jumping with fluency and speed, with few if any mistakes, in order to reach the conclusion. This was now getting through to him. If he found himself jumping where angels feared to tread he was reaching a stage where the name on that suspect list was becoming more predictable; the only difficulty was going to be…proving it.

The following day's racing on the Friday was much like the first. The track had a good covering of grass and the going was on the easy side of good.

Giles and Laura decided to walk the Grand National course to get acquainted with all the fences. These were made of green spruce on a wooden frame. They inspected the daunting Becher's Brook followed by the smallest fence, and after that the sharp Canal Turn where previously horses had been known to fail to make the ninety degree left-hand turn and end up in the canal.

They skirted Valentine's and the next three fences which took them to the other part of the Melling road that crossed the track. Turning left brought them towards the two fences that would complete the race on the final circuit. After that was the mighty Chair, the biggest fence in the race, and the Water Jump.

When they'd completed the circuit they crossed to the stands, had lunch with Freddie and made a check on the declared runners for Saturday's big race. The weather was looking a bit iffy and Giles suggested he might leave a little early and take Laura into Liverpool where they would have dinner and go to the theatre. Giles thought it would be a great opportunity to let Laura see the city where he and Freddie had become friends when they were in the RAF at West Kirby.

Once they were back in Southport Laura went to phone her mother and came back with startling news. She was to call again on the morning of the big race because her mother had a premonition which was similar to the one many years ago when she'd correctly predicted a big race winner by an outsider.

Grand National day, Saturday 8th April, 1967 started damp, but a few showers were unlikely to dampen the enthusiasm of the large crowd. Giles and Laura were at the racecourse quite early and met Freddie in the grandstand. They had a light breakfast and were discussing the cryptic prediction made by Madame Eva Zigana at RAF Winkleigh when who should appear but Madame Zigana herself. Giles introduced her to Laura.

'Have you, by any chance, placed your wager on today's race, Mister Oldsworth?' Eva directed her question to Freddie.

'Yes I have,' Freddie replied without hesitation. 'Your rather enigmatic prognosis coincided with my own belief, Madame, at least as far as the *putting two and two together and making eight* part is concerned. I have backed the favourite Honey End whose name is made up of eight letters. The other horses with names of eight letters were of no interest to me and the latter part of your diagnosis of a conundrum was a load of double Dutch.'

'That reminds me,' said an anxious Laura. 'You must excuse me. I have to make a call to my mother.' She rose and hurriedly left the group.

It wasn't long before she was back. 'The lines were very busy,' she said, slightly out of breath. 'But luckily I got through to Mother.'

'And?' said an eager Giles.

'My very good witch of a mother confirmed her premonition after reading the list of runners for the big race in the morning paper.'

'Well?' said the three curious listeners.

'I've just placed a small wager on a rank outsider in the National. It's a 100 to 1 shot with the bookmakers but I've placed the bet with the Tote which looks to be giving much longer odds. I don't suppose it has any chance but I'm not going to let Mum's prediction go unsupported.'

'A 100 to 1 shot is it? Giles nodded as he spoke. 'Well they don't win that often but the first Grand National that Freddie and I went to was won by a horse named Caughoo and it was an outsider at those odds so...who knows?'

'But does it have eight letters in its name?' asked Freddie.

'As a matter of fact it does!' Laura came back with her answer after a thoughtful pause.

The expression on the face of Madame Zigana was significant. 'There may be the largest number of runners in today's race than in previous years, and in particular we'll have two to watch.'

The early races were interesting spectacles but the big race was what the racing fraternity was concentrating on. As the runners left the paddock and paraded in front of the stands, before cantering down to examine the first fence, the tension was beginning to mount. The crescendo when the starter let the runners go, was at fever pitch and the roar of the crowd was probably heard in Liverpool.

Most of the field cleared the first fence. All except one that is. Popham Down, who got over the first, fell over another runner and was brought down. The horse carried on riderless.

The early pace set by Castle Falls, Princeful, Kapeno, Rondetto and Rutherfords, was frenetic and the favourite, Honey End was kept under control and not allowed to become involved. The odd mishap occurred on the first circuit but crossing Becher's, second time around, there wasn't a single faller. At this stage of the race, the riderless Popham Down, was on the inside of the course. As he approached the twenty-third and easiest fence he appeared to be tiring and he suddenly veered to the right hammering into Rutherfords and unseating his rider. Chaos was becoming madness as Limeking went down and other runners piled into each other. Jockeys on both sides of the fence tried to get hold of their mounts; loose horses were running all over the place, some even running back the way they'd just come.

Out of all this mayhem one horse appeared moving to the right to find a gap. It managed to jump the fence and, having been in last place for most of the race, now found himself in the lead. When Honey End was remounted and set at the fence for the second time, which he cleared, he found himself in pursuit but thirty lengths behind. Following on was Red Alligator but hard as they tried they couldn't catch the one in front. That one was a horse by the name of Foinavon…another with eight letters in the name.

The race had barely finished with Freddie's selection in second place at odds of 15-2. 'Well so much for Madame Zigana's prediction.' Freddie uttered as he looked dejectedly at his betting slip. Laura was in a totally different mood as she excused herself once more. 'I won't be long,' she said laughing and hugging Giles. 'I must go and collect my winnings. It wouldn't surprise me if mother's premonition and the Gypsy girl's were the same.'

She was gone and back in no time as few people had backed the winner, Foinavon. 'You lucky girl, Laura, Did you manage to get 100-1?' Freddie asked giving her a pat on the back.

'Well not really. You see I backed with the Tote and the horse was paid out at 444-1.'

The surprised look on everyone's face was given an added dimension when Giles interrupted. 'Don't you see,' he said. 'Madame Zigana made another statement when she inferred that you would be successful in this year's big race, Freddie. She mentioned something like paying special attention to your lucky number…and that is the number four and there were three of those numbers in the odds paid out by the Tote.'

'But what real connection did that have with my name?'

'That's fairly simple, Freddie,' stated Laura, the girl from the big house near Lockerbie who as a child solved conundrums with the boy who was now her fiancé. Your name, Freddie Oldsworth has the initials FO, the first two letters of Foinavon and the remaining letters *in avon* is where you live; beside the river Avon. Easy peasy if you'll pardon the expression. Mother was certain her dream could become reality. And Eva was equally certain if you were able to follow her line of thought. The race turned out to be another fable like the one from Aesop. It resembled the Tortoise and the Hare.'

'What's more,' exclaimed a thoughtful Giles. 'The race was another perfect example of accurately *jumping to conclusions.*'

The time spent in London's South Kensington flat was an opportunity for Laura and Giles to put their heads together and attempt to solve a few more conundrum-type puzzles as well as getting to know each other more.

Eating out at Simpson's in the Strand, and a couple of nights at the theatre somehow cemented their relationship and Giles was glad of the input Laura was able to give to clarify the many things which were still vaguely obscure.

'Let's start with the tragic death of the magician's assistant Allison, Laura,' Giles suggested one afternoon. 'I spoke with Martin Drummond and mentioned that the new assistant was the magician's daughter. Martin thought that was a motive for murder on the part of the magician. What do you say to that?'

'It could also work the other way round and provide the magician's daughter with a motive for murder. Anyone could kill for a good part!'

'Yes, Laura. That's true but what if neither of those allegations were correct. What if the murder of Allison was a necessary prelude to a future atrocity…a smokescreen that would cloud the issue at a later date?'

'You're doing something with your face again, Giles. What are you up to?'

There was no reply forthcoming from Giles. 'Can I see that list of suspects once more, Giles? There is one name that wasn't on the original list but you added later. I've been thinking about that name.'

Handing the list over to Laura, Giles clasped his hands behind his neck and sat back ready to hear what she had to say.

'There,' said Laura as she scanned the list. 'You added three names, Giles, and one of them made me do a bit of thinking.'

'Well it wasn't Allison,' said a chastened Giles. 'I certainly regret adding her name. I didn't think the others were serious contenders. Whose name made you think about the spate of accidents?'

'Signor Gomez, the trainer of Khan, the tiger.'

The frown on Giles' brow, as he looked across, was followed by his apt question. 'I'd like to know why Rodrigo crossed your mind as a likely suspect?'

'It was Allison's escapades that made me wonder. Not the fire in the clown scene but the cage illusion when Khan and Allison were meant to change places.'

'Go on, Laura. I'd love to hear a bit more.'

'Well, you originally thought Allison might have been responsible for causing the equipment in the cage to malfunction, the magician himself could have been the culprit. But there was someone else who could have tampered with the mechanism…the person who secured the tiger in the false back of the cage…the trainer of Khan, Signor Gomez.'

'That is an interesting point of view and one to be given consideration but can you implicate Signor Gomez with the other accidents?'

'Where was he when Allison had the fainting spell in the tyre illusion? Could he not have been one of the assistants wheeling in the tyres?'

The lines at the outer edges of Giles' eyes and the silence that followed Laura's train of thought were enough to suggest that her exposition had some merit.

Taking the slip of paper from Laura Giles put a question mark against the name of Signor Gomez. He looked up at his fiancée. 'I knew we'd make a good team, my love. Rodrigo must now come into the equation and will have to be interviewed and given close scrutiny as regards other incidents… but, my dearest, I cannot rule out the one name on the original list that shouts out at me.' He pushed the paper back to Laura and pointed at a name that made Laura gasp.

'You're not serious, Giles…are you?'

'Deadly serious, my dear!' he said, his features showing real concern.

Chapter 18

DEAD MAN'S CHEST

The city of York was in readiness for a spring and summer of welcome visitors as Giles and Laura arrived at the Knavesmire, after settling at a coach-house inn.

The vans of the Tropicana Circus were already there in numbers and preparations had started for the erection of the massive tent. The Knavesmire was the York racecourse where, two hundred and thirty years ago, Dick Turpin, murderer and highwayman, had been hanged at the age of thirty-three, after being tried and convicted of horse theft at York's Assises. The area, recognised as the Ascot of the North, was now being made ready to become a place of fun and high drama with some of the world's top artistes in action.

As they threaded their way through the maze of trailers and trucks, searching for the circus boss, all expectation of fun disappeared. The screams emanating from nearby were blood-chilling. Giles and Laura were almost first on the scene. They got there just behind a group consisting of two leading acrobats in leotards and wearing warm coats, and Ingrid Dahlberg the impalement artist.

Miss Dahlberg was standing at the rear of the instantly recognisable trailer belonging to Ramon Mordomo. She was having difficulty calming herself and was being comforted by a female acrobat when Giles arrived.

'What on earth is going on?' enquired a ruffled Giles.

The impalement artist was unable to answer. All she could do was point to a narrow window which had the glass broken. All the windows on that side had the curtains drawn but the curtain on the broken window had been pulled to one side thus allowing a clear view into what lay beyond.

Peering through the broken pane Giles could see what looked like the figure of Senhor Mordomo. He was seated behind his desk, leaning back in his chair with his head tilted backwards and slightly to one side…and his face had turned a blueish colour.

'It's the boss,' Ingrid managed to blurt out. 'And I think he's dead!'

Unable to take his eyes off the tableau of horror at the far end Giles could hardly believe what he was witnessing. It was not the apparently lifeless body behind the desk that brought on disbelief, it was the *objet d'art* designed by the Frenchman Lalique, which was embedded in the man's throat. The vintage car mascot, a collector's item prized by Ramon, was seemingly now the cause of his death.

'We'll have to put a call through to the police. But what made you look through here?' Giles asked.

'I came round as I wanted to have a word with Ramon but his trailer door was locked. It looked as if the door was locked from the inside so I knocked but there was no reply.'

'Yes?'

'I came round here. All the windows were locked but this one had been broken. I put my arm in and moved the curtain to one side…and the sight in there was ghastly.' She was starting to sob as she spat out the words.

'What the bloody hell is going on?' The well known Portuguese voice made everyone turn.

'Good God, Ramon! You're alive!' exclaimed Ingrid. 'But that body in there? Who is it?'

'I'm sure I can answer that,' said a rather disturbed circus supremo. 'I believe that is Sebastian, Sebastian Capuzzo, our esteemed ringmaster.'

'Ringmaster no more!' commented one of the acrobats.

'Sebastian made a habit of using my premises for a bit of relaxation and always wore a false moustache to confuse passers-by. We were going to use him as a credible double but that is now out of the question. I think we should call the police…but let's get inside and confirm his condition and identity.'

'Make sure no-one touches anything.' Giles insisted.

Ramon sent for several riggers, while Laura busied herself tending to Ingrid Dahlberg. There were several minor cuts on Ingrid's left arm.

'How did that happen?' Giles asked as he went over to Ingrid and examined her injuries.

'I think it probably happened when I put my arm in to open the curtain.'

Two riggers arrived promptly with tools which, with some ingenuity, they used to undo the hinges and release the door away from the lock.

Another visitor arrived at the scene asking what was wrong. It was Signor Gomez.

Entering through the opened doorway Ramon was closely followed by Giles who suggested that the others should remain outside.

Going over to the broken window Giles was sure the pane had been broken from the outside. The gap in the shattered glass was only big enough to allow an arm and shoulder to go through and, with the door locked from the inside, Giles was convinced he was, once again, involved with a locked-room mystery. It was extremely doubtful if any human being could have entered via that broken window unless…!

Taking a handkerchief from his pocket Giles went over to the humidor and opened the box. The humidor was almost full of cigars all of them with wrappers. There was no partly smoked cigar in the ashtray but the ornate cigar lighter felt vaguely warmish through the hanky in Giles' hand.

'It's beginning to look like an attempt on my life,' uttered a shaken circus boss as he tried to recover his composure. 'But how could that have been done?'

'I'm not sure, but I'll find out.'

'I think you'd better, Professor. You're the locked room wizard.' Ramon looked seriously concerned as he glowered at Giles. 'Something must have got in without Sebastian being aware…unless it was magic, Professor Dawson!'

'The terms, supernatural and magical are often used to explain events that are apparently impossible, Senhor. But be in no doubt, such events always have a logical explanation if one examines and explores all possibilities. It was Sir Arthur Conan Doyle's Sherlock Holmes, I believe, who put it much better than I can.'

'You may well be right, Professor. But a magician or illusionist can create what seems to be the impossible even though the secret becomes perfectly logical only when the mechanics of the trick are explained. Come to think of it, I have an illusionist as one of my suspects. Is it possible that he could have devised some devilish device that plucked the *Spirit of the Wind* from the desk and, with tremendous force, plunged it into a man's throat without him making any effort to prevent it happening?'

'I think you're bordering on the realms of fantasy and delusion without considering all the other alternatives.'

'I suppose you mean, for example, that someone, with the necessary skill, could have thrown the Lalique mascot from the break in the window.'

'You're putting words in my mouth, Ramon. If that was indeed what happened, it means the object must have been removed from the trailer beforehand.'

'Assuming that was the case,' said the circus owner. 'And the mascot had been taken from my trailer, who had the skill to throw with such force and accuracy?'

'I know what you're getting at, of course. It could only be the person with the cuts on her arm from reaching through the broken glass,' stated Giles. 'Is that what you're implying?'

'Yes! Ingrid Dahlberg, one of my original suspects.'

It wasn't long before the police were on the scene. Detective Inspector Brian Rowlands made himself known to those who'd been present when the body of Sebastian Capuzzo was discovered. He took statements from everyone and was especially pleased to become acquainted with Giles.

'It's good to know that you are working with Senhor Mordomo in trying to establish who may be trying to terminate his ownership of the circus. It would appear to have reached the stage where someone is also trying to terminate his existence and you may be the best person to get to grips with this assassin.'

'We'll get to the bottom of this, I can assure, you but it may take some time, and I will keep in touch.'

Some hours later the Barnsley chop, cooked to perfection provided the main course at the old coach house inn and was badly needed to help counteract what had been a difficult day. The gruesome murder had come out of the blue, and blue was the predominant colour. After dinner the need to discuss the death was paramount to Giles.

Upstairs in the cosy little bedroom the chat moved to the individual statements given to the Yorkshire detective and it was Laura who eventually posed the question. 'Did he ask what you made of the unsuccessful attempt on Senhor Mordomo's life?'

'Yes, he did, Laura. Yes he did.' Giles answered with a smile and a gentle nod of the head.

'You are doing that thing with your face again, darling!'

'Yes I am, my dear. Yes I am. At least I sincerely hope so.' Giles paused and his brow furrowed as he continued. 'What,' he asked, with a beguiling voice and a twinkle in his blue eyes. 'What if the intended victim was the ringmaster and not the circus boss?'

'That would throw a different light on things I suppose.'

'Yes it would, wouldn't it?' The blue eyes appeared a little colder and his features changed to deadly seriousness.

'Come on, Giles. You saw something in that trailer today that you're not disclosing to anyone. Am I right?'

'Not quite, Laura. I am about to disclose it here and now and you are to be the first to know.'

'And…? Well don't keep me in suspense, Giles.'

'I noticed something in there as you suggest. I'm not yet sure of the significance of what I saw but there was something quite meaningful…on the Dead Man's Chest!'

By noon, on the following day, the trailer belonging to the circus boss was restored to its former elegance. The police surgeon and photographer had made their examination and taken details at the scene of the crime, the body of Sebastian Capuzzo had been removed for a pathologist's report. The door and window had been repaired and all traces of the macabre killing had been wiped clean.

The subdued atmosphere among the Tropicana crew was now tempered with the attitude that, in a few days time, everyone would be required to produce quality acts before a capacity audience. Rehearsals were now at a critical stage and circus life was always going to be one step away from tragedy, despite the many triumphs attained during each season.

Wandering around the various trials Giles was able to let Laura have a good look at the quality which would appear before a York public in less than a week.

The understudy ringmaster was a South African by the name of Mark Kimberley. It didn't take Giles long to discard him as a possible addition to

Ramon's list of suspects as he was on holiday when the first set of incidents occurred.

Spotting the colourful booth of Madame Zigana, Giles coaxed Laura to accompany him to meet the fortune-teller extraordinaire who had correctly forecast the winning horse in the recently run Grand National.

'Good day, Giles, and I'm best pleased to renew acquaintance with your lovely fiancée.'

'Likewise, Madame Zigana.' said Laura, returning the compliment. 'Giles told me that you are always extremely diligent in doing your homework.'

'That's very true, Miss Ramsden.'

'Please call me Laura. I'd prefer that.'

'Thank you, Laura. I would be so glad if you would do the same and call me Eva. After all we put one over on the boys at Aintree, did we not?'

'That was certainly the case though I'm not convinced that success was due entirely to homework. Have you, by any chance, done any research about the city of York?'

'To be honest with you I do not have to look into my crystal ball to let you both know that this vast area, known as the Knavesmire, was also home to the Tyburn where the Three-Legged-Mare was situated.'

'The Three-Legged-Mare?' The puzzled expression on his face was enough to suggest that Giles had never heard of the name.

'It is a little piece of York history that, as a historian, you will undoubtedly welcome with some degree of satisfaction. The Three-Legged-Mare was the title given to the gallows at Tyburn. It was where Dick Turpin the highwayman was hanged for horse theft. The gallows was removed over one hundred and fifty years ago but now we've had another execution close to the same spot.'

'But not for horse stealing, Eva,' Giles tilted his head as he spoke. 'I can assure you of that. But if you accumulate anything more that might be of use to us please don't hesitate to get in touch.'

'There is just one thing, Giles.'

'Yes?'

'Something I mentioned to you before. You have been followed for some time now and you will continue to be followed. You must be on your guard! Someone in this circus is out to silence you. You really have to be very careful where you go especially at night. The city of York has a maze of narrow streets where, under darkness, you would be vulnerable to attack if you should venture there.'

'I will take your warning to heart, Eva. I'll bear everything in mind. Now we must go and take another peep at Ingrid's Wheel of Death.'

On entering the large tented area they were just in the nick of time to catch the start of the knife-throwing rehearsal. It was the first time Laura had seen a knife-thrower at work and she watched the rehearsal enthralled. When the practice was over Giles suggested they drive back to the city centre and find somewhere for a cup of tea.

They discovered a tea room in St Helen's Square. It was Betty's Tea Room. Inside it wasn't long before a neatly-attired waitress took their order and informed them that Betty's Tea Rooms were world famous in North Yorkshire. The décor having been inspired by the ocean liner, Queen Mary, after the person who established the tea rooms sailed on the ship in 1936.

As they sipped their Russian tea amid the elegance of this unique establishment, Giles decided to seek out some information from Laura.

'Was there anything in particular that made a special impression on you when you watched Ingrid throwing her knives?'

It took a little time for Laura to answer. When she did, the answer came partly as a question. 'I was expecting to see Ingrid throwing at a man but with the necessary accuracy to avoid hitting him. But she was alone and the person on the rotating wheel was a dummy. Is that how she will do the act before an audience?'

'No, Laura. The dummy is only occasionally used when there is a danger of the act going wrong and Ingrid was still a bit upset after the ordeal yesterday when she discovered that Sebastian had been murdered.'

'She didn't appear to be too upset though and she performed her act without hitting the dummy target.'

'She is that proficient, Laura. She is one of the world's best knife-throwers if not the best. Her father taught her at an early age. Did anything else impress you?'

'Yes there was something else.. Apart from the accuracy and strength of her throwing arm…she threw with her right arm.' Laura put a hand up to her mouth before she continued. 'Ingrid was right-handed.'

'And…?' said an inquisitive Giles.

'It was Ingrid's left arm I treated for cuts after she pushed her arm through the broken window.'

'Which probably means?'

'It means it is unlikely that she threw the Lalique mascot that killed Sebastian.'

'Good girl. Well spotted! It wasn't Ingrid unless she is equally proficient with her left arm as she is with her right. But if it wasn't Ingrid…who was it? Or what was it?'

'What do we do now?'

'I think a visit to the Pathology Department at York County Hospital in Monkgate is called for. We may discover if the post-mortem has been carried out and whether it clarifies the mysterious death of Ringmaster Sebastian Capuzzo.'

The hospital staff were courteous to a fault when Giles and Laura asked to see the pathologist. The senior member of the team, Sir Lionel Spencer, made it crystal clear that every post-mortem differed depending on the circumstances and this one would take some time for conclusions to be reached.

'The peculiar scenario in which the death took place is going to complicate things, Professor Dawson. From details given by the police surgeon and the Inspector who visited the crime scene the man obviously died in a room which was effectively sealed apart from a broken pane of glass. There wasn't a great deal of blood from the wound caused by the object that pierced his throat which may suggest that he was dead before being impaled. There is some evidence that suggests that he may have died by injection or inhalation of some deadly substance.'

'Is that possible?'

'Yes, his colour may be the result of some agent entering the body in a sufficient dosage to cause death. But, if so, why was he stabbed when there was no need to go to such elaborate detail?'

'In your opinion, could the Lalique car mascot have been thrown from the broken window or fired, in some way, using a gun or crossbow device?'

'Why do you ask?'

'Well, if the man was already dead, might the killer have used the car mascot in order to try and implicate someone else?

'You mean someone in the circus renowned for throwing?'

'Yes. Why not?'

'If the man was already dead, how would the criminal know this when all the windows were locked and the curtains closed? And if the person was not dead the breaking of the glass would surely have alerted the victim who would then have taken evasive action.'

'Exactly my own thoughts, Sir. Thank you for providing me with some of the answers I required.'

'I'm not entirely sure I'm on the same wavelength as you are, Professor. I cannot see how I have answered your questions when I don't yet know if I have answered them myself.'

'You mentioned earlier that there was some indication that the dead man might have inhaled some sleep inducing agent before he died.'

'Yes! But how was that possible? He might have smoked something before entering the trailer. But then again, the killer would not have dared breaking the glass for fear of warning the victim in advance. There was, apparently, no evidence that the man smoked after he was inside, and if he had taken a contaminated cigarette or cigar the remains of such would surely have been found. The death was a complex one, Professor. The throwing of such an implement was difficult enough even if the man was asleep. If he was awake it would have been impossible; the breaking of the glass making it more so. At the moment we're stumped, Professor Dawson. We'll provide you and the police with all the details at our disposal, as and when we have them. I'm sure you'll work things out in due course, though I wonder if you have considered the possibility that someone or something entered the trailer and plunged...? Need I say more?'

'What was all that about, Giles?' Laura questioned him, as they got into the car, before heading back to the circus encampment.'

'It's exactly as I knew it would be. Despite all the skill of the medical team they are at a distinct disadvantage if they do not have all the evidence. They can only go so far and the answers they seek can only be attained if the facts are revealed.'

'I do believe, Giles that you know a lot more than you are prepared to divulge. I have an uncanny feeling that you either have all the facts or that you can put all the pieces of the jigsaw puzzle together to make a calculated guess. Am I right?'

'You've always said you could read me like a book. Draw your own conclusion, my dearest.'

'Since childhood, you and I have collaborated in the solving of enigmatic puzzles and I have every reason to believe that you have more than a shrewd idea of how this evil deed was done. Count me in, squire. We work well as a team.'

Chapter 19

YOU MAY BE NEXT, PROFESSOR!

Several large circus trucks were arriving at the Knavesmire when Laura drove her car into the large area in the centre of the racecourse.

The circus boss was supervising the arrival of the wagons when Giles got out of the car to speak to him.

'We have just been along to the District Hospital and had a word with the Pathologist.'

'Has the hospital come up with any results?'

'Early days yet, I'm afraid. They are just as baffled as we are.'

'I still think you are the one to sort all this out. I believe I can still count on you.'

'I have not the slightest doubt about that.'

'When you do, you will have earned the bonus I have lined up for you. Now let me introduce you to a new and original bonus for our great circus.'

'Would that be something brought here in those wagons?' Giles asked as he nodded towards the men unloading the trucks.

'Yes indeed! What you see is the necessary equipment, but the real bonus is the lady who will be using it…and she is not in the wagons. Come, let me introduce her to you.'

They followed Ramon to a gaily coloured trailer where an attractive young dark-haired woman was busy doing some warm-up exercises. She turned when the group approached and her radiant smile was a welcoming signal that impressed Giles.

'Miss Sirpes, allow me to introduce Professor Giles Dawson and his fiancée Miss Laura Ramsden. Giles is the historian of illusion and magic who has been of enormous assistance in bringing the craft of stage magic into the circus ring.'

'Delighted to meet you, Miss…?'

'Sirpes, Giles but please call me Gayle.'

Giles took her hand which he kissed gently. 'Now am I expected to guess what role you are about to play in this talented show?'

'You mean, of course like a piece of mentalism or mind magic,' the circus boss suggested, his tone hinting that even a mentalist would have great difficulty in providing a suitable description of this gorgeous woman's athletic prowess. 'Remember you were unable to guess correctly the art of another of our female performers.'

'That is true. And I expect to be equally astonished when you explain what Gayle does in a circus such as this.'

'Gayle is going to work on a swaying pole high above the circus ring. An act, I believe, that was first devised by the Chinese. It has now been transformed by this young woman who will perform a multitude of daring balances on the pole in conjunction with the trapeze and *without a safety net.* When you see her perform later this evening, I promise you that, as a historian of magic, you will have to suspend disbelief.'

The eagerly-awaited performance on the swaying pole was about to be witnessed by a large number of the circus crew,

as Giles and Laura took their seats close to the ringside. The hushed buzz of anticipation was unmistakable as they sat down and raised their heads to look skywards. The slender pole, which was securely anchored in the centre of the ring, appeared to reach almost to the topmost part of the circus tent and there was no visible means of ascending the structure.

The sudden applause which heralded the appearance of the young woman Giles and Laura had been introduced to earlier that afternoon, brought everyone's attention to the stunning girl who now stood in the centre of the ring.

She was attired in a floor length glittering cape and when she disrobed her fantastic figure was clothed in an alluring body-hugging leotard which complimented her curvaceous torso. Her lustrous Prussian blue costume, her dark hair, tied back, allied with her golden skin, lit by the circus lighting, made a sensational spectacle.

After stepping on to a mat at the foot of the pole she slipped off her dainty footwear and, with not the slightest hesitation, started to climb the pole using hands and bare feet. Without so much as a pause or stumble she ascended and the higher she went the more the pole began to sway at the top. She moved upwards like a tree-climbing female panther but with the poise of a ballerina.

Whenever she stopped she moved around the pole and, with arms and legs, presented balletic postures that were graceful to watch. At times she let go with hands and arms using only her legs to maintain her grip on the pole, and on several occasions she slipped downwards to suddenly stop using only the power of her legs.

The seemingly effortless movement around a swaying pole and the numerous artistic postures brought admiring gasps from an audience used to watching death-defying aerialists. As the moments ticked by a trapeze was brought into action and made to gently swing towards the pole.

The astonishing 180 degree turn as Gayle left the pole and grasped the bar of the trapeze followed by another turn to leave the swinging trapeze and finally clutch the pole brought spontaneous applause from those watching with bated breath. Gayle made a theatrical gesture of thanks as she steadied herself on the upright pole, but she wasn't finished.

She climbed upwards to the top of the pole which was now starting to sway quite a bit more. At the top there was a small round platform and, gripping that with her hands, she gently eased herself into a handstand and, placing her raven-haired head on the platform, removed her hands and maintained a headstand. With her legs and feet stretched skywards and arms outwards for balance she allowed her body to move from side to side to counteract the swaying of the pole.

Remaining in that position for almost thirty seconds before returning to the vertical again, she did a theatrical bow to her audience, before starting her downward descent to an ear-splitting clapping of hands from a circus group who knew they had another wonderful act to amaze the public.

Gayle was helped into her robe and disappeared to her trailer. Ramon approached Giles who could only shake his head when the circus supremo asked 'Well, what do you think?'

'You have another winner there,' Giles said as he watched the circus crew removing the pole. 'And without a safety net! Extraordinary and quite exceptional.'

'My arms and legs ache as if I'd gone through that routine,' added Laura. 'Gayle must be exhausted.'

'Yes,' said a beaming circus proprietor. 'And she may have to do that twice each day when our season starts next week.'

It was pitch dark outside the old coach house inn while Giles and Laura were deep in conversation in the cosy little lounge.

'What thoughts do you have after watching that incredible performance this evening, Laura?'

'It was an accident waiting to happen,' Laura declared, her voice demonstrating her obvious concern. 'It really wouldn't take a lot to create some demonic alteration in the safety devices at this circus which could cause that young woman to fall.'

'That is a good assessment of the situation, my love, The ground is hard and a long way down from the top of that pole and, without a safety net… death is almost inevitable!'

'Someone in that circus will consider this a golden opportunity to make Senhor Mordomo give up control.' Laura added, shaking her head

'You may well be right, darling, and one more fatality could be disastrous.'

'And another female, particularly a star like Gayle, may be more than enough, Giles.'

Getting to his feet Giles crossed to the window and looked outside. Rubbing his hands he turned to Laura. 'If you will put your warm coat on and accompany me I think we should go to the narrow streets of this great city and enjoy a leisurely, but captivating, ghost walk.'

Wearing his Crombie overcoat and armed with a street map of Old York, which he'd borrowed from the coach house lounge, Giles walked arm in arm with his Laura towards the city centre. Lots of people were wandering amid the lights from traffic. The engaged couple headed in the direction of the towers of York Minster and, studying the map of the alleyways of Old York, prepared themselves for a meander along the time-worn streets of a city which was reputed to harbour ghosts of yesteryear.

They started their walk through the left-hand archway of Bootham Bar, most likely the oldest gateway into Roman York. This took them into the main cross-street of High Petergate where there was peace and tranquillity as there was in the Precentor's Court. It was here, away from the hustle and bustle of modern traffic, that the towers of York Minster could be seen to advantage.

From there they entered into the tree-lined path of Dean's Court near where the fortress of the Roman Legions was established. Strange names like the "Hole-in-the-Wall Pub" and "Mad Alice Lane" conjured up images of a past which lingered still in this city. The occasional lamps in wrought-iron brackets, which lit the shadows of narrow alleyways, took each walker who ventured after dark, into a world where Dick Turpin and Guy Fawkes may have wandered.

Huddling closer to Giles as they passed through Stonegate, Laura was informed by Giles, reading from the map he carried, that it was probably here where Fawkes was born; and that this was one place where on each 5th November, there was no bonfire burning the guy.

The alleyways known to some residents as the snickets and ginnels of York eventually led to what was the city's most noted street…the Shambles.

The blurb, on the street map, stressed that this famous of all medieval streets was where the butchers displayed their produce on benches and meat-hooks. The hooks and benches were still there. It wasn't difficult to imagine this narrow street with an open sewer running down the middle and the stench from that, plus the smells from the slaughterhouses which were probably situated behind the living quarters nearby.

Imagination can play a lot of tricks on people in the dark if they are exposed to buildings which haven't changed much over the years, and they are plied with gruesome details of how things were. But it required no stretch of imagination to notice and become aware of what was hanging from one of the meat hooks as they advanced down the Shambles.

In the subdued light the lifeless body of a man could be seen to hang grotesquely from a hook. As they approached the hanging man it became clear to Giles that, attached to the body, a note was pinned to the man's clothes. Then, and only then, did it become evident that, hanging from the hook, wasn't the body of a man but the dummy that Ingrid Dahlberg had used as the target during her impalement practice. Giles looked at Laura and shook his head before removing the note which read… *You may be next, Professor.*

'This isn't at all funny, Giles. I'm scared. Really scared. Aren't you the least bit afraid of what might happen?'

Taking her hand in his Giles gave it a tender squeeze. 'I don't believe whoever played this practical joke intends carrying out this threat. This, I'm sure, is just another way of informing me that any success I may have in solving this problem could be dangerous, but only when it is clear that I am succeeding. The longer I keep secret, any success I have, the less danger I'm in. Someone is testing the water and although the threat may be real, I still have the whip hand. I'm being paid to solve a serious problem and if I let the guilty person know that I'm afraid to continue I'll have given up the initiative. Trust me, Laura. When the time is right I'll make my move...but not yet.'

'What are you going to do now, Giles?' Laura's voice was shaky as shock and fear seemed to have set in.

Putting a comforting arm around his trembling Laura and giving her a gentle squeeze Giles asserted convincingly. 'I'm going to pin this notice back on the dummy, my dear, and pretend I never saw it... or, better still, pretend, like Rhett Butler, in Gone With The Wind, that...*Frankly, my dear, I don't give a damn!*'

The smile that lit Laura's face in the subdued lighting of The Great Shambles, was like a breath of fresh clean air in a street of butchers which had previously ponged with terrible smells.

Arm-in-arm they briskly continued their walk down the street where once upon a time, Margaret Clitherow, the wife of a young butcher had lived. She was found guilty of hiding a Jesuit priest and was later pressed to death beneath a door heaped with stones. Yet another tale of York's demonic past.

As they left the darkness of the street of butchery, a decision was instantly made to return to their lodgings at the old coach house and enjoy a nightcap to nullify the nasty experience with the hanged dummy.

They had barely entered the brightly-lit bar when Giles was informed that there was a phone call for him. When he picked up the receiver the familiar voice of Freddie was on the other end.

'Can you book a room for me for two nights? I'd like to come to York where I'll be at the Spring race meeting in a few weeks time, but I especially want to see you again and that pretty girl of yours. I need you to fill me in with an up-to-date version of exactly where you are with your Holmesian efforts in the circus puzzle.'

'I'll do that right away, sport. The place is not too busy yet and I'd value the opportunity to explain how things are progressing. I also understand there is to be a dinner in the racecourse building the day after tomorrow and that will give you another chance to rub shoulders with those who are shortlisted as likely suspects. And that pretty girl of mine will be so glad to see you after that fiasco of a Grand National.'

'No need to rub it in, Giles, old son. I'll see you tomorrow.'

After breakfast on the following morning Giles reckoned a return visit to The Shambles, in daylight, might be productive. Their discussion in Bessie's Tea Room centred on the disappearance of the hanging dummy. Who'd removed it was anyone's guess. It could conceivably have been the local authorities, but Giles was in no doubt it was taken seconds after he'd pinned back the notice. Being watched was par for the course, but this was no game of golf he was engaged in.

Whenever a happening occurs in life, whether it has a grisly or happy end, if it cannot be explained then the world of the supernatural or ghosts may be considered. York, being Europe's most ghost ridden city, was a likely location to provide such an uncanny explanation when trying to rationalise the inexplicable death of Sebastion Capuzzo, the circus Ringmaster. With that thought in mind and the imminent arrival of Freddie that evening, the subject of ghostly interventions would be discussed when examining the ghastly ending of Sebastian's life.

Once Freddie was unpacked it didn't take long for him to join Giles and Laura in the cosy lounge and the conversation turned immediately to the gruesome affair at the circus.

'Can you describe everything you know of what might have happened in that trailer?' asked Freddie, eager to get up-to-date information.

Giles looked forlornly at his ex-RAF friend. 'I'm afraid I can only tell you what we saw when we entered the crime scene.'

'You say we, Giles. Who were we?'

'Ramon and I were the only ones to enter. We made sure no one else was involved.'

'What was your first impression?'

'The door was locked on the inside and the key was still in the keyhole. Ramon sent for technicians who eventually managed to free the lock after a struggle.'

Freddie gave a nod of understanding before raising his eyebrows.

'And…? He said.

'Sebastian, who looked incredibly like Ramon, was seated behind the desk. His head was back, and the car mascot with the sharp wing, designed by Lalique, was embedded deep into the dead man's exposed throat.'

'Did you examine the man to check if he was dead?'

'No! Ramon did that. But he was dead alright; his colour made that fairly obvious. I went over to the broken window.'

'What did you discover there?'

'It looked very likely the glass was broken from the outside. The broken glass was on the inside of the trailer.'

'Was the curtain open or closed?'

'It was open. All the other curtains were closed.'

'What did you do next?'

'I went over to the desk and, using a handkerchief, I opened the cigar box. The cuspidor was pretty near full of large Cuban cigars, all of them still in their wrappers.'

Another nod from Freddie begged Giles to continue.

'Again, using the hanky, I picked up the cigar lighter. It was slightly warm, though that may not be significant.'

The gentle shake of Freddie's head and the puzzled expression was immediately followed by an obvious probe.

'What were your conclusions after giving the situation some thought?'

'It was similar to the other deaths I've been involved with…another mystery, defying logic. If the murder was committed by someone or something inside the trailer the victim would have been aware of the attack…unless.'

'Unless what, Giles?'

'Unless he was asleep…or was already dead! There was no sign of a struggle.'

'And?'

'You're very persistent, Freddie. If Sebastian was asleep, the murderer would surely have recognised the victim as not being the intended Ramon. And, if he was already dead there would have been no need to use the Lalique mascot...unless'

'There you go again, Giles. Unless what?'

'Unless, my dear old Freddie. Unless the victim was meant to be Sebastian!'

'That had never crossed my mind. But, if that was the case, why was the window broken as if from the outside?'

'Unless, of course, to attribute blame to Ingrid Dahlberg.'

'Who?'

The circus impaler. And the use of the car mascot would add credence to that theory.'

'Yes, of course. Go on, Giles.'

'On the other hand, if everything was done from the outside the victim would have been alerted by the breaking of the window unless he was asleep or drugged.'

'What if the window had already been broken before Sebastian entered the trailer?'

'What if, Freddie? The entire episode is a mish-mash of *what ifs.*'

There was a short pause as Freddie stared at his friend. 'Who discovered the crime?' He asked.

'It was Ingrid, whose scream brought Laura, me and a few others, to the broken window. She said she'd found the window broken, had put an arm through and opened the curtain. In the act of doing so she'd received cuts on her arm. Laura attended to those.'

'Tell me about the gap in the broken window...was it large enough to allow someone to enter?'

'Not a normal human being!'

'If she put her arm through the break in the window why would she do so when the curtain was closed? What would make her suspect that something was wrong on the other side if the curtain?'

'That, I'm afraid, is one of those strange happenings that is so difficult to explain beyond reasonable doubt.'

'Could she have thrown the mascot?'

'I suppose it's not outwith the bounds of possibility but she is right handed and the cuts from the jagged glass were on her left arm.'

'Hmm!'

'If the implement was thrown or projected, in some way, from outside the trailer then the deadly mascot must have been outside to start with.'

'And whoever was responsible had to be sure that the intended target would be totally unaware of the breaking glass in order to draw back the curtain.'

'Unless, Freddie, the curtain on that one window was not drawn when Sebastian went into the trailer and locked the door. That would have allowed Ingrid a view of what was behind the desk. The problem with that is…if the curtain did not obstruct the view, why was it necessary for Ingrid to put her arm through the break in the glass?'

'You and I, Giles, are not entirely convinced that ghosts play a part in the actions of the living but neither of us can discount their involvement when other explanations are impossible to reach.'

It was Laura's turn to enter the conversation after a lengthy spell of silence. 'You did mention something you found on the dead man's chest, Giles.'

'So I did, darling! So I did!'

'Well, Giles? It wasn't fifteen men by any chance, was it?' said Freddie with a wry grin on his face.

'No, it wasn't, Freddie. Nor was it a bottle of Rum, Yo, ho, ho!'

'Well, let's be having it, Giles. Don't keep me in suspense.'

'What I found doesn't make things any easier, Freddie. In truth it tends to make things more difficult. What I found was some cigar ash!'

'But there was no other evidence of a cigar having been smoked and no wrapper. Am I correct in saying that?'

'Yes!'

'The plot does thicken, my friend. And in a city renowned for its ghosts there are many who would put that theory to the test. I think this would be a good time for us to imbibe something a little stronger than the table wine. I believe it could be your turn, Giles, to order some Courvoisier brandy from the bar…for the three of us, while I have a chat with your intended. We can then continue our discourse when you return…and, by the way, it seems you have another locked-room mystery on your hands.'

'The opposite of the magician's assistant's murder that took place in full view of several hundred curious onlookers.' Laura chipped in.

When Giles returned he said a waiter was bringing a tray of drinks. As he sat down Freddie leaned across to him and said, 'Tell me, Giles. Are you any further forward with your suspicions? Do you still believe that the killer's name is on that scrap of paper Ramon gave you with the names of the suspects?'

Thanking the waiter, bringing the drinks, there was no response to Freddie's question and Freddie knew that he often had to be patient and wait for an answer as Giles drifted off into his world of decision making.

Sipping from his cupped glass Giles smacked his lips, smiled and, looking directly at his friend, gave his reply. 'I am,' he said. 'More than ever convinced I know the identity of the killer I'm also convinced I will eventually have a confession...but not in writing!'

'You never cease to amaze me, Giles. But, knowing your prowess with the art of misdirection, I have to take your word that you know where you're going. Just be very careful. I don't want to lose you as a friend!'

'I don't want to lose you either, Giles,' Laura said, as she took Giles' hand. 'You now mean more to me than just a friend.'

'Count me in on that as well,' said a grinning Giles, as he raised his glass. 'Let's drink to that.'

Chapter 20

THE INVISIBLE EXECUTIONER

After breakfast on the following morning a waitress called Giles to the phone. When Giles returned he found Laura chatting to Freddie in the lounge.

'Well,' said Freddie, leaning forward and jutting out his chin. 'Laura tells me that was probably a very important phone call and the look on your face appears to confirm that. Are we about to hear bad news?'

Licking his dry lips Giles gazed first of all at Freddie, and then at Laura, giving both of them, what could only be described as his utmost attention tinged with seriousness.

'Well, I'm not sure whether it's good news or bad news. That was a call from the York pathologist and he has asked me to come and meet him again as he has some news for me. His findings seem to suggest that the death of Sebastian Capuzzo could be more complicated than he first thought...and that was bad enough.'

'Would you mind if I came along with you, Giles? To hear a pathologist giving his results of a post-mortem would be a first for me.'

'I think we should all go,' said Giles, clasping Laura's hand. 'If we have to analyse what we hear I'm sure three heads will be better than one.'

On arrival at the York County Hospital the trio didn't have long to wait before the pathologist welcomed them, ushered them into a private room and closed the door. When everyone was seated the pathologist gathered some papers together and opened the meeting with an apology. 'I don't think I gave you my name at our last meeting,' he said; his comments directed at Giles. 'My name is Lionel Spencer and, as a pathologist, my job at a post-mortem is to examine the deceased and ascertain the cause of death. That can sometimes be very difficult and can take some time. However an answer is usually found and is accepted with a high degree of confidence. In the case of Sebastian Capuzzo the answers were more difficult to find and not easy to explain.'

'No need to apologise Sir Lionel, your name was known to me when I visited you last time but you sound as if you are about to add a much deeper mystery to what was already a mysterious incident?' Giles' words registered with the pathologist whose wan smile and slight nod of the head suggested he was about to do just that.

'I can provide the facts that contributed to a death and can, in many cases, explain how certain substances which are found in the body may have got there. Nonetheless what I cannot do is explain exactly who put them there. That is for you and the police to decide. The obvious instrument of death would appear, on the face of it, to be the metal object that pierced the ringmaster's throat causing an obstruction that prevented him from breathing.'

'In other words he might have died of asphyxiation?'

'Yes, Professor, he might have died of asphyxiation; obstruction of the oxygen supply by occlusion of the air passages. But there is a further complication. In his body there is positive evidence that the man suffered from curare poisoning. Curare is a muscle relaxant extracted from the bark of a tree and used by South American Indians in blowpipes propelling a poisoned dart – later synthesised as d-tubocurare. I do not wish to confuse you with alarming medical terminology but I do want you to realise that this drug would paralyse all the muscles of the body – including the respiratory muscles – and so cause the subject to succumb after a few minutes of being unable to breathe. Asphyxiation would have resulted in that case. The drug could only have been administered intravenously by hypodermic needle…or more sinisterly by an arrow tipped in the substance or by a poisoned dart via a blowpipe. An arrow could have been fired from outside the trailer but as a blowpipe can only be accurate over a short distance and the needle must be used while beside the person; the drug would have to be administered by someone, or something, already in the trailer along with Sebastian.'

Giles looked at Freddie and frowned before speaking. 'I think you are hinting that there may have been an invisible executioner in that trailer.'

'That, I'm afraid, is for you and the police to decide. Let me tell you one more thing. Although I discovered a mark on the neck that could have been caused by a needle or a poisoned dart...if a dart had been used, the dart would still have been in the dead man's flesh when the body was discovered and no dart was found. Similarly no arrow was found either.'

'Thank you, Sir Lionel. I'm not too sure that what you are telling me makes me any the wiser but it may offer clues when I have time to digest things.'

'You're welcome, Professor. There is just one more piece of information that you may want to digest.'

'Yes?'

'The dead man's body showed traces of cocaine!'

As the trio left the County Hospital Freddie's chilling words were uppermost. 'What do you really make of all that, Giles? Curare, poisoned darts at close range? Another reason for an invisible executioner to enter the equation, I suppose.'

'Not forgetting the cocaine, Giles? Said Laura looking at her fiancé, as she pressed the point.'

'Ah, the cocaine,' said the smiling detective. 'I hoped I might be informed of that.'

'You cunning fox,' commented Freddie as he watched the interplay between the other pair. 'You're looking smug again, Giles. What are you up to?'

'Oh, nothing really. It simply leads me to a name I can't seem to get out of my head which might confirm my previous thoughts.'

When the trio returned to the Knavesmire they headed straight for the trailer of Ramon, where they found him in conversation with the circus doctor.

'Come in, Giles and bring your friends with you. The doctor has just received a call from Exeter Hospital and I expect you'll want to hear the news.'

The doctor stepped forward and shook Giles by the hand. The pathologist at Exeter Hospital called me a few moments ago.' he said, taking a piece of paper from his pocket and putting on his glasses. 'He explained that Allison had been given a barbiturate, known as Thiopentone.' The doctor looked across at all three visitors. 'Thiopentone or Sodium Pentothal is suitable for intravenous use which will lead to unconsciousness in ten to thirty seconds.'

'How long would that unconsciousness last?' Giles asked, his eyes narrowing as he awaited a reply.

'It would last for several minutes before recovery took place. Pentathol was commonly used as an induction agent and would be followed up shortly afterwards with a muscle relaxant. That would allow a tube to be inserted into the trachea so that air could be blown into the lungs by a ventilator; thus maintaining oxygenation and life.'

'That would mean that Pentathol must have been administered as Allison was being covered by the tyres.'

'That's correct. And it would appear that a muscle relaxant must have been injected intravenously either, as she was being carried on the stretcher to the rest area, or in the rest area itself. Allison would have been unable to breathe and death became inevitable.'

'Was it not possible for the nurse in attendance to have done something to prevent Allison's death?'

'Yes! But only if she'd known that two injections had been given. Remember, it was thought that Allison had fainted through pressure of work and that a period of rest would bring her back to normal. The circus nurse did consider giving Allison an injection of Insulin in the belief that she might have been diabetic but she decided against that. Had she given Allison Insulin she would certainly have killed her. It was only after Allison had died that scarring and local inflammation was apparent on Allison's upper arm and shoulder suggesting that someone had used a needle but had missed the vein and injected into the tissues around it.'

On the journey back to the little hotel Giles mused over the findings at the post-mortem of the magician's assistant at RAF Winkleigh. Before leaving Ramon and the circus doctor, Giles had delivered the verdict of the pathologist he had been to see at the York County Hospital. The findings matched in many ways: the main difference being the metal car mascot which had effectively blocked the windpipe of Sebastian.

'Another case of the invisible executioner at work.' stated Giles when all three were back in the lounge of the coaching house.

'That, of course,' said Laura. 'Assumes that, in the case of Sebastian's death, the injection of curare was done using a needle or a blowpipe at very close range...and that begins to smack of the supernatural.'

'How else could it be done?' Freddie posed the question.

'Well, I'm no expert,' said Laura. 'But I do believe Big Game Hunters, on Safari, use tranquilising guns to sedate wild animals allowing them to be caged for transportation to zoos. Tranquilising guns fire darts and there is someone in this circus who must have a similar type of gun!'

'What a clever girl you are, my love,' said Giles livening up out of a moody spell of mild depression. 'The one person who must have such a projector is Rodrigo, the tiger trainer, and he could have fired a poisoned dart by shooting through the broken window.' Giles turned to face Freddie. 'What Laura has just said intrigues me,' he said nodding slowly to his ex-RAF friend. 'She recently made a good case for having Signor Gomez on the list of suspects and her offering about a tranquilising gun tends to give her suggestion more credence. There is, unfortunately, one thing that throws a major doubt on the animal trainer using the dart gun from outside...the dart would have ended up inside the trailer – and no dart was ever found on the body.'

'There seems no answer to that.' Freddie expressed; his face showing extreme concern.

'Have no fear, Freddie. There is an answer to everything if you care to search in the right direction. One thing I'll grant you Laura, Signor Gomez will have to be interviewed and I shall do that at the party which Ramon intends to give in the racecourse building prior to the opening of the circus season.'

By the time the celebration party, to be held in the main racecourse building, was ready to be held, word had got around regarding the concluding statements of the respective pathologists concerning the deaths of the magician's assistant and the ringmaster. As was normally the case, when accounts moved throughout a close community from mouth to mouth, the originals became embellished out of all proportion and fact became myth. This was no exception, but one thing was abundantly clear –

the circus accidents were no longer accidents when the two murders were examined.

Giles wandered around the guests, most of whom were the top circus performers. At a meeting with the chef preparing the meal, he learned that each star performer was having a special meal prepared to prevent any physical upset which might interfere with their performances.

While coming into contact and conversing with the hierarchy of the circus elite, Giles made sure that Laura and Freddie were being well catered for. His main focus of attention though, was directed at finding the swarthy figure of Signor Gomez and asking him some questions.

Strangely enough it was the man dressed in smart breeches who drew his interest. The man, who was in conversation with the leader of the circus band, turned and Giles recognised him as the trainer of Khan.

'Good evening, Rodrigo,' Giles said, as he shook the South American's hand. 'I wonder if you would spare me a moment of your time. I have a few questions I wish to ask.'

'Certainly, Professor. I have no problem with that, but I think we should find a more private place.'

'Give me a few seconds, Signor. I have a friend here who knows his way about this grandstand as he's been here racing on many occasions. I'll just ask him for some directional help.'

Luckily Freddie was nearby and it took no time at all for him to show his friend and the trainer to a private room where they could speak freely.

Once inside and with the door closed the two men pulled up a couple of chairs.

'Am I now on your suspect list, Professor?'

'You were always on my suspect list, Signor.'

'But you didn't interview me when you questioned the others.'

'That's right. No, I didn't…that's why I'm doing so now.' The tiger trainer shifted awkwardly in his chair as he awaited the flood of questions he expected. 'Do you own a tranquiliser gun, Rodrigo?'

'Yes, I do. It happens to be an essential piece of equipment for anyone keeping wild animals. And Khan, despite what some people say, is a wild animal.'

'Where do you keep the gun?'

'I have one in my trailer.'

'You say you have one in your trailer. Does that mean you have more than one?'

'Yes! I have two guns.'

'Where is the other one kept?'

'Inside the wagon with Khan.'

'Hmm! When did you last use one of the guns?'

'Not for several months, Professor.' The trainer's eyebrows rose then they fell as he frowned. 'I always have a gun ready when the cage illusion is being presented. I was almost at the point of using it when the illusion went wrong and Allison was left in the cage with my Khan. But I didn't use it then…and I didn't use it to kill Sebastian!'

'How can you explain the door of Khan's cage being unlocked?'

'I can't. But maybe you can? After all you are supposed to be the detective.'

'Maybe I can, Signor. But you may have to wait a bit longer before I worry you with a truthful explanation.'

'I'm sorry if I sounded scornful, Professor. We're all a bit on edge in the circus and you could well be the man to put a stop to things. Can I ask you a question?'

'Yes, if it has a bearing on what has been happening in the circus.'

'From what I've heard about the strange death of our esteemed Sebastian I believe it has a bearing.' The pause before Rodrigo continued added intensity to his question. 'Do you believe in the supernatural, Professor?'

'Do not believe all you see or hear!'

'What the bloody hell is that supposed to mean?'

'Not very much I'm sorry to say,' said Giles as he scrutinised for any clues forthcoming from the animal trainer's demeanour. 'It was just something I seem to have heard recently.'

'Well, do you?'

'Do I what?'

'Do you believe in the supernatural?'

'That is a question I was asked while on a previous assignment and my answer hasn't changed.'

'Well, Professor?'

'I do not disbelieve in the possibility,' said Giles with a slight shrug of his shoulders as he spoke. 'There was an incident recently at another racecourse when I encountered an apparition at what should have been an empty racecard kiosk…but that needn't concern you. Let me just say that a vivid imagination can play a powerful part in life. Imagination along with mystery was the great double act of the writer Edgar Allan Poe.'

'Your imagination, Professor, must be very vivid if you think I should be one of your suspects and had anything to do with the death in Ramon's trailer. If what killed Sebastian was a poison dart it was not projected by me or with my tranquiliser gun. And if it was delivered by a blowpipe it must have been done at close range by someone inside the trailer…and that, to me, suggests the supernatural!'

'What you are saying demonstrates the power of imagination. I do not subscribe to your assumption and I prefer to examine other possibilities.' Giles shook his suspect by the hand. 'Thank you for your cooperation. Please return to the evening celebrations and I wish you lots of success with Khan during the season.'

When Rodrigo had left the room and closed the door Giles sat for a moment in deep contemplation, with eyes shut. His thoughts were interrupted almost immediately by a knock on the door. Laura entered and went over to him. 'Freddie told me this was where you'd be so I waited until I saw Rodrigo leave the room. How did you get on?'

'I think it went quite well…and he has, not one, but two tranquiliser guns!'

The stunned look on Laura's face, as Giles took her hand and led her out of the room, was tantamount to a realisation that her assessment of who might have murdered Sebastian could be correct.

'Don't get carried away, Laura. I doubt if it's going to be quite as easy as you think. For the time being, though, he stays on the list.'

Along with Freddie, Giles and Laura were invited to join the circus boss at the evening meal. The conversation turned to the forthcoming public shows about to start on the open space in the centre of the racecourse.

'As you well know, by now, my Tropicana Circus is ready to entertain, amuse and thrill a North of England audience before moving to London.' Ramon's voice was as edgy as his body language. 'I hope we have a trouble-free run both here at York's Knavesmire and at London's Alexandra Park.'

'We subscribe to that.' All three said as one voice.

'*Obrigado!*' Ramon said as he expressed his thanks. Looking around at his three guests his tone changed to one of bitterness and uncertainty. 'I'm afraid, though, that we may be heading into a period of great difficulty during which a few more accidents, in front of a paying audience, could break my resolve.'

'I will honour my contract and do everything in my power to prevent that happening, Senhor.'

'Have you reached any conclusions, Professor?'

'All I can say, at this stage, is that I have a person in mind who, given a little more time, may be revealed as the evil person in this circus.'

'Is that person on the list of suspects I gave you?'

'Yes, Ramon. Although I have to admit I added a further three names, the one I believe to be guilty is on the original note you gave me.'

'Good work, Giles. It will be a great relief to me to end this nerve-racking ordeal and the sooner the better.'

After coffee Giles excused himself and moved around the galaxy of circus stars; finally meeting up with Lizzie, the rider of the Andalusian mare.

'I'm not sure if I've been of any help to you, Professor Dawson, but I did mention to Senhor Mordomo that I was keen to assist you in every way I could and he thanked me for that.'

'Have you explained that to any of the others?'

'No. I don't want anyone on that list to know that I'm on your side.'

'Good girl. Lizzie. But be on your guard; I don't want you getting hurt.'

At the old coach house, after the celebration evening was over, Freddie suggested a nightcap before turning in. While he was gone to the bar a waitress came to the lounge with an envelope addressed to Professor Dawson.

Opening the envelope Giles drew out a small sheet of notepaper on which was a message.

Come and meet me at midnight tonight. I have some very important news for you. I will be in the street known as The Shambles. You will not see me until I appear from my hiding place in one of the doorways. Come alone and you will be well rewarded.

See you at midnight.

219

Giles studied the letter for quite some time before looking up at Laura whose face registered extreme concern. Freddie arrived with three brandies and as he put the tray on a table he became aware that something was amiss.

'What has been happening while I was away? You both look as if you've had a fright.'

The Prof gazed at his friend, took one of the brandy goblets in one hand and, without a word being spoken, passed the hand-written note across.

Taking a sip of brandy Freddie fumbled for his reading glasses and then became occupied with the note. The tension in his face, as he removed the spectacles and peered over the note, was a warning of what he was about to mouth to his close friend.

'Don't tell me, Giles. You're surely not going? Not alone at least. For God's sake man, this is madness. It could be a trap.' Giles sat and listened to the ranting of a friend whose opinions he valued, even when they disagreed. His lips pursed and his breathing deepened; he knew full well that Freddie had his best interest at heart and was possibly offering the most sensible advice. But it was clear to Giles that if he was to succeed, he would have to take chances while trying to solve this hellish affair. He looked at his watch. There was less than two hours to go till the time stated in the letter…only a few minutes during which he must decide to either take the bull by the horns or give up the chance of possibly making a breakthrough.

'Please don't get in a flap, Freddie. I feel I'm on the verge of picking out a name and proving who is the guilty one, beyond reasonable doubt, but I need to have a bit more to go on before I can convince myself that my theories are correct. This meeting tonight might be a mistake but it could just be the piece in the jigsaw that completes the picture. I'm going to go there but not without taking precautions.' As he said those final words he glanced at Laura and smiled.

'You can go alone if you must, Giles, but the cavalry won't be too far away.' Laura said, clinking glasses with a bemused Freddie.

It was pitch dark as Giles approached The Shambles. A cold breeze was blowing and Giles pulled the collar of his Crombie overcoat up around his neck. His hands were deep in his coat pockets and an eerie silence pervaded the darkened street. There was no one about and the only sounds Giles could hear were his own footsteps. His imagination began to work overtime and his steps slowed, in contrast to the increasing beat of his heart. His loneliness was briefly shattered by the yowl of a scampering cat from out of the creepy shadows…a noisy movement which caused him to contemplate a speedy return to the comfort of the coach house. He resisted the temptation and continued down the street wondering if this was a wild goose chase or whether someone would materialise out of a gloomy corner.

His thoughts were engaged in how this narrow medieval street, the only street in the city to be named in the Domesday Book, got its title. His thoughts were miles away in a different age when there was a very slight rustle from one side, followed immediately by a thump that hit him high up on the back of his neck. As he staggered on unsteady legs he caught a vague glimpse of a cloaked figure disappearing out of sight. He put a hand up to his coat collar where he could feel something hard embedded in the material. His legs felt weak and he was on the point of sitting down when the assistance of two welcome friends helped him to recover. They guided him to a part of the city where they were able to assess what damage, if any, had been done.

It was Freddie, with the aid of his scarf, who extracted the object which was sticking out of Giles' coat collar. When they reached a point where there was better lighting all three could recognise what the object was. It was a dart, and the kind of dart which could be projected via a blowpipe. The invisible executioner had been at work again, but thanks to an overcoat the assassin had failed. Or had he? Was it just another shot warning Giles to back off?

Chapter 21

THE THREE-LEGGED MARE

The morning after the escapade in the shadows of The Shambles Giles was loathe to rise early and spent an extra hour in bed.

Laura brought a light breakfast up to him and, as he munched a piece of wholemeal toast swallowed down with hot tea, she tried to remonstrate with him about the folly of his ways in putting himself at risk…especially with a person who refused to offer identity.

'You might have been killed, Giles. You must admit you gained nothing by accepting that assignation.'

'On the contrary, darling,' asserted Giles as he seemed to come out of his cocoon-like mood. 'I don't think I was the intended target last night. That, I believe, was a warning shot across my bows and, strangely enough, that confirmed what I suspected. If someone had wished me dead last night it would have happened in The Shambles.'

'How can you say that, Giles?'

'It was one more warning to make me give up the chase and, my dear, I have no intention of doing that.'

'But don't you think you may be out of your depth compared to those in this circus. You could be up against more than one, Giles, and in racing parlance you are still in the novice class and could be handicapped out of any chance of success.'

'You are perfectly right to criticise my actions, Laura, but last night assured me I'm simply up against one person. And that person is beginning to realise that the net is closing.'

'So what do we do now?'

'We must be diligent. Keep our eyes open for any sign of an accident which the public might accept as a piece of misfortune in a circus act that constantly attempts to defy death, but which has probably been caused deliberately by the person on that list.'

'That's not going to be easy.'

'No! In fact it's going to be rather difficult, and I have a strong feeling that two artistes may be the next ones to be involved, and they're both young and female!'

'You very seldom get it wrong so count me in. I'm with you all the way, Giles, so what's the next move?'

'I think another visit to the pathologist is called for. I want that dart examined; the one that Freddie pulled out of my coat collar. We need to know if it was poisoned and, if so, with what.'

The return journey to the County Hospital was like something straight out of "The Wizard of Oz" and Giles was almost on the point of whistling *We're off to see the wizard* as the three companion sleuths travelled their own yellow brick road through the hospital corridors to meet the forensic wizard inside.

The medical scientist had the dart placed in a clear plastic packet and sent to the lab for tests. 'It shouldn't be too long before we have a result,' he said, once he heard of the nocturnal event in The Shambles. 'We can then assess how close you were to death.'

The short wait for the result of the tests on the dart was interspersed with the pathologist's comments, such as 'You must be involved in a very dangerous game, Professor' and 'Whatever possessed you to try and solve such a complex and life-threatening puzzle?'

When the lab assistant reappeared with the dart he gave the object to the pathologist along with a note. Sir Lionel passed the packet containing the dart to Giles, and started to read what the note conveyed. In a few seconds the beginnings of a smile on the medical expert's face broadened into a huge grin. 'Yes, Professor, as I said before, you must be involved in a very dangerous game. Your dart was as lethal as a prick from a drawing pin. It had not been dipped in anything stronger than water so had you died it could only have been from a heart attack due to fright.'

Grinning almost as much as the pathologist Giles could only say 'That clinches it,' as he and Laura gave Freddie a send off when he left to return home to his wife and family in Evesham. When Freddie had gone, Giles took Laura to Bessie's Tea Room. After a light snack they headed to the Knavesmire for the first afternoon performance of Ramon's talented circus at York's racecourse.

When it was over, the capacity crowd had been entertained to over two hours of high quality acrobatic acts; alongside the glamour, side-splitting humour and artistry of elegant equestrianism; plus the mystery and magic of ringside illusions. Everything went as smoothly as Swiss clockwork and the circus elite were perhaps wondering if the afternoon success was a forerunner of things to come.

The crowds leaving the racecourse after the extravaganza were vocally complimentary and many said they would come again. Everyone seemed to have a special fondness for a different act, but the general opinion was that the entire programme was an enormous triumph from start to finish. As Giles acclaimed 'Not an accident in sight.'

Leaving the Big Top and heading back to the coach house for dinner Giles reflected on that statement about there being no accidents. He regretted having to admit that before every storm there was usually a calm. The prospect of disaster happening after such a wonderful start to the season, was unthinkable but, unfortunately, not unlikely.

Dinner at the coach house was delicious yet Giles had extreme difficulty in eating. His vitals were knotted and he imagined what stomach ulcers must feel like. The possible outcome of unwelcome catastrophe to one of the female performers in the next few hours was, according to Giles, almost inevitable if Ramon's *gauntlet of fear* was still a problem.

The evening performance started well with every seat taken. Giles and Laura had the best seats as usual. When the opening acts of acrobats and jugglers were followed by Hank, the funambulist, giving a flawless display on the high wire, Giles could feel the tension drain from his body. Before he knew it, the clowns had him relaxed and ready to watch the first of the illusions when Annette successfully replaced Khan, the tiger, in full view of the audience. The action, accompanied by the music played by the circus band, was non-stop and when Chuck and his firemen clowns brought roars of laughter from those watching, Giles was convinced the noise would be heard as far away as York Minster.

The suspense as Leonardo climbed the staircase of swords was electric and the superb equestrian artistry of the young girl from Exeter riding her white Andalusian horse was poetry in motion. The applause for young Lizzie was so prolonged that the ringmaster had to ask for special attention to be paid to the next performance as it was one of extreme danger. While he was making a plea for a restraint of noise during the next act a pole was being securely harnessed in the centre of the ring. The pole clearly stretched upwards towards the roof of the giant tent. Being fixed at the base and unconnected at the top, the structure could be seen to be swaying gently by the hundreds of eyes looking upwards.

Into the ring stepped the young woman being introduced as Gayle. Removing her dressing gown and shoes she bowed to the crowd and, without any fuss, started to climb the pole using hands and feet. As she climbed, the band was playing the kind of music that enhanced her movements and Yoga-type positions on the swaying pole.

Round and round she went: sometimes stopping with her hands only being used to retain a hold on the pole and on other occasions, to the gasps from those watching, using only her legs to maintain a grip.

When a trapeze was released and made ready for the next part of the act, the ringmaster made a special request for the audience to exercise strict control over applause during dangerous moves when Gayle would be performing between the swaying pole and the swinging trapeze.

There was a hush inside the Big Top as Gayle timed her movements on the swaying pole to coincide with the swing of the trapeze. The band slowly and gently set the pace; the music complimenting each action as Gayle moved from the pole to the bar of the trapeze and back again. But something was wrong. There was hesitancy in Gayle and her indecision was disturbing.

Peering upwards Giles tried desperately to figure out what was causing the upset. Gayle moved from one piece of apparatus to the other and she caught the trapeze bar with one hand, the other hand clawing empty space as she knocked the trapeze sideways. Giles had noticed a flash of light as

Gayle was about to make the transfer movement and there was another flash shortly afterwards. Now he knew what was happening.

The lights in the circus were positioned to avoid dazzling the aerialists, but this was different. The next flash of light that blinded Gayle as she struggled to achieve perfection appeared to be a reflection from one of the instruments in the band. It was coming from a bassoon and that was being played by the band leader himself. Another flash as Gayle tried to grasp the pole, which was swaying away from her, brought an uncontrollable gasp from an anxious crowd. It was an effort of miraculous proportions which prevented a fall as the young acrobat clung to the pole with her legs while her body travelled downwards, head first, before she could wrap her hands around the swaying device.

A roll of the drums and the crash of cymbals plus a final fanfare from the entire circus band gave the perspiring audience the signal to applaud and cheer a very courageous effort as Gayle descended to the centre of the ring below.

An angry Giles was finding great difficulty in stopping himself from having a confrontation with Felix Reiser, the band leader, but his first duty lay in finding out how Gayle was after such a physical ordeal.

Leaving Laura in her seat Giles went directly to the rest area where the circus nurse was tending to Gayle who was lying down.

'How is she?' asked a very concerned Giles. 'It was touch and go out there, and she could have been seriously injured.'

The nurse took him to one side. 'She is surprisingly unscathed,' she said. 'It was her bodily strength and agility that saved the evening and, like most circus performers, her sheer will to survive was probably the dominant force. Nevertheless she will need time to completely recover and she may have to cancel tomorrow's performance or modify it by leaving out the trapeze.' Giles looked over towards the resting athlete who was lying with her eyes closed. 'You can go over and have a word with her, Professor, but only for a minute or two.'

The Prof went over to Gayle who turned her head and opened her eyes as he approached. 'I do hope you haven't come to criticise my performance,' she said, attempting a grin that became more like a grimace. 'I'm afraid I wasn't quite at my best this evening.'

'On the contrary, I thought you were magnificent. It was a blinding light reflected from an instrument in the band that nearly caused a fall. A fall that would have been devastating for you and would have been added to the list of circus accidents plaguing Senhor Mordomo.'

'Was it an accident, Professor?'

'I'm afraid I don't know. It could have been accidental by the way it happened, but it could have been a deliberate attempt by someone wishing to add to the previous accidents. I just don't know; I'll have to reserve judgement on that.' He nodded, gave her a smile and added, 'Keep on your guard and get well soon.'

The first half of the circus programme was almost ended when Giles sat down beside Laura. Lizzie, astride her white horse was enthralling the watching crowd and the routine was so captivating that neither Laura nor Giles spoke until it was over and the short interval had started.

'How was she, Giles?'

'Who?'

'The girl who nearly fell off the pole.'

'Oh, sorry. I was in another world when you asked.'

'You very often are, Giles.'

'What?'

'In another world, precious. But I love you for it.'

'You're quite correct, Laura. This circus is another world and the more high profile it is, with the artistes attempting feats that have never been successfully done before, the more likely you are to have accidents. Accidents with the consequence of career-ending injury or life-ending death. I'm damned if I know what category this evening's event on that pole came under.'

They watched the remainder of the acts, all of which were performed with excellence and without incident. There was a telephone message for Laura when they were back at the coach house. It was from Doreen, the housekeeper at Maskelyne Hall, to say that Laura's mother was not too well. Although it was quite late in the evening Laura phoned Lockerbie and said she would come home right away.

Left on his own Giles had a nightcap before preparing for bed. His head was buzzing with a myriad of murderous meditations when it eventually hit the pillow.

With Laura gone, sleep was infinitely more difficult. It would be quite some time before she would arrive back home. Giles was aware she would not call him until morning and the night would be long and apprehensive. He was restless and when a fitful sort of slumber overtook his agitated body his fertile imagination took over.

A flashing light intermittently shone through his bedroom window; he tried to open his eyes but the light kept blinding him. When he did manage to catch a glimpse of his lit-up room all he could make out was a hypodermic needle floating in space and hurtling towards him like a javelin. It was being propelled by an invisible executioner and, as it came towards him, it was changing shape. That blasted flash of light came again and everything was a blur. His eyes hurt but he was determined to identify what the changing object was. It was something Laura had told him about – or was it someone else? Get a grip, Giles, he told himself. That was a lot better…he was gripping tightly now but what he was gripping was a pole high above the ground and the object closing in on him was a blowpipe and some invisible force was blowing poisoned darts at him.

He woke in a cold sweat, looked at his watch and realised he'd been in bed less than an hour. He rose and, unsteadily, went to the bathroom where he splashed his face with cold water.

Crawling back to bed he lay for a while as his breathing returned to normal. He was missing Laura and, in a way, he was also missing Freddie, but he was dead set on getting to the bottom of this whole business and finally reaching a conclusion with a conviction to follow.

He turned over, pulled the blankets around him and in no time at all was in the land of nod. Tomorrow was another day and he would show the circus community that he was not prepared to abandon the fight. Perhaps, he thought, his determination may have returned following the conversation with Gayle as she lay exhausted after her ordeal.

At breakfast he received a phone call from Laura to say that her mother was not too seriously ill after a heavy cold had developed into a chest infection. Her mother was responding to treatment and Laura said she would remain at Maskelyne Hall until her mother was fully recovered. She expected to be joining Giles when the circus moved to Alexandra Park.

Feeling a bit more like himself after speaking to Laura, Giles decided to stay in his room and make a special effort to analyse most of the important events which had taken place since he accepted the task at the circus.

Jotting down the various happenings in chronological order as best he could, Giles wrote down the wire walking problem for Hank, the funambulist and the vibrating wire; the metal gauntlet that was thrown in the old control tower, the names of the film actors who had identity changes which was left in his trailer at RAF Winkleigh; the fire scene involving Allison and the clowns; and the injuries to Leonardo when he hand-balanced on the staircase of swords. All of these incidents could have been the responsibility of any of Ramon's suspects. Giles could not pinpoint any one person: though the name which stood out for him was capable of involvement in any one, or all of them.

Thinking back to those early days at the winter quarters of the circus, Giles had a problem trying to remember the several times when Khan's cage had been left open. One person was the most obvious suspect, but again, any one of those considered guilty could have managed to release the tiger.

'There was the occasion when Lizzie wasn't given her dressing gown after performing on the Andalusian mare; but that could just have been a pure mistake,' muttered the slightly embarrassed lecturer in magic, becoming aware that he was talking to himself.

Scribbling on the paper Giles added the cryptic message addressed to him in the control tower. Whoever wrote that knew he was to be sailing north on a cruise ship and that surely narrowed the field. That person was the one throwing down the gauntlet and challenging him to answer the clues which would reveal the person's name.

There was the fire and the smell of kerosene when the light aircraft was arriving, not forgetting the near disaster when Allison and Khan failed to exchange places. There were so many incidents which could have been the nasty work of any of those suspected.

Continuing to scribble notes on the pad Giles stopped abruptly as his thoughts turned to what turned out to be a major incident and a despicable one at that – the death of young Allison during the tyre illusion. The killer had to have been one of the tyre mechanics wearing masks to avoid identity. Why did Allison have to die? The reason was surely to pave the way for the later attempt on Ramon's life. But he was getting away from what had taken place between the two deaths.

He looked at his watch and decided it was time for tea. If only Doreen…? Giles smiled and went downstairs to ask for some to be sent up.

The trip to Rum and the big Edwardian house known to this day as Kinloch Castle wherein he was followed and, most likely, offered false clues to put him off the scent, was next on his catalogue of incidents. But the biggest clue of all was there, inside that big house and within his grasp. As he sipped his tea Giles reasoned that given time or hearing some unconnected phrase, he would come up with an answer. He frowned and was startled by his own thoughts. That was it!

There was a phrase he'd heard and he'd taken it out of context and assumed wrongly. He was now sure it had a relevance to something that was in or near the dining room of Kinloch Castle.

Identity problems and the names of those film actors had to tie in with the phrase he'd heard and the secret that was close to the seats of Rhouma in Kinloch Castle. But that would have to wait until good fortune struck in the shape of another phrase or word that led him in a direction where success was lying in waiting.

On the way downstairs to lunch Giles' brain, for no reason at all, began to ponder over the whispered voice who purported to come from beyond the grave. A devilish attempt to introduce the supernatural must have been the work of Allison's killer and Giles would not forget that.

After having a light lunch, Giles decided to attend the afternoon circus performance. The early acts produced no surprises other than the clever use by clowns on the high wire pretending to lose balance and hilariously coming close to a fall only to recover at the last minute and hug each other in desperation. As the first half was nearing the finish the ringmaster announced that, owing to injury, the lady who was to perform on the swaying pole was indisposed and would not attempt her death-defying act until the evening. This announcement was met with muted groans from the audience but everything soon perked up as into the ring came the Andalusian mare with Lizzie astride her.

The band started playing gentle waltz tunes in quite slow time and the white mare, with her rider riding bareback, was in perfect time with the music. Hooves were beating and her head was nodding in such perfect unison it was impossible to say whether the horse was in time with the music or the music in time with the horse.

Throughout each phase of the routine the superb segue as the music effortlessly went from waltz time through to polka and then into the quicker Viennese waltz, was matched by the equally-superb segue by horse and rider. It was as much the transitional changes from one tempo to the next which generated the excited and appreciative applause, but as quickly as the applause started so did it die.

There was the slightest of stumbles from the mare as the band changed tempo once more. Lizzie looked down at the horse's legs as if noticing something was amiss. The animal started to limp and slowly teetered into the ringside. The young rider was off in a flash as the white horse tried to regain balance but the stricken mare was now standing on three legs and was shaking as if in a fever.

Several attendants were quickly at the horse's head to gently guide it out of the ring while the young rider was helped into her robe.

It took Giles only a few seconds to leave his seat and make his way to the circus stable where the sick horse was being examined by the circus vet. Giles kept out of the way until the vet came over to him and introduced himself as Barry Gilmour.

'I don't think we've met, Professor, but I know you'll be anxious to hear about this case.'

'Was it an accident do you think?'

'You can be the best judge of that when I explain something to you.' Giles nodded for him to continue. 'The horse is a non-ruminant herbivore and such animals prefer to eat small amounts of food steadily throughout the day. Their digestive system is delicate and consequently overeating is bad for them. When that happens, or when they eat something that doesn't agree with them, they are susceptible to colic.' The vet's expression became serious. 'This sudden illness can cause poor performance in a dressage horse and the animal will refuse to perform the manoeuvres it has had no trouble with in the past.'

'So you think that may have happened in this case?'

'Yes I do, Professor. What's more, a non-ruminant herbivore must never be fed lawn clippings!' The corners of the vet's eyes screwed tightly as he made the statement and Giles' eyebrows went up as enlightenment dawned.

'Where better to get lawn clippings than a racecourse preparing for the opening of its flat season in a few days time? The injury was created by someone not in charge of the horse's welfare?'

'I'll know better tomorrow but meanwhile Bianca will have the best of attention and I'll keep you informed.'

'Bianca? What a lovely name for an incredible mare.'

When he left the stable Giles wondered at the cruel irony; the three-legged mare – twice on the same piece of ground…the Tyburn on York's Knavesmire.

Chapter 22

OUT OF THE FRYING PAN…

It was a rather depleted evening show given by Circus Tropicana that day. Gayle performed a modified routine on the pole, discarding the part of the act involving the trapeze, and Lizzie didn't appear with Bianca, the indisposed mare.

Although the evening was trouble-free, Giles made an appointment with Ramon to explain to him what the latest incidents had meant to his progress in his attempt to solve the *gauntlet of fear* curse.

The circus boss was angry at the way things were going and deplored the unforgiveable injury to the mare.

'Be honest with me, Professor,' he said. 'Are you making any headway in this puzzle or is it now time to look for more professional help?'

'You are at liberty to seek out the services of someone with a good track record of detection, Senhor but, whoever comes in, will have to start at square one whereas I have already covered a considerable amount of ground. As my racing pal would say, this was never going to be a sprint and stamina will win in the long run.'

'Does that mean you are getting somewhere?'

'I'm sure of it, even though the latest mishaps have clouded the issue a little.'

'Are you prepared to give me some idea as to when you might be able to give an answer and stop what's happening to my circus?'

'If I am unable to bring this culprit to justice before midsummer I'm prepared to return the bulk of the retainer you gave me.'

The Portuguese supremo slapped his desk. 'Let's leave it at that then,' he said. 'We now have a timescale that satisfies me and I believe you are a man of your word. I will watch your progress with interest.'

Following his meeting with Ramon, Giles considered a visit to Gayle might be worthwhile, but as it was getting late and as she was probably resting, he decided such a meeting could wait until morning. He would then combine that with a visit to the vet and get the latest news on Bianca.

He headed back to the old coach house inn and made a phone call to Laura in Lockerbie. The good news was that Laura's mother was making good progress at home and that her daughter was tying up some loose ends at her own work place and would be ready to join Giles quite soon.

Before turning in for the night Giles made a few notes regarding his next moves. The start of the circus season would soon be over in York and the entire extravaganza's next spell would be in the north of London area and the aristocratic space of Alexandra Park. He would have to be ready for London. Also, as the middle of summer wasn't too far away, when he'd guaranteed to the circus boss he'd return the bulk of his retainer fee if he was unable to bring the culprit to justice, he was acutely aware that he must remain focussed.

The early morning sunlight flooding his room, wakened Giles out of a restful sleep. After a light breakfast he was soon fit and ready to pay his respects to the two females who were the latest victims of circus accidents.

The vet was already at the stable when Giles arrived to question him. 'It was definitely grass clippings which caused our mare to suffer, Professor. And that means it was not self-inflicted.'

'And what is your prognosis? When will Bianca be fit enough to give of her best again?'

'We'll give her a trial fairly soon and make a decision. But I expect her to be performing in a day or two. Exactly how well is questionable. We'll have to wait and see, but she has a sound constitution and could surprise us all.'

'Do you believe this was an attempt to kill Bianca?'

'No, Professor, though it could easily have happened. The amount of grass clippings was only sufficient to incapacitate her; probably just enough to prevent her performing at her best. It looks like an attempt to cause distress to Bianca as well as Ramon.'

On leaving the stable, Giles wasn't long in finding the youthful and supremely-fit Gayle who was exercising in the Big Top itself. 'You seem like your old self again Gayle.' He said when she'd stopped her exertions.

'Thanks for the old, Professor. I have to confess, though, that when my limbs started to ache after the flashing lights caused me to fail to grasp the trapeze I did think senility had caught up with me prematurely. But the show must go on and one of the vital rules of circus life is that after a fall, the quicker one gets back into harness the quicker you are likely to succeed.'

'I'll let you get back into harness then, Gayle. Take care and good luck, but remember danger doesn't always come from where you expect it.'

The next few days were spent keeping a watchful eye on all the acts and trying to detect any deterioration which might end in accident. Nothing of serious note occurred and Giles was pleasantly surprised to see the mare, Bianca, and her talented rider, Lizzie, back to form after the collapse in the ring. With Bianca giving her scintillating demonstration and Gayle thrilling the audience with the swaying pole and the trapeze, everything was back to normal. Giles though, was less than convinced. As far as he was concerned, just as he'd said to Gayle, danger doesn't always come from where you expect it.

With the final performances at York over, the circus folk were speedily in the throes of dismantling everything and loading wagons for the journey south to Alexandra Park. That would be their home for the next few weeks.

Giles was packed and ready to catch the train to London but decided to stay around and savour the organised chaos of a huge complex being packaged and sent on its way in time to re-establish itself at another venue in preparation before delighting yet other audiences.

He watched, in awe, as large numbers of riggers made light work of bringing down and folding the giant canvas. For a second or two, his concentration was distracted to such an extent that he was not really aware that he was in the way of a group working feverishly to fold the tent just as the ground staff do at Wimbledon with a tennis net following a heavy shower of rain.

The next thing he knew was that he was bustled from behind and found himself sprawling into the thick material on the ground and being rolled over until daylight disappeared and his lungs became tight and he was unable to breathe.

He kicked with all his strength but that was short-lived and he was virtually semi-conscious when, eventually, he found himself lying on his back with a myriad of male faces gazing down at him.

'The boss warned us not to lie down on the job but it's bloody obvious he didn't speak to you.' One of the riggers sniggered as he spoke. An out-of-breath Giles was helped to his feet and, with his balance unsteady and his dignity in tatters, he teetered away from the seething crowd, thanking his lucky stars that he was still in one piece.

What was that he'd been telling others – about danger not always coming from where you expect it? Time, he thought, to take heed of his own words.

He returned to the coach house to collect his bag and call a taxi to take him to the station where he'd catch the next train to London. He made two more calls: one to Lockerbie and one to Evesham to alert those at the other end that he'd be at his South Kensington flat when they wished to contact him.

The journey by train was always a chance to relax and clarify what his next moves should be; and this journey was no exception. He made a few notes. One being that a return visit to the St James's Club in Picccadilly would be useful to find out if their premises would be available should he want to hold another meeting there.

Something was drawing him there. He desperately tried to analyse what that was and all he could think about was a phrase he'd heard at the big house on Rum. What was it?

He settled down to have forty winks but he'd hardly closed his eyes when he was shaken awake with six words on his mind…"he was the most trusted man."

He looked around at others wondering if he'd said the words out loud. Nobody seemed in the least interested. So, getting back to those words and where he'd heard them. It was when he'd returned to hear Major Mackintosh and his wife discussing George Bullough's gentleman friend, Sir William Bass. He'd assumed that the words had been expressed about Sir William… but what if they'd been talking about someone entirely different? What if the gentlemen at St James's Club were able to throw a different light on those words?

He dozed off again and, although he went into a trance-like state, his mind was fully concentrated on that one name...a name that seemed to ring out like a fire alarm. He was convinced that, sooner or later, he would trip over a clue which would be incontrovertible proof of his belief. Was it possible that something he saw or heard, at the St James's Club, would light the blue touch paper and ignite the explosion which would bring an end to his circus problem? That would, of course, put paid to the other saying *do not believe all you see or hear.*

Being in his South Kensington flat when he arrived back in London it was quiet. Quiet compared with the hustle and bustle of the dismantling of the Big Top and his conflict with the army of riggers who very nearly suffocated him in the folded canvas. The apartment building was a peaceful haven where he didn't need to watch his every step.

Looking at his watch Giles decided he'd done enough for one day. He ran a bath and came to a decision that the following morning would be soon enough to pay a visit to the gentlemen's club.

The St James's Club was quite busy for a spring morning. The doorman welcomed Giles and ushered him inside to where the manager greeted him. After being given an assurance that if there was a suitable room available in the Club when he required it, all he had to do was give them a telephone call.

He spent some time being shown around and was intrigued by a large room used specially for the game of Baccarat. It was something he was totally unaware of when he'd lectured in the Club to the circus bosses and the stage magicians.

When he was about to leave he was invited to join members in the smoking room where they were having morning coffee. Once he was comfortably seated in one of the leather arm chairs he was in no hurry to leave and wanted to spend some time in conversation with the group of gentlemen smoking their cigars.

Topics varied from the weather to how the markets were doing on the Stock Exchange. However Giles managed to get around to the reading matter in the Club after he spotted the number of books available; many of them by the popular P.G. Wodehouse.

'Can anyone explain why Wodehouse is a favoured read by members of the Club?' asked Giles as he savoured the aroma of ground coffee beans allied with the quality cigar smoke. 'Is it the light entertainment of Bertie Wooster and his valet, Jeeves; or is there an alternative but less obvious reason?'

'I think I can answer that on behalf of all of us, Professor.' The monocled gentleman, who spoke in a cultured voice, was sitting in a corner with a copy of "The Guardian" newspaper. 'My name is Charles Meldrum and many of us were fortunate enough to have a manservant who made our lives almost trouble-free as did Jeeves for Wooster. But that, unfortunately, was in the past. There aren't so many of them nowadays and it can be nostalgic to delve into the past even if only through the pages of a novel.'

'Thank you, Mr Meldrum. That makes a lot of sense, but it couldn't have been easy to choose a manservant or valet in real life. After all the impeccable Jeeves was the fictitious imagination of an author of the old school.'

'I suppose it was,' said the spry elderly Charles Meldrum as he folded his paper. 'But we lived in different standards then and made absolutely sure of our choice. It was vital that the gentleman's gentleman was beyond reproach.'

There was a general murmur of approval and someone called out 'He just had to be the most trusted person and we made sure the best person for the job was chosen.'

'Will someone please say that again?' Giles could hardly get the words out.

A sea of faces looked at the agitated, Giles.

'What do you want, Professor?'

'Someone said something that reminded me of a phrase I'd heard before.'

'Well,' said Charles Meldrum. 'I think I was the last one to speak and I think I said the valet had to be beyond reproach.'

'No,no, it was after that. Someone shouted out.'

'Oh,' said a portly gentleman. 'I'm sure I heard someone say "he had to be the most trusted person" and I'm sure we'd all agree on that.'

'That's it!' Giles said, almost knocking over his coffee cup in the process. 'That's definitely what I wanted to hear. Now if you'll excuse me …!' He rose and headed for the door leaving the gentlemanly occupants, bewildered and unable to understand what had been said that had caused such a transformation in their visitor.

The Club doorman removed his cap and scratched his head as Giles passed him and hailed a taxi. He thought it unusual for someone leaving St James's not to let the uniformed person at the door have the honour of calling the cab.

On the journey to his flat, Giles had time to dwell on what he'd learned and it suddenly dawned on him that what he'd discovered, though it may have had a distinct bearing on the phrase he'd taken out of context at Kinloch Castle, he was really no further forward with what it meant as regards the secret which was supposed to lie near those blasted seats of Rhouma.

A rather subdued Professor of Magic became elated again when he spotted the two cars outside his flat when he'd paid the cabbie.

Inside he found Freddie and Laura preparing coffee. 'Hello you two,' he said 'When did you get here?'

'I just got here a moment ago, having come from Newmarket. Laura was here when I arrived.'

'I drove overnight from Lockerbie. The roads were quiet and I got here early but you were gone.'

'It's great to see you both and I've just had some good news. At least I thought it was good news. Now I'm not so sure.'

'Let's all have a coffee and you can tell us what you've been up to, Giles. After that I'll probably lie down for a while.' Laura said as she stifled a yawn.

'I would certainly advise that, my love.'

'Let's get down to brass tacks then,' said a perky Freddie. 'And later on I'll guide you both to Ally Pally and the Frying Pan.'

Freddie guffawed as soon as he saw the surprised look on the faces of his two companions. 'Ally Pally and the Frying Pan.' he said. 'They're one and the same. They're some of the names Alexandra Park racecourse has been called. But I'm afraid the track has been called many other names that are distinctly worse.'

'Why the frying pan?' enquired Laura.

'Because of its shape,' was the reply. 'Though I sometimes think it could be described a little more flatteringly. Being situated close to the city it has been attended by large crowds of well-to-do Londoners enjoying the racing including evening meetings. But, because of its shape and sharp turns with the wrong camber, it has been loathed by jockeys and trainers due to the frequent numbers of accidents.'

'And that's where Ramon's circus is now headed,' said the enlightened Giles. 'The Big Top will be erected inside the racecourse.'

'Wouldn't it be rather ironic if the course continued to have accidents even when there was no racing?' Laura said as she gripped Giles by the hand.

'Only this time on the inside of the track as opposed to the track itself.' Freddie added in reply. He turned towards Giles as Laura poured the coffee. 'Come on, squire,' he said. 'Tell us what you've been up to and what news you're undecided about?'

Recounting what had taken place at St James's Club, Giles ended by pointing out what he considered was the clue which finally put an end to the enigmatic conundrum that had been posted on the notice board in the relic of the control tower at RAF Winkleigh. 'I was so sure that fitted the puzzle,' Giles said, rather less than satisfied. 'I really believe that the little room off the Dining Room in Kinloch Castle, might well have housed the valet or manservant of Sir George Bullough, rather than the piper, when family guests dined. But therein a secret was supposed to lie…a secret that was to reveal something special according to the writer of the puzzle and…' he paused and seemed at a loss for words before struggling to continue. 'Now I'm not so sure. It makes no more sense than it did before I linked the *most trusted person* as a person on the staff of Sir George. I appear to be back at square one.'

'But wasn't there some implication about two names in the conundrum. A lot was made of that. So much so that there has to be a connection with this secret.' Laura said as she drained the last of her coffee and started to close her eyes.

'Come on, pussycat,' said Giles as he assisted Laura to her feet. 'Let's get you to the bedroom where you can lie down for a couple of hours.'

Alexandra Park, six miles north of London; looked magnificent in the late afternoon sunshine when Giles, Freddie and a rested Laura arrived. A fairly large crowd had gathered to watch the giant canvas being erected on the land inside the actual racecourse of Ally Pally, The nervous tension in Giles became visibly evident as a tremor went through his frame.

Laura glanced at her fiancé with apprehension, in the realisation that he would be in a contemplative mood, for this racecourse would almost certainly be the finale of his attempt to solve the impossible.

At the same time Freddie appeared to have the same thoughts when he put an arm on his friend's shoulder and, in a soft voice, murmured 'Could it be that we have another racecourse where the final act takes place as did Kempton Park with Arkle?'

'And two courses with the name Park after the title,' responded Giles as he looked round. 'One more coincidence, wouldn't you say?'

It was Laura's turn to add another dimension to the conversation. 'It really would be a coincidence if the girl, you both met at Kempton, turned up here as well. Now that would be spooky! What was her name by the way?'

'Katie! Katie Starter!' Freddie hardly got the words out before a lovely London-Irish voice called out as they neared the racecourse grandstand.

'What on earth are you doing here?' the voice asked as Katie rushed over from the main office.

'We could ask you the same question.' A nonplussed Freddie shook his head as he spoke.

'I was invited here for an interview by the racecourse authorities as they've been a bit short-staffed of late but there's no racing today, and there won't be any for a few weeks. So what brings you here today?'

'You remember my friend, Giles?'

'How could I forget him?'

'Well, he happens to be involved with the circus that you see and it concerns a bit of detective work.'

'If it involves a bit of mystery I think he should be good at that… remembering my dad and all that. There *is* a mystery I'm sure you can solve for me. Could one of you please introduce the lady who is obviously with you?'

'I'm so sorry, Katie. This is Laura and she happens to be Giles' fiancée.'

The two girls shook hands. 'Giles, you are a very lucky man,' expressed Katie as she turned to him. 'But I have no doubts that Laura will also be very lucky. I think you'll make a great team and I wish you every success with your mystery. Now I'm afraid I must go but we may meet again. I certainly hope so.' With that she was gone and the two ex-RAF friends just looked at each other and smiled.

Moving to the inside of the course the trio caught sight of one or two people they recognised. Most of what was happening was being organised by the crews turning the piece of ground in the centre of the racecourse, into the site for an international circus of repute. Whether it would still be that when the time came to present his conclusions Giles was uncertain. One thing he seemed sure of was that he was ready to roll up his sleeves and, like the best close up magician, tell his audience that there was nothing up there but his wrists and arms, and then perform the impossible.

No attempt was made to go anywhere near those working on the large tent, least of all by Giles. His recent struggles to breathe sufficiently in order to maintain life while enveloped in the giant canvas, were still fresh in his mind.

'You've gone a little pale, Giles, old son. Freddie said, his voice charged with concern. 'Are you having second thoughts?'

'About what?' asked Giles, shaking his head and shrugging his shoulders.

'Don't beat about the bush, Giles. I'm talking about this *gauntlet of fear* thingamabob. Has it got to you at long last? For heaven's sake don't be afraid to admit defeat.'

'Freddie's right,' begged Laura. 'Remember the old adage..."better to have loved and lost than never to have loved at all".'

'You may well be right, Laura, about the adage I mean, but what I'm involved in is far removed from love. This could be described using another four-letter word. That word is evil.' The pause, as Giles waited before continuing, gave extra emphasis to what he was about to say. 'I'm going to see this through to the bitter end...and that end will probably be staged here inside the innocent looking structure being assembled inside Alexandra Park's Frying Pan.'

'Are you absolutely sure you know what you're doing? Remember this could be totally out of your control and even the best detectives would find that a daunting prospect.'

'I realise what you're saying, Freddie, but I doubt if anyone, stepping into the unknown, can be absolutely sure they're doing the right thing. Even the most gifted performers in the history of the greatest show on earth, have succumbed though they believed that their act on the tight rope or trapeze was faultless.'

'Do you believe you're faultless, Giles?

'No, I don't. But all along someone has been tricking me. Not in the way the stage magician operates but tempting me in the belief that I was unable to see through it. As an historian of illusions I'm willing to accept the challenge and I'm determined to bring this person to account. All I require is the support of two very close friends.' He smiled at Laura and took her hand in both of his. 'And a slice of luck allied with the unintentional help of the guilty person.'

'You sound as if you have a plan, Giles. What do you intend on doing next?'

'It might be a plan fraught with danger, my dear Giles,' commented Laura. 'But you'll have the support of those two close friends. So what do we do next?'

'Let's take a walk up to the Palace. I'd like to make some enquiries there.'

'Count me in as well, Giles. Laura and I are with you all the way, but just beware…the mystery may deepen and you could be *out of the frying pan and into the fire.*

Chapter 23

...AND INTO THE FIRE

The evening was still young when the trio got back to the South Kensington flat and Laura proposed that they start to examine the circus problem in a different way to see if they could come up with something that might open a new door to discovery.

While they all got down to business, a Chinese takeaway was only a phone call away and a meal was ordered to be delivered in about an hour's time.

'Where do you think we should start, Laura?' Giles enquired as he thumbed through some papers. 'I must admit that I have exhausted most of the accidents apart from the two murders and so I think a change of plan might be in order.'

'When we were having a look at Banquo's Walk near Torcastle you mentioned an identity problem, Giles. I've thought long and hard about the identity, not only of the killer, but the way the subject has raised its head from the very beginning.'

'That sounds like it might be worth delving into,' said an interested Freddie. 'Can you be a bit more explicit Laura?'

'I'll try my best but I'll certainly need help from Giles. I think we have to go right back to the time when you were so sceptical about the real identity of RAF Winkleigh and had grave doubts about Giles accepting the task at a place that, according to the RAF, never existed.'

'That's right, Laura, and even the incident with Giles at the racecard kiosk at Kempton Park when he described someone he saw who, in reality, was already deceased. That was unquestionably a problem of identity.'

'Spooky goings on,' said Laura. 'But it was the names of the well-known people left in Giles' trailer that started me thinking in a more intense way. Those names which were assumed when they went into the entertainment business were meant to be a major clue and not a distraction; I'm sure of that. They suggested the wrongdoer could have two names and that suggestion is made over and over again, so I think we should examine that possibility.'

'You may well have hit on the best way to tackle this problem, Laura,' agreed Giles, as he sorted through his papers. 'It has become more evident that the one I'm looking for is someone with a double name and a motive which sets this person apart from the others.' He spread out the written riddle which was posted to him on the notice board at RAF Winkleigh. 'This could be the next clue of real importance,' he said pointing to the words in front of him. 'The entire conundrum makes a play on characters and events with a double role.'

'Yes, Giles,' Freddie revealed. 'From the Hitchcock movie with the leading actor having a pseudonym playing the part of a man in the film with a double identity; to the isle that was known by two titles and the race with more than one description, finally ending with a secret in an Edwardian dining room which could lay claim to a second identity problem that, if solved, could reveal a person who organised a host of serious accidents ending in murder.'

'Putting it like that,' said a muddled Giles. 'I'm not at all convinced that we may find it easier to go in this direction than working on the two murders.'

The ringing of the door bell halted the discourse. Giles left the room and returned with the delivered Chinese meal. Laura set everything out on the dining table and Giles produced a bottle of wine.

Conversation was brief during the meal and much of it centred on the attempt to identify the guilty person.

'When you went over to the States, Giles, and met the Harvard criminologist, was there anything in particular that gave you an inkling as to how the death you were investigating, might have taken place?'

'No, not really Freddie. There were several instances that concentrated my mind.' Giles replied as he refilled the wine glasses while Laura cleared the table. 'Come to think of it, the criminologist had a well-thumbed copy of a novel entitled "The Three Coffins" by John Dickson Carr in which was a chapter entitled "The Locked-Room Lecture". I knew the novel as "The Hollow Man" when it was published in this country and there was something in the pages of that novel that helped to set me off in the right direction.'

'Can you think of anything similar that might have the same effect, Giles?'

'No! Nothing comes to mind although I'm always prepared for something comparable to happen.'

'Are you still convinced,' Laura asked as she returned from the kitchen. 'I mean about the name you put forward as the person who is below suspicion?'

A startled Giles just managed to catch his glass of wine before he knocked it sideways. 'Convinced? Yes, I'm still convinced, but I'd like you to repeat what you've just said.'

'You're doing something with your face again, Giles. I was asking if you were still convinced about the name you pointed the finger at. You know, the name you believed was the guilty person.'

'No, Laura. You didn't use the expression, the guilty person. The words you did use set a bell ringing.'

'I think I used the phrase "below suspicion", Giles. Does that mean anything to you?'

'Yes it does, if you'll give me a moment to think back.'

'You showed me a name, Giles,' said Freddie. 'Was it the same as the one you showed to Laura?'

'Yes it was, Freddie. But it is the expression *below suspicion* that intrigues me.'

'I knew it,' said Laura scrutinising Giles. 'It was that something you were doing with your face. Something has had a profound effect on you. Please enlighten us.'

The phrase "Below Suspicion" was the title of a novel by the same author who wrote "The Hollow Man". The book was published, around 1950, I think, and featured a barrister by the name of Patrick Butler. The barrister appeared in another novel six years later entitled "Patrick Butler For The Defence" but when it was published in this country the final word in the title had a spelling change to Defense.'

'Very interesting,' said Freddie, looking a trifle bewildered. 'But why should a slight change in the spelling have such an effect on you?'

'I suppose I seem obsessed with anything that smacks of a double identity.'

'Well then, my dear Giles, I think there's something there that could be of much more interest.' Laura ventured with some enthusiasm.

'And what would that be?'

'The barrister in "Below Suspicion" had a surname that is yet another name for a valet or manservant which you associated with the small room in Kinloch Castle which you felt held a secret.'

'That is curious. A butler could certainly be a person who, not only was the male servant taking care of the head of the household, but would also be the head of all the other staff in that household…and would probably be *the most trusted person.*' Giles nodded with satisfaction written all over his face as he contemplated what he'd just said.

'It would definitely make a slight mockery of the crime mystery if it turned out to be the butler whodunit.' Freddie offered jokingly.'

'Give me a moment,' said Laura as she left the table. 'I have an idea that might be worth looking in to.' She returned from the bedroom with a couple of pocket dictionaries. 'I found these in your room, Giles.'

'They're Spanish and Portuguese dictionaries; I thought they might come in useful when I joined the circus but they were really unnecessary as everyone seemed to speak fairly good English.'

Thumbing through one of the pocket books Laura stopped at a page which she passed to Giles.

He gazed at the words on the little book then he turned to Laura who was hurriedly going through the other one. He said nothing as Laura passed over the second booklet making a point of fingering a piece that elicited from Giles just one word. 'Wow!'

The dictionary was passed over to Freddie who, when he'd accepted the implication, looked up and gave Giles a nod and a smile. 'Does that make you satisfied, Giles? And what's the next step now that the identity problem seems to be over?'

'The puzzle I had trying to identify the culprit may be over, Freddie, but I may now have an even bigger problem; I have to prove it and that's not going to be easy. I may well be out of the frying pan and into the fire.'

'I think we should sleep on it, Giles,' expressed Laura. 'And in the morning we can make a move. This might be the time for you to lay down the gauntlet and put the fear into someone else.'

After a good night's sleep Giles decided that it was now time to start the ball rolling and give the circus prior warning that he would soon be giving everyone an explanation of his findings for trying to bring someone to justice. Today would be the final preparation day for the circus to have everything ready for the opening of the short season at Alexandra Park.

Laura was still fatigued after her drive from Scotland and she was advised to remain in the flat and take it easy; while Giles paid a short visit to the racecourse at Ally Pally. Freddie was going to the racecourse at Sandown Park to have a word with some of the staff. Laura would be on her own for an hour or two, but Giles promised he'd not be away too long.

The vastness of the Big Top had a somewhat eerie atmosphere when Giles entered to find a small group making sure that the seating arrangements were in good order. He couldn't help but feel the surge of adrenalin as he looked upwards and caught sight of the trapeze which would be in action at the climax of the show. The time was fast approaching when the accidents that had bedevilled the circus for the past six months or so, might almost be at an end. The burden was his: it was going to be up to him to bring the disasters, and in particular the murders, to a final conclusion.

Biting his lip, Giles left the tented emptiness and went over to the booth where Madame Eva Zigana was quietly preparing for visitors wishing their fortunes to be told.

'I'm sorry to barge in like this, Eva, but there is something I want to ask of you.'

'If I can help you it will give me great satisfaction, Giles.'

'You were one of those I questioned in the old control tower at RAF Winkleigh.'

'That's correct, Giles. I was one of the suspects and I expect that I still am?'

'For what I am about to say I have to confirm that you will be asked to attend a news conference along with all the other suspects. It will be held very soon when I intend to put my cards on the table, Eva, and reveal the identity of...' Giles discontinued his discourse as he watched the lines appear on the smooth skin of the fortune- teller's face.

Madame Zigana did not answer for several seconds. She stared at Giles, the frown on her brow expressing her immediate feelings. 'You will be insisting that I, along with other suspects, attend a meeting to give you the opportunity to name one of us as the guilty person and yet you wish to ask a favour of me?'

'Not quite true, Madame. I will not be insisting that you attend the conference. That will be done by Ramon, your circus supremo. He will ensure that everyone is there before any revelation is made. The other part of your enquiry is true, Eva. I do wish to ask a favour of you. I have a very strong reason for wanting your presence when I ultimately make my allegations, and I wouldn't be asking you to grant me a favour if I thought you were criminally involved…and I have a good idea that the favour I ask will be something you will enjoy doing as a teller of fortunes.'

The furrows on Eva's brow disappeared as she turned her head to one side and gave Giles a smile. 'Please tell me what you want of me?'

'Thank you, Eva. There will come a time when I will give you a sealed envelope. In that envelope there will be a prediction – similar to what a mentalist magician might do. The prediction will be the name of the person I believe to be guilty. I do not wish the envelope to be opened unless I can produce sufficient evidence to support my claim in a manner which will convince those who are innocent, or…' the pause was dramatic, '…or,' he repeated. 'In the event of my death! I depend on you to carry out my wishes.'

'Are you reasonably confident that you can bring the guilty person to justice, Professor Dawson, or do you anticipate that there is a fifty-fifty chance that you might die in the attempt?'

'You, my dear Eva, are the most likely person to make an accurate forecast of what the immediate future may hold for me. I'll leave that prediction in your capable hands.' Giles moved towards the door of the booth, stopped and turned back; with tongue in cheek he said 'Just a little piece of advice, Madame. As one exponent of the art of magic to another can I possibly ask you to look into your crystal ball and, with a touch of levity, dream up an ending that gives me a better than fifty-fifty chance?' With those words Giles left to make a few more calls.

Lizzie Lisbet, the equestrian artiste, was with her mare in the circus stable when Giles called in to speak to her. Everything was set fair for the London opening. Both horse and rider were in good form and Giles made sure that Lizzie was informed as to what he intended doing and that he wanted her to be in attendance at the conference when it was called.

His next visit was to Gayle Serpis. She was wearing a full-length body-stocking and was engaged in some gentle stretching exercises as she prepared for her twice-daily act on the swaying pole complete with trapeze. She was willing to attend any press conference which was called and was intrigued that there was a distinct possibility that the circus disasters might be nearing an end and a guilty person might be brought to justice.

There was only one more visit to make before returning to the flat. Giles thought it prudent to call on Ramon, take him into his confidence and put him in the picture regarding the way things were going.

'I came to wish you the best of luck for tomorrow when the new season begins. I know you'll be a bit apprehensive, Ramon, but I may soon have some better news for you'

'That's kind of you, Professor, very kind indeed. I'm sure we need all the good luck we can get and if you have some better news for me that would definitely help.'

'I believe I'm on the verge of solving the problem your circus has and I will be calling a press conference as soon as I'm confident of making an announcement. When that happens I want you to direct all those who were listed as suspects to attend that conference which will probably be held across the park in Alexandra Palace. I'll contact the Press and give them the information.'

'Have you really come to a decision, Professor?'

'I'm sorry but that will depend on what may take place at that meeting. I hope to be able to clarify things when we all meet in the Palace.'

They shook hands and Giles left to walk the short distance to the Alexandra Palace railway station. He was looking forward to getting back to Laura who would probably be rested by now.

With the first part of his strategy to reveal the identity of the killer now complete, Giles was annoyed that the journey to his London flat seemed to take longer than he wished. It crossed his mind that it might not be a bad idea to renew his driving experience and purchase a car. The money he'd received from Ramon would certainly come in handy for that…unless he was forced to return it due to his inability to reach a successful conclusion.

He was still musing over everything when he got back to the flat. That was short-lived as once again he was in for a rude surprise. Laura's car was gone.

He let himself in only to discover a note on the dining table. It was addressed to Freddie and was written in a hurried scrawl.

Dear Freddie,
A phone message from someone at the circus has asked me to come as quickly as possible. Giles has had a nasty accident and he may be in intensive care.
Laura

Giles wasted no time in calling a cab. Luckily he was able to have the assistance of the cabbie, Colin Forbes, who drove him to Ally Pally in record time. Despite the friendly chat the journey to the circus was a nightmare for Giles. Someone had made a hoax call – but for what purpose? Laura could now be in grave danger. If that was the case it would constitute a threat to Giles unless…? Was this another shot across his bows? Was someone trying to make him pull out of his effort to solve the impossible?

The black cab had hardly stopped when Giles jumped out and rushed to where he thought the rest area might be. It was empty and there was no sign of nurse or doctor. He wandered around asking everyone he bumped into but nobody had seen Laura. Some didn't know who she was. He was frantic and although contemplating the worst scenario he tried to stay calm and reason things out.

The entire centre of the racecourse was teeming with what seemed hundreds of men apparently occupied in fine-tuning preparation of the giant tent and clearing all the un-needed steel poles, ropes and clutter. None looked to be a threat to Giles or the missing Laura and that at least was a comfort to him.

Giles pushed his way through the working throng until, by a strange quirk of fate, he heard a voice that was distinctly recognisable. The sound came from the trailer of the equestrian youngster, Lizzie, and Giles almost fell in the door, without waiting for an answer to his knock.

The relief etched on Laura's face was matched by the calm, now shown by Giles, as they embraced each other.

'I'm so glad you're safe and well, Giles. I hurried here as quickly as I could. Were you involved in an accident?'

'No I wasn't. I read the note you left for Freddie and I came here by taxi.

I can't understand who called you…or why? Was it a man or a woman, Laura?'

'I think it was a man's voice but I'm not certain. I can't swear to it.'

'Well, I'm certainly ready to swear to it.' Giles was furious as he continued. 'Whoever called you was intent on mischief and I'm damned if I'm going to allow that to happen again. I may be *out of the frying pan and into the fire* but it's the person responsible who is going to be burned.

They spent a little time with the young girl from Devon. After explaining what the next steps would be they thanked her for the time she'd devoted to Laura.

The drive back to the flat was less stressful than the trip Giles had made by cab after reading Laura's note. He was adamant that it was now or never as far as throwing down the gauntlet was concerned; and the quicker it was done the better. If he was correct in his assumption about the killer, he was sure that the only way to prevent another death was to carry out his proposals at the conference. The prospect of a third murder was horrific especially if it was within his power to prevent it happening.

The first thing Giles did when they were safely back in the London flat was pour drinks for everyone, after which they sat down and talked over how he was going to approach the confrontation with all those on that suspect list. Obtaining a conviction sustainable in court would probably require a confession in some form or other. His explanation to Laura was met with strong opposition as she considered it life threatening but Giles insisted that it might be the best way to bring this whole matter to an end.

Chapter 24

THROW DOWN THE GAUNTLET

There was a distinct buzz of excitement and anticipation in the Conference Hall of Alexandra Palace when Giles and Ramon entered to make their announcements to the circus elite. Members of the Press were in attendance to learn if a solution to the criminal problems of the Tropicana Circus was imminent and, hopefully, to hear the identity of the murderer.

All the named suspects were there including the magician's assistant, Annette Wagner, who had replaced the first murder victim Allison Somerfield. Lizzie Lisbet, the equestrian rider of Bianca; and Gayle Serpis, the acrobat on the swaying pole and trapeze; plus the replacement ringmaster, Mark Kimberley, were also in attendance.

The meeting opened when Ramon got to his feet. He looked a little uneasy as his gaze searched around the sea of faces seated before him and, without saying anything, he brought out a cigar. Taking plenty of time he put a light to the Havana, took several puffs and blew a few smoke rings into the air.

'Some five or six months ago,' he began. 'I was going through hell because of the number of strange accidents that were taking place in my circus. I was under the impression that someone in this show was deliberately causing these disasters to force me to relinquish my control of this great spectacle. I was at my wits' end until a unique opportunity came about.' He paused, took another few puffs of his cigar and turned to look at Giles.

'When this gentleman, Professor Giles Dawson, invited circus owners and stage magicians to a meeting, to highlight the possibility of introducing illusions into the circus ring, I grasped at the chance to ask for his help.' He paused once more and, placing a hand on Giles' shoulder, he nodded and took a puff of his cigar before continuing.

'Professor Dawson had been renowned in most of the daily and evening newspapers because of an outstanding performance in solving a fourteen year old mystery. I believed he was the best person to break this hoodoo… this *gauntlet of fear* I was under and, when he accepted my offer, I prayed that a time would come when a meeting of this sort would take place. I do not know how successful he has been, but I'm confident he will be able to provide us with all the essential facts. How much still remains to be resolved will become clearer this evening. Ladies and gentlemen, please welcome the historian of the Great Illusionists, Professor Giles Dawson.'

Rising to a muted applause Giles took the large cigar handed to him by Senhor Mordomo but made no attempt to have it lit. He looked out to the group facing him and could see Laura and Freddie sitting among the journalists just behind the suspects. 'When I first took on this intractable task,' he said. 'I was instantly reminded of an adage by a distinguished author. I believe it was G.K. Chesterton who said that "If a job was worth doing, it was worth doing badly." That Chestertonian paradox has constantly been with me and there were many occasions when I despaired…when I was aware I was doing badly. I recently made a promise to Senhor Mordomo when the circus was in York. I told him that if I was unable to solve his problem by midsummer, I would repay him the bulk of the retainer he gave me.'

'So you've given up the ghost, Professor?' yelled one journalist. 'How much are you going to repay?' shouted another.

Holding up a hand to silence the hecklers, Giles waited until he was ready to continue. 'You were all called here tonight so that I can keep the promise I made and, even though we're a few weeks short of midsummer, I am going to do just that.'

'First, I'd like to take you through all that I've gleaned from start to finish before finally revealing my conclusion. After that I may be asking for a little helpful co-operation from the guilty person. That person… the instigator of all the accidents and the murderer of Allison – the magician's assistant, and Sebastian – the ringmaster, is here in this room tonight.'

The commotion following that last statement grew rapidly into a hullabaloo as several journalists raised their arms.

'When I've explained what my early thoughts were, I'll give you all a chance to ask questions. In the meantime please bear with me.' Giles bent down to speak to the circus boss after Ramon had calmed the situation somewhat. The Portuguese owner produced a lighter which he handed to the historian. Giles took his time while lighting his cigar, then handed the lighter back.

'At the very beginning,' he said. 'I had to admit I was confused by the sheer size of the problem I was being asked to investigate. The numbers involved were so great, when taking into account the complement employed in the circus, that I came to the conclusion the complexity of the situation was beyond my control.' He paused to draw on his cigar. 'I repeat,' he said. 'Beyond my control, that is, until Senhor Mordomo came to my rescue and lightened my load.' Giles took another puff, blew out the cigar smoke and smiled. 'Senhor Mordomo produced a list of suspects for me and I have that in my pocket. The murderer's name is on that slip of paper.'

The hubbub in the hall reached disturbing proportions and Giles had difficulty in bringing back a resumption of order to the proceedings.

When peace was restored Giles asked one of the attendants in the hall for an ashtray. He took another draw on the tobacco leaf before placing the cigar in the ashtray. 'My first encounter with an accident was on hearing from Hank, the circus funambulist, about his fall from a vibrating wire. That was quickly followed by one of the worst things a tented show could possibly suffer...that of fire. The fire happened during a hilarious performance by Chuck and his clowns and fortunately took place in a hanger where it was dealt with speedily.' He picked up the cigar, tapped it with his fingers to knock the ash into the tray, took a look at the glowing end then put it down again.

'After the fire, there were the lacerations to Leonardo on the staircase of swords and the impending disaster when the tiger, Khan, ended up with the magician's assistant in the same cage. Both of those incidents could have resulted in death. I am also reminded, when thinking of the Royal Bengal Tiger, about the times when Khan's cage has been left open in mysterious circumstances. Looking back at the variety of misfortunes it was distinctly possible than any one of several people could be responsible for all of them, or a different person might have carried out each one. It was all confusion until two incidents happened which seemed to be connected. The first of these was a note left in my trailer with four names on it. They were the names of well-known people in entertainment who had changed their names from the ones they were given at birth.'

The silence in the room was electric as Giles stopped to have a sip of water from the glass in front of him.

'The second of the two incidents,' Giles persisted. 'Was a written conundrum posted on the notice board in the old control tower of RAF Winkleigh.'

One of the journalists raised a hand which, for the moment, Giles ignored. 'In every line of that conundrum,' he continued. 'There was a clear-cut reference to people, places and objects, with double names or double meanings. It had to be either a help pointing me in the right direction or an attempt by someone to lead me up the garden path.' He stopped and pointed to the hack with the hand raised.

'Geoff Granger, *The Daily Telegraph*.'

'Yes, Mr. Granger I'll take a question from you at this stage.'

'Thank you, Professor. I believe I'm correct in saying that part of the conundrum was directing you to visit some remote island where you might find the secret you were searching for. Is that true and, if so, did you go there?'

'Where did you get that information from Mr. Granger?'

'I'm sorry but as you probably know I'm not at liberty to reveal my sources.'

'I thought that would be the answer I'd get,' said a smiling Giles. 'But I will try and answer your questions. Yes, the conundrum did direct me to an island and yes, I did go there.'

Another hand was held high; this time by a female.

'I'll take one more question,' he said pointing to the lady. 'Then I'd like to carry on a little longer before I give you all a chance to quiz me.'

'Eleanor Johnson, *The Guardian*.'

'Yes, Miss Johnson?'

'When you mentioned about that written conundrum you were unsure as to whether it was sent by someone trying to help by pointing you in the right direction, or if it was a case of being led up the garden path. Can you tell us what your assessment of the situation was at the time you first read it and what it is now?'

Reaching for the cigar, Giles put it to his mouth and made an effort to bring it to life once more. It took several attempts before a red glow appeared. 'A moment ago,' he said holding the cigar upwards. 'I wasn't sure whether this cigar was lit and doing me a favour or whether it was dead and making my own existence more difficult. I have to admit that was probably the way I felt when those names and the riddle were brought to my attention. You see, if the aim was to help me who would be doing it and why? It would make no sense for the person causing the *gauntlet of fear* syndrome to do so as it would be self-destructive. What other option was open to me? Only that of the garden path remained. But if that was the case, the person leading me in that direction would only do so if I was making significant progress in solving the problem. My only conclusion was similar to that Chestertonian paradox I gave earlier. I came to believe that someone was trying to help me by leading me up the garden path in the belief that I would fail.'

'I'm afraid that also makes no sense, Professor,' the lady journalist of the Guardian proclaimed. 'Do you honestly expect us to believe that?'

'No, Miss Johnson. I've had great difficulty believing it myself. But if you will allow me to carry on I may be able to change your mind.'

'Do what you can, Professor Dawson. If you can make me change my mind and the mind of the other members of the Press here tonight you will need to be a very skilled illusionist indeed. And I doubt that – I doubt that very much. I will say, however, that should you achieve the impossible, my paper will acknowledge that feat in no uncertain terms.'

'Thank you. I will look forward to reading your column in *The Guardian* after I supply you with the nom-de-plume of the murderer.' Giles was still holding his cigar and, after a few more puffs, he stubbed out the glowing prop as a nurse or doctor might use a hypodermic needle. 'The tragic and dramatic death of Allison Somerfield, as she was performing an illusion, introduced another element into the equation. Her death, in my opinion, was unnecessary. I therefore asked myself...why did she die? If previous accidents were to continue, true to form, she could have been incapacitated just sufficiently to ruin her performance. But no! She was killed by the use of Pentathol. If this had been used correctly, and followed by a relaxing agent and given the required air blown by a respirator through a tube into the lungs, she would have survived. I came to the conclusion that she had to die. She had to die in order to become a prelude to a more important death.

This started to put the cat among the pigeons. For then I knew at least one more death would take place. What I did not know was the name of the victim or the time and place of death.'

Reaching for the glass of water Giles took another sip and looked towards the ceiling as if trying to summon another power to aid his thoughts. He cleared his throat as he gazed at his audience once more.

'My short, but eventful, visit to the Isle of Rum was, I believe, a turning point in my investigation. Although nothing conclusive came of it certain skirmishes, as my caretaker friend Major Mackintosh would have stated, led me, not up the path you understand, but led me to focus my attention on items of some significance. Unfortunately I was unable to be conscious of what they really meant until much later, when everything slotted into place.'

'You're beginning to talk gibberish, Professor!' yelled out someone.

'Yes, I probably am,' agreed Giles, taking another puff of the cigar he still held in his hand. 'Gobbledygook was all it seemed to be at the time. I was getting nowhere fast. It was the city of York that changed everything and the strange death of Sebastian Capuzzo, the Ringmaster. The whole thing smacked of the supernatural; that is until another alternative could be considered.'

'Did you consider such an alternative?' questioned an impatient journalist wanting answers.

'I thought I asked you all to allow me to finish before I accepted questions. But yes, I did have a different view on that murder…a view that coincided with my thinking about the name of the guilty person. The only problem was I had no way of proving it. Until now, that is!' Giles paused to take a sip from his glass. 'I will take another question.' He pointed to one of the newspaper men with hands raised.

'Bob Lawson, *The Observer*.'

'Yes, Mr. Lawson?'

'You say you know the name of the murderer and that you can now prove it, yet you seem reluctant to give that name an airing. I also note that there are no members of the police in this hall tonight and I wonder why not?'

'For the simple reason, Mr. Lawson, that there isn't going to be an arrest made tonight and I'll explain why in a few minutes.' Giles watched and waited until the uproar that followed his statement had sufficiently subsided.

'The murder of Sebastian Capuzzo was a complex one. It appeared to have been committed by someone from outside who could deliver an induction agent intravenously from an impossible distance, or by someone inside using a hypodermic needle who would have had to leave a room which was locked in order to escape detection and still ensure a locked room. The only other alternative which could be considered was that the assassin was invisible: before, during, and after the killing. So many things had to be considered. The victim could have been made drowsy if he'd smoked a cigarette or cigar that had been treated with heroin, cocaine or some other barbiturate. But, when the room was eventually unlocked, no cigarette or cigar was found.'

'Does that mean you have no idea how that murder was committed?'

'On the contrary, Mr. Lawson. Although I can't give you a demonstration, or claim that I know exactly how it was carried out, what I do know is that the evidence was there which confirmed my suspicion about the identity of the killer.'

Giles looked at his audience for more signs of immediate questioning but, as none was forthcoming, he continued his talk. 'Subsequent accidents,' he said, in a subdued tone. 'Were more than disappointing; they were life-threatening. There was the senseless upset on Bianca, the Andalusian mare; and the near fatality of Gayle, on the swaying pole. The pole affair might just have been the result of carelessness by the circus band but the interference with the mount of young Lizzie was an act of cruelty. Accidents are likely to go on unless I put a stop to them, once and for all.'

A hand shot up from the row of journalists which Giles pointed to.

'Bob Langley, *The Sunday Express*.'

'Yes, Mr. Langley?'

'Can you really put a stop to these accidents, Professor and if so how do you intend doing it?'

'If I had been asked that question a few weeks ago I would've been unable to give an answer except to shake my head. Now I'm about to tell you what I'm going to do. As I said earlier, the person responsible for the accidents and the murderer of two members of the circus elite, one and the same person, is in this room. Tomorrow, at some time during the evening performance, I want this person to meet me.' Giles stopped and beckoned Senor Gomez, the animal trainer, to approach him. They had a short discussion before Rodrigo returned to his seat. Giles nodded. 'As I was saying I want this person to meet me in the wagon that houses the cage of Khan, the Royal Bengal Tiger.'

He had another sip from the glass of water and took a few puffs of the cigar before he laid it down in the ashtray, leaving his hands free.

'This person has not only caused a series of accidents, been responsible for two murders, and brought dread and fear in their wake, but has goaded me throughout. I've been challenged at every turn. All the time I was conscious of the fact that this same person seemed to think that even though I was supplied with clues, however cryptic, I would be unable to come up with a solution. I would like the chance to hear what the real motive was because I don't believe it was to take over the circus.'

Bending down Giles brought, from under the table, a grey leather gauntlet which he banged on to the table almost spilling the glass of water. 'It is now my turn to throw down the gauntlet and challenge this person to meet me where Khan will be the only creature who can hear our conversation.'

Another hand shot but this time the hand belonged to one of the suspects.

'Yes? Giles said, pointing to the gentleman.

'Michael Wagner, Professional Magician.'

'Yes, Mr. Wagner? I know who you are – yes, but the press don't '

'Do you honestly expect one of us to come and face you and answer leading questions?'

'Yes, Mr. Wagner. Yes, I certainly do and I'll tell you why…I've had no problem with any of you doing so in the past. The person I'm interested in has an ego problem and will do anything to have it fed to excess. If Khan was able to digest all that is said tomorrow night, what a star he'd be in Circus Tropicana!'

The magician sat down and Giles took a piece of paper and an envelope from his inside pocket. He scribbled something on the paper, folded it and placed it in the envelope which he sealed.

'As a magician, Mr. Wagner, you will understand what I am about to do.' Giles plucked his cigar from the ashtray and took a couple of draws before examining the glowing end. 'In this sealed envelope,' he said. 'I have written the name of the murderer of Allison and Sebastian.' There was a hushed murmur as he set fire to the envelope, using the burning end of the cigar, and watched it burn safely into the ashtray. 'That name, now an ash, has been transported by magical powers to the safe-keeping of someone sitting here as a potential suspect.'

Giles' smile was more of a beam as he picked up the leather glove and added. 'I throw down the gauntlet, this *gauntlet of fear*, and challenge this person whose name I have just burned, to meet me tomorrow night in the presence of Khan.' Giles paused briefly. 'And to all of you,' he said, gesticulating to the members of the Press. 'I extend an invitation to attend the evening performance of the circus when you may have enough copy, of the scoop category, for your next column.'

Chapter 25

THE WRATH OF KHAN

Giles did not attend the afternoon performance of the circus on the day after the Alexandra Palace conference. He spent most of the afternoon in the Palace building, accompanied by Laura, wandering around trying to appreciate everything on show. This was the place where the BBC News had its headquarters and where Pink Floyd, along with others, had just performed in a successful "Love-in" concert. There was a good bar and the toilets were spotless, but as far as Giles was concerned his mind was elsewhere. Freddie had gone to meet some of the staff in the racecourse offices of Ally Pally, where he could check on the latest racing news, but he promised he would be in the circus tent that evening, ready to lend support if needed.

The weather was fine, quite warm and dry when Giles had gone into the Palace. But, by the time he and Laura had finished having a bite to eat in the canteen, it had clouded over and light rain was falling.

It was beginning to get ominously dark as they left the building and rain was still falling when they met up with Freddie.

'This is the kind of weather the racecourse often gets,' said Freddie as they searched for shelter. 'Light rain on a hard surface can make the ground slippery, especially on bends with the wrong camber and that often brings about disasters.'

'Is that a dreadful omen, I wonder?' Laura asked, grasping Giles' hand more firmly. 'I don't mind admitting I'm scared!'

'That makes two of us, my love. I don't mind confessing that I'm afraid as well, but I won't be alone if the guilty person comes to accept my challenge. I'll have Khan in there with me, and we may get a chance to see if he is the pussycat Hank thinks he is.'

'I'm sorry, Giles, but I hardly think this is the time and place for jokes, however well-meant.'

'You are, of course, absolutely correct, darling, but I have to do this.'

'There is something I really must ask you, Giles.'

'I'm listening.'

'When you did that magic piece of spiriting the envelope away in a burning flame last night surely that was a bit of magic mischief designed to lure the unsuspecting onlookers into believing you were sending that name somewhere safe? Does someone have that name? And, if so, is it safe?'

'Yes, my dear. It was deliberately used to misdirect at least one person and someone does have that name and it is safe…probably safer than I may be in the wagon with Khan and…? But I'm prepared to take that risk as this may be the only chance I'll have to lay the ghost that has plagued this circus. And prove, once and for all, that I'm not the easy touch that someone thinks I am.'

The rain had stopped when Giles saw Laura and Freddie go safely into the circus tent for the evening performance. He then walked the short distance to the large wagon which housed Khan's cage. There was nobody about as he approached the silent truck.

Before attempting to go in he looked up at the sky that was loaded with dark cloud. He opened the door, which was unlocked, and went into the dimly lit area. The Bengal Tiger was lying in his cage and the strong animal smell was vaguely comforting as Giles moved to the far end of the wagon where he found a place to sit. Khan rose and came over towards the Prof who watched the beast with more than a passing interest. In the subdued light the tiger seemed to fill the cage and looked anything but a pussycat.

The silence in the confined space was interrupted by the padding sound of Khan's huge paws, the increased breathing of the historian of magic and the approaching footsteps at the door of the wagon. The door opened and two men came in. One was Rodrigo Gomez, the trainer of Khan; the other Giles did not recognise. The cage door was opened, a tunnel affair was attached and Khan was led out.

No word was spoken and when he was left alone Giles realised what had just taken place. The tiger was being used by the magician in the illusion where his daughter, Annette, was to be substituted. Rodrigo and the keeper's assistant would be ensuring that Khan would be securely placed in the small cage and, when the illusion was over, the tiger would be returned to his own wagon for the remainder of the night.

Giles got to his feet and walked about for a spell. When he sat down he began to feel sleepy and it was the slight noise of Khan's return which brought back instant alertness. Once again no word was spoken and Giles was soon left on his own to watch the giant tiger lie down.

The minutes went by and the sounds from outside signified that the rain had started to fall again. There was a distant rumble of thunder and Giles could not help feeling that an evening in his London flat, enjoying a Whisky Mac with Laura and Freddie, would be preferable to this lonely vigil beside one of the world's wild animals, while waiting for another wild animal to arrive.

He tried to look at his watch and began to wonder if his throwing down of the gauntlet challenge was going to be accepted, or whether the attempt to confront the guilty person was about to backfire.

He made an effort to visualise what might be happening at the circus as faraway echoes of hilarity mixed with gasps of surprise were mingled with the crashing din of applause. At times the noise from the circus became faint as if it had become impossible to compete with the sound of the storm brewing outside.

The evening wore on and Giles was on the verge of sleep once more when there was the unmistakeable, though slight, creak from the wagon door as it was evidently being opened cautiously. The bad weather had ceased and Giles tried hard to keep his eyes focussed on the door which was slowly opening. It seemed ages before a cloaked figure could be observed and in the gloom it was almost another example of black against black as the figure entered. It was difficult to determine the gender of the intruder, but that was of no consequence to Giles, for he knew who it would be and the name in the sealed envelope would reveal the truth if anything happened to him. What was now required was to obtain a public confession that would finally put an end to the circus debacle. But how that might happen was in the lap of the gods? ...He switched on the little tape recorder he'd brought just in case the gods required some help.

A shiver travelled down Giles' spine as a disembodied whisper came from the figure in black to open the creepy conversation. 'I'm here, from beyond the grave…' The voice, muffled by the masked face, was impossible to discern as male or female. But Giles was in no doubt as the murmur changed to a deeper tone. 'You, Professor, will be joining me, and your short career as a detective will soon be over.'

'I wouldn't bet on it! Why did you have to go to such lengths?' Giles asked, hoping to extract an answer. 'What were your bloody motives for submitting the circus to acts of such hellish depravity?'

'That should have been obvious to you, Professor. I had to kill Sebastian. He had to die as there was an old score to settle. Your coming to the circus was a golden opportunity for me to have an alibi; for when Ramon hired you, I believed I could get away with murder, while he thought someone was trying to take over his circus. The accidents were a smokescreen. I was also consumed by a desperate urge to prove that as a detective you were a non-event! What better than to kill two birds with one stone? I could demonstrate my vast superiority to everyone here and to show that you in particular would be unable to prevent my actions or solve the mystery.'

'Don't kid yourself! I know who you are and have known for some time now and the name in that sealed envelope will confirm my suspicions.'

'I doubt that, Professor. I doubt that very much. Now you listen to me! I am going to leave here and lock the door behind me.' There was a metallic click as the cage door was slipped open. 'You will not be able to escape and with Khan for company, I believe the final seconds of your life will be a blood bath. Khan's claws will rip you to shreds and death by misadventure should be the likely outcome at your inquest.'

There was a demonic laugh as the cloaked figure made for the wagon door. Khan padded his way towards the gap in the cage. But instead of heading towards Giles, the beast turned and followed the figure in black towards the open door. There wasn't time for the door to be closed and Khan pushed his way out as the cloaked figure dashed towards the safety of the circus tent, slipping on the wet turf. Khan, following close behind, started to gain in the chase. Giles was not slow to join the pair in Indian file, and was in full view of the action as the figure in black and the Royal Bengal Tiger went into the tent via the artistes' area.

The Wheel of Death knife-throwing act was in full progress when the person being pursued made a dash across the ring. Giles, who was behind

Khan, heard the swish of the throwing knife and then the dull thud as the blade sank into human flesh. The cloaked figure stumbled, carried on for a few more strides, before collapsing face down on the floor of the ring. The stumbling figure had hardly hit the floor when Khan was there placing his huge front paws one on either side of the knife that protruded from the limp back.

Signor Gomez and his assistant were quickly on the scene and soon had Khan securely under control and ready to be returned to his cage.

Giles went forward. Along with Ingrid Dahlberg, the impaler, and Mark Kimberley, the ringmaster, they eased the mask from the inert figure's head to reveal the identity of the person in the black cloak.

The person was male and startling gasps came from everyone who recognised him. He was the same person whose name Giles had secreted in a sealed envelope. It was the circus boss…Ramon Mordomo.

The quick-thinking ringmaster, Mark Kimberley, went to his microphone and asked the audience to put their hands together to show their appreciation of the wonderfully choreographed illusion, which they had just witnessed as a finale to the Wheel of Death. The cloaked figure was stretchered away to a hesitant applause that gradually increased almost to a standing ovation.

The alert, Mark Kimberley, was given a congratulatory pat on the back by Giles before he followed the stretcher out of the tent as the band began playing some rousing music to introduce the next act.

Inside the rest tent the circus doctor confirmed that Ramon Mordomo was still alive and that an ambulance would be on the scene shortly. The members of the Press, who demanded an explanation from Giles, were told he would supply everything they required as soon as the evening performance was over.

The spectators, who'd been lured into thinking they'd watched a brilliantly choreographed piece of theatre during the knife-throwing act, had long since gone. Most of the circus artistes had changed out of their costumes and were gathered together in the vast emptiness of the Tropicana tent. Giles, after giving statements to a Scotland Yard Chief Inspector, was now at the ringside getting his thoughts in order.

Members of the Press, with notebooks at the ready, were anxious to obtain copy in time to meet their deadline for the following day's newspapers. For some time they'd been pressurising Giles to make a start. As the Prof moved to the centre of the ring, only the distant rumble of thunder could be heard. He looked out at his audience who were conveniently seated where he could address them without turning around.

'I will try my best,' he said. 'Not to keep the members of the Press any longer than is needed while I explain how I arrived at my conclusion. Unlike much of the detective fiction of the Golden Age, when all the suspects were each accused before the dénouement was delivered, I am happy to reverse that process and explain to the innocent seated here, how it all transpired.'

'Before you start, Professor Dawson, can you possibly tell us when you finally decided that none of the original suspects was guilty?'

Giles smiled as he looked across at Michael Wagner, who'd just asked the question. 'That's a tough one,' he said. 'All of the early accidents could have been carried out by any one of those names given to me by your circus boss. In fact there was a time when I believed there was a possibility that the accidents were the ruthless responsibility of all the suspects together, just as a well-known authoress wrote in one of her early novels.'

The low murmur as the circus elite looked at each other ceased as soon as Giles began speaking again.

'There were two very important factors that started to change my mind. The first was the murder of Allison, the magician's assistant and the second was when I interrogated most of you in the old control tower at RAF Winkleigh. When Allison was killed one of the vital clues was the wearing of face masks by those bringing the tyres into the ring. The decision to use the masks was made jointly by you, Michael, and by Ramon. You were in full view of the spectators during the illusion and that left Ramon as someone who could have used a hypodermic. When a needle was probably used in the rest room, who was closest to Allison and warning others to give her breathing space? Why…Ramon! And that made me very suspicious.'

Ingrid Dahlberg was the next one to ask a question. 'During the interrogation in the control tower,' she began. 'What surprised you most, Professor?'

'I know what you're getting at, Ingrid. Yes, I was surprised at the sudden demonstration of your skill with a knife but that wasn't the real surprise.

What did amaze me was that most, if not all, of the suspects answered my questions in a satisfactory way and didn't appear to be trying to cover guilt. I then started to think back to when the knowledge of my cruise was mentioned. If I remember correctly two people were present: Eva, your clairvoyant, and Ramon. One name was beginning to enter the equation with regularity and that name was on my mind during that interesting trip to Rum. I was being followed and when I considered who would be the most likely person to employ someone to do the following I came up with the same name...Ramon! At that stage there was no proof in sight – only surmise. The double identity given to me on two occasions, with the four names of screen entertainers and the conundrum asking me to go north, gave me something else to think about. That is, until the gruesome murder of Sebastian, your ringmaster.'

Wandering across the ring Giles stopped and said a few words to Madame Zigana. She rose and left the tent and Giles returned to the centre of the ring.

'The death of Sebastian was so complicated. The question that first had to be answered was whether it was committed from the inside or the outside. Had it been done from the inside it brought in the supernatural and I discounted that. But from the outside it also presented many problems. I had to decide how the ringmaster could be unaware when the window was shattered? The breaking of glass would make such a noise. True I suppose... but only if the window was broken after Sebastian had gone inside and not if the glass was broken before he entered the trailer. And who might have arranged that? Ramon could conceivably have done that and closed the curtains so that the broken glass would be unnoticed by a person on the inside.'

At that point Madame Zigana entered carrying a glass of water and an envelope. Giles took the glass from which he had a good drink.

'How could a dart be fired without Sebastian realising it was about to happen?' asked Felix Reiser, the band leader. 'Surely he would have noticed or heard the weapon.'

'Yes, I'm sure he would...if he'd been in full control of his senses and not in a state of drowsiness. I found cigar ash on the dead man's chest which suggested to me that a contaminated cigar may have been used, not to cause unconsciousness, but simply to make Sebastian drowsy. The post-mortem confirmed that the dead man's body showed traces of the barbiturate cocaine…' Giles was cut short as the band leader butted in.

'How on earth could the killer be certain that the contaminated cigar was smoked unless every single one of the cigars had been given the same treatment?'

'That, Felix, is easy to explain. You see, I know for a fact, that when Ramon was expecting a visitor he would leave one or more cigars unwrapped and pre-clipped ready for use. When I examined the cuspidor all the cigars were wrapped so he could easily have left a contaminated cigar without a wrapper and if pre-clipped that would be the most likely one to be selected. A dart could then have been fired from the broken window without much fear of detection.'

'But if that had happened,' persisted Felix. 'Both the cigar and the dart would have been in the room when the body was found.'

'Yes, Felix. That's what you'd expect unless…'

'Unless what, Professor?'

'Unless…? What if the incriminating evidence was removed by the first person to enter the trailer after Sebastian was murdered? Yes, it was Ramon!'

There was a loud crack of thunder as the implication of that statement dawned on the listening group. Giles picked up the glass of water and moved to the ringside where the clairvoyant was seated. 'Before I go on,' he said. 'Madame Zigana was my safe deposit for the sealed envelope. I thank her for that.' He nodded an acknowledgement 'Would you please open it Eva and read what it says.'

The fortune teller did what was asked and opened a folded sheet of paper. In her best voice she called out. 'There are only two words – Ramon Mordomo.'

'Thank you, Eva. Thank you so much.' There was a brief hiatus as Giles took a long swig of water, put the glass down and returned to the centre of the ring. 'To get back to the death of Sebastian there was the problem of the Lalique car mascot. If it was thrown from outside, the mascot had to taken outside beforehand, and who better to do that than the owner – Ramon. The throwing of the object was more difficult to rationalise. Miss Dahlberg was the knife-thrower but a thought struck me…something I believe Miguel, the senior member of the Velazquez trio of trapeze artistes, said when I asked him about the circus boss during interrogation in the control tower. He said the boss had the ability of many of the top performers. That meant that Ramon could have thrown the mascot and if it had failed to hit the ringmaster it wouldn't have made any difference as Sebastian was probably already dead.'

'Despite all the indications I still couldn't prove that Ramon was the guilty party. I had to ask myself why. The circus boss clearly had the opportunity. Although the obvious person that would use a tranquiliser gun was Rodrigo, the other one with the clear opportunity was the circus boss. He had the capability to commit murder…I'm certain of that! But what was the motive? If, as I believed, Sebastian was killed in order to try and convince others that the real target was the circus boss then that was certainly a strong motive! To eliminate someone without throwing suspicion on yourself is a powerful motive but why was I called in? Presumably it was to validate the fear syndrome he was drumming up to free himself of guilt. But that would have been mistaken if I successfully solved the mystery. I therefore assumed there was another motive. I had to give credence to one of vanity. To get away with murder and, at the same time, prove that you are much cleverer than the one employed to find the killer is also a strong motive especially for someone with an inflated ego.'

Young Lizzie, the circus equestrian, raised a hand surprising Giles who nodded as he spoke. 'Yes, Lizzie? Can I help?'

'Regarding what you've just said, does that mean you think you were hired as a kind of smokescreen?'

'Yes I do, and Ramon was not impressed by anyone who tried to help me.' There was a short pause as Giles seemed to be thinking back and searching his powers of recall. 'Do you remember telling me that you mentioned to your boss that you had agreed to help me by keeping a watchful eye on everything?'

'That's right. Yes I did, and you warned me not to mention that to anyone else.'

'Well, Lizzie, I believe Senhor Mordomo took exception to that and had your wonderful mare doctored with grass cuttings. That's how evil the man was. But I still couldn't pin anything on him. I knew I was unable to provide enough proof in order to get a conviction. That is… until the secret I was to seek at Kinloch Castle was unravelled by my fiancée and a character from the pen of P.J. Wodehouse. That fictional character was Jeeves, the valet of Bertie Wooster. There was also a phrase put to me in a question by the lady I'm engaged to, Laura. That phrase was "below suspicion" and those two words took me back to another novel by that same title. In it was a character by the name of Patrick Butler and the curious thing was that *butler* was another name for valet. I began to think it would be a strange irony if it was the butler whodunit. But the music hall joke was too serious to be taken lightly'

'You are joking, Professor, aren't you?' blurted out Hank Findley.

'Quite the opposite, Hank. By looking up a foreign dictionary we found that the Portuguese translation of butler was *mordomo!*'

The mild commotion amongst ex-suspects and those from the Press was quietened when Giles held up both hands. 'Although my suspicions were then confirmed it was still speculation. If I was correct in my assessment of Ramon's motives, especially his vanity and belief of superiority, I bargained that he might accept my *gauntlet of fear* challenge and try to eliminate me at the same time.'

'What is likely to happen to Senhor Mordomo now?' The leader of the clowns, Chuck Marstow spoke in anything but a clownish voice.

'He will be sent for trial as soon as he's recuperated and a jury will decide whether he is guilty or...'

His answer was abruptly cut short as the circus nurse came into the ring and rushed towards him. There was a hushed conversation before the nurse left in a hurry. Laura noticed that Giles was doing something with his face but it was quite the opposite of what she normally saw. He gazed at the faces waiting to hear his final words. There was a flash of lightning followed by a clap of thunder and the sound of torrential rain on the canvas structure. Giles looked upwards. 'It never rains but it pours!' he said, his shoulders drooping. 'I've just had word from the hospital. Senhor Mordomo has just died. It seems he died after seemingly taking a cyanide capsule.'

Laura rushed forward to take Giles by the hand. 'Let's get you back home, darling. You've had your fill of murder and need a rest. With a bit of luck, everything will be set fair when you help me with the illusions this new theatre company want, when they stage their mystery thriller based on Cinderella – the fairy tale with a happy ending...?'

NOTES FOR CURIOUS MINDS

The RAF airfield at Winkleigh in Devon played a valuable and secretive part in World War II. Construction was begun one year after the war started and, although it wasn't ready for use until 1942, the airfield was operational with airmen and aircraft from the USA, Canada, Poland and Great Britain. The "Black" squadron was one of the groups specialising in missions using camouflaged Lysander aircraft to transport secret agents into and out of occupied Europe. So secretive were all the assignments that Whitehall never admitted that RAF Winkleigh ever existed.

The St James's Club was in existence in the Piccadilly area of London in 1967 and, for those who may wish to find fault with the floating apostrophe, the club's name was as the spelling above shows. When gentlemen's clubs in London were going through a difficult period the club moved to different premises in 1981 and is now The St James's Hotel and Club in Mayfair.

The Isle of Rum is the largest of the Small Isles of the Inner Hebrides in the district of Lochaber, Scotland. The name became Rhum for much of the 20th Century because Sir George Bullough did not wish to be known as the Laird of Rum. For the purpose of this novel the present spelling is used throughout. The Isle is a wonderful place to visit and there is a regular MacBrayne's ferry from Mallaig.

Kinloch Castle, the large Victorian/Edwardian House, is owned by Scottish Natural Heritage. At the time this tale takes place it was in the ownership of The Nature Conservancy a predecessor of SNH. It still attracts the public who can see, at first hand, how the gentry lived, and entertained. a century ago. How much longer this will be available is uncertain.

The racecourse at Alexandra Park no longer exists but was still in use for horse racing in 1967. It was affectionately known to racegoers as Ally Pally, and because of its shape was nicknamed "The Frying Pan." They called it many other names; most of them much worse. Due to the tight turns, slippery surface, and the camber running away from the inside, it was a tricky course for jockeys and their mounts, and accidents were not unusual. In the late sixties evening meetings were popular, but as betting shops did not stay open in the evenings the Levy Board received no money and refused to fund the course. Alexandra Park racecourse closed three years later in 1970 described in the words of one journalist as "in a storm of indifference."

The 1967 Grand National was contested much as described in the novel. Foinavon did win the race coming from last to first because of the multiple disasters at the twenty-third fence. The smallest fence on the course is now called the Foinavon Fence. Foinavon did win at odds of 100-1 and the Tote paid 444-1.

'Enter Three Murderers' was a stage direction in Shakespeare's Macbeth.

"Double, Double Toil and Trouble" – Quotation from Act 111 Scene 111 Macbeth.

My thanks to Georgina McMillan – Administrator and Company Secretary Isle of Rum Community Trust for putting me in touch with George W. Randall and Douglas King of The Kinloch Castle Friends Association and to Scottish Natural Heritage. Their association with the Isle of Rum and Kinloch Castle was deliberately omitted from the original acknowledgements as that would have given the game away.

My thanks go to Dr Mary Elliott who has commented on a draft using her long local knowledge of Lochaber and brief stays in Kinloch Castle.